A
Splendid
Passion

A Splendid Passion

by
Marianne Evans

WARNER BOOKS

A Warner Communications Company

Copyright © 1980 by Nicholas Demetropoulos
All rights reserved.

Jacket art by Elaine Duillo

Warner Books, Inc., 75 Rockefeller Plaza, New York, N.Y. 10019

Printed in the United States of America

"What shall I be this time?"
the eleven-year-old Phémie asked her cousin Florimond as they began their game of "let's pretend."

"You can be the maiden," he told her.

"I was the maiden last time," she complained. "Why do I always have to be the maiden?"

"Because you are a maiden. Even if you do wear a a shirt and trousers like a boy, you are still a girl," Florimond teased as her face grew red with anger.

Eustache, her uncle, smiled indulgently and came to her rescue. "All right," he said, "you can be the hero today. Run get the swords."

When Phémie failed to return, he sent Florimond after her. "Eustache, come quickly," Florimond called; and, with a sudden stabbing of fear, the older man hurried upstairs to find Florimond holding Phémie high in his arms. Scattered about the floor was her beautiful long hair.

"Now," she announced, "I won't ever have to be the maiden!"

Eustache collapsed against the door, laughter and relief flooding over him, but his voice was sober as he said,

"My child, you'll have to be a maiden someday."

To C.E.M., S. vM.M.

Enjoy.

1

"Are you hurt, sir?" she asked, keeping her distance. He looked up at her but made no effort to rise from where he sat leaning against a worn tapestry in the long corridor.

"No, I am not hurt." He replied courteously, taking off his hat and inclining his head in a slight bow.

"I heard someone calling for help. . . ."

"Much to your credit, my girl. Come forward into the light so I can see you."

"Perhaps, then, you are drunk," she suggested with increased wariness. "If you'll excuse me, sir . . ."

"Halt! Do not desert me, I beg of you. You're a well-spoken girl. Who taught you your manners?"

"I have no time for visiting. If you're not hurt, I must be on my way."

"One can need help even if one is not hurt," he protested, satisfied to see her hesitating in her flight. "You see, I am lost. These underground passages all look alike."

"Oh, is that all?" She laughed lightly, and he was pleased

by the sound. "How long have you been here?" She stepped closer, but not close enough for him to reach out and touch her, if that had been his thought.

"My, you are a pretty thing." He complimented her matter-of-factly, and she had the grace to blush. She couldn't have been more than sixteen years old, of slight stature but not delicate. Her thick hair was golden brown, wound in a heavy knot at the nape of her neck. He couldn't see the color of her eyes, as she kept them averted shyly.

"You must be mad," she ventured, half fearful, half fascinated.

"Most assuredly. Anyone who lives in this court must be more than a little mad."

As her old-fashioned black dress revealed only her face and her hands, he concluded that she was some old dowager's maid. He was certain that he'd have remembered if he had ever seen her before, but there were hundreds of people living in the King's palace whom he'd never seen.

"If you're ready, Monsieur, I'll guide you back to the part of the palace where you belong."

"I'm not so certain I want to go back." An idea had been germinating during the awkward pauses, and he needed only a moment before it sprang, in full bloom, into his mind. "I do need your help, however."

He got to his feet painfully, stamping impatiently to stop the pins-and-needles sensation. At this little dance, she started to back away, but he caught her wrist, delaying her flight.

"Don't be afraid. I'm not going to hurt you. On the contrary, I'll pay you well for your assistance."

As he expected, she ceased struggling, and when she looked up at him, her eyes were the brightest green he'd ever seen. The sight of them almost made him forget his plan, but only for a moment. "I want to hide down here. Do you know any place where I'll be safe, and, I hope, comfortable?"

"Why?" What have you done?" she asked suspiciously, and he allayed her fears with quiet logic, saying, "I've done nothing! If I were a fugitive, would I have been calling for help? I merely want to play a trick on some of my friends."

Evidently she had come to expect such behavior from King Louis's courtiers, and admitted to knowing a hiding place. His feet and legs were greatly improved as he followed her with only a slight hobble. Without warning she stopped, turning to him once again.

"You must promise me that once your game is over, you'll never return to this place or tell anyone else about it."

"My dear girl, even if I wanted to, I'd never find my way down here. You can even bind my eyes when you finally guide me out."

"You must promise!" she insisted.

"Oh, very well. My oath on it."

This seemed to satisfy her, for she led him a short distance down the corridor and halted in front of one of the tapestries.

"Get a torch," she commanded, and he seized one from a wall bracket. Glancing both ways down the corridor to be sure that they weren't being spied upon, she quickly pulled aside the tapestry and pushed him rudely into the dark, gaping hole.

"It's quite safe, truly," she assured him, and he moved cautiously into a large room that had been recently cleaned and refurbished. Before he could turn about, she took the torch from his hand and used it to light some candles on a refectory table, then left him for a few moments to return the torch. The first sight his eyes lit upon was the gleaming crystal at the front of the room. As he made his way up the shallow dais steps to where an altar stone was still in place, he saw that it contained an array of fine wines. Without asking, he poured some into a goblet, drank it off thirstily, and then refilled it. At the bottom of the steps she watched him with obvious disapproval, and he hastened to try to win his way back into her good graces.

"Forgive me, but I've been down here since late afternoon with neither food nor drink. It must be almost time for supper."

"Long past," she corrected, but her disapproval vanished. Wisely he left the subject alone, instead exploring the room that had once been a chapel. Beside the refectory table there was a wardrobe, a comfortable chair, a desk, and a commodious bed. The privy was in a recess at the back of the room, concealed behind an ornate screen. The candles flickered in a draught of fresh air coming through a grill in the ceiling. Nowhere in the decoration was there a hint of a feminine hand, and he turned to her, the question in his eyes.

"It belongs to a friend of mine. He is away for a time, so there's no need to worry."

"Your friend shows excellent taste in his surroundings, his wine, and his companionship." He smiled kindly, completely unprepared for her outburst.

"I know you intend that as a compliment, sir, but I do not care for it. If you must know, he and I have never been down here at the same time. He has been more than generous in allowing me to avail myself of the solitude, and I'll not allow you to cast aspersions upon his motives."

"My dear, please." He held up a hand to stop the outraged protest. "I don't need to know any of this, and I'm most sorry if my unfortunate comment has caused you a moment's distress. We must be allies, but that does not mean I claim any right to know of your personal life. With your permission, I shall stay here for only a few days. You must act as my ears and eyes up there, telling me all that is happening. That is all I ask of you. Will you do it for me?"

"I don't know." She hesitated, plainly dismayed. "There is so little I hear."

"Doesn't your mistress have any friends? Is she so deaf that she doesn't listen to gossip?"

"But what am I to listen for?"

"Anything that is said about Georges du Broussac. I'll wager that my name will be whispered all over the palace by tomorrow morning."

"You are this man?"

"Forgive me, I've not introduced myself. I am du Broussac. May I ask your name?"

"Agnes," she answered, and he didn't think to ask if she had a surname. "You'll not have to wait until tomorrow morning. I have already heard something."

"You see? I knew you could help."

"I heard your name mentioned. They were laughing a great deal."

"So they would be," he said darkly, but she paid him no attention.

"They said that all the passageways were being watched, and as soon as they knew from which direction you were coming, they would all gather to give you a welcome."

"A welcome, indeed! I can well imagine." He was thoughtful for a moment, before laughing himself. "How perfect! So they are watching all the passages, are they? And when they don't see me come out, what will they do?" He asked the question of himself, but Agnes replied, "They'll come down looking for you, if they are your friends."

"Even if they are not my friends, they will come down. Yes, even to the door with the white cross. And they won't find me, my girl. Then, in two, or perhaps three, days I suddenly reappear—well-fed, well-wined, and well-bedded. Just when they are despairing. Then who will laugh?"

"I don't think your game is very amusing, but it is not my place to say," she commented absurdly, but in perfect seriousness. "You mentioned being well-fed and well-wined. I must insist, Monsieur, that you do not drink any more of this wine. My friend knows that I don't drink it myself, and will suspect that I've brought someone else down here. It is a betrayal of his trust. I will bring you your own wine, and some food, if you can let me have the money."

"I've no money with me," he admitted, shame-faced, but she saw nothing strange in his confession.

"Then you'll just have to eat and drink whatever I can provide. Perhaps you'd best give up this game of yours, Monsieur du Broussac."

"Never! Whatever you bring will serve well enough. You'll be paid for it, I promise."

"Very well, then. I'll get whatever I can for now, but tomorrow I should be able to do a little better."

"You're a saint," he called after her, rubbing his hands gleefully, as she hurried away. Surely the angels had led him to this place. Everything had been provided for his arrival, even a lovely girl with whom to pass his lonely hours.

Much to his disappointment, the first meal was an abomination rather than the novel picnic he'd anticipated. But he was even more crestfallen because she stayed only long enough to deliver the "delicacies" for his repast and was gone before he uncovered the basket. When she handed him the receptacle there was a bright gleam in her eyes. If he'd known her better, he'd have recognized the expression as pure mischief. There was a hard crust of bread that must have been baked days before. There was no meat, only a cheese, but most of it was covered with an unappetizing green mold. The liquid in the wine bottle was undrinkable, so he broke his word and availed himself of his unknown host's refreshments, promising himself to replace it as soon as he was able. The food he threw down the privy so he wouldn't hurt the girl's feelings. The wine softened the hardship of going without food, and he was quite pleasantly drunk as he fell asleep on the comfortable bed.

It wasn't until late the following day that the girl finally appeared. This time the gleam in her eyes was unmistakable, and his complaints died before they were spoken.

"You are a master of understatement, Monsieur. Your name is not being whispered, but shouted all over the palace today."

In fact, upstairs in the palace the gossip was rampant. How ridiculous it was that du Broussac, that social leper, had made an invitation to compromise to the most sought-after lady of the court! How fitting it was that she had agreed to the rendezvous and had led him unknowingly to the room with a white cross upon its door—the place where all the castle privies emptied!

"Are they looking for me, then?" he asked eagerly.

"Indeed," she replied, "cooks, gardeners, lackeys, valets, maids, footmen, guardsmen, costumers, hairdressers, courtiers; all are in an uproar, searching everywhere."

He whooped with laughter, delighted that his scheme was turning out so well.

"Everyone knows of your lady's jest, and there are some who suspect you of merely hiding. That is why I'm so late, and empty-handed. No one is permitted below stairs with a basket, as it might be smuggled food. But soon they will relax their vigilance," she reassured him. "This morning most people believed you lost, but since finding the lady's note by the open door of the . . ." she paused, unable to find a delicate enough word, and he commented shortly, "Exactly. Go on, go on!"

"The possibility that you might have thrown yourself in is growing in popularity."

"Oh, my God!" He shook with laughter and stamped his feet with glee.

"That is not all." Agnes was having a difficult time restraining herself, and at the prospect of more information, he gulped noisily and managed to control himself. "The lady herself had a fit of hysterics a short while ago. It was a fine show."

"Tell me!"

"Well, she began by screaming, then loosened her hair, tearing patches of it out, and ripped her gown from her breast. She blames herself for your misfortune, vowing that if you have, indeed, lost your life for love of her, she will do perpetual penance."

This intelligence did not throw him into gales of laughter, as she half expected. Instead, he wiped his eyes, saying simply, "And so she should."

"Is that all you can say?" she asked, amazed at his calm.

"No." He considered carefully before continuing, "I could

say that I'm terribly hungry, or apologize for drinking your friend's wine. What would you have me say?"

"I don't know." She was obviously perplexed, and sat in the chair he'd deserted to replenish his empty goblet. When he returned he perched on the refectory table, his eyes softening as he looked down on her puzzled expression. She blushed at his proximity, having forgotten how handsome he was in the time she'd been away. He'd not put on his wig, wide-brimmed hat, or ornately embroidered coat when she'd come in, and she found the unadorned du Broussac even younger-looking and more attractive.

"I am sorry about the food," she apologized timidly, uncomfortable in the long silence.

"Do you truly mean that?"

"Of course. As I told you, it was impossible . . ."

"Do you wish to make amends?" he interrupted, pretending disinterest. Quickly sensing a trap, she retorted, "For giving you shelter and doing all that I can to help you in your absurd game? I think not!"

Her reaction was not at all servant-like and he eyed her with suspicion.

"You never told me who your mistress is."

"And you've not asked how your wife is responding to your disappearance."

"I'll be honest with you if you'll be honest with me."

"You're in no position to bargain."

"I don't believe that you're a maid at all."

"After things have quieted a bit, I'll guide you out of here," she replied, pretending not to have heard him.

"You'll not escape that easily. Tell me, what is your name?"

"I've already told you. Or don't you believe me in that, as well?"

"I mean, what is your family name?"

"Lapalisse." Agnes supplied the information casually, and if he had expected a stunning revelation, he was doomed to disappointment. After a few moments of searching his memory, he was forced to admit, "I don't know the name."

"I scarcely expected you to. Tell me, what is your wife's maid's family name?"

"I have no idea."

"And why should you? I'll wager even your wife doesn't remember it."

She made her point very neatly, and he was compelled to put aside his suspicions except for one nagging doubt.

"You don't speak or act like any maid I've ever known."

"I was born in my mistress's household, and attended her daughters, even while they were having their lessons. I listened closely."

"And what of her sons? Did you attend them, as well? Or perhaps her husband?"

"That's small gratitude for all I've done for you. I should have left you out there, rotting in your own stupid plan for revenge." With a flash of temper she started to rise, but he reached out, slapping her soundly across the face. Falling back in the chair, her hand on her cheek, she stared up at him with wide-eyed amazement, too shocked to feel any pain. He appeared completely unconcerned, reprimanding her kindly, "That's not the way a servant talks to her master."

"You are not my master," she reminded him, almost crying with indignation.

"In this room, at this moment, I am your master. I do not like to be scolded like an ill-mannered boy by a person of rank. Coming from a mere servant, it is intolerable. Do you understand, my girl?"

Suddenly she became aware of her danger. It had been folly, befriending this strange young man. She'd thought she would be safe as long as he believed her to be a servant; it would seem that she had been mistaken.

"Do you understand?" He repeated the question, his tone noticeably sharper.

"Yes, I understand," she replied meekly, and this seemed to satisfy him.

"Go and bring me some wine, as a penance for speaking so rudely to me."

As she rose to comply with his command, her mind worked furiously. When she reached the display of bottles, he directed her to the one he wanted. Picking it up, she turned to descend the steps, but instead, threw the bottle at his head. When he ducked, she leaped off the dais and ran for the corridor. Before she had reached the tapestry, she felt his arm catch her about the waist and his hand cover her mouth. He dragged her struggling back into the room, almost squeezing the breath out of her.

"I've had nothing to eat for two days, and I've been drinking our host's excellent wine," he warned disjointedly, successfully containing the twisting, thrashing girl. "I'm in a very dangerous mood, and if you don't behave, I'm most likely to do something we'd both regret. Believe me!" The threat was naked in his words, and she didn't have to see his expression to realize that he meant what he said. Abruptly her struggles ceased, and he tentatively removed the hand from her mouth. Her chest heaved with her exertions as she tried painfully to regain her breath.

"Do I have your word that you'll not scream or try to escape again?"

"I'll not scream." His grip about her waist tightened, and she winced with the pain.

"And escape?"

"I'll escape if I can," she replied honestly, and he realized that there was nothing he could do, short of keeping his arm around her or somehow tying her in the chair.

"What am I to do with you?" he asked, exasperated, and she shrugged her shoulders. Her hair had come undone during the struggle, and as he touched its silky thickness he felt her stiffen.

"It smells so good." He bent down and she heard him inhaling deeply. "What fragrance do you use?"

"Soap," she replied unencouragingly, causing him to laugh.

"How quaint! Our ladies spend small fortunes on perfumes, smothering themselves with scent, and never smell as good as you do. Will you lie with me, Agnes?"

The query was so sudden that she was bereft of speech. "Please," he added as an afterthought. When no reply was forthcoming, he commented lazily, "I've never raped a woman before. It might be an interesting experience."

"You are mad!"

"With hunger for you." His free hand went to the back of her dress and began fumbling with the hooks. "You promised not to scream," he reminded her when he felt her quick intake of breath. "And if you struggle, I'll give you a good beating."

"Oh, please," she cried, "I've shown you nothing but kindness. Don't shame me like this."

"Shame you?" It took a moment for him to realize her meaning. "Are you a virgin, Agnes?" he asked incredulously, and the flush in her cheeks gave him his answer.

"It's hard to credit. . . ." He turned her to face him, holding her by the shoulders as he gazed at her with more than casual interest. "What a rare creature you are!" Still she averted her face. "I suppose you believe that a girl should go to her marriage bed without blemish?" When she didn't answer, the blush deepening, he became adamant, "I won't permit it!"

As she looked up at him wonderingly, he explained, "It's not right that some clumsy oaf should terrorize you on your wedding night. You should be gently awakened to passion, my child, by one who would treat you as a delicate flower ready to blossom. There are such delights I could teach you."

He bent down slowly, and, as if she were fascinated by his melodious voice, she lifted her lips trembling to his. The kiss was gently searching, not rudely insistent, and she moved closer to him as his arms went about her.

"My darling girl," he whispered, kissing her eyes, her cheeks, her ears, delighting as he felt her shivering response. Under his practiced fingers, her gown was unfastened and falling from her shoulders before she realized that it was being done. She hardly noticed when the gown fell to the floor and he carried her to the bed.

He'd never known a virgin before, and after the first awkwardness had passed, he was charmed by her faltering attempts at lovemaking, finding her a willing student. When he slept, she'd leave quietly, returning with food and water for washing. So they passed almost a week in solitude, forgetting the turmoil upstairs caused by his disappearance. One day she returned after a longer absence than usual with startling news. The King was expected shortly.

Georges realized the King would hardly be pleased to find his court in an uproar. With regret, Georges had Agnes guide him back to his own world. When he strode into the great hall, leaving her behind, he was quickly surrounded by his peers, all relieved to see him and questioning him eagerly. As she hung about on the fringes of the crowd, she heard him explain that he had wandered lost for a time, and when he had been almost fainting from hunger, a beautiful creature had led him into a secret chamber, where she kept him a prisoner in her bed. As this was greeted with hoots of laughter, he swore with great sincerity that it was true, dramatically tearing open his shirt to display the marks of Agnes's passion upon his body. No one noticed the girl running from the hall, tears flowing from her eyes.

When the King heard snatches of gossip about the affair, he commanded du Broussac into his presence to tell the whole story. Much gratified by this show of royal interest, the young courtier described all that had befallen him without minimizing his humiliation at the hands of the great lady, but exaggerating his interlude with Agnes. All in all, he made it believable, and the King was so entertained by Georges's adventures that he was restored to favor and was rewarded with a prominent place in the King's closest retinue. Because he was closely watched with envy by most and skepticism by a few, he never attempted to return to "the secret chamber" below. He could, and did, surreptitiously watch the faces of passing women, but soon gave up his search for Agnes as a lost cause. She faded from memory as du Broussac pursued his newly awakened ambition. It did not take long, however, for his unruly tongue and overweening pride to cause a fall from favor so complete that he was exiled from court. He became a wastrel who eventually succumbed to his dissipations.

Agnes left the palace and escaped to a convent as soon as she discovered that she was pregnant. In giving life, she lost her own.

2

King Louis did not often grant private audiences to members of the lesser nobility, but the name of the man who made the request was one he remembered from his childhood. There had been a Lapalisse who'd warned of the nobles' intent to capture the royal family in open rebellion and who had helped the Queen Regent, her minister, and the boy King flee from Paris. Never had he been permitted to forget that night of terror, but he had not heard from the Baron for years. As soon as the man entered the council chamber, Louis saw that this could not possibly be the same man. After accepting his obsequious homage, the King began, "I have cause to recall a service performed by a Lapalisse long ago. . . ."

"My father, Sire," said Eustache Lapalisse. "You do him honor to remember, and he would have been pleased."

"Is he dead, then?"

"Many years past."

"Why did he disappear? My mother and Cardinal Mazarin wanted to reward him for his bravery."

"He would not have accepted a reward. And as for leaving, the nobles made life very uncomfortable for him here."

"That I can well imagine. But it was no slight service he performed, at great danger to himself. Ask me a boon so that I may pay my debt at least to his memory."

"Forgive me, Sire, if what I say sounds ungracious, but twice my family has been struck with tragedy through the actions of your court. After the rebellion, we lost our lands and were forced to move to the border country, where we have lived almost in poverty."

"Why didn't your father appeal to the Crown?"

"For what? He saw his service to you as one of duty and love. To have asked for help would have put a price on that which he held invaluable—his honor."

"I think I can understand that, although there aren't many here who possess the same quality. You said there was a second tragic occurrence?"

"Yes, Sire, and most recently. As I explained, we are poor. When my wife died two years ago, I went mad, and was no fit guardian for my young sister. A distant connection of our family, an elderly lady of good repute, suggested that Agnes come to court, promising to take care of the child and perhaps find a suitable husband for her. Because I was so consumed with self-pity, and refused to accept that duty myself, I doomed my innocent sister to death."

"My God!" Louis, sincerely shocked, led the weeping man to a chair, then, with his own hand, poured him a glass of wine. When Lapalisse was restored to a semblance of control, he continued in an unsteady voice, "I thought Agnes was safe because my dearest friend, the Duc d'Amberieu, wrote that he would give her his protection, as well. But both the lady and the Duc were lulled into believing that she was secure. She never entered into court life, preferring to serve the lady in little ways: reading to her, writing her letters, things of the sort an old lady required. As you undoubtedly know, the Duc had a secret retreat; an old chapel, I believe he said."

"Yes, I remember when I gave him permission to convert

it into a private chamber where he could work uninterrupted."

"He kindly gave Agnes permission to go there whenever he was not using it. My sister had always been a solitary child, preferring quiet, secluded places where she could be alone."

"Why was she never presented?"

"The Duc wanted to make the arrangements, but Agnes begged for a little time before being brought to the notice of the court. How little it mattered. I thought she was here at court; Théophile thought she had returned home. Only the old lady knew the truth and promised Agnes never to reveal it. I knew of nothing amiss until I received a message from the Mother Superior of a convent just outside the city. Upon my arrival I was shown my sister's grave and entrusted with her infant." He paused, trying to compose himself before continuing. "Before the birth of the child, Agnes seemed to know that she would die, and accepted her fate with great peace. She wrote me this letter," he pulled it from under his shirt, "telling me what had happened to her, even her final humiliation in the great hall when her seducer bared his chest for all to see and made sport of his time with her. But she did not tell me his name."

"May I read the letter, please?" Louis evidenced the good manners that were characteristic of him no matter with whom he was dealing. When he'd finished reading it, he spoke with sorrow.

"How gentle and good she must have been. She bears no shame for this deed. What may I do for you?"

"Allow me to search the vile creature out, Sire. Allow me to challenge him for killing my sister."

"I cannot permit any such disruption of my court. It would serve no purpose but to bring discredit upon your sister and stain your family name."

"But you said there was no shame attached to her."

"In our eyes. But those wild animals do not possess such tender sensibilities. They feed upon ruined reputations as vultures feed upon carrion. Let her sleep untroubled, Lapalisse. Retribution has already overtaken the villain."

"You know him, then?" he asked eagerly, and Louis nodded slowly.

"I knew him slightly. An amusing scoundrel of good birth. I heard of the episode in the great hall, and was as entertained by his tale as the others. He is no longer with us." He said this so solemnly that Lapalisse was content. "Trust me, my friend, when I tell you that he has destroyed himself, and it would be useless to search him out yourself. You must give me your word that you'll not pursue the matter. What would become of the child if a duel took place? If he killed you, or you killed him and were executed by the state for murder, what would become of the child?"

"But what have I to offer her?"

"Now that is something I can do. I will arrange that you become her guardian, and will deed her land and monies to assure her future so that she will always have a home and will never be forced to come to court. Before you leave Paris, you'll have documents giving her freedom of the realm and permission to travel where she will."

"These are great gifts, Sire, and I am truly grateful."

"Nonsense! It is I who am grateful for having the opportunity to repay a long overdue debt. It is a small price for a kingdom. I ask only that you write a report on her progress yearly. I promise you that she'll not be forgotten."

"Baron Lapalisse!" the innkeeper called as Eustache started up the stairs. "A moment of your time, please." The man stood in the doorway leading to the kitchen, motioning for Eustache to join him. "While you were out I admitted a visitor to your rooms."

"You took a great deal upon yourself! Did he give his name?" Eustache frowned angrily.

"I thought you might be expecting him."

"I am expecting no one." He was about to lecture the innkeeper but decided against making too much of it. "Very well, I'll see to it myself."

"Shall I bring some wine to your room?"

"That won't be necessary. And the next time I have a visitor, kindly have him wait downstairs."

"Eustache!" His visitor was Théophile d'Amberieu, his old friend, who embraced him unashamedly, pounding him on the back in his exuberance.

"It has been too long, my friend." He responded to Théophile's greeting with equal warmth. They stood back from each other, judging the toll the years had taken. Eustache had aged with tragedy, but Théophile, while aged by dissipation, retained all the flair and vitality he had possessed as a youth.

"You rogue!" He blinked away his tears. "You haven't changed at all. My God, it's good to see you again. What blessing from heaven brought you to Paris? Not that I would have it otherwise," Théophile d'Amberieu said. "And how is dear, sweet Agnes?"

"Agnes!" Eustache exclaimed guiltily; already he'd forgotten her. He tried to control himself, but in the comforting presence of his friend the tears flowed of their own will as he told the tale. Finally, wiping his eyes, he concluded, "I promised His Majesty to tell no one, but I know I can rely on you to hold your tongue."

"Of course, my friend. I just can't understand how such a thing happened. I share the blame, you know." He wasn't dry-eyed himself. "I truly believed that her innocence would protect her even in this hellhole. Do you know his name?"

"No, and I'm not permitted to discover it. His Majesty made me promise."

"I made no such promise!"

"Please, Théophile, don't attempt it. Agnes is at peace, and I don't want her name on these people's lips. All of Paris would know, and the city has a long memory. The child mustn't suffer."

"The child lives?"

"Yes. I have named her Euphémie."

"The name of a truly noble lady whose memory I hold

dear. This has been a great shock. Perhaps your grief will be lessened by your knowing that it is shared." He put his arm about his friend's shoulders. "I had planned a celebration for our reunion, but now . . ."

"Pray don't change your plans."

"So be it! I promise to show you every delight this wicked old harridan of a city has to offer."

Being with his friend again had wrought a small miracle in Eustache. Not since before his wife's long illness had he laughed as frequently or as freely. Only occasionally did he regretfully realize that he, rather than Agnes, should have made the journey to Paris. Théophile had insisted upon returning to the convent with his friend to see the babe for himself. He immediately took to her, carrying her about proudly. Eustache regarded his friend fondly.

"It is too bad that you never had children of your own," he remarked gently, knowing it to be a sensitive subject for Théophile.

"With that dried-up twig I was forced to marry? On our wedding night she confided to me that she had always wanted to be a nun. I've never forgiven her for not telling me before the ceremony. The only time I'd bed with her was in hopes of producing an heir, out of family loyalty. God in heaven, what sacrifices a man will make for his name! I think she used to pray that she wouldn't have a child. But what of you, my friend? What of children for yourself? You're not too old to remarry."

"I've never wanted to since my wife died, but there is Florimond. He's a fine son, Théophile; eight years old and the size of a boy half again his age. You'll see him later."

"Why didn't you ever acknowledge him, since you don't wish to remarry?"

"There was Agnes, and I had thought to name one of her sons as my heir, if she had lived and had a life like other women."

"But the boy is your son, even if your union with his mother wasn't blessed by the Church."

"There is so little I possess to leave any heir, but I've adopted Euphémie as my own daughter, and my only heir, so it's just as well I didn't marry."

"Will you share her with me, Eustache? May I also be her father?" Théophile's entreaty was passionate and his friend agreed, "Gladly!"

"I warn you, I'll take my duties seriously. Once a year I will visit our daughter and make certain that you're taking proper care of her and bringing her up as a lady. And, hear this, if you're not bringing her up in the proper way, I'll thrash you within an inch of my life." He handed the infant to the waiting nurse, and, arm in arm, the two men left the place ringing with their laughter.

3

"What can I be this time, Eustache?" the eleven-year-old Euphémie asked in all earnestness.

"You can be the maiden," the young man answered before Eustache could reply to the girl's question.

"I was the maiden last time," she complained. "Why do I always have to be the maiden?"

"Because you are a maiden. Even if you do wear a shirt and trousers like a boy, you are still a girl." Florimond was only teasing her, but she took him seriously, becoming angry.

"I am only a girl when Théophile comes to visit."

"That's enough, Florimond!" Eustache decided it was time to end the argument. "This is my game, and I will assign the roles. Do you both agree to stand by my decision?" When they agreed, he continued, "Florimond, you will be the villain."

"That fits you more than a maiden's role fits me," Euphémie interjected, and Eustache silenced her with a look.

"And I shall be the maiden," Eustache announced.

The girl jumped with delight, while Florimond conceded gracefully, winking at his father.

"All right, little hero," Eustache told her, "you can go and get the swords."

After she had run off across the lawn and into the house, Florimond laughed. "I hope one day she'll want to be a maiden, Eustache."

"There's plenty of time, yet. Look at the way she eagerly dresses up for Théophile during his visits."

"It's just another game to her."

"It was hard work getting her to agree to wear nothing but girl's clothes for so long a period."

"Not when you began assigning the role to her, and making up a story for it. It became just another adventure."

The two men sat in companionable silence while they waited for the child. Eustache had kept the promise he'd made at her birth, sparing no effort to ensure that she would be well-prepared for the moment when she would face life alone. Euphémie was given the same education as had been given Florimond earlier. She learned to ride as well as a man, and was given rigorous training in fencing and hunting. She was also taught how to read and write in her own language, and was familiar with the classics in Greek and Latin. Her only real difficulty was in mathematics, but she received enough background to enable her to manage the estate that would one day be hers.

Louis had kept his word, as well, and before she could form any permanent memories of the house in the mountain valley, the family moved to the south, where she blossomed in the mild climate and gentle countryside. She was never told of Agnes, accepting Eustache as her father and his dead wife as her mother. Despite Florimond's warning, Eustache was oblivious to the danger that the portrait of life that he painted in such adventurous hues and tones might have an effect opposite to that he wanted. Florimond, being far more objective about the child, was concerned about her love of fantasy and, at propitious moments, had tried to warn his father, but all attempts had failed. In one way only had Euphémie disappointed Eustache. She hadn't retained her homely shield, but showed promise of becoming a lovely young woman. She was quite tall for her age, and very athletic. Her light hair had darkened over the years to a shade of rich honey. Her face didn't possess what the world considered beauty, but it had a winsome quality. She had none of the awkwardness of most girls her age, but an easy, animal-like grace. Her spontaneous laughter was infectious. Her stubbornness, that bordered on the obstinate, was forgiven by the overindulgent Eustache, rather than being corrected.

"Phémie!" Florimond shouted, using the endearment that had been given her almost from the first. "Where has the urchin gotten to?" As Florimond ran into the house in search of his "sister," Eustache experienced the feeling of well-being he had whenever he watched the two of them. His belief that his son loved the girl as much as he did and would be with her after he had died was a source of great comfort.

"Eustache! Come quickly!" the young man called from the house, and with a sudden stabbing of fear, the older man hurried as fast as he could, visions of disaster to the child haunting him. He found Florimond and Phémie upstairs, and what he saw made him fall against the doorway, laughing in relief. Florimond held the struggling Phémie high in his arms. Scattered about the floor was her beautiful long hair, shorn by the girl herself. The young man set her on her feet roughly, still keeping a grip on her, while he ran his free hand through what was left of her hair.

"Look what she's done to herself now," he complained, exasperated. Phémie stopped struggling and addressed him logically.

"Now I won't ever have to be the maiden, will I?"

"But your hair . . ." the youth began, and Eustache took his part.

"You did a very bad thing, Euphémie. What will Théophile say?"

"You can tell him I had a fever and the surgeon cut it."

"You'll have to be a maiden someday, my child. What will you do then?"

"Don't be angry, please," she entreated the two men in her life. "I'll be good from now on, I promise. And," she addressed this to Florimond, "I'll let you be the hero whenever you want, and I'll be the villain."

Florimond could only shake his head hopelessly, realizing that further censure was useless.

"Well, it's been done, and we can't undo it," Eustache said sensibly, and Florimond had no choice but to concur.

"Let's see if the damage can be repaired. It looks pretty hopeless." Picking up the knife, he tried to even the length a bit. When he was finished, Phémie was thrilled with the shaggy hair just barely covering her neck. "I'll get the swords now."

"It would seem that I'm to be the maiden from now on." Eustache laughed, and his son retorted sourly, "You'd best let your hair grow, and borrow some skirts from one of the women. As for me, I'm going to find a good hiding place. Théophile will be here shortly, and I'm not going to take the blame for this."

Florimond did not underestimate Théophile's reaction to the fiasco. Phémie donned her dress for his arrival and felt no trepidation at all, having absolute faith in Eustache's ability to soothe the reaction that was certain to come, and come violently, from the Duc.

As was usual, Théophile's humor, when he arrived at the chateau, was excellent. His booming laughter could be heard all the way into her room as he greeted Eustache and called for his "daughter." Phémie ran down the stairs, out of the house, and straight into his outstretched arms, hugging him closely. As he looked down on the child's head, all tenderness disappeared, replaced by horror.

"What, in the name of all the saints, happened to this girl?"

"She suffered a fever a short while ago," Eustache supplied sheepishly. "The surgeon had to cut her hair."

"Thank God he's a better surgeon than he is a barber," he

responded caustically. "And I don't believe you for a moment, Eustache Lapalisse. Where is Florimond? Was this his handiwork?"

"He's hiding from you, Théophile," Phémie volunteered innocently.

"I'll have his hide!" the Duc roared, and when Phémie didn't supply the truth, Eustache warned, "You'd best tell the truth, Euphémie. You must never allow someone else to suffer for something you, yourself, did."

With faltering voice, she related the whole of it to the Duc, whose expression became darker and darker with the telling. Forbearing to make comment in her presence, he sent her to find Florimond. When she had run off, he turned to Eustache.

"I have never approved of the unsuitable education you've been giving that child. But now I hear of fencing and play-acting; villains and heroes and maidens. What am I to think, Eustache?"

"I know how you must feel, and I am sorry that you've found out. I would ask your forgiveness, my friend, but I can't bring myself to do it. Looking at Euphémie at times I think of Agnes, and realize that even if she'd had a weapon to defend herself, she wouldn't have known how to use it."

"That won't do any more, Eustache." He was severe in his disapproval. "You promised to prepare her for life as it really is, but you have romanticized it with your own love of games. All this talk about villains and heroes and fair maidens. My God, man, life is not like that! A man is both a villain and a hero, depending upon the circumstances he finds himself in. Neither heroes nor villains are born; they become one or the other in a crisis, and once that crisis has passed, they go back to being just men. What if Phémie encounters someone who meets her requirement of a hero in that one instance? She'll go on thinking he's yet a hero, and when he proves otherwise and cannot live up to her opinion of him, she's likely to be very unhappy."

"It's not that serious," Eustache commented, shrugging his shoulders.

"Whether you realize it or not, my friend, Euphémie will not always be a child. One day she'll be a woman, and will seek a husband. What kind of a choice will she make with a background of this nonsense? These games must stop."

"I must agree with you, Your Grace." Florimond joined them, having sent the girl on an errand.

"My boy!" The Duc embraced him warmly. "It hardly seems possible, but you have grown even taller."

"I can't agree with you." Eustache continued the argument, becoming petulant, feeling that his son had betrayed him.

"She's a woman, or will be one day soon. And women, like heroes and villains, are not born good or bad. Who will protect her when you and I are gone, and Florimond marries and has a family of his own? Your preparation for life is doing nothing but making it necessary that she have constant protection."

"You are too harsh!"

"Not at all. I love her too, Eustache, and I want to see her happy as much as you do. These games are great entertainment, I know. They are as entertaining for you as they are for the child. You must not let your own enjoyment blind you to Euphémie's safety. I beg of you, send her to a convent school where some of the damage will be erased by the good sisters. They will teach her decorum and a sense of responsibility as a woman and a lady."

"No!" Florimond blurted, unthinkingly, then flushed at his misstep as the men looked at him, one surprised and the other relieved.

"You showed good sense a moment ago, young man. What is the reason for your change of heart?" The Duc's attitude changed toward him, and Florimond was not unaware of the chill.

"I agreed with you about the games, Your Grace, but I cannot about the school. It would break Phémie's heart as well as her spirit to be sent away. She seems wild now, but all she needs is gentling."

"Are you equating Euphémie with a horse?"

"Children and horses are much the same." Florimond refused to be intimidated. "They sense things more than they think them through and are much more manageable with kindness."

Eustache saw that there would be an open breach, and hastened to offer a compromise.

"I'll make a bargain with you, Théophile. I'll not allow the games any more if she may remain here with us."

"My dear friend," he had become distant, even from Eustache, "you are her guardian. I can only offer suggestions having no legal power over her."

"I've never used that against you." Eustache was stung by the injustice. "Florimond has been in opposition to the games for quite a while now. And you just said that he was sensible. I'm willing to accede to his judgment, if you are."

"No more villains or heroes?"

"Agreed!"

"I only pray that the damage is reversible," Théophile replied, still disturbed by the whole situation. "You must promise me that you'll work very hard to undo what you have done."

"You have my word," Eustache promised readily, and the thaw was complete. Putting an arm about the shoulders of Eustache and his son, the Duc propelled them into the house, his good humor restored.

Eustache kept his word about the games, knowing full well that Théophile, if he was convinced it was for the child's welfare, would go to Louis for support. Phémie accepted his edict without demurring, and this behavior was so unusual in the girl that Florimond suspected that she had overheard much of what had been said by her elders.

She even accepted, without complaint, the dancing master whom Théophile sent to instruct her and Florimond. The youth thought that he was far too old for such nonsense, but the Duc had asked it of him as a special favor, so he attended, but under protest. Phémie had little difficulty in mastering the intricate steps and patterns of dance, as well as the various degrees of curtsey required when one was presented to each rank. The master never spoke of the nobility as people, only ranks, much to his students' amusement. First, there was the royal family, of which only the King's brother remained; then the Princes du Sang, which included all the King's other relatives. Third in the great pyramid were the Ducs et Pair, of which Théophile was a prominent member. These personages were also given the title of Cousin du Roi and were allowed to sit in the presence of the Queen, even at her table. Next, the Princes Légitimes, the acknowledged illegitimate children of the King and their descendants. Following were the Princes Etrangers, independent princes but subject to His Majesty. Finally, there were the various Marquises, Comtes, Barons, and the very lowest of all, Chevaliers.

Florimond found such lessons an absurdity, but Phémie was fascinated by tales of the glittering court, the scene of a countless number of possible adventures. She kept these dreams to herself, knowing that such thoughts would be disapproved of, and rising before her always was the specter of convent school.

4

Shortly after Phémie's sixteenth birthday, a fever raged through the countryside and many people lost loved ones, including Florimond and Euphémie Lapalisse. With overwhelming sorrow, Théophile rushed from Paris to be with the young people and to settle the estate of his old friend, Eustache. Upon his arrival, the members of the household, including the servants, were called into the drawing room, where the Duc informed each of the various bequests and gifts that Eustache had meant for them.

When all had departed, leaving Phémie and Théophile alone, Phémie demanded, "What of Florimond? Is there no mention of Florimond in the will?" She had remained very calm during the reading, but now jumped to her feet, facing Théophile angrily.

"He did not acknowledge Florimond before his death, Euphémie, so he could not mention him to this document."

"Then there is another document?"

"Yes . . ." he admitted reluctantly. "But there are other things to discuss, more important things, my child."

"There is nothing more important than Florimond." She disagreed, and he scolded, "You are being most ill-mannered. If you cannot contain your impatience, and realize that perhaps I am a better judge of what is or is not of importance at this time, I suggest that you retire to your room."

No one had ever spoken to her in that way before, and she was shamed. "Forgive me, Théophile."

"I appreciate your concern for Florimond. Believe me, I have not forgotten him. At this moment, your future is of first concern to me. With Eustache's death, your position becomes very dangerous."

"I don't understand."

"It is very simple. You are not of age yet, and there exists the possibility that you will be made a ward of the Crown."

Phémie sat down abruptly, paling. "Is it truly possible? Couldn't Florimond be made my guardian?"

"A bastard whose father never really acknowledged him? I'm afraid not, my dear."

"I hesitate to ask so great a boon, Théophile, but what about you? I promise I'd never be a burden, or troublesome to you in any way."

"You could never be a burden, Euphémie, but I don't believe it would be possible. I'm an old man, and it would be a mere postponement of the inevitable. Once you've been made a ward of the Crown, I'm afraid an arranged marriage would follow very shortly."

"He wouldn't do that! He promised . . ."

"The precious papers! I am fully aware of their existence. But, legally, you could not take advantage of them until you are of age. Besides, those promises were made to Eustache in your behalf. If Louis changes his mind, and determines that marriage would be best for you, you would then come under your husband's guardianship and the papers would have no real value."

"What can I do?" she asked wildly, feeling trapped, with no recourse to mercy.

"There is a way, but I hesitate presenting it to you." He cleared his throat. "As I said, I am an old man, and have always regarded you as a daughter. A few years ago it was my plan to adopt you as my legal heir, and in that way, the Lapalisse title and estate could fall to Florimond. But . . ." He held up a hand, motioning her to silence as she was about to speak. "When I approached His Majesty concerning the matter of adoption, he could not grant my request. Oh, he was most regretful, but the law was clear. You could receive a portion of my fortune, but the rest, along with the title, would fall to the Crown. I am loath to have this happen, Euphémie. In fact, I am so loath to have this happen, I am willing to prevent it at any cost. Even His Majesty's disapproval."

"Would you really?" She was wide-eyed at his daring. "That is very brave of you, Théophile."

"It is very important to me. Not only because I would be unhappy seeing the estate in the hands of His Majesty, to be doled out to that pack at court for favors, but because I believe a man should have a right to choose his own heir, male or female. Everything I possess will be yours, Euphémie, if you'll forgive my boldness and consider becoming my wife."

She was not as surprised as he thought she would be, merely leaning back in her chair and waiting for him to continue.

"Needless to say, I would never expect to consummate the marriage. As my wife you would be safe from being made a ward of the Crown, and also from any marriage Louis would want to arrange, naturally."

"And as your widow?" She was not hesitant of speaking so in his presence.

"You would, by marriage, be a Cousin du Roi and exempt from any such arrangement."

"You are certain he couldn't force me?"

"Absolutely. He may try to influence you, but he cannot

command you. Also, if you were my wife, the Lapalisse title would be vacant."

"Florimond!" she exclaimed simply.

"Exactly. I have a document written in Eustache's own hand, and properly witnessed, acknowledging Florimond as his son."

"Why didn't Eustache release it, himself? It would have meant so much to Florimond."

"It would have left you unprotected, my dear. In the event of your marriage, however, I was to submit the acknowledgment, along with a petition that the young man be given the title and certain monies Eustache set aside for him."

She considered for but a moment, then stated with dignity, "I have a very deep affection for you, Théophile, and would be honored to become your wife."

The Duc burst into laughter, and the girl became confused. "Didn't I say it right?"

"A woman with far more years than you couldn't have said it more properly." He became serious again, admitting ruefully, "I may not always have seemed a kind and patient man, and I can only hope that what I am about to say will not be misunderstood as to be anything but in your best interest, and Florimond's interest, as well."

"Please continue."

"To be perfectly honest with you, Florimond is not really prepared to step into his new role. He lacks polish, my dear, and this will go against him when he is presented to the court as the new Baron Lapalisse. I can arrange a postponement of that presentation until he has attended a university and has traveled. Nothing gives a man polish as much as travel."

"I can appreciate the necessity of what you suggest. And as to my interest?"

"You cannot remain here without a relative's protection, and I don't want you exposed to court life at your age."

"Then it's the convent school, after all." She laughed at his expression. "I overheard when you were talking with

Eustache and Florimond. I used to listen to conversations I wasn't intended to hear. To be quite honest, that is how I learned that Agnes and not Eustache's wife, was my mother." She had calculated the effect this might have on him and was not disappointed. "Do not look so dismayed, Théophile. I overheard that many years ago, when Eustache was telling Florimond about it, and I have grown accustomed to the truth. Remember those games Eustache would allow us to play? I used to pretend that the fair maiden was my mother, and I was the hero defending her honor in the palace chapel."

"You poor child!" he commiserated, and she flared angrily, "Save your pity. I have learned a great deal about acceptance of an unpleasant situation. Did you see Florimond tonight? Not even to have his name mentioned in the will! His heart was breaking, but he accepted. My cousin is far more understanding than I would be. May we call him in now, please? He will be so happy that Eustache did not forget him."

At the school for young women of noble birth, Euphémie had her first experience with boredom. She was forced to wear dresses every day, as well as wigs and the rest of the paraphernalia considered proper by the unbending, gray-faced ladies who were responsible for the bodies as well as the souls of their charges. The only time she was allowed to return home was for the Christmas holidays, when Florimond would return also. At these times, she reverted, joyously and without restraint, to her old ways. Théophile could no longer make his annual visit because of his duties at court and increasing ill health. However, he was a faithful correspondent, and she looked forward to receiving his letters.

The only benefit she gained from the school, in her estimation, was her friendship with Mignon Chazelles, whose father was the Governor of a far-flung colony. The two girls were completely opposite in temperament and behavior, as Mignon was shy, sweet, and gentle. Until Phémie's friendship, the wealthier girls had bullied her mercilessly, so the Duchesse had become her protector, as well. When Mignon was called back home, the parting was heartrending for both girls. Phémie was required to stay almost four years longer, more alone than she had ever been in her entire life. The day that she received news of the death of her husband, and dear friend, Phémie became her own mistress and left the school of her own volition. No one, she vowed to herself, no matter how well-intentioned, was ever going to enforce his will upon her again.

5

Charles de Montais was a very inconspicuous fellow; his life at court was free from strife and struggle. He worked very hard to get it that way, and harder yet to keep it that way. He was successful in his efforts to remain separate from any friendly or romantic entanglements, confining himself to brief interludes rather than long-term affairs. He never entered into political intrigues, cliques of power, or kept the company of ambitious men. He listened to gossip—who could prevent it in the scandal-hungry court?—but never repeated it. He abhorred the practical jokes that were so dear to the courtiers' hearts. He played cards, more as a social gesture than from the desperate need to win, as with his peers. He danced very well, was a master of the compliment, especially to the older ladies, and could ride on a hunt without disgracing himself. In the eyes of others, he was completely inoffensive, non-competitive and harmless, so was well-liked and the receiver of many confidences. In his own eyes, he considered himself a casual observer by talent rather than vocation. He was fascinated, and more than a little repelled, by the people surrounding him.

When he married, far beneath his station, the lovely, empty-headed daughter of a wealthy merchant, he became the target of a great deal of ridicule. His wife's subsequent amoral behavior brought further ridicule to him, but Charles rode out the storm, as publicly unperturbed as ever, until the gossips' attention was drawn elsewhere. While he may not have been blessed with a faithful and loving wife, he had found a friend, that rarest of commodities, in his father-in-law, who saw to his every need and comfort.

His very inconspicuousness brought Charles, unknowingly, under the scrutiny of his King. Louis was so accustomed to being besieged with petitions and requests for favors that the one man who had never asked him for anything interested him. Occasionally noticing de Montais in the throng about him, Louis would be reminded of his puzzling behavior. The man had the reputation of being a fool. His wife was extremely indiscreet in her affairs of the heart and skated dangerously close to the edge of scandal time and time again, just barely escaping banishment from the court. While Charles was unfailingly polite to his vicious and erring wife whenever they chanced to meet, she was particularly abusive. The Comte would merely sweep her a bow and retire gracefully, always to his credit; he wore the horns she'd given him better than any man Louis had ever seen.

The King was prejudiced against women who took pleasure in abusing their husbands, so he tried to make his courtier's life more pleasant. Without prior warning, he had de Montais's furnishings moved from a cubicle in the upper attic of the Louvre to a suite of rooms on the ground floor. Louis received a very proper note of gratitude, but the man still didn't approach him, although Charles, he knew, was being assailed with requests of others to present petitions for them during the time of his new-found favor. One night, one of those courtiers who found talking to Charles such a comfort had imbibed too heavily and told him far more than he realized. The drunken indiscretion passed unnoticed by the man, and Charles made no effort to have him enlarge upon the remark, allowing him to pass on to safer subjects until he passed out. After a lackey removed the man to his own quarters, Charles requested an interview with the King through the usual channels. Since he had not petitioned for a private meeting, Charles was neither surprised nor dismayed to find the antechamber crowded with people when he arrived at the appointed time, and he wore the usual vacant expression he'd cultivated with such care when he approached the King.

"Sire!"

"De Montais." Louis acknowledged Charles's bow, eyeing with great curiosity the box his courtier was carrying.

"My esteemed father-in-law, the merchant LeForge, has, for several years, been indulging in a favorite pastime that he was not permitted when his house was cluttered with women."

"I congratulate him!" Louis commented with a wry expression, and his audience was required to control their laughter, as everyone knew of the difficulties he was having with the favorite, de Montespan.

"When I told him of your latest bereavement, he requested that I present you with this small gift as a token of his great regard." Charles placed the box on the table, removed the top, and stepped back, allowing Louis to look within. With an exclamation of delight, the King lifted out the beautifully marked springer puppy, nuzzling it fondly and letting it lick his face.

"What a wonderful gift! You need not thank him for me, de Montais; I'll write him myself."

"Such an honor would greatly please him, Your Majesty. He has had great success with dogs, so he took the liberty of sending along a menu for feeding, if it please Your Majesty."

Louis accepted the paper Charles handed to him and as he read it, his expression didn't change in the least. With great care, he handed it back to his courtier, commenting, "It is not unlike my own."

Charles accepted the reply with good grace and took his leave immediately. He had not expected the news he had secreted within the so-called menu to please the King and could hope only that he had not overstepped his position by warning him of an impending disaster. Not until a few days later was Charles informed, unobtrusively, that he was wanted by the King. The hour appointed was long after the court had retired, so the courtier entered the royal apartment unobserved. Louis was sitting up in bed, waiting for him.

Their conversation was lengthy, the King questioning him about his marriage, his friendship with his wife's father, and his reaction to the attitude of the court toward him. Louis was well informed concerning all his courtiers, and everything Charles told him merely confirmed the information he'd already been given. What he had not known was that de Montais had purposely cultivated the facade of a fool, that he was a confidant of highly placed men as well as ladies, and that his only ambition was to serve his King. Louis immediately saw the possibilities of de Montais's unique position; the man had already been instrumental in helping the King to prevent a major scandal which would have involved a member of the royal family.

Charles became Louis's very secret and very special ambassador at large. Whenever they met, whether for the assignment of a task or the delivery of a report, it was always clandestinely. Most of his duties involved the delivery of messages too personal to be handled by a royal messenger; or the feeling out of possible political negotiations too unofficial to be handled by a minister. His assignments were as close as the Palais Royale and as far flung as England, Flanders, or Spain.

It had been Charles who informed Louis of the epidemic poisonings taking place right under his royal nose. De Montais had his first suspicion when a great lady of the court, who was used to confiding in him, told him of the poisoning by a lady and her lover of the lady's husband. There were no names given, but his informant's terror convinced him that there might be some truth to the remark. The more he investigated, not yet telling the King of his suspicions, the more alarmed he became. From sources of information that no one else would ever have been able to tap, Charles followed a trail that ultimately led him to Madame de Montespan. The lady, it would seem, had been frequenting a certain Madame Voisin, a self-claimed witch, for many years. Her latest contact with the woman had been for aphrodisiacs to revive her royal paramour's flagging interest. In the past she had resorted to love philters, spells, incantations, and, it was whispered to him, even a Black Mass. Not for a moment did he believe de Montespan would attempt poisoning her lover, but he realized, however, that the Voisin witch could easily substitute, for a fee and without her noble client's knowledge, a poison in the place of her usual prescription.

The first time Louis became ill, Charles put it down to natural causes, for the King had a tendency to overeat. The second time, following so closely upon the first, spurred Charles to action. The courtier didn't wait until the King had fully recovered from his "indisposition." Approaching the trusted servant who was their liaison, de Montais gained admittance to the King's presence at the usual late hour. As always, Louis listened to the whole story, interjecting a pertinent question where Charles, in his anxiety, hadn't been too clear. When he reached the part about Madame de Montespan's also using the potions of Madame Voisin, he prefaced his comments with his belief in that lady's innocence. At the conclusion, the King agreed that the lady was undoubtedly innocent, but could have been duped easily. As de Montais was about to leave, Louis stated that he was fully aware of the service performed by his faithful courtier and promised, someday, to be able to reward him in full measure.

The scandal of the poisonings first broke over Paris, and then the court. Louis appointed one of his favorites, Louvois, to work in liaison with LeReynie, the head of the Paris police. It was agreed that Parliament should not become involved because of its obvious favoritism to the upper classes, so the Chambre Ardente was assigned to begin proceedings. For three years the investigations and trials continued, with Madame Voisin, among others, condemned as a witch and meeting her death at the stake. Her list of crimes—the Black Mass, sacrificing babies, abortions, poisoning—was formidable; yet under extreme torture, she never once mentioned the name of Madame de Montespan. Many other prominent names were mentioned, even some of the King's friends. Louis remained firm, telling the Chambre to continue its inquiries, no matter where they led.

Despite this edict, the Chambre proved as ineffectual as it had been feared Parliament would be. A few wealthy ladies of the bourgeoisie were sent away to repent in convents for the remainder of their lives. The largest scandal came after the first year of investigation. Warrants had been issued for the arrest of a Comtesse, for the murder of her husband; a Marquise, for doing away with her father-in-law; a powerful and popular Maréchal for murder and resorting to witchcraft; a Duchesse for murdering a valet who knew about her affairs of the heart and the attempted poisoning of her husband; and, most scandalous of all, one of the Queen's own ladies, a Princesse, who was accused of murdering her own baby. All but one of the nobles were acquitted; the Comtesse fled the country and never returned.

When the Chambre finally closed its doors, it had earned the derision of the whole world. De Montais had been spared the investigation and attendant publicity. He had proved too valuable to the King to have him involved in any way. He attended the trials and discussed the latest developments with as much horror as anyone. Louis hadn't assigned him a task during the years of scandal, as the courtiers had awakened with a shock and were watching everyone else too closely. It wasn't until after the court had been moved to the new palace of Versailles that he was finally sent for. Charles found his new assignment actually dull, but he accepted it gratefully; anything was better than remaining at Versailles during the chaos of moving.

Traveling south at the King's behest to the Lapalisse chateau, Charles was disappointed to learn that the Duchesse d'Amberieu was making her annual pilgrimage to her husband's estate in Bretagne, in the company of her cousin, the Baron, and that the only approach to the isolated chateau was by sea. Upon reaching Brest, he was able to hire a guide, a native of the village he intended to visit. During the remainder of the voyage to the coast of Mer de Gascogne, he tried unsuccessfully to learn something about the d'Amberieu widow. No one at court had known of a second marriage of the Duc, and he wondered why the King had not "requested" the Duchesse's presence at court before now; or why she, herself, had not tried to find a place at the hub of the universe, which Versailles was fated to become. The Duc had died shortly before the poisionings became common knowledge, but he had been an elderly man who had been ill for some time before his death. Since he hadn't left Versailles for several years, and his wife had not been presented at court, there could be no suspicion that she had helped her husband out of this world. The verbal request de Montais carried was an invitation. The more he thought about his assignment, the more puzzling it became.

His guide was amiable enough when conversing on neutral subjects, but became deaf at any mention of the Duchesse. If he had been less polite, Charles would have had a complaint. As it was, the fellow's attitude lent even more intrigue to the mission. At their destination, the guide accepted his fee and was over the side even before the courtier came on deck. Charles surveyed the rugged cliffs and small cove with distaste. The "village" was extremely dismal. There had been rain that morning, and everything looked gray from where he stood. Even the boats pulled up onto the sand were bereft of any color. There was no gaiety here; only a small knot of men standing near the shore staring at the ship anchored in the bay. Charles climbed into the longboat and was rowed ashore. As he approached the men, they removed their caps, and Charles asked directions to the chateau.

"You'll not get there in those shoes," a voice said from

behind him, and turning, he saw a young woman, her gender barely discernible in the fisherman's boots, trousers, shirt, and jacket she wore. To his credit, de Montais recovered gracefully from his surprise.

"Is it far, mademoiselle?"

"In the mud? Yes, it is far."

"Perhaps I could borrow some boots." He looked hopefully at the friendly faces about him. "I'll pay a fair price."

"That won't be necessary; I'll take you in my cart."

"You're very kind, mademoiselle."

"If you'd ever ridden in an ox cart, you wouldn't say so. And you'll have to share your passage with a load of fish."

"If they won't object to my presence, I won't object to theirs."

The woman smiled appreciatively, and one of the men commented, "You're a rare fish yourself, monsieur."

Charles laughed with them, bowing in farewell, then followed the woman to the cart. It was true that he'd not had many dealings with the *hobereaux*, the provincial nobility; but, even so, it was not usual for a woman to dress as his present guide did. Everything about her was natural, from the curl in her short, honey-colored hair to the sprinkling of freckles across her high cheekbones; her walk was more of a stride, and she moved with the easy, animal-like grace of those who spend most of their time out-of-doors. His trained eye noted that, despite the common cut, her clothes were of the finest material and her boots were made of Spanish leather. The clothes could have been handed down to her, but the boots were her own. Her manner was as natural as the rest of her; there was nothing subservient or shy about her, but then, there hadn't been about the fishermen, either. She was certainly taking a chance, wearing those trousers among the men, he thought, looking at the long, well-shaped legs with appreciation, and wondered if her morals were as easy as her manner.

When they reached the cart, she rearranged the baskets of fish to make a place for him. He had barely time enough to seat himself on the straw before the cart started off with a jerk. To his dismay, she was walking along beside, prodding the beasts with a stick.

"Mademoiselle, I beg of you!" he protested, "I cannot ride while you walk."

"Don't be distressed, monsieur. One cannot drive oxen as one would a team of horses. I would walk whether you were here or not, so compose yourself." She spoke so matter-of-factly that she left no room for further discussion. "How do you like Bretagne, monsieur?" she asked conversationally once he had settled back.

"It's not as pleasant as the Lapalisse estate," he commented slyly, and the look she gave him was penetrating.

"Every place has its own kind of beauty. I love the sea, and the rocks, and the sky. Nowhere else have I seen clouds like these." She pointed up to the high, billowing clouds above them.

"I preferred the trees and greenery of the Lapalisse estate," he persisted doggedly, but she only shrugged.

"The good God made us all different."

"Have you ever been there?" he asked directly, and she smiled slightly.

"Oh, yes; I spent most of my life there."

"Are you in the service of the Duchesse?" he asked, feeling very uncomfortable with the need for such directness.

"No, I'm the cousin of the Baron Lapalisse."

"I do beg your pardon, mademoiselle!" he exclaimed, horrified by his error, but she didn't appear to take offense, waving his apology away lightly, and asking, "Do you come from Paris or Versailles?"

"Versailles," he admitted slowly, watching for her reaction. When it came, it puzzled him, as most everything about her had done. She became very thoughtful, commenting softly, "That is indeed far away; not only in distance and time."

"I don't understand you," he said frankly, and she looked over her shoulder at him for a moment.

"It's of no matter. Tell me, is Princesse Antoinette still one of the Queen's ladies?"

"Nothing was ever proven against her, or any of the others."

"It would seem that their position at Versailles protected them."

"So it would seem," he agreed sourly. "The trials were a farce."

"What do you think of the poisoners' return to court?"

"I have my own cook, mademoiselle, and drink my own wine."

"Say no more!" She snorted shortly. "A fine place, your Versailles. 'The City of the Rich!' It's more like the City of the Corrupt. But you seem like a decent enough fellow, though."

"There are a few of us, mademoiselle. The Duc d'Amberieu was one of our number."

"From what I've heard, he found the intrigues a source of entertainment. I believe he admitted to being eminently suited to that way of life. Would you say the same for yourself?"

"No, I would not!" he answered quickly, hoping he didn't sound pompous as he continued, "I only wish to serve His Majesty."

"A very noble ambition."

How shallow he must sound to her, he thought, and wondered why he had admitted such a private feeling to a stranger.

"I was not doubting your sincerity, monsieur." It was as if she'd sensed his regret in being so honest with her. "My uncle, the Baron Eustache Lapalisse, bent every effort to teach my cousin, his heir, and me the same sentiment. We were also taught that the people at court were there to serve themselves. The King once told Eustache that the courtiers were like wild animals and he dared not turn them loose on France. Could you leave Versailles and live elsewhere, if you wished to?"

"Where would I go, even if His Majesty permitted it, which is doubtful? Our family lands were sold before my birth; the house in Paris was disposed of when my parents moved to the court. What would I do? I spent my childhood and young manhood in schools and the university, but learned nothing in particular. I have no relatives. We are all prisoners, even His Majesty."

"Are you married, monsieur? Do you have a very beautiful wife?"

"Yes, I am married to a beautiful woman. Unfortunately, I am not the only man to have found her beautiful."

"Forgive my impertinence, monsieur. It was none of my affair." She was ashamed of herself and was silent for a few moments before saying, "My name is Phémie."

"And mine is Charles. You're a very strange person, Phémie."

"Not so strange as undisciplined. It is only rarely that there is a need for me to hold my tongue. Florimond—that's my cousin, the Baron—is always warning me, but like any unruly child, I won't listen. I fear I've hurt you."

"Not you, my dear. I'm not usually so sensitive upon the subject of my wife. Are you married?"

"No, thank the good God! There are enough problems in life without a husband."

"What else is there for a woman but a husband and children?"

"For most women, nothing; I envy them only for their children. There are a great many advantages to freedom, Charles. Can you imagine any man who would approve of the way I choose to dress? Or my going to the inn for a glass of wine with the fishermen after we'd been out in the boats?"

"I can well imagine that your mode of life would be frowned upon by most men. But there are advantages to marriage, as well."

"What? Having a roof over my head or food in my belly? I have everything I need. Perhaps you meant sharing my bed? I can do that without marriage, if I were of that mind. Versailles is not noted for its chaste women, Charles, so you must know how easy that is. I've not met the man . . ." She paused, having the grace to blush. "You make it easy to forget that we've not known each other for long. You have a wonderful ability, putting people so at ease that they tell you anything; even things they'd not say to their closest friends. You should have been a priest."

"I've never thought of that." He laughed with her, and they were comfortable with each other again.

6

"There's the house." She pointed in the distance and he turned, seeing an ancient stone house balanced on the cliff. He'd known that they were climbing, but was unprepared for the broad plateau stretching to the horizon, where it met an incredibly blue sky.

"It must be very old."

"I don't think anyone knows its exact age. The d'Amberieus were originally Northmen and made their home in Normandy. There was a quarrel of some sort, so they left the settlement and came here alone. The oldest part of the house is like a fortress. It looks as if it were carved out of the cliff, doesn't it?"

"As though Nature were the architect, and fashioned it without the help of man."

"How nicely said! It's not as primitive as one might think. You'll see when you get inside."

"Did you know the Duc, Phémie?"

"We were related by marriage, and he was like a father to

me; very loving, but very stern. He wanted me to be a lady, I'm afraid." She shook her head wonderingly. "If you can imagine such a thing."

"I think I can. You're more of a lady than many I've met."

"I know you mean that as a compliment, but I don't want to be a lady. I can't think of anything more stifling."

"What do you want, Phémie?"

"An adventure; a real adventure," she replied unhesitatingly. "Not just going out on the fishing boats or looking for treasure . . ."

"Treasure?" He was amazed. "Here?"

"And why not here?" she countered, on the defensive. "But I talk too much . . ."

"No, please," Charles entreated, "don't stop. I promise never to tell anyone."

"Forgive my bluntness, but you're from Versailles. I don't think I can trust you."

"Believe me, please. I swear I'll never reveal your secret."

"Your sacred oath?" She demanded eagerly, and he agreed, "On my hope for heaven."

She was silent for a moment, making up her mind, then relented, "I should talk to Florimond first, but since you've given your oath, I can tell you this much. There is a riddle written in the d'Amberieu family Bible that is supposedly the key to some mysterious treasure. Florimond and I have looked for it every time we come here, but to no avail."

"What is the riddle?"

She hesitated, apparently undecided, and he misunderstood the reason for her reluctance to tell him.

"Come now, I've given my oath," he prompted, but she shook her tousled head, "It isn't that! I'm just afraid you'll think it's a child's game, as Florimond does. It doesn't make any sense, you see, and Florimond thinks that it was made up to entertain children."

"A riddle can't help sounding like a game, for that is exactly what it is. But it's also the best way to keep something secret. And the more senseless it sounds, the more difficult it is to find the real meaning."

"All right, then." She was easily convinced, and recited, after noisily clearing her throat:

> "In my father's castle
> Keep a tower bold, tower deep
> From the burning cross count nine
> Then twelve on high in a line."

"It says nothing about treasure."

"I know, but Théophile said that it led to an ancient family treasure," she responded petulantly, as if tired of arguments.

"But why all the secrecy if it belonged to the family?"

"Théophile thought that perhaps they expected an attack of some kind. Why else would they need to build a fortress? He would laugh at the possibility that when they left the other Northmen, they didn't leave empty-handed. He used to say that they were probably nothing more than pirates, and were afraid the others would find them. When the family became 'civilized,' and took a French name, only the riddle remained."

"Did he have any proof? Were there any other records?"

"No, only the riddle written in the Bible. He was certain they were pirates and looters; he said all the Northmen were."

"He had a very low opinion of his ancestors," Charles commented lightly, and she shrugged.

"He had a right to any opinion he chose; it was his family, after all."

"Of course. I did not mean to offend you." He was quick to apologize, but she only laughed.

"It means nothing to me. I think he was secretly proud of his family's dishonorable past. I don't know whether he believed in the riddle when he told us about it, but he did admit that, as a boy, he'd had many hours of enjoyment in looking for it."

"Will the Duchesse permit me to assist you?"

"Oh, her!" She dismissed the mistress of the house with a

casual gesture, obviously considering it of such little importance as to be unworthy of further comment.

"And your cousin, the Baron?"

"I'm very disappointed in him. I'm certain he believed in the beginning, but now he says it is only for children; meaning me, of course, but I don't care. If we find it, he'll look the fool, not I." The last was said with feeling, and Charles saw the specter of failure rising before him. Unwittingly he had entered an armed camp and become allied with its least important protagonist. Least important? he asked himself; least important to what? To his mission, certainly, but otherwise, no. He suddenly saw her not as a young woman capable of caring for herself, but as a neglected waif surrounded by powerful relations. She'd spoken only of her uncle, never her parents, so she was probably an orphan thrown on the charity of her wealthy family. His first duty was to his mission, of course; but after that, it if were permitted, he would help her find the treasure. It was undoubtedly the only dream she possessed.

"At first we counted nine paces from every crucifix and cross-beam in the house," she was saying. "We dug up flagstones from the floor and loosened stones in the walls. All to no avail."

"Without understanding the beginning of the riddle, the second part leads nowhere."

"But it is there, Charles. Every time I enter that heap of stones, I know it's there. Can you understand?"

"I think I can. But if we find it, we'll have to tell the Duchesse."

"Why?" she demanded, and Charles saw a possible source of real trouble.

"Because she is the rightful owner; it belongs to her family."

"Nonsense! It belonged to the Northmen, and they're all dead. I know!" She was suddenly struck by an idea, and the courtier braced himself inwardly. "We'll smuggle it down to your ship to avoid any difficulty. She'll never know it exists."

"That's madness!" He laughed. "Smuggling, piracy, stealing off in the night. And what would you do with your loot?"

"I'd buy a great ship, one that can sail all the oceans of the world. I'd go to New France, or the Indies, and have some real adventures."

"Why not go to Versailles? There is enough adventure there to last a lifetime." At his misjudged comment, the laughter died out of her face.

"I know little about Versailles, but I do know that the court is a place of sorrow."

"Ah, it matters not." He tried to lighten her mood. "When I was young, and at school, I used to make up riddles to confound my friends. I became quite good at it, but it has been a long time." His ruse was a success, for the face she turned to him was beaming. "You must have been sent here by the good God," she stated, awe-struck.

"No, but by someone very much like Him."

She'd taken him past the front of the house, its facade solid stone, with only slits in the wall. He was reminded vaguely of something he'd learned in his youth but couldn't quite call to his mind. By the time they'd reached a side door, it had completely slipped away. When the woman stopped the cart, they were met by a man of about his own age. The newcomer wasn't tall but extremely muscular, giving the illusion of height. His face was broad, the features rather flat, suggesting peasant stock, with that strangely pleasant ugliness that was so prevalent among the lower classes.

"You brought back an odd fish, Phémie." His friendly grin removed any intentional insult, and Charles guessed that only the cousin of whom she'd spoken would converse with such easy familiarity, thus he was saved from making another embarrassing mistake by thinking him to be in the service of the family.

"Poor Charles!" She laughed at his comically painful expression. "This is the second time someone's mistaken you for a fish."

"Permit me to introduce myself." Charles bowed. "I am the Comte Charles de Montais."

"And I am the Baron Florimond Lapalisse, at your service, Monsieur le Comte." He returned the bow gracefully, despite his ill-fitting shirt and trousers.

"Charles is going to help me look for the treasure," Phémie said defiantly, and her cousin's smile faded.

"That nonsense! You promised—" he began, but she interrupted hurriedly, "Charles gave me his sacred oath, and if you don't tell her, the Duchesse will never know."

"Oh, my God!"

"She's very old, Charles," Phémie ignored her cousin's outburst, "and never leaves her room." Charles regarded her closely, his eyes narrowing, but he said nothing. Florimond noticed his expression, and began to laugh. "You've gone too far this time, cousin. Your fish is no fool."

"I don't understand . . ."

"I am beginning to, Your Grace." Charles bowed, and Florimond was shaking his head, embarrassed at the awkwardness that he alone felt.

"This is the Duchesse Euphémie d'Amberieu, Monsieur, if you can believe it. I am ashamed of her and must apologize."

"Nonsense, eh . . . Florimond, if I may make so bold, and please, call me Charles. Phémie and I got along famously, and it would be a pity to have to start all over again."

"You are a gentleman; unfortunately my cousin is not a lady and doesn't deserve your kindness."

"Please, my dignity has suffered enough. But it isn't every day that my ox cart is driven by a Duchesse."

"I wish you two would stop talking as though I were not here. I've apologized once for my bad behavior."

"And that is more than enough." Charles came to her defense gallantly. "It was a most noble apology."

"I doubt that." Florimond looked at her darkly, but obviously felt that enough had been said. "Tell me, Charles, what brings you all this way? Do we owe this pleasure to chance, or purpose?"

"This is no chance! His Majesty wishes the two of you to be his guests at his birthday celebration. There is the Grand Ball, of course, and he charged me to wring a promise of several dances from Her Grace. There will be other festivities, as well." He finished lamely, dismayed by the expression on Phémie's face.

"The court!" she murmured quietly as her cousin put his arm about her shoulders, as if to comfort her.

"So it's come at last. We knew it would, one day, and now that it has, I'm glad. You've seen too little of the world . . ."

"It's only an invitation." She looked up at him hopefully, but he shook his head, reading her thoughts.

"Louis has been too generous for you to ignore his personal invitation."

The courtier was startled by the content of their conversation; the very thought of someone "ignoring" an invitation from the King was heresy in his mind.

"Louis has been unobtrusive," she corrected firmly, but then relented. "He has been kind; I believe that he was truly stricken by Agnes's fate. It's a high price to pay for these years of peace. . . ."

"No price is too high for peace, Phémie. Are you afraid . . ."

"Of course I'm afraid. I've lived too long with Agnes's ghost not to be afraid."

"He didn't invite you to live at Versailles, just to attend the Grand Ball. We could stay at the d'Amberieu house in Paris," he suggested hopefully, and she laughed, surrendering. "Your presentation is long overdue, and it would be great fun seeing you making a leg to the ladies. Very well, we will go to the Grand Ball."

"You devil!" He grabbed her by the arm to prevent her escape and swatted her on the hindquarters.

"Florimond!" she admonished him, looking more worried than outraged. "What will our guest think?"

"Your guest is beyond thinking!" Charles felt a sudden warmth of emotion come over him, and a sorrow as well.

How empty his own life seemed, when he watched the easy affection between the cousins.

"That is the only way to remain sane in our company, Charles. We have kept you too long standing outside," said Florimond. "First, we'll find you some clothes that will let you breathe. And then we'll eat and drink. I can personally, and heartily, recommend the widow's wine, if not her beauty and charm." He threw an arm about each of them and led them inside.

They entered directly into a red-tiled, spotlessly clean kitchen. It was another new experience for Charles, and he examined each pot cooking on the fire, questioning the cook with not only politeness, but real interest. After the poor woman's initial shock, she became voluble, explaining her craft proudly. While maintaining a very proper dignity, she offered him tastes of the dishes she was preparing, a privilege she'd never allow the cousins. Charles was enchanted by the different spices and herbs. His mouth, he told his audience, fairly watered for the noon meal, and he could not resist tearing a piece from the still warm loaf of sour bread.

"Madame," he lifted his hat to her, "your food would grace the King's board."

As they left the room, Phémie stole a look over her shoulder at the beaming woman, whispering, "She'll be impossible to live with, now."

"How much would you consider for that treasure?"

"Nothing in the world would induce me to part with her; she is the Lapalisse family treasure, as was her mother before her, and as her daughter will be after her." Florimond clapped him on the shoulder, offering, "But you are welcome at my board anytime. She'll come with us to Paris, and then you'll see what she can do with real food—a rack of lamb, a side of beef, or a brace of fowl, and honest vegetables. She is an artist, my friend."

"A fish stew is a fish stew," Phémie said impatiently, but with a glint of humor in her eyes. "All you men can think of is your bellies."

"Not quite, my dear Duchesse, but almost." He winked

over her head to Florimond, who grinned broadly. As they progressed through the chateau, Charles saw that the house had indeed been civilized by succeeding generations of the d'Amberieus. Along the cliff side of the house were small and large drawing rooms, a music room, a dining room, and a gallery containing portraits of the family ancestors. Each room had huge windows overlooking the sea, and the views of the rugged cliffs and wheeling gulls against the clouds and sky were beautiful. While Phémie waited below, Florimond took their guest upstairs. The rooms all faced the sea, and no expense had been spared in the windows even here, in the least lived-in part of the house. When he had undergone the transformation and returned to the dining room where Phémie awaited them, Charles found himself the object of a lengthy, and rather bold, scrutiny that made him feel extremely self-conscious.

While Charles had always been tolerant of other people's appearance, he had been extremely critical of his own. His acquaintances called him slender and well-made; he called himself scrawny. His arms and legs were thin and sadly lacking in shape. The hair on his head was receding and gave his already high forehead a startling prominence; without his wig he felt almost naked. He felt at a further disadvantage being deprived of his customary court costume, for the high neckcloth that was part of the masculine attire in a more civilized atmosphere effectively covered the large lump at his throat that had the distressing habit of bobbing about when he swallowed. But of all his shortcomings, his face, without the distraction of wig and other finery, was the worst of him. The features were even, but his eyes were far too deepset, his nose too pinched, and his mouth too thin. He had the look of the esthetic, however, and his smoldering dark eyes were quite attractive to some women who considered him mysterious.

"Why, Charles," Phémie wondered, "you look like one of those hermit saints hanging in the church."

"Your Grace is too kind."

"It was not intended as a kindness," she replied with

what apparently was characteristic forthrightness. Charles, having spent his entire life among subtle, and even devious, people, found her frankness disconcerting. Fortunately their meal was brought in, cutting off any further comments concerning his appearance. The cook served them herself, giving their guest the finest morsels of fish, the plumpest pieces of vegetable, and the crustiest cut of bread. Charles complimented her with an enthusiasm she found satisfying. When the door closed behind her, Phémie giggled girlishly, neglecting, for once, to make any comment. Charles attacked his stew with relish, certain that his jaded palate had never known such a treat. He doused his bread liberally in the rich juices and thoroughly enjoyed himself. After their plates had been removed, they relaxed over an excellent wine, and Charles realized that he'd not been so at ease in a very long time. Stretching luxuriously, he then turned to Phémie.

"Now I must earn this bounty. I think it would be best if I looked at the Bible you were speaking of."

While Phémie was off on the errand, Florimond suggested, after a few moments of companionable silence, "Wouldn't you rather rest? I always sleep in the afternoon myself."

"Pray, don't let me deter you," Charles insisted. "My presence must in no way interfere with your custom."

"What custom?" Phémie had returned, bearing the book in her arms.

"Florimond was telling me how he takes his rest in the afternoons."

"Nonsense!" she said shortly, ignoring her cousin's expression of dismay. "He's usually out digging up rocks to repair the walls in the pastures." She looked at Florimond, puzzled. "Why would you say anything like that?"

Charles intervened, saving Florimond the need to explain. "So I would feel comfortable in doing so. It was a courtesy. . . ."

"Mercy." She actually looked embarrassed. "I'm not going to do very well at Versailles, am I?"

"Most certainly not!" Florimond agreed heartily, but the

moment had passed, and she only shrugged, "It matters little."

Relieving her of the burdensome book, he set it carefully on the table before him, handling the aged manuscript with respect. Phémie leaned over him, her arm about the back of his chair for support, and Charles was very much aware of her proximity as she opened to the page where the riddle was written.

"Tell me the riddle again, Phémie," he requested after reading it through, and she complied readily,

> "In my father's castle
> Keep a tower bold, tower deep
> From the burning cross count nine
> Then twelve on high in a line."

Florimond shook his head, disgusted. "No one but a child could have written that."

"My dearest fools, you've got it all wrong."

"That's the way Théophile recited it," she protested, turning to her cousin for collaboration. "Wasn't it, Florimond?"

"It was indeed! He filled Phémie's head with dreams of treasure; a child's story for a child."

"Then it's little wonder that he didn't find it, or anyone else of his ancestry who listened to the telling of it, rather than reading it. Listen to the way it is written:

> 'In my father's castle keep
> A tower bold, tower deep
> From the burning cross count nine
> Then twelve on high in a line.'"

Both were silent for a moment, then Florimond exploded, "Castle keep!"

He rushed from the room, and the others followed behind, Charles catching up the wine and goblets and Phémie a candle-tree and flintbox. He led them into a room at the front of the house, and Charles's first suspicions were justified. It was made of stone and was obviously the early immigrants' complete house—a combination of kitchen, bedroom, and dining area. The only furnishings consisted of a long table and several hard chairs, but there was evidence of where the beds had been built directly into the far wall. A wholly cheerless place, and rather sinister in the semidarkness, it didn't improve after the candles were lit. There wasn't one window, and only the small, narrow door leading into it from the civilized part of the house. Charles noted the slits in the outside wall for the defenders' bows, and with a flash remembered the drawings he'd seen of castles in schoolbooks.

"But we've been all over this place," Phémie protested. "It doesn't fit the riddle at all."

"Not your interpretation," Charles agreed, passing his hand over the huge, circular column of stone that ran from ceiling to floor in the middle of the room. He thought it an elaborate support, where several smaller ones would have done as well and been far easier to construct.

"They would have been safe here," Charles mused, looking about him. "And that"—he pointed to the column—"is the only tower I've seen."

"The tower! By all the saints, it must be the tower." Florimond embraced the courtier, dancing around with him.

"It must be." Charles disengaged himself from the bearlike grasp, unaccustomed to such familiarity.

"What of the burning cross?" Phémie asked, barely concealing her excitement.

"It's almost too simple," Charles complained, taking his wine to a chair and making himself as comfortable as possible, his feet resting on the table. "There is your burning cross." He gestured negligently toward the oddly shaped fireplace. It was very tall, narrowing at the top, and reached almost to the ceiling. The mantel intersected it in such a way that it did, indeed, resemble a cross. Florimond placed himself directly in front of it counting off nine flagstones, which brought him hard up against the column.

"Now you must count twelve stones up," Phémie directed, breathless in her excitement. Florimond counted carefully, reaching the twelfth, then paused, wiping his sweating hands on his trousers.

"Do you really think . . ." Phémie joined the courtier, stooping beside his chair, her charmingly flushed face raised to his. "Oh, Charles, might it be?" Overcoming the impulse to kiss her, he patted her on the head, turning his attention to the man.

"Try pushing it, Florimond," he suggested, then smiled down at her as the cousin set about his task. "There'll be no treasure behind the stone, my dear." Her face showed her disappointment, mingled with disbelief, so he hastened to explain, "The riddle said 'tower deep,' and that means that the treasure, or whatever it is, can only be underneath."

"It's moving," Florimond shouted, and Phémie jumped to her feet. Charles caught her wrist, preventing her from running to the column.

"We don't want it falling on you," he chided gently, releasing his hold.

"No fear of that, Charles," Florimond called, "it's hinged."

"Phémie, do you think you could find us some gloves?"

"You won't do anything until I return?"

"I promise," he assured her, and while she was gone, he poured the sweating Florimond a liberal goblet of wine. Phémie had returned even before he'd finished drinking it off, and Charles noted with amusement that she'd brought a pair for herself. The three took themselves to the column, and Florimond reached his gloved hand into the dark cavity.

"Nothing in here, except a piece of . . . chain, it feels like."

"Excellent! Don't do anything yet. Phémie, you stand on this side"—he placed her in position carefully—"and I'll stand here." He stationed himself midway between the cousins. "We must all remain absolutely silent. The chain may open yet another cleverly concealed doorway, but it would be too much, after all these years, to expect it to do so easily. You, my girl, must keep your eye on the tower before you and pay no heed to what the excellent Florimond is doing. I will do the same on my side. We may see nothing but will undoubtedly hear something, so do be quiet."

"May the 'excellent Florimond' proceed now?" he asked jocularly, and Phémie giggled. Charles nodded, quelling her outburst with a fierce expression.

"Not too hard," he cautioned. "You mustn't break it."

Bracing himself against the "tower" for leverage, Florimond got a good grip on the chain, pulling with all his strength. In the silence, the movement of stone could be heard.

"I see it!" Phémie exclaimed breathlessly. "It's opening."

"It's still giving," Florimond reported, "but my God, it's stiff."

"Let me help," Charles offered, noting with alarm that Florimond was becoming very red. When Florimond refused his assistance, the courtier rushed to the girl's side. "It's opened enough for my hand. I'll try to move it from here." So together the men worked, each at his own position, and before long, the aperture was wide enough to pass through.

"Whew! What a stench!" Florimond complained when he joined the others. "Phémie, bring the candles." As they waited, he continued, "We'd never have found it in a thousand years without you, Charles."

"Don't thank me until we see what lies hidden below."

"It doesn't matter what's down there." Florimond grinned mischievously. "We won't have to search for it any more, and I can find some peace. Give Phémie a few more years, and she'd have had the house torn down." When Phémie joined them, each man took a candle, but as the girl was about to do the same, the courtier stayed her hand.

"You stay up here, Your Grace."

"I will not," she snapped angrily, but he insisted, reasonably.

"We don't know what we'll find down there. If anything befalls us, there must be someone to get aid. If all goes well, you may come down."

Despite her disappointment, she saw the wisdom of his

plan and nodded mutely. Both men had to bend almost double to get through the opening. Florimond led the way down the narrow, steep stairs spiraling deep into the "tower." The going was necessarily slow, each man pressed tightly against the wall of the column. When they had reached the bottom, Charles had counted sixty steps. The room in which they found themselves was about a quarter of the size of the "keep" above, cut from solid rock. Stacked against one wall were shields, against another, spears. There were double-edged broadswords, battle axes, and armor—breastplates, helmets, and even mail. It was an impressive collection of weaponry, and Florimond was enjoying himself hugely, putting on a breastplate and helmet, and arming himself with shield and broadsword.

"Those Northmen must have been giants, to fight like this. They weren't dancing about in these outfits. Can you imagine how big their arms must have been to carry such a sword into battle?" He swung it in an arc over his head, striking the wall a resounding blow accidentally. The sword fell from his numbed hand with a clatter.

"Are you all right?" Phémie called anxiously, and Charles laughed, reassuring her.

"We've become weak, Charles; drawing room creatures more at ease bending our knees to ladies for exercise than lifting one of these." He kicked at the broadsword, rubbing his wrist.

"If you have finished playing soldier," Phémie joined them, scolding, "perhaps we may begin looking for the treasure."

"This is the only treasure your husband's ancestors were interested in protecting." He indicated the weapons in profusion about them.

"You haven't had enough time to make a real search," she accused him boldly, and he agreed, "Granted, but I have seen that this room is solid rock; no hidden doors down here. As you can see for yourself, there isn't a chest of treasure in sight."

"I don't understand it." She was frankly disappointed and

Charles smiled gently, explaining, "These weapons were worth more than all the gold and silver in the world to the Northmen. If I remember my history correctly, they were more interested in survival than in precious jewels."

"The way you're talking, one would think that you didn't have a fortune of your own, cousin, and that you needed a treasure." Florimond was short-tempered, unnecessarily cross with her, Charles thought, but knew he'd no right to interfere.

"It's just that it would have been so much more exciting . . ." She paused, shrugging off the disillusionment. "Life has always been like that, hasn't it? The searching is so much more adventuresome than the finding." Before leaving them, she smiled briefly, and, it seemed to him, courageously at Charles. When they were once again alone, Charles set to work to find something, anything that would compensate her for "the finding." Finally, he discovered something he believed would please her and hurried up the stairs to show her. But she was nowhere to be found in the whole house. The servants only knew that she'd left, but neither the direction nor when she'd planned to return. There was nothing for him to do but wait, and he took the time offered to clean and polish the dagger he'd found. It wasn't much of a treasure, but even in its present condition, he could see that it had a fine blade and its handle was exquisitely wrought. In the meantime, her cousin had brought up a broadsword and shield, and, although he couldn't understand why Charles attached so much importance to his cousin's feelings, he willingly shared his metal-cleaning soap and cloths. After they had worked at their tasks for a while in silence, Florimond cleared his throat and asked, reluctantly, "Tell me, Charles. Are you married?"

"Why, yes, I am." The question startled him, and he laid aside the dagger, waiting for Florimond to continue.

"Then perhaps you'll understand. I know we've just met, but if I'm nothing else, I'm a good judge of men and horses. You're a splendid fellow." He said the last gruffly, almost as if he were embarrassed, and still Charles waited, all the more curious. Florimond hesitated a moment, as if deciding whether to say what he had on his mind or to let it pass, but the courtier was looking at him so closely that he went on just out of politeness. "You see, I've met a girl . . . a wonderful girl. She's the daughter of one of the minor landowners near the estate in the south. Her breeding isn't as impressive as the Lapalisse lineage, but since my father acknowledged me and made me his heir to his own property, her father is willing to overlook the fact that I was born a bastard to a tenant's daughter on our land." Florimond hurried on, "She's a sweet and gentle girl, and will make a perfect wife for me. Except for Phémie!"

"Phémie?" he asked, incredulously, and the other nodded, the pain naked in his eyes.

"If it were any other woman than Phémie; a woman like my Giselle, sweet and gentle . . . But my cousin is too accustomed to being the mistress of the house. Even with the title of Baronne, Giselle would be too shy and simple to assert herself."

"Surely Phémie would step aside and respect your wife's right . . ."

"You don't understand. When Eustache died, he left the title to Phémie for her protection. He could not leave her the estate, as it was already hers, given to her shortly after her birth. However, Eustache left a secret will, acknowledging me as his son. It was to be used only after Phémie married. That was why she allowed Théophile to persuade her to become the Duchesse. She insisted that he present the will, and her petition that the Lapalisse title be passed to me, to the King."

"Are you saying that she married the Duc so you could come into an inheritance?"

"One that was rightly mine," he said defensively, and Charles asked, trying to understand, "Then what is your complaint?"

"The inheritance included only the title and a small fortune. The King would not approve her petition that the estate revert to me with the title."

"You have money of your own. Why can't you buy your own estate?"

"I want this one." His reply was petulant. "It adjoins the small holdings of Giselle's father."

"Ah, I think I'm beginning to understand."

"We've wanted to marry for the last three years."

"Has Phémie prevented it?"

"No, not Phémie, actually," he admitted grudgingly.

"Then the girl's father?"

When Florimond didn't reply, he pursued, "Is it the father who wants the estate, and whom Phémie sent away?"

Still no response.

"Have you agreed to his plan?" he demanded roughly, compelling the man to answer.

"It's a good plan! There is only Phémie . . ."

"Why haven't you offered to buy it? Or haven't you told her all this?"

"I've told her that I wish to marry Giselle, and that I wish to purchase the house and part of the land. She only laughed."

"I can't believe that. You must have misunderstood her."

"You don't know her, Charles. She has this Godforsaken place, and Théophile's house in Paris. She doesn't really like the estate, but she won't sell it to me. She has already said as much."

"What do you expect of me? I only met you both this morning. Anything I would say would be an impertinence at best."

"But she likes you, Charles. I can see it in her eyes."

"Yes, but how long would that liking last if I interfered? I cannot endanger my master's invitation. The King's business must come first—at least, with me." He could see at once that his logic fell on deaf ears. Taking pity on the poor creature, he relented. "Oh, very well. I'll do whatever I can, but I don't promise any success."

"I was right!" Florimond's expression brightened perceptibly. "I knew you're a good fellow. I'll never forget this."

"Hold a moment! My intervention will probably come to

nothing. You must promise, whether I succeed or fail, you'll see that Phémie doesn't change her mind about attending the Grand Ball. Otherwise, we have no bargain."

"You need have no fear of that. I'll not dissuade her."

Leaving the house, determined to find the girl, Charles had a feeling of regret. The mission was completed, and he was becoming far more involved than he had intended. He'd not the first idea as to where his search should begin. She could have struck out across the pastures, or even returned to the village. He walked aimlessly to the cliff edge, and, in desperation, called out her name across the sea. Suddenly, he heard an answer and saw her apppear from behind an outcropping of rock far below. It was a difficult descent, and he was breathless by the time he reached her. Taking him by the hand, she led him over the rocks to a sheltered spot out of sight of the house. Without a word, they sat together; she staring out to sea while he recovered from his exertions.

"I've brought you something I found in the tower," he said at last, handing her the dagger, and she examined it, her eyes glowing with pleasure.

"It's very beautiful. Did you clean it yourself?"

"Not very well, I'm afraid. I'm unused to doing such labor, but I enjoyed doing it for you."

"How kind! It's a fine blade, isn't it?"

"One of the finest I've ever seen," he stated truthfully, and she took his hand, saying, "It wasn't a waste, then?"

"Nothing is wasted, Phémie. We may not always find the treasure we hope for, but if we search diligently, we'll find something of worth."

"How comforting!" She commented seriously enough, but he caught the twinkle in her eyes.

"Rather like what a priest would say, don't you think?"

"Are you very religious, Charles?" The suddenness of her question was not as startling as the gravity with which she asked it.

"I don't often think about matters of religion," he replied carefully, but she was impatient with his caution.

"Being at Versailles, you're not expected to be a theologian. All I'm asking is, simply, are you a religious man?"

"Very well, I am a religious man, but not in the sense you mean. Every day the Court goes in procession to mass. In the chapel, only His Majesty faces the altar; the rest of us face him. I go through the ritual; confession, communion, all the outward forms. But I worship at the altar of our King and the France he rules."

"But what of heaven, and hell?"

"I'm too involved in this world to concern myself with the next."

"But you're a good man, Charles. How do you account for that?"

"Easily, my sweet innocent. I'm a decent fellow, I admit that. But my decency, or goodness, as you call it, comes from duty, and a code of what is right and proper. I don't cheat at cards because it's not the behavior of a true gentleman. But there's something else, too; I don't need to win. Have you ever wondered that perhaps a man does an evil thing because he needs something desperately? I don't need anything, so it's not at all difficult for me to be good. How do I know what I would do if there ever came a time . . ."

"The nuns called it a time of temptation, and they say if a person is good, and has faith in God, then he'll overcome the temptation and do what is good."

"That's a nice story for children," he said, gently amused, and felt her stiffen with offense. "Wait before you say anything," he cautioned, fearing a storm of protest. As she held her silence, he continued, "The good nuns see very little of the world, and even less of men. If a person overcomes a temptation, it merely means he didn't want it badly enough. He weighed the one side against the other, and decided the prize wasn't worth the risk. If a man wants something, really wants it, then nothing will stop him from getting it; neither God nor the threat of hell. In my world, only one thing would stop a man—the displeasure of his King. That is the risk he would run, if he were found out."

"Then Louis is your god . . ."

"Exactly! And banishment from court our hell."

"Surely you don't pray to the King—that is, if you pray at all."

"There have been occasions when I pray, and it is to the God of your nuns that I address my prayers. But most of the time, He is far, far away, and I am here. Man was born in sin, Phémie, and I'm no different from any other. But I have arranged my life to my own satisfaction, and so I never enter into 'temptation.' It's no honor to me that I'm not a thief or a cheat; it's merely a felicitous arrangement between me and the world I live in."

"Even your marriage?" Her words were like the thrust of a rapier, and he parried gracefully.

"Nothing more so than my marriage. Oh, I entered into it with good faith, which is more than I can say for my wife. I believed her to be the embodiment of all the virtues. On my wedding night I found I had wed a harlot. The damage was done and couldn't be undone. But it has turned out for the best, after all. My wife's father is most anxious to atone for his guilt in foisting an exceedingly impure daughter on a well-meaning, rather naive young man and has done everything possible to make generous amends."

"And you're satisfied with such an arrangement? Wouldn't you be happier with a wife who loved you, even if you were poorer?"

"Most certainly not!" he replied, horrified at the suggestion, and she shook her head.

"Is this the same man who was praising the joys of marriage to me only a short while ago?"

"If you remember the discussion correctly, my reference was to a woman, and it's different for a woman." He dismissed her argument carelessly, then turned more seriously to his own case. "At first I had hoped for both—a loving wife and a generous father-in-law. If it had turned out the other way—poor but in love—I'm certain I'd be far less happy now than I am. One can become accustomed to being without love, but I don't believe I could ever become accustomed to poverty. Nor would I want to make the attempt."

"Then you don't miss love?"

"Do you?" He turned the discussion toward her. "Haven't you become satisfied with your arrangement?"

"Do I miss love?" she mused, her eyes unseeing as she looked out to sea. "Since I have never known love, how can I say I miss it? No," she smiled mischievously, "I don't miss love."

"You're not being honest!" he protested bluntly, and she laughed.

"But I am. You used the word love. If you'd asked about romance, my answer would have been quite different."

"You're playing with words. You know what I meant."

"As to being satisfied with the arrangement of my life," she continued as if there had been no interruption, "you know that I am. In a way, we are much alike. You have accepted the loss of love in return for all the comforts you could wish for, and I have accepted the lack of love for the abundance of personal freedom."

"But one day you'll be alone. Florimond will want to marry."

"He does now, to a silly, stupid girl with a sly, ambitious villain of a father."

"You don't approve of the girl?"

"It's not for me to approve or disapprove. Personally I believe she'll make an excellent wife for my cousin. She likes the country life as well as he and regards him with an emotion akin to awe. No man could ask for more in a woman. But the father sees himself installed in the Lapalisse chateau, mismanaging the estate as ruinously as he did his own."

"Doesn't Florimond know?"

"All the fool knows is that he's in love. It turns my stomach!" The contempt in her voice made him laugh.

"Tell him, then. You'll be doing him as well as yourself a disservice if you remain silent."

"I can't agree with you. If I told him, he'd not only disbelieve it, but would think I'm jealous and attacking the girl through her father. All I can do is let him find out for himself."

Charles was amazed that such sound reasoning could come from a woman who had been so sheltered all of her life. He looked at her sharply as she laughed softly. "The villain has shown the patience of a saint, but only because he believes the prize is worth waiting for."

"The prize?"

"Yes, he waits for the estate itself. Florimond has offered to buy part of it, but I can't sell it to him."

"Because of the King?"

"Oh, so that's the way of it. Florimond has told you about it, has he?"

"Only that it was given to you by His Majesty, and he wouldn't permit it to revert with your cousin's title."

"True, but there's nothing to prevent me giving it to him, as a wedding present."

"Is that your plan?" He saw the difficulties fading before his eyes. "But he can't marry her until the estate is his. The father won't permit it."

"Why didn't he tell me that himself? If he's such a fool, perhaps he deserves both of them."

"Are you going to give it to him anyway?"

"The light is failing." She jumped up, holding her hand out to assist him. "If we don't go now, you'll not be able to make the climb until the morning."

It was all she would say, and he had to be content.

7

Since the King had told him that he was to place himself entirely at the Duchesse's disposal, Charles overcame his first feeling of panic and remained at the strange house while Phémie made her preparations for the journey to Paris. She had a strong sense of duty toward her husband's people, and spent most of her days in visiting the ailing and infirm, the aged and confined.

From the first day of the courtier's arrival, Florimond used his presence as an excuse to put off seeing to the repair of the walls and outbuildings. With Phémie gone most of the day, he took upon himself the duties of host and drinking companion, but after a few days of listening to the ravings of a frustrated, drunken fool, Charles found himself looking forward to escaping to the quiet hideaway where he had found Phémie that first day. He looked forward to Phémie's return from her rounds in the late afternoon. He didn't know exactly when, in those eight days, the great change had come over him, but he realized, to his sorrow, that he had done the one thing he had vowed he would never do again—he had fallen hopelessly in love. Even more surprising was the change that had taken place in Florimond in the few days he had been there. Gone now was the easy affection between the cousins; no longer did he suddenly throw his arm about Phémie, either to hug her like some great bear or to swat her playfully. Charles could see that Phémie was not only amazed at the difference, but deeply hurt, although she never complained. That he was inadvertently to blame, Charles knew full well, but he could do nothing to reverse what had been bound to happen eventually, anyway—with or without his presence. Florimond had never had anyone before in whom he could confide; now he had the impetus to set flowing the flood of bitterness and resentment that he had been harboring for years. Florimond had been constantly in the company of his strong-willed, aggressive cousin, and if assertiveness had been her only sin, it would have been bad enough. But that she should own the one thing that would bring him happiness, and seemingly refuse to part with it, was the real problem. He was, quite simply, not his own master; he was not even allowed to make his own mistakes. This was easy enough for Charles, being an observer of human behavior, to understand and to sympathize with in the beginning, but as his feelings for Phémie became more pronounced and Florimond's complaints against his cousin more virulent, the courtier's sympathy began to wane. He hated Florimond as much as he loved Phémie. Thus on the eighth day after his arrival, he welcomed with relief the news that they would be leaving in two days. At breakfast Phémie promised that this would be her last day of visiting and that she would devote the rest of her time to making final preparations. After she'd left, Charles humored his host by whiling away the morning with cards. As they played, Charles was grateful for the training he had received at court. Neither cousin, he was certain, suspected his true feelings. As the morning wore on, Charles noted, with increasing alarm, his companion's prodigious drinking and was not surprised when he threw in his hand with disgust.

"I can't follow the cards, Charles. I'm in such distress." The tears sprang to his eyes and he buried his face in his arms, knocking over the bottle of wine at his elbow. "Oh, God," he cried, sweeping the tipped bottle from the table, his voice overflowing with anguish, "when am I to be free of the woman?"

Charles wisely held his silence, schooling his expression into one of disinterest, using the pretext of saving the cards from being stained to keep his gaze averted.

"Listen to me!" Florimond demanded, grasping Charles's wrists painfully, and the courtier freed himself abruptly, holding himself in remarkable control.

"My dear fellow," he was at his soothing best, "I am neither deaf nor in the next room. Calm yourself before you fall into a fit."

"How can I be calm?"

"After imbibing so much wine, you no doubt find my request difficult, so perhaps you'd best take yourself off to your room until you are once again composed."

"If I could have some more wine . . ." he suggested hopefully, yet afraid that he'd lose his audience.

"If you do that, you'll become raving, and I'll have to lock you in the keep."

The prospect of so slight a man attempting to put him anyplace made him see the ridiculousness of the situation and calmed him momentarily.

After a long silence, Florimond began again. "Do you know that she hates Giselle's father?"

"Are you referring to Phémie?"

"She hates him, truly she does, Charles."

"Did she tell you that?"

"No, but he knows it, the poor man. He can't understand why Phémie is so averse toward him. He is the kindest gentleman, always shows such an interest in the place. He once made a suggestion concerning the harvest, and Phémie had the discourtesy to turn on her heel and walk away. I wanted to give her a sound scolding, but she was gone too quickly. He's made several good suggestions and I've passed them on to Phémie, but she won't even consider them. All she'll say is that I should take a closer look at what he's done to his own place. But he's learned from his mistakes, and wants to point out the pitfalls to me."

"Well, it's her estate, and from what I've seen of it, she must be doing the right thing." Charles was deliberately calculating the effect this would have on Florimond and was satisfied when the man became extremely uncomfortable.

"Yes, but she's only a woman. Anyway, it's the overseer who's responsible. Théophile found him for the place, and the fellow has her ear. She won't even listen to me. She keeps the household accounts well enough, and should restrict the rest of her activities to a woman's position. Everyone thinks that I'm a witless creature . . ."

"Does Phémie know that?"

"I don't know. She cares so little about people's opinion of her that it would be useless to make such a complaint."

"But she has been so generous to you . . ."

"Generous?" He snorted contemptuously. "It should all belong to me. She was only Agnes's daughter, not Eustache's." Charles noted this bit of information without showing any interest in the statement. Florimond went on without pause, "I am the son of his flesh and his rightful heir."

"But there was nothing but love compelling her to petition the King for you."

"What use did she have for the title? She had captured one of far greater worth, and a fortune that makes her one of the wealthiest people in France. Do you truly believe she married Théophile for such a noble reason as to see her bastard cousin get what was rightfully his? Well, I'll tell you something. She's just as ill-born as I am, and worse. At least I know who my father was."

"Why, you are a fool—an ingrate who has been living off his cousin's bounty and now that she's no longer convenient to have around, wants to push her out, expecting her to leave her beloved estate in the care of dolts."

"You can't talk to me like that!" Florimond's face flushed as Charles's insult penetrated his besotted head.

"At least I'm telling you what I think of you to your face, which is more courtesy than you're showing Phémie. How do you dare say such things about her before a stranger? You're so dense that you can't even see that your evil, selfish cousin approves of your empty-headed Giselle, believes that she'll make a perfect wife for you, and is pleased that you're planning to marry. She wants nothing but your happiness, knowing full well that when you marry, she'll have to leave."

"But that isn't enough. She'll still be mistress of the estate. I'll be like a tenant farmer, under the orders of her overseer."

Charles watched his tongue, knowing it was not his place to tell Florimond of Phémie's wedding gift.

"I'll look like a fool," Florimond complained miserably.

"How else, after acting like one? But you can comfort yourself. Giselle's father has acted even more of the fool."

"He'll never forgive me, and he'll never permit the marriage. He'd put her in a convent rather than let her become my wife. I must acquire the estate somehow."

"If you're aware of such a dark side of his nature, how could you ever entertain the thought of letting him have his way with Phémie's property? This fellow is obviously vulgar, and greedy."

"But Giselle isn't!" he stated vehemently, and Charles conceded, "I'm not one of those who believe that the sins of the father are visited upon the children. She is undoubtedly all you say, although I find Phémie a far more reliable source for that information."

"Has she spoken well of Giselle?"

"Very well indeed! Haven't you listened to anything I've said? She even thinks that your Giselle would be a perfect wife for you. Why don't you speak with your cousin? From what I've seen, Phémie is certainly a reasonable person, and between the two of you a plan could be devised that would be fair to both."

"You don't know her!" he repeated, disconsolate.

"It's no good talking to you, Florimond; you only hear what you want to hear, and are deaf to anything that doesn't suit you. I can see that you have a problem, but it is of your own devising. No one else is to blame."

"My mother knew the truth of it," he went on, unheeding. "She knew what it would be like the moment they brought Agnes's babe into the house. Everyone thought that Agnes was sweetness and kindness itself, but Mother knew that behind her angel's face was a soul of darkness. She said that Phémie—"

"Cease! Drink from your own cup of poison. I hope you choke in it."

"You don't mean that, Charles." Phémie's voice came from the doorway, and Florimond leaped to his feet, knocking over the chair. "Don't upset yourself, Florimond. You'll get the rash again, and Giselle won't find you so attractive." As she joined them, Charles pulled a chair up to the table for her, and she smiled her thanks to him. "I thought you two were going to play cards while I was gone, and when I return I find you fighting like a pair of children." She scolded them good-naturedly, and Charles regarded her with suspicion.

"How much have you heard?" Florimond asked brutishly, and the courtier could almost smell the animal fear possessing him.

"Only what Charles just said, but there must have been a great deal I missed to have brought it to such anger," she claimed, all innocence, and Charles realized that she was lying. Her cousin visibly relaxed, picking up his chair and taking his place again. "What were you two arguing about?" she pursued guilelessly, and Charles, always the diplomat, filled the awkward silence with, "Something that only men would argue about, and in their own language."

Florimond's glance toward him was filled with gratitude.

"Therefore not fit for a lady to hear." Phémie laughed lightly. "I'll ask no more questions, but I do think you should apologize to Florimond."

"If Florimond weren't my friend, I would never have

been so harsh. One is only polite to people one doesn't care about." He prayed he was taking the correct course. Obviously Phémie was placating her cousin, and Charles could only follow her lead, finding the situation intriguing.

"Is it true?" Florimond asked, stretching out his hand to the courtier, who took it with all appearance of warmth. "I was so afraid. You know, you're my only friend."

"I was merely trying to help you out of your difficulty."

"What difficulty?" Phémie asked, avoiding looking at Charles, and Florimond explained, "Charles says that you approve of my marriage to Giselle."

"That decision has never been mine, my dear. You may marry your sweet Giselle any time you wish."

"What will you do?"

"Oh, I hadn't thought too much about it. If the Paris house is pleasing, I might stay there until I can make more permanent plans."

"But you'll be alone."

"Nonsense! I'll have a house full of servants to watch over me, and Charles will be close by to act as escort, if such a task won't be too odious for him. There have been many widows turned out in the world who've had no family at all to care what happens to them."

"If you're living in Paris," he began, watching her slyly, "you'll have no need for the estate."

"No, I suppose I won't," she agreed simply, not volunteering anything.

"What are you going to do with it?" He was rather agitated despite his pretense of calm, and she laughed.

"I was planning to give it to you as a wedding present, but if you have a better plan . . ."

"Oh, is it true? You're not just teasing me, are you?"

"It's true enough. As soon as you're married, it is yours."

He fell on his knees before her, kissing her hand. "I've always said it. You're the kindest, most generous—"

"Stop!" Phémie laughed again, and Charles noticed that her gaiety didn't ring true. He was sickened by the slobbering hypocrite, but forced himself to smile.

"All I ask is that you care for it as I have."

"I give you my sacred oath. Charles can be our witness."

"We've never needed a witness before," she said softly, but he paid her no attention, saying, "We have a bargain, then. As soon as I am married, the place is mine."

"We have a bargain. Now, if you've finished your card game, we can eat. And then I'd like to borrow Charles to help me pack."

"Of course, my dear." Florimond became very expansive, laughing heartily and rubbing his hands together in a self-satisfied gesture. "Since you are being so understanding about this, is there anything I can do in particular?"

"It just happens that there is, cousin. I would be very pleased if you would come to Paris for your presentation. Eustache would have been so proud, and it would make Giselle happy. And while you're in Paris, I would like to choose the fabric for her wedding gown, as a personal present to your bride."

"That's really very decent of you. Giselle was so afraid of your feelings about our marriage, and this will show her that you truly approve."

"Then it's all settled. I'll tell them in the kitchen that we're ready to eat now."

When she'd gone on her errand, Florimond clapped Charles roughly on the shoulder. "I have been a fool, my friend, and I'm grateful to you for all your help. Everything has worked out just the way I wanted."

"Savor it, dear fellow; it will be one of the few times that Fate is so kind."

"Fate!" He shouted the word joyously. "Fate will provide everything a man of courage demands of her. One day I'll prove that to you. But listen, Charles, I would like you to be my groomsman when I marry. I could find none better."

"That would be an honor, but I can't promise. If my duties at court don't prevent it, I'll be there."

"Fair enough! One other thing, do you think Phémie will be offended if I don't invite her? There is no liking between her and Giselle's father."

"I don't think so. You'll have a new family to consider, and Phémie is a sensible woman." The words almost stuck in his throat, but he knew that it was what Florimond wanted to hear. Never before had he witnessed such complete betrayal, and he felt rather sick in the face of it.

"Will you do me another service, and tell her? I'll be leaving before the ball, so you could tell her after I'm gone."

Is this the man of courage? wondered Charles, who would have found the situation amusing if it weren't so hateful to his new-found love.

"That would be the easiest way." He placated Florimond, hating to play the hand that Phémie had dealt him when she'd first come into the room.

"You are a good fellow! Now everything is settled, and I shall know some happiness at last."

But at what a price, thought Charles, relieved as Phémie returned with the servants bearing their meal.

After eating, Florimond claimed an unaccustomed but understandable weariness, attributing it to all the excitement, and after excusing himself, retired to his room to sleep until the evening meal. Once they were alone, Charles whispered, "My poor Phémie! Are you all right?"

"There's no need to whisper. He'll be asleep as soon as he lies down. I gave him a powder, and he'll not stir for hours. Oh, Charles!" She reached out to him and he put his arms about her, holding her tightly. "I wish I could weep. It's as though he had died."

"It's my fault. I shouldn't have excited him."

"No, that's not true. It would have happened anyway, and it would have been far worse if you hadn't have been here."

"I've not served you very well, but if there is anything I can do, you must tell me. You said earlier that you've prepared for this."

"Not for his betrayal; I could never have prepared for what he said this morning. I was prepared to give him the estate and allow his father-in-law to manage him."

"But that's been taken care of, hasn't it? He gave you his sacred oath to continue things as they have been, without interference."

"And you believed him?" She laughed harshly, bitterly. "He'd promise to go to hell and back to get his hands on that estate. That is what I must accept. The fool will allow the place to be turned into a desert." She walked to the window overlooking the sea, and Charles went to stand beside her, wishing she were still in his arms.

"What can you do?"

"Nothing. The papers giving him the estate on his wedding day were signed when Théophile died and I became my own mistress."

"A generous gift to one who has no love for you." He hated to remind her of it, but the words were spoken before he thought.

"How well I know it now. I always thought of him as Eustache's son. I don't remember his mother."

"Breeding will tell, my dear." His gentle smile removed the pious snobbery that might have been mistaken in his words.

"I haven't thanked you yet for your defense of me or for keeping his friendship. You are really very kind."

"Kind? I felt like a traitor."

"You mustn't. You did just what I'd hoped for."

"Well, you did seem to prefer peace to open warfare. But I can't understand why you wish him with you in Paris. I should think that you'd want to be as far away from him as possible."

"It was Eustache's dream. He thought so highly of him . . ."

"A father's pride in his son? If only he could see him now."

"It would break his heart. Florimond even had Théophile deceived into thinking him a fine fellow. My husband thought himself so wise in his knowledge of men. It would seem that we've all been blind. I'm truly grateful that you're here."

"I pray that someday I'll merit that gratitude. If there is anything I can do for you to make your stay in Paris less painful, all you need do is ask."

8

The carriage passed through the thick, iron-studded gates of the walled estate, and Phémie was delighted with the broad avenue and its belt of old stately trees that hid the house from view on the street. They had traveled all night, and as they arrived at the estate, the ground mist was just lifting in the early light of dawn. She shivered with anticipation as the carriage negotiated a curve in the drive and the mansion came into sight. Before reaching the house, Phémie ordered the driver to stop, and she jumped to the ground, Charles following.

"Isn't it beautiful?" she exclaimed as she gazed at the huge mansion with its leaded windows, fluted columns, and extensive terrace. The courtier only nodded, rubbing his hands briskly in the cold dawn, envying Florimond, who was asleep in the warmth of several traveling robes. He hadn't known what to expect, never having been invited to the house while the old Duc was still alive, but it certainly wasn't the immaculate condition of the establishment evidenced. The lawns and trees were well cared for, and recently, which bespoke the presence of gardeners. Even in the gray light it was obvious that every window was polished and the outside walls were scrubbed spotless, indicating a staff of house servants was at work. D'Amberieu had been one of the few courtiers who could afford the financial drain such an estate would demand. As Phémie was determined to walk the rest of the way, there was nothing he could do but fall into step beside her. As the light became better, he noticed that smoke was coming from a back chimney, and he realized that even without a master in residence, the servants were up and about.

When they reached the house, the carriage following, the front doors were thrown open and a man stepped out, his greeting as chilly as the early morning air.

"What is your business here?"

"This is your mistress, man," Charles answered, glad to see that Phémie had had the good sense to pull her cloak close about her, hiding the boy's clothing in which she traveled.

"Your Grace!" The man bowed, stepping aside. "We did not expect you for several days." Phémie merely nodded, walking past him into the house. Charles woke Florimond, then followed her in. The entry hall was huge, hung with tapestries and banners from days long past. The room was cold, not only in temperature but in décor, much like a meeting hall, with padded benches along the walls.

"Damn, Phémie, this place is like a tomb." Florimond turned to the man behind them, acting very grand. "Here, fellow! I'm the Baron Lapalisse, and this is the Comte de Montais. I don't know about the Comte's needs, but I want a room with a warm bed, and a hearty breakfast served to me after I've changed."

"One moment, Florimond," Charles protested, "I do think we should see what Phémie wants."

As Charles spoke, a line of servants entered the hall, an older woman leading them. While they ranged themselves in orderly fashion, the woman curtsied before Phémie, then turned to the others.

"If you gentlemen will be patient, one of the footmen will show you to your rooms."

"Who the devil are you?" Florimond demanded rudely, but he quailed as she pulled herself up into full dignity.

"I am the housekeeper, Matilde, and this is my husband, Henri." She indicated the man who had admitted them, and he bowed to Florimond, but with noticeably less deference than to Phémie. She was a formidable gorgon and Charles felt like a small boy being introduced to an old dragon of an aunt. Florimond was as intimidated as the courtier, but Phémie merely smiled, amused by the setdown administered to her cousin.

"Of course we'll wait upon the Duchesse's wishes," he capitulated, and Charles avoided looking at Florimond's embarrassment.

"Do as you want, Florimond," Phémie said carelessly, then to the woman, "Would you please arrange for my cousin's comfort, madame?" The gorgon nodded, smiling frostily, and called for one of the footmen to be of service to the Baron. As Florimond, looking extremely sheepish, hastily took his leave, she turned to Charles.

"And you, Monsieur le Comte?" she asked if she were dismissing him, and Charles excused himself, following the retreating Florimond. Once they were alone, Matilde's tone softened, and she asked, with unsuspected kindness, "Will Your Grace's maid be arriving shortly?"

With her usual sensitivity to the type of person with whom she was dealing, Phémie looked rather forlorn and lied without blinking.

"I'm afraid not, madame. The girl found a young man in the village near the chateau in Bretagne, and I released her so that she might marry."

"Ah, these young women!" Matilde commiserated, shaking her head. "Never to be depended upon. One of the girls here is quick, although she's had no training as a lady's maid."

"My demands are few; I'm certain she'll do well enough."

"And a hairdresser?" Matilde suggested, looking dubiously at Phémie's untidy locks, and again the Duchesse lied gracefully, having been prepared for such a question years before.

"I suffered a fever and the surgeon was forced to cut my hair."

"You poor child! Well, I expect it will look better when it's been cared for. Now I imagine you're tired from your long journey . . ."

"Not at all, madame. There is something I wish to be done at once, if possible. I had no idea that the house was kept so well staffed."

"The Duc's bankers were left instructions—"

"Of course. I understand," she interrupted gently. "But my cousin's servants are traveling with our luggage carts. They shouldn't be more than a day or so behind us. Could you sent a messenger to tell them to proceed directly to the Lapalisse estate?"

"I will arrange for it immediately, Your Grace."

"You're very kind, madame. Now, if I may meet your staff, then, while I'm changing, you may join me in a cup of chocolate. I have a thousand questions."

"I would be honored, Your Grace."

When Charles ventured downstairs in the late afternoon, after a much-needed sleep, he found Phémie alone in the drawing room directly off the main entry hall. At the surprised expression on his face, she whirled about, the skirt of her gown rustling noisily. Laughing, she kissed him lightly, and his heart leaped within his breast. If he'd loved her before, in her boyish garb, it was nothing to what he felt now, seeing her as a woman. She was not beautiful, in the popular conception of beauty, but was exotic in her difference. Her lips were not too full; her eyes almond-shaped, almost oriental in their length, and a true green; and, most strange of all, she wore no cosmetics. The honey-colored hair was shining clean and bright as the sunlight caught it through the open windows.

"Oh, Charles, you should see my apartment! There's a drawing room, a small salon, a bath chamber, and the bedroom. Théophile had them all done over for me in gold and white. And then there's a library and a chapel all my own. It's so beautiful!"

"And your gown?"

"I have wardrobes full. Théophile took one of mine for fit, and left instructions that every year I was to have a complete wardrobe in the latest fashion. There are even court dresses, and a ballgown. And the bankers came early this afternoon, bringing the d'Amberieu family jewels. You've never seen anything like them, Charles."

"So now you are Euphémie, the Duchesse d'Amberieu."

"Oh, no, never to you! I'll always be just Phémie, won't I? This is only a game; I must be a lady for Madame Matilde, and the rest. But not to you, Charles."

"All right, play your game; I'll not give your secret away. But for now, my dear, I must leave you. I've been away from court for a long time, and His Majesty will be anxious for my report."

"But you'll be back tonight, won't you, Charles?" She grasped his hand in both of hers, pleading.

"I don't know, Phémie." He sounded doubtful. "I usually don't see His Majesty until quite late."

"I don't care what the hour; I'll wait up for you."

"If His Majesty permits, I'll be back. That's all I can promise."

"You can tell him how important it is, how much I need you. He'll allow it; I know he will."

"I'll make every effort. Why don't you take a rest after dinner? Then, when I return, I'll tell you about my visit with the King."

As Charles was driven away from the house, he felt more elated than he'd ever felt before; she needed him. She needed him! And he would never fail her, no matter who stood in the way. One day, he prayed, she would love him as he loved her. But following the prayer came the brutal reminder that even if she did love him, what could come of it? He had a wife.

When he returned, it was very late, but he could see the light shining from the drawing room where he'd last seen her. As he alighted from his coach, the door was thrown open and Phémie ran into his arms, almost knocking him off balance.

"I knew you'd come back to me. I've been so afraid."

"Florimond again?" he asked, his tone sinister, and she nodded, her head against his shoulder. "Where is he?"

"Sleeping." She giggled nervously. "I gave him another powder."

"You must be careful; he might guess."

"No, he thinks it was the journey. He was drinking again, and saying wild, mad things."

"The house is full of servants. You have nothing to be afraid of."

"I only feel safe when you're here." She stepped back, taking his hand. "Come inside. Did you get anything to eat?"

"More than enough. I would enjoy some wine, however. I hear your husband possessed an excellent cellar."

She led the way inside, not relinquishing her grip on his hand until he was sitting down, and he experienced a flood of warmth at her nearness. Once inside the drawing room, she closed the door quietly and asked, in the whisper of a fellow conspirator, "What of the King?" She handed him a glass of wine, then sat at his feet, gazing up at him.

"He's in very good spirits. Florimond's presentation is four days hence, in the afternoon. The court is a veritable beehive of tailors and dressmakers, cobblers and jewelers, hairdressers and wigmakers. The confusion is amazing."

"But what of you?" she asked anxiously, and he relieved her fear without delay.

"I'm to place myself at your disposal, Your Grace, and do all I can to make your sojourn in Paris as comfortable and pleasant as possible. I didn't tell him that perhaps you'd be staying here longer than a brief visit. I think he'd prefer having you stay at court, but he didn't press the matter when I told him how much you were enjoying the d'Amberieu chateau."

"Thank you, Charles. That means more to me than you'll ever know. By the by, did you see the Comtesse?" she asked, as an afterthought, and he was puzzled.

"Which Comtesse?" he asked, wondering if he had forgotten something, and she stared at him, wide-eyed.

"Why, your Comtesse, of course."

"Oh, that Comtesse! No, I was fortunately spared that delight." He laughed with her, reaching out and tousling her hair. "She'd left several messages with my valet while I've been away, asking for money, as usual."

"I thought her father was very rich; rich enough even to indulge his daughter's husband in his slightest wish," she commented mischievously, and Charles took it in good humor.

"It would seem that his daughter's husband, by his soberness and responsibility, has earned the old gentleman's approval, while his daughter has lost it. The daughter must approach the husband for anything she wants beyond her allowance."

"Are you going to give her what she needs?"

"She always receives what she needs, Phémie." He was suddenly serious. "But not always what she wants."

"Charles, forgive me for asking, but do you still love her?" Her question was asked so earnestly and she regarded him with such sympathy that he restrained the hoot of laughter he felt rising to his throat, choking on it, tears coming to his eyes.

When the fit passed, he was able to answer with equal earnestness, "No, my dear child, I feel nothing for my wife."

"I don't believe you," she retorted with her usual frankness, taking as evidence the tears in his eyes. "It must be terrible to love someone who doesn't love you in return."

"It's not too terrible, as long as there is hope that someday the one you love might love in return."

"And do you hold that hope for your wife, Charles? Do you think she might come to her senses and realize what a wonderful man you are?"

"I do not hold that hope for my wife," he replied firmly to her first question, and to the second, "As for her coming to her senses, it would be too late. I'm too plain for her tastes, my dear; she likes her meat well spiced." As he expected, the cruder aspects of his remark were completely beyond Phémie.

"What do you mean, well spiced?"

"Only that she has no use for men who believe in treating women with respect and kindness."

"I know what you mean. They bore her! Théophile wrote me of women like that. He called them 'creatures to be pitied,' and said that they didn't like themselves very much or they wouldn't allow men to abuse them."

"The Duc was very wise," he commented drily, and she was struck with a new idea.

"Why don't you beat her? She'll probably love you for it."

"Simply because I don't want her to love me, although I've been sorely tempted to do as you suggest. On the contrary, I wish her well of her abusive lovers, and will leave the beating in their more capable hands."

"It was only a thought . . ." She shrugged, losing interest in the matter.

"And I thank you for it," he teased, but she ignored it, asking instead, "Do you have a mistress, Charles?"

"My dear, a lady does not ask a gentleman such a question."

"Nonsense! I thought we are friends, and not a lady and a gentleman."

"Despite our being friends, you are still a lady, at least in my eyes, and I like to believe myself a gentleman."

"As you will, Charles. But if I had a lover, and you asked me, I'd tell you."

"I don't doubt it, but please, leave me with my illusions."

"I have too many of my own not to grant your request.

But answer this, if you will: do you believe a man and a woman can really be friends?"

"For a time, Phémie, yes, they can be friends."

"And after that time?"

"They either drift apart or become lovers."

"I wonder what it would be like, being your mistress," she asked sleepily, and he hesitated a moment before asking in return, "Would you want to be my mistress?"

"If what you say is true, and there would be no other way to keep you close to me, I suppose I would have to be."

"My God!" He exploded with laughter, and she lost her drowsiness. "That's not very romantic, nor is it saying much for my attractiveness as a lover."

"May I be honest with you, Charles?"

"When haven't you been honest?"

"I don't mean exactly honest. It's just that I've said things to you that I meant at the time I've said them, and will mean them again but now I have other thoughts—serious and secret thoughts."

"I understand. What is it you want to tell me?"

"I talk wildly at times, without giving thought to what I'm saying. Like all this talk about lovers and mistresses. To be honest, Charles, I don't want to be anyone's mistress."

"But you don't want to be anyone's wife, either."

"Not right now. I was speaking the truth when I said I value my personal freedom. I should have been born long ago, when the husband went off to tournaments and to wars, and the woman was her own mistress."

"So, even to 'keep me close to you,' you wouldn't consider becoming my mistress?" he asked lightly, his voice concealing the sinking feeling he felt inside. He was so concerned with his own emotion, he didn't notice the twinkle in her eyes, nor the mischief that crept into her tone.

"I can't lose my maidenhood to you, Charles. It belongs to another."

Nothing she had ever said had surprised him so, and that was saying a great deal.

"What madness is this?"

"It's really very simple; I just believe in the old way. It was a custom many years ago; our tutor told me about it. I think he was trying to instill virtue in me."

"What did he tell you?" he asked, impatiently amused, yet worried because he knew that she held so many strange opinions.

"In history, before there were kings, as we know them, there were lords, and they had certain rights in regard to the women living on their lands."

"Good God! The Droit du Seigneur!"

"That's it; how good of you to remember. I never could."

"But Florimond will be the master of the estate."

"Don't be foolish, Charles. You were doing so well."

"The King!" He breathed the two words out, rather than speaking them, but she heard him and clapped her hands, laughing.

"Exactly!"

"My poor, poor child!" he said pityingly, shaking his head. "There are a hundred women, and more, who are vying for His Majesty's favor."

"I said nothing about vying for His Majesty's favor, did I? Do you think I want to become his mistress, and perhaps wake up poisoned one morning? Thank you, but no."

"But you said—"

"All I said, if you remember, is that he has the first claim to my maidenhood. No more than that. And if he doesn't want to take his right, as my sovereign lord, then I am free to look elsewhere."

"But that just isn't done any more," Charles protested, not knowing whether she were serious or teasing. "What are you going to do? Just walk up to him and offer yourself?"

"That's not the way it was done, Charles. If the lord wished to exercise his right, he would approach the woman."

"Yes, but only on her wedding night, not years after she had married. If he didn't claim her on that first night, she belonged to her husband."

"But Théophile never claimed me himself. So it's the same as if I am just married."

"It is not! And well you know it." He was losing his temper, and she was amazed.

"Why, Charles, you're angry. Every woman in France is in love with Louis Bourbon, yet you act as if I were wicked."

"Are you in love with the King, then?"

"No, of course not. I've never seen him."

With an immense effort, Charles kept his voice even, "And never having seen him, you're willing to let him lie with you. Are you hoping to be left alone with him? Do you think your beauty will so overwhelm him that he'll take your maidenhood on the top of the council room table or behind a hedge in the garden?"

Charles leaped to his feet, throwing his glass in the general direction of the fireplace and pacing the room in his rage. "I heard that he once took a servantwoman in Madame de Montespan's anteroom while waiting for his favorite to dress. I imagine that he did the wench enough courtesy to take her in comfort, perhaps on a couch. Doesn't your exalted position as the widow of one of the most powerful men in France demand at least the same comfort as a serving woman? Or do you picture yourself as some poor peasant girl working in the fields on her lord's property? Tell me, Your Grace, what do you see yourself as, in this dream of yours?"

For once Phémie had no ready answer. Her mouth gaped and her eyes were wide with surprise at his rage.

"You fool!" he continued without waiting for her reply. "Do you think that court is a game? Do you think Louis plays so lightly with his women? Do you think, once he has possessed you, that he'd let you go with a godspeed? You must be mad; there can be no other explanation for such thoughts."

He suddenly noticed that she was scrutinizing him closely, an expression of speculation in her eyes. "Why are you staring?" he demanded rudely. "What have you got to say for yourself?"

At his questions, she lowered her eyes, and in doing so, noticed that when he threw the glass, the wine splashed her skirt.

"You've spoiled my dress," she complained, pouting, completely disarming his anger. "I put it on just for you, and you've thrown wine all over it."

He knelt down in front of her, his mood changing abruptly. "So I have." He shook his head in mock despair. "I'm afraid it's ruined."

"Charles?" She reached out, touching his arm timidly. "Why did you become so angry with me?"

"Because you're my very dear friend, Phémie, and I don't want to see you get hurt."

"I won't get hurt, I promise. Only people who love get hurt."

"How well I know that!" he agreed ruefully, and she smiled softly, her eyes downcast. "Are you laughing at me?" he asked, amazed, and when she looked up at him, her expression was perfectly solemn.

"Will you kiss me, Charles?"

For a long moment he looked into her eyes, then leaned forward, kissing her firmly, and, he hoped, brotherly on the forehead.

"That's not what I meant." She was obviously disappointed, and he said, resolutely, "I know what you meant. But I'll not play your game, Phémie. If I were more of a man or less of a friend, I might be tempted. I fear you've set a very dangerous course in your quest for romance, and since I'm the nearest man, and comparatively safe, you feel you can play with me. But I'll do all I can to protect you, even from yourself."

"Am I really such a fool?" she asked, more of herself than of him. "I thought you cared for me, and not only as a friend."

"We've not come to that yet, Phémie."

She flushed slightly at the rebuke and stood up, steadying herself with difficulty.

"I think I'll retire," she stated, with an attempt at dignity. "Thank you for your patience, Charles."

"Go to bed, child. This has been a full day for you."

She walked to the door, pausing a moment to ask, "Do you still like me, Charles?"

"But of course, my dear."

"I must be mad."

"No, only tired. And I am sorry about the dress. I'm certain my father-in-law will have something in his warehouse."

"That won't be necessary. Good night."

After she'd left him, he poured himself another glass of wine, noting with amazement that his hand was trembling. His rage had been a very real thing, based purely on a jealousy he had no right to feel. She could have been his at the height of the emotional moment; she had offered herself to him when she asked for the kiss. But he knew even during the moment of temptation that afterward she would hate herself, and him as well. So close; they had been so close to the embrace of which he had dreamed. All he needed to do was take her into his arms, but it would have been for one night only. In the morning he would have had to leave her forever, and he was not going to sacrifice a lifetime for a night of passion.

9

If there was a slight awkwardness between his cousin and the courtier, Florimond was insensitive to it at the table the next morning. After his drugged sleep, he was out of sorts, but very full of himself and his plans, which he divulged to them pompously. Charles was getting bored with his company, but he had agreed to take him into Paris so that he might buy a few things for his bride. Phémie gave him a purse, more than sufficient to purchase the promised fabric for Giselle's wedding gown. While Charles was waiting for Florimond, an unexpected visitor arrived. As he took his unwanted guest into the drawing room, he was relieved that the cousins were elsewhere.

"How did you find me?" Charles asked, without ceremony, and the man laughed.

"It was no great feat. His Majesty mentioned the arrival of the Duchesse, and that you were to be her escort to the ball. You're doing very well, as usual, de Montais."

Charles cut him short. "I've no time for you today, Tremon. I'll be at Versailles in a few days and will listen to you then."

"You'll listen to me now." Tremon was just as short. "I have some letters here from your honored wife, the Comtesse de Montais. I suggest you read one before I go on." He tossed it to him contemptuously, and Charles caught it deftly. It didn't take him long to read it through, his face flushing angrily.

"What do I care for filth?" He threw it in the fire, and the man laughed.

"I have more; many more. Your wife's writing is distinctive, de Montais, and her sentiments to me most descriptive. I don't believe you would care for her to be exiled from the court over the scandal if these were revealed."

"My wife's banishment from court could do nothing but good; I would simply send her to a convent. An arrangement that would save me a great deal of embarrassment in the future."

If Charles hoped to disappoint him, he was himself disappointed, for the other merely laughed.

"But what of the virtuous LeForge? Would he react so carelessly to his daughter's disgrace? I think not!"

Tremon realized by the unguarded expression of dismay on the other's face that he had struck home and laughed triumphantly. "I thought you would appreciate my reasoning."

"How much do you want?"

"Please, de Montais, don't be so graceless." He was feeling his power, and teased, "We are merely acting the roles of merchants; I am selling and you are buying."

"Get on with it!" Charles was in no mood for dallying, and the fellow had sense enough not to push him too far.

"I've certain debts, de Montais; if I don't pay them, I'll have to leave court."

"I wish I could sympathize with you. How much are you asking for your merchandise?"

"100,000 *louis d'or!*"

"Don't be ridiculous!" Charles snorted disgustedly. "If

you owed that much, the whole court would know it. Now try the truth, and don't be greedy."

"If I didn't need you, de Montais . . ." the man began threatening, and Charles knew that he could be very ugly when provoked.

"How much is it?" He reminded him of the business they were about.

"10,000."

"I'll give you five, nothing more. And you can go to the devil if you don't take it."

"7,000, and you'll never hear from me again."

"All right, but I don't have it here. I'm going into Paris today. I'll bring it to you when I come to Versailles."

"No, I'll wait here."

"I can't permit that. I don't want anyone here to see you."

"The Duchesse might not approve of your business, is that it? Well, if she has the d'Amberieu fortune, I can't blame you. I'll wait outside, near the gate. No one will see me."

"But it will take me hours."

"Two hours, de Montais; no longer. If I have to leave here without my money, the letters will be all over the court by tonight."

"Very well, two hours," Charles capitulated, but added, "Before I give you a *sou*, I'm coming to the house. If I learn that you've disturbed anyone here, you can start running from your creditors."

"We understand each other, then. I'll avail myself of your hospitality"—he took a bottle of wine from the side table— "no longer."

True to his word, there was no sign of Tremon as the coach bearing Charles and Florimond passed through the gates. Once certain that they were not returning, Tremon rode onto the property again, tied his horse in the belt of trees near the gate, and settled down with his bottle to wait de Montais's return. He was very pleased with himself and with the Comtesse de Montais. She needed money as much as he did; and when he had gone to her as a lover, begging her help, it was she who had thought up the scheme. She wrote the few letters he was carrying upon his person, and would write more when next they required funding. Since it was not his own money, de Montais would not kick up too much of a fuss the next time they approached him. The only drawback to the plan was that it placed him in the power of a woman; she could carry on the scheme with another man, and did not need him, while he did need her, or rather her father. He was at a distinct disadvantage, he thought, but one he could live with far more easily than living with the alternative. If only there were some way to reverse their positions . . .

Waiting was hot work, and he'd finished his wine in less than an hour. It took him but a few minutes to decide that he was thirsty again and to start through the trees toward the house. When he reached the last tree, he weighed the distance across the open lawn against his chance of getting to the house undetected and knew that there was little hope for success. Keeping to the shadow of the trees, he quickly crossed the drive and worked his way to the side of the house where the stables were located.

When he was certain there was no activity around the stables, he dashed across the open space to the protection of the wall. He felt slightly foolish, but was enjoying the challenge of commandeering another bottle of wine from the drawing room and escaping unnoticed. He had just about decided that he could reach the terrace and work his way to the open window he sought, when he heard someone approaching. Pressing hard against the wall, he held his breath, hoping that whoever was coming would not catch sight of him. He could hear the rustling of skirts as the woman passed into the stable without seeing him. Moving silently to the door, he peered into the dim interior but couldn't see anyone. It must be one of the housemaids, he thought to himself; perhaps chickens were kept in there, and she was gathering eggs. In the darkness of the stable, he could hear her moving about, and found that he was no longer bored; this was an adventure to his liking. He darted into the stable, closing the door quickly behind him.

"Who is there?" she demanded, and she sounded more than a little frightened. He laughed a deliberately sinister laugh, making his way almost silently in the direction of her voice.

"Florimond, is that you?"

When he didn't answer, she spoke again, pinpointing her location for him even more definitely. "Answer me!"

Before she could cry out, he was upon her, covering her mouth with his hand. As he expected, she fought him wildly, and with no mean strength for a girl, but he overpowered her, forcing her down on the straw. Frantically she tried to bite the hand over her mouth, but he knew how to avoid that. He lay on top of her, laughing in pure enjoyment. Her fists beat at him ineffectually, and what had begun as an escape from boredom became very serious to him. The heaving body beneath his excited him. Everything added to the mounting passion he felt: the warm smell of the stable; the scent of flowers worn by his victim; the smoothness of her face; and, more than anything, her panic. This was the way it was meant to be, he thought; not the easy dalliance that existed at court, where the women so often were as bold as the men, and the roles became confused. But here, in the darkness, was the primeval truth between man and woman —master and slave. He would conquer her, beat her to submission if necessary, but she would be his, as she was meant to be.

"Submit!" he whispered, tearing at her bodice with his free hand. Her furious struggle renewed with his demand, and she almost escaped the hand pressing so hard on her mouth that it hurt her. As she tried to scream, his mouth claimed hers, biting her lips until they bled, and the taste of blood seemed to drive him mad. Her bodice was ripped free, and his hand found her naked breast. Suddenly she lay quietly under him, responding to his kiss and caress, her body moving again, but slowly, maddeningly. He became aware of a sense of disappointment; she was surrendering too easily. As he relaxed his hold on her, she gathered all her strength, and heaved, pushing him away from her. His head smashed against a stall, and he lay still.

When Charles returned from Paris, alone, having left Florimond exploring the merchant LeForge's warehouse, there was no sight of Tremon. Searching the woods, he found the horse and the empty wine bottle. Charles knew the Master of Horse only slightly, but knew that his word was not good, especially when it came to gambling. He raced to the house, calling for Phémie, but no one seemed to know where she was. As he started upstairs, his driver approached him, and, having the sense to keep his voice low, asked Charles to come to the stable. By the expression on his face, Charles realized that something was amiss and rushed out of the house. The scene that awaited him in the stable set his heart throbbing painfully. Phémie lay on the stable floor. He put his ear to her breast, and almost sobbed when he heard the strong heartbeat. Blinking away his tears, he covered her with the remnants of the torn bodice.

"Is Her Grace still alive, Monsieur le Comte?" his man asked fearfully, and Charles reassured him, "She has only fainted."

"And the man?" Charles had reason to be thankful that his man was so well trained and did not approach the scene too closely. He put his ear to Tremon's chest and caught the sound of a heartbeat. The beast was still alive, he thought, but when he turned away, he only shook his head.

"Go to the house and tell them that Her Grace has been attacked by a dog and to prepare her room. I'll bring her in."

When the man had run off, Charles hurriedly moved aside Tremon's coat and opened his shirt. With great deliberation, he unsheathed his sword, placing its point directly over the man's heart, then shoved it in. After a spasm, Tremon lay still, and Charles fastened his shirt and placed the coat back where it had been. With a handful of straw, he wiped his blade clean, replacing it calmly, then picked Phémie up gently, and carried her to the house. As she was being attended to, Charles, with the help of his servant, buried Tremon in the trees behind the stable. When he returned, he found Matilde waiting for him.

"Did you kill the dog, Monsieur?" she asked quietly, and Charles replied carefully, "He is dead, Madame, but for Her Grace's sake, I think we should tell everyone that he ran off."

"Where did you bury him?"

He suddenly realized that she knew it hadn't been a dog that had attacked her mistress, and wondered what she would do.

"Why do you want to know, Madame?"

"So I may keep the servants from becoming too inquisitive if they come across the grave."

He smiled wearily, placing his hand on her shoulder. "In back of the stable, deep in the trees."

"There is no reason for them to go back there."

"But the gardeners—"

"I'll see to it that they restrict their activities to the lawns until winter. The snows will cover our secret."

"You're a good woman, Madame."

"And you, Monsieur, are a true gentleman. I'll be with the child when she awakens, and will send for you."

"No, it is best that she sleeps. When she begins to awaken, give her a powder in a cup of warm wine. I don't know where she keeps them."

"I do, Monsieur. It will be done as you suggest."

"Good. I must go now and get the Baron in the city. He can be told only as much as the servants, no more."

"I understand, Monsieur."

There remained only Tremon's horse to be disposed of, and Charles decided to do the most obvious thing. He rode the horse boldly into Paris, realizing that there was little chance of any courtier being in the city, and set it loose not too far from the waterfront warehouse of his father-in-law. As he was driven to his destination in his own carriage, he was confident that some citizen or other would find use for such an animal, and would not be too quick to report its finding to the authorities. It was a gamble, but he had no other choice.

When Charles was finally relieved of his vigil at Phémie's bedside by Madame Matilde, he was deeply concerned. The experience had left the girl understandably terrified, and she had clung to him weeping until she had fallen once again into a fitful sleep. He viewed the murder of Tremon as more of an execution, justly administered to an animal who'd caused so much anguish to one he loved. Phémie, even in her distraction, had accepted the tale that her assailant had run off, and promised that she would support his explanation of the dog. The servants had accepted it readily, recounting various incidents of wild dogs in the city, and Florimond had not seemed very much interested in his cousin's misfortune.

It had been a long night for Charles, and he was weary beyond belief. The last thing he wanted was a private, pre-dawn interview with Florimond; but there he was, poking his head out of the door when he heard Charles approaching. He motioned wildly to the courtier, holding a finger to his lips, and wouldn't speak until they were seated next to the heavily curtained windows of his room.

"I know you must be tired, Charles," he said by way of apology. "Phémie can be a nuisance when she wishes."

Charles felt the hot words of defense spring to his lips, but decided prudence would be a wiser course, and kept silent. There would be time enough later to tell Florimond what he really thought of him.

"I wouldn't detain you if I didn't think it was important, and you might be interested in what I have discovered."

"Another gift for Giselle?" he asked politely, and Florimond laughed.

"You might say so. First tell me, did you actually see the dog that attacked Phémie?"

Charles was about to mutter a careless "yes" to his inquiry but suddenly became suspicious, and very alert.

"No, not actually," he commented easily, watching the other's excitement growing before his eyes. "I heard it from one of the servants. It's a terrible thing when one can't walk about one's own property without being attacked by wild beasts. Phémie needs our protection."

"My cousin doesn't need protecting by anyone." He laughed harshly, full of triumph. "Your friend attacked her, and she killed him."

"My friend?" Charles felt the cold clutch of fear in his heart. "I don't understand."

"The man you took into the drawing room shortly before we left for the city. He must have come back and seen Phémie go into the stable. When he attacked her, she killed him, and rightly so. But why did she hide the fact? If she had admitted it, no one would have blamed her. There must be more to it than a simple rape attempt. Perhaps she met your friend and lured him to the stable."

"You know Phémie wouldn't do such a thing; she's not that sort of woman. I don't know where you learned all this. Who told you such a wild tale?"

"No one. I found the grave they put the poor fellow in. It's behind the stable."

"It's true, then!" Charles seemed amazed. "And you're certain it was the man who visited me earlier?"

"I have eyes, don't I?"

"I can't believe that Phémie would have tried to conceal such a thing. When they found her, she had fainted."

"Well, perhaps she didn't bury him. It must have been Madame Matilde's plan. She's capable of such a horror. Henri probably buried him at his wife's insistence."

"How was he killed?"

"A stab wound to the heart. She probably did it with that dagger you found in the keep."

"Are you going to tell her you know?"

"Not yet, my friend. I have everything I need now, and I don't want to warn them. They'll just move the body, and I'll have no proof." He laughed again, and Charles saw him in his full villainy for the first time. He meant to hold his secret until he needed something from Phémie. If she happened to deny it to him, he would threaten her with disclosure of what he thought was her crime.

"Who was your friend, by the way?" he asked innocently, but Charles wasn't to be taken in.

"You have all the information you need. Someday I might find a use for the other myself."

"What do you mean?" he asked sharply, afraid that Charles would use the information to strip her of the d'Amberieu fortune.

"Not what you're thinking! I'm certain you've guessed by now that I find Phémie very attractive."

"You devil!" Florimond laughed heartily, relieved that his source of wealth was not to be threatened. "I wish you success of it."

"Of course, I would prefer it if she would come to me willingly. But if I grow tired of waiting . . ." He shrugged lightly, grinning.

"Won't do her any harm. She's needed bedding for a long time."

"Well, my friend, the hour is late." He rose, stretching, and hoped that his pose of weariness was real enough to let him escape.

"Don't you want to see the grave?"

"It's not necessary. Your word is good enough. We'll meet later and discuss your plans."

"You're a good friend, Charles."

"No effort is too great for those I care about. Until later, my friend."

Once within the privacy of his own room, Charles threw himself down on the bed without disrobing. He was sick, not only with apprehension, but even more with the hatred he felt for the man. Florimond held a sword to Phémie's heart and would not hesitate in using it if it suited his purposes. Charles could not allow her to live under such a threat. She would deny knowledge of the man's death, but it would start her thinking, and she would soon realize who had killed her assailant. Lying there, he could envision her turning from him in horror. She would never permit him to see her again. That was the worst of it. The least of it was that when she denied her part in it, Florimond, as well, would realize the truth and would merely transfer his demands to Charles. To be under the power of the beast would be hell on earth. Either way, Florimond would win, and Charles vowed that he could not permit that. It was actually very simple—Florimond had no right to life as long as he threatened Phémie. The only difficulty was in planning a way to execute him before he could tell his bride of his discovery, and before she could tell her father. Yet it would have to happen far away from Phémie. An accident! he thought. Somehow he must arrange an accident. But how?

By the time the afternoon of Florimond's presentation arrived, Charles was no closer to a solution of his problem than when he had first learned of it. Phémie was rapidly gaining control over her fear. At times she could even smile at his attempts to lighten her mood, but there was no gaiety in her eyes, and she steadfastly refused to leave her apartment. The night of the Grand Ball was but a few days away, and Charles was seriously dismayed by her withdrawal. Shortly before he and Florimond were to leave for Versailles, he was told that she wanted to see him. He found her at the desk in the library, and she put down the book she'd been reading. As she looked up at him, smiling, he was gladdened to see a hint of the former mischief in her eyes.

"So you are off for the great adventure."

"I could wish myself elsewhere." He made a face of disgust and she hastened to apologize.

"Forgive me for burdening you with this tiresome excursion. You must be terribly bored with all the problems we've thrust upon you."

"My darling Phémie, you have brought light into the dark corners of my life. I've not known one moment of boredom since the good God directed my path to yours. I pray every night that I may be worthy of your friendship."

"Enough!" she pleaded, blushing prettily. "You must be very successful with the ladies."

He had been perfectly sincere, but decided that he'd best fall in with her lighter mood.

"My dear, in order to survive at court, one must be very attentive to the ladies. It is they who make all the rules of social grace. To fail with them is to fail at Versailles."

"You know those people so well. What will they expect of the Duchesse d'Amberieu?"

"They didn't know of your existence until recently. I think they will expect someone like the Duc's first wife. That lady spent a goodly amount of her married life in a convent. An older woman, undoubtedly; religiously solemn, dignified, and respectable. There is very little speculation about you."

"You sound as if I should be grateful for that."

"And so you should. The court's favorite sport is destroying other people with gossip, especially if those people don't offer any defense. It is not a pretty sight."

"I don't know if I'll have the courage to go there. I was so dependent on Florimond before all this happened."

"Florimond would have been of no assistance at all," he protested jealously. "He knows no more of court life than you. Do you not believe that you can depend upon me? Have I not enough strength to protect you from them?"

"My dearest fool, of course you do." She smiled with such tenderness that his heart melted. "Someday I shall be able to repay you for everything you've suffered for me." Someday he would remind her of that promise, he thought to himself as he kissed her hand lingeringly. But aloud all he said was, "I want only your happiness."

At the presentation, relieved that Florimond had acquitted himself surprisingly well, Charles entrusted him to the care of a lesser luminary of the court while he was occupied with the King. Louis received him warmly in the council chamber, asking for the latest report on the Duchesse. Charles was prepared for this and had decided not to mention the attack of "the wild dog." Louis would probably have commanded her removal to the palace for her own safety. After being charged with conveying the King's warmest regards and telling her how anxious he was to make her acquaintance at last, Charles made his exit, thankful that the ordeal was over. He had charted a dangerous course, and if Louis ever learned of the attack upon Phémie, the courtier would be lucky to find no more than a home taken from him.

That was the least of his considerations at the moment, however. He was committed now to this game, and the danger involved was worthy of the high stakes. Before collecting Florimond, he began by making several discreet inquiries among some of his lady acquaintances. Between snatches of light gossip and discussion of their ensembles for the ball, he secured the information he was seeking. None of them realized that she had been questioned nor that any specific information had been given. He was very pleased with the results.

10

That night the companions held a farewell dinner in Phémie's cousin's honor, and all three were in high spirits. Florimond was celebrating his upcoming marriage, already having written the patient Giselle that he had at last persuaded his stubborn cousin to relent. Phémie was rejoicing at the imminent departure of the troublesome Florimond, and Charles was pleased at the discovery earlier in the afternoon of one who could perform a valuable service for him. There was a great deal of laughter, and relationships seemed to return to what they had been when Charles first arrived in Bretagne.

After Phémie excused herself, the men retired to Charles's room, where they spent several hours in conversation. Charles promised that he would stand beside Florimond when the latter married; and, in return he tried to wring an oath from the lout that he would tell no one of his discovery of the assailant's body. Florimond took exception to the aspersion cast upon his betrothed's loyalty and discretion, but

Charles finally convinced him that none was intended. He was successful in limiting the promise until after he were indeed married, reminding him that at such time Giselle's interests would be those of her husband and no longer of her father. At last Florimond saw that such knowledge could prove to be a weapon in the hands of someone tempted to improve his own fortunes, and, bowing to the courtier's persuasiveness, gave his sacred oath to remain silent. Charles rejoiced at his victory, becoming very effusive as he bade Florimond farewell. He had purchased the time he needed so desperately to arrange that Florimond's wedding would never take place.

On the night before the Grand Ball, Charles absented himself from Phémie's company on the excuse of visiting his father-in-law on business. It had cost him a heavy purse to pursue his inquiries toward arranging a meeting, while keeping his own identity anonymous. Rather than taking his coach, with the revealing crest on the doors, and its driver, who could well give witness against him in the future, he left the chateau on horseback. Several miles outside of Paris, he recognized the landmark he was to watch for and found the overgrown path leading to the river. As he neared his destination, he was required to dismount and lead the horse to the water's edge. He concealed the animal in the undergrowth, as instructed, put on the full mask, and waited. This was accomplished none too soon, for darkness quickly fell, and he doubted if he would have been able to find the place without light. After almost an hour, a craft bearing a lantern approached his place of concealment. As the barge touched the shore, he stepped out into view, ready to give the hooded man a severe tongue-lashing for keeping him waiting so long past the appointed time. The fellow forestalled him by saying, "My apologies, Monsieur, but I had to be certain you were alone."

"Of course I'm alone. Those were the instructions."

"You must understand. After the recent trials, it is necessary for us to take precautions, for your protection as well as our own. These are dangerous times."

"I admire your caution," Charles admitted grudgingly, and the man continued, "We do not know you, and you will not know us. If you were a spy for the authorities and led them to this spot later, it would be of no avail. We never use the same meeting place twice. Nor will you know where I am taking you. If you'll step aboard, Monsieur." Charles jumped onto the barge and took a seat where the man indicated.

"Beside you, you'll find a hood. Please put it on," he directed as he pushed off from the shore. Charles did as he was told, not surprised that the hood provided for his use had no eyeholes. He made no effort to determine their direction, or to keep track of the time they spent on the river.

At last they touched ground, and Charles was told not to remove his hood. The fellow was a courteous and careful guide, leading the courtier away from the river and finally into a house, where he was permitted to see again. They were in a narrow hallway, dark except for one lighted candle. It was an old, ramshackle place, dank and musty. His guide, taking up the candle, led him into a room off the hall, where there were several monks' robes hanging on pegs. Here Charles divested himself of his clothing, donning a robe approximately his size, relieved that it at least was clean. He was then led up the rotting staircase and cautioned to keep close to the wall. At the end of the long hallway he was ushered into a surprisingly comfortable, well-appointed room. He accepted a glass of excellent wine, and was left alone. Presently a woman entered and sat opposite him.

"I am the one you've come to see, Monsieur. What is it you wish?"

Charles stared at her open-mouthed, shocked by her appearance. Here was no ugly, harsh-voiced, common old woman, as the witches of Paris had been. This was a cultured lady with gentle speech and impeccable manners. She wore only a half-mask, so he saw that she was both young and beautiful. Her slender figure was draped in a nun's robe, and her dark hair was bound in braids and wrapped about her head.

"You're a witch?" he asked, incredulous, and she smiled gently. "Most assuredly, Monsieur. Did you expect another Madame Voisin, perhaps?"

"Why, yes. I don't mean to offend you, but I thought all witches . . ."

"Those crones were not witches. They read the cards, performed abortions, and mixed poisons. They were not true servants of my Dark Master."

"I think I'd best tell you, before we go any further, I don't believe in your Master."

"It is not required that you believe." Her voice remained kind. "I have more than enough belief for both of us."

"You're a very unusual woman, Madame. I can imagine you have quite a few conversions to your credit."

She laughed charmingly, shaking her head. "It is not my mission to convert people. That is left to those with lesser talents than those with which I have been blessed."

"Blessed?" Charles asked teasingly, and she replied, "My Master is as capable of blessing his followers as is your god."

"Then you also call him god as we do?"

"But of course. I believe that god exists, but not in the world during our time. We are not in opposition to god, only to those who claim to be his followers."

"I don't understand."

"My Master rules this world, Monsieur." She continued in her calm, plausible way. "You have only to look about you to know that I am speaking the truth. It is the clerics who are the hypocrites. They bring the people to their knees for their own power and glorification, not for their god's, or for their so-called Christ. The ancients knew the truth of it— that there are two gods. There is the God of Light whose time has long passed but will come again and the God of Darkness whose time is now and will pass only to come again after the time of Light."

"Doesn't your Master inspire you with fear?"

"No more so than your god inspires you with fright.

When I am called from this life, I will join my Master in His Kingdom." She laughed again, a sane, happy sound. "Your Hell is my Heaven. But enough of religion. How may I help you?"

Charles moved uncomfortably in his chair, unable to meet her eyes, and she said sympathetically, "I think I understand. You have come here to avail yourself of my Master's powers, yet without offering homage to Him as you would to your own god if you were petitioning him for favor. But you must remember, Monsieur, that there are some things in this life for which one cannot approach your god. Let us say that we want someone sped from this world into the next. The methods of the Voisin woman and her confederates were plain and simple murder. Poisons that sickened their victims, causing them much suffering. Your religion has taught you that murder is wrong, and I agree. But that same religion also teaches that one should rejoice at the doorway of death, and the approaching union of the soul with its god. We merely assist that soul in obtaining its ultimate desire quickly and without pain."

"But what if a person is unshriven; what if he doesn't have the presence of a priest?"

"It is only the clerics who made that rule. Even if it were not so, you mustn't limit the mercy of your god by the standards of the clerics. Do you think the one you call Christ would deny such a soul forgiveness for something that was beyond its own control? No, Monsieur, you must look to your own soul for this act, and not be concerned about another's."

"Are you trying to dissuade me, Madame?"

"Not at all. It means nothing to me personally. You are the one who left the letter at the baker's and who followed the instructions I arranged for you. We are strangers and will never meet again, unless you have future need of me. I will not attempt to convince you nor to dissuade you. You have taken this path for reasons of your own, and by an act of your own will. I am merely serving my Master in the way that pleases Him best. If such a service is to your advantage, and you wish to use it, then you must decide, and live with that decision. I cannot help you in that."

Charles was thoughtful for a moment, finishing his wine, then stated, "If I had not already made that decision, Madame, I would not be here. You are certainly not what I expected, and I appreciate your truthfulness. There are two people I wish to speed on their way to the next world. As you said, my reasons are my own, and I'll be grateful to you for the fastest and least suspect way you can provide."

"There is a way I have perfected. It will appear as if they had died in their sleep, peacefully. There will be no pain, only a drowsiness, and then death. They'll not struggle, or cry out . . ."

"I salute you, Madame," Charles said with sincere admiration. "It is more than either of them deserves. What is the cost?"

"No cost, Monsieur," she admonished, laughingly. "Only a donation, as your clerics would say. It is not usual to give two at the same time, however . . ."

"Five thousand is all I brought with me."

"Three will be most generous."

"You are a wonder!" he said in sincere admiration.

"It may be worth five to you, Monsieur, but I don't want to cheat you. I am a moralist, despite the fact that I worship at a different altar."

"That reminds me, will a . . . ceremony be necessary?"

"But of course! Otherwise, it will be useless."

"Do you sacrifice humans during your ceremony?"

She hesitated only a moment before answering, "Your cause is not serious enough for such measures. Madame Voisin was a butcher; we are not. Would it have prevented you from continuing if I had said yes?"

"No, Madame," he replied with surety. "My own survival depends upon the effectiveness of your method. If it is all you say it is, I would stop at nothing."

"You will not be required to take an active part in the ceremony, but your resolution is imperative. Ask me nothing now; you will be instructed when the time is near."

After Charles had counted out the money and had a quick glass of wine to fortify himself, she led him into another part of the house, to a dimly lit room where she left him.

Charles was so deep in thought that he did not know he was being watched until he heard a man clear his throat. When Charles looked up, startled, he saw that a priest had joined him. At least, nowhere had he ever seen a man more fitted to the image of a priest. His innocent, strangely unlined, cherub's face was wreathed in a halo of white hair. His blue eyes were lively, filled with humor and kindness. His voice, when he spoke, was gentleness itself.

"I imagine this all a little puzzling to you, my son. Julia undoubtedly explained much of it to you; she's very good at it. But if you have any questions, I'll be happy to answer them."

"Yes, Father . . ." He paused, embarrassed. "If I may call you that."

"Please do. I was once a cleric in your religion, but was saved and enlisted in the service of the Master. I am yet a priest, a true priest of the true religion, so 'Father' will do just the same."

When he spoke of "the true religion," a fierce light came into his eyes and Charles felt uncomfortable in the presence of such naked fanaticism.

"What is this room?"

"It is a chapel, once consecrated to the worship of your god. We must always hold our mass in a place such as this, and there are very few here in France. Usually we can only find them in old ruins like this. It's different in England. The Protestants have caused the clerics to flee, and there are hundreds of deserted monasteries and churches suitable to our needs."

As he spoke, a young man in monk's robes entered and began lighting tapers on the altar. As the illumination increased, Charles saw that the altar was draped in black; the tapers were black as well, and the crucifix hung upside down. There was a skull in the place of a chalice. A short distance from the altar a kneeler was placed. The walls were covered with tapestries depicting several stages of intercourse between a woman and a giant goat, with various demons looking on.

"Can you tell me about Julia?" he asked, tearing his eyes away from the interesting tapestries. "I don't mean anything that would betray her or identify her."

"I understand. Many men have asked that question. It is whispered that she is a succubus."

"What is a succubus?"

"A demon who takes the form of a beautiful woman and drives men wild with desire." He was smiling angelically as Charles drew in his breath sharply.

"Do you believe such nonsense?"

"For shame! Simply because you don't understand something, you mustn't ridicule it. Personally, I believe that every woman is a succubus. The false god created Adam, a poor, weak creation, and our Master created Eve. There is nothing weak about woman, and nothing in the world has led men so often to our Master as woman."

A bell rang in the distance. The ceremony was about to begin, and Charles's relief was mixed with a perverse curiosity as he was led to another chamber to wait. He had commissioned the dark deeds. Surely he should watch; thank Heaven or Hell that he must not.

Minutes passed into hours in the dank chamber where Charles sat, and he slept fitfully, wakening suddenly at the sound of bestial growls and shrill, feline screams that punctuated the silence. Then there were low moans that sounded much like the satiated agony of exquisitely painful sexual union. It was over. Charles was guided down a flight of stone stairs to where his clothes had been deposited. After he was dressed, he felt the hood slipped over his head again, and he was led out into the cold night air. Being outside cleared his head, and he breathed deeply as if to wash away the evil humors that had invaded his body. Once in the barge, he reminded his guide, "She was going to give me something."

"I have it here, Monsieur," the guide replied, handing

Charles a small packet, and Charles slipped it into his pocket, patting it to make sure that it was secure. "The packet is small," the man assured him, "but it is sufficient. The best time to use it is when the person is asleep. All that is necessary is to drop it into a fire, and leave the room quickly."

When they reached the other side, Charles thanked him warmly and tried to press a coin on him for his services, but he would not accept it, waving to him in a friendly fashion as he rowed back out into the river.

When he arrived at the chateau, Charles went directly to his room, knowing that Phémie would have retired hours ago. Bolting his door, he hurriedly unwrapped the parcel and found two wax figurines, one male and one female. He didn't try to understand how Julia knew the genders of his victims; her powers were beyond him. Now that he had his weapons, he believed that the worst was over. It was simply a matter of carrying out the instructions, and he would be free. He undressed, humming, and lay down on his bed, feeling an exultation that he'd never known before. Soon Phémie would be his! But at the thought of Phémie, he felt a dimly remembered passion flowing through him, and as it became stronger, he closed his eyes, trying to conjure up the image of the woman he loved. But it was to no avail. All he could see was the haunting face of the witch, Julia.

11

He won't like this, Charles groaned inwardly, the troubled dreams of the night before forgotten. His thoughts were concerned only with the reaction of the King, as he and Phémie waited for him in the council chamber off the royal apartment. If only she had allowed him to see her choice of costume before they left the chateau. But no, she had been adamant, refusing to remove her hooded cape, so Charles could not see what she was wearing until they had reached the private chamber. Despite all logic, he suspected that she was trying to displease the King deliberately. Ever since he'd met her, she'd said and done things that no sane person would do. He could imagine the expression of dismay, and then naked disapproval, on Louis's face and the accusation he would hurl at his courtier for permitting such an outrage. Phémie, he decided disloyally, needed more than a protector; she needed a keeper.

When Louis entered the room, he nodded casually in Charles's direction, then concentrated on the woman who was in a deep curtsy.

"My dear child," he began, taking her hand and assisting her to rise; but he got no further, his eyes widening. If Phémie were self-conscious under the close scrutiny, she didn't betray it. The King was speechless as he moved around her. She seemed to have stepped out of another age —a more simple age. Her gown was simplicity itself; the neckline began at her chin, and the trainless hem just barely grazed her ankle. She was completely covered, only her face and part of her hands showing. Yet never had Louis seen a more erotic costume. The material at the neck had been cut in scallops, and her face looked like a flower rising from its calyx. The fitted sleeves were long, extending in points over the tops of her hands. The bodice was like a second skin, clinging to the naturally firm young breasts temptingly. The skirt was flowing rather than full, and he suspected that she wasn't wearing any petticoats. It was violet, the color of widowhood, and the golden chain, with its great emerald pendant, was slung low across her hips with the jewel dangling below the knee. Upon her shining, carefully tousled hair was a golden circlet; she wore no other jewelry. The only cosmetics she used were a light dusting of rice powder, which barely concealed her freckles, and a bit of color on her eyelids. Her slippers were a shade of deeper violet, and heelless, as she was quite tall. The scent she used was as light as a spring shower. The complete picture was a celebration of freshness and natural beauty.

"Do I displease Your Majesty?" she asked softly, as he came full circle to face her once again.

"What do you think, de Montais?" He consulted the other man for no other reason than the lack of anything to say, so complete was his surprise.

"I think it is different, Your Majesty," he contributed, tight-lipped, and Louis laughed, taking her hand in his once again.

"That means he does not approve. And I'm not yet certain whether I do or not, but you certainly don't displease me, my dear."

"Your Majesty is too kind," she murmured, her gaze on

his pointed red shoes. "If you'll not think me too bold, I have brought a small gift as a remembrance." Charles stepped forward, handing her the package, and she, in turn, handed it to Louis.

"Another surprise. How pleasant!" He opened the finely wrapped package, revealing the dagger Charles had discovered in the keep. "This is very ancient, isn't it?" he asked appreciatively, and Charles told him of their adventure in Bretagne. "My dear Euphémie, it's a gift as unusual as the giver. May I offer you some wine?" He filled a goblet for her himself. Without any awkwardness, Charles excused himself, saying that there were some acquaintances he would like to visit, and Louis dismissed him eagerly. As he left, he heard the King ask if she liked dancing, and her delightful laughter mingled with his as she told him of the dancing master Théophile had insisted upon when she was a child.

The halls were almost deserted as he made his way to the upper reaches of Versailles. The courtiers were all closeted away, preparing for the ball. Occasionally he passed a hurrying servant, but they took no notice of him. Finally he reached the room of the Master of Horse, entering it without knocking. For a moment his heart stopped when he saw the figure lying across the bed, but he soon ascertained that the woman was his own wife.

"Elisa!" he whispered harshly, not wanting to be heard by anyone through the paper-thin walls, and he shook her by the shoulders until her head rolled loosely.

"Clement . . ." she murmured, drunkenly, and Charles let her fall back on the bed. There were empty bottles thrown about, and from the disordered state of her gown, he guessed correctly that she hadn't been sober for several days. Making a thorough search of the room, he failed to find the letters he was after. The only explanation must be that his wife had destroyed them first. It was unexpected good fortune, finding his wife here, and in a helpless condition, so he built a small fire in the grate. As soon as it was burning well, he took the female wax figurine he had secreted in his pocket and dropped it on top of the fire. Once outside, he hesitated, trying to decide whether to go on to her room and raise the hue and cry for her, or to return to the royal apartment and wait for Phémie. He decided on the latter course in case someone had seen his wife enter Tremon's room; he didn't want her found too soon. He could scarcely believe how easy it had been, and felt that perhaps the obscene mass had helped him after all.

The Grand Ball was a triumph for Phémie. The courtiers giggled behind their hands at her outlandish costume, her short hair, and healthy, natural coloring. She was an object of ridicule to those she had wished to avoid, and so they had avoided her. Not once did a courtier approach her for a dance, nor was she asked by any to join their table for cards. But the victory was hers, for she completely captivated the King.

Once the opening ceremonies were completed, they danced often, strolled through the gardens, sat together and talked, both of them laughing a great deal. Charles remained nearby, for occasionally the King was required elsewhere and would signal the courtier to entertain the Duchesse. At these times Charles couldn't help but notice the blush in her cheeks and the excitement shining in her eyes. However, she would not talk about the King, asking him questions instead concerning Versailles. Then Louis would reclaim her, and the two were off to another dance, or another glass of wine, their heads close together as they whispered to each other.

Toward the end, when Charles saw that they were unlikely to need him for a while, he approached an acquaintance and asked him to accompany him in search of his wife, saying that he had a message from her father. The courtier understood Charles's need of company, as everyone knew how abusive she could be, and went with him to Elisa's room. As Charles expected, there was no reply, and the gentlemen returned to the ball. Charles's companion promised to tell Elisa, if he saw her, that her husband wished a moment's speech with her. Charles was so pleased with his foresight that on the way home from the ball, he allowed Phémie to rhapsodize about the King's wit, the King's charm, the King's courtesy without taking offense. When he escorted her to her apartment, she forestalled his good-night by asking him to sit with her for a few minutes. He complied, wondering why she was suddenly so uncomfortable in his presence.

"Charles," she blurted out, "His Majesty has asked me to join his hunting party. I don't know how long I'll be gone."

"About ten days is usual." He was delighted with this news, and she was surprised by his reaction.

"You don't mind? You have no objections?"

"None at all. I think you'll enjoy yourself, as all formality and protocol are relaxed on those little journeys."

"You are truly the kindest man!" She hugged him gratefully, and he patted her shoulder in his most brotherly manner.

"My dear, I do feel I must warn you. You'll be in a den of lions, with no friend beside you."

"His Majesty is my friend, isn't he?"

"He is now, but if it amuses him not to be, he will follow that course and leave you to your own defense."

"If I don't like it, I'll come home again."

"And I'll be here waiting for you." He lied easily, already preparing secretly for his own little journey.

12

If anyone had told her before she left, she wouldn't have believed him, but Phémie was bored! All day long the men hunted, barely tolerating the presence of the women who chose to accompany them, and at night it was no better. The women, who wouldn't acknowledge Phémie's position despite the much valued "for Duchesse d'Amberieu" that had been chalked on the door of her private room as a mark of royal favor, were waiting for the right moment to attack her. The men were little better, forever talking of horses and hunting, and bragging about their exploits during the day. It was beyond Phémie's understanding how the King could find these people entertaining, but he did, laughing at their tales and adding his own. He even enjoyed talking with the women about clothes and jewelry! Fortunately the musicians were close at hand; it made her corner far from the center of conversation less lonely. She could at least listen to the music. Louis ignored her, leaving her to her own devices, but often she felt his gaze upon her.

One evening, evidently tired of waiting for Phémie to take part, Louis decided to bring her into the group. As the courtiers took their places on the pillows scattered about the main room of the lodge, the King suddenly called out, "A footstool for the Duchesse d'Amberieu."

He pointed to the space directly in front of him but a few feet distant, and Phémie slowly came forward, feeling all eyes upon her. As she took her place on the footstool, she smiled slightly, keeping her voice low, and saying, "Am I to be this evening's amusement?"

"Either you or the pack."

"I hope we prove entertaining."

"We share the same hope." He nodded in a parody of graciousness, then spoke to the group. "What shall we do tonight, ladies and gentlemen?"

Sensing that this was to be more sport for their diversion, they consulted eagerly among themselves, while Phémie and Louis gazed at each other, waiting for the challenge. The young woman, thanks to Charles, wasn't totally unprepared for this attack, and rested easily, able to smile at the King. There was a light in her eyes that puzzled Louis. He thought at first that he had taken her off balance; but if he had, she'd recovered with amazing speed. Finally one man spoke up. "Let's tell stories."

The others agreed in a chorus, and another took up the challenge. "Perhaps the Duchesse would honor us."

Again the chorus approved, and one of the wits added, "That is, if she knows any tales."

"Yes, I know a few," she replied, still looking at the King.

"About the farm?" another asked, gleefully, and her answer came quickly, "No, about love."

"A love story?" Came the eager question, "Between a goat and a sheep?"

Everyone laughed at this, even the King, and Phémie's eyes gleamed mischievously. Louis noticed the new light in her eyes and was watchful of her reply.

"You might say so. It's about a king and a maiden."

There was no laughter now, with the exception of Louis's,

as he concurred with her, "And so it might be, Madame; so it might. What is the name of this wondrous tale?"

"'The Story of King Florus and of the Fair Jehanes.' If you have heard it, Sire, please tell me and I'll not bore you with the retelling of it."

"I've not heard it. You may begin." The King leaned back, giving his approval, and she started the story as if they were alone and she were telling it to him only.

"It is really three stories in one. We begin with King Florus, who married a beautiful young princess, she but fifteen years and he seventeen. They were very happy, as young lovers are; she with her handsome, brave lord and he with his fair, admiring bride. But a dark cloud passed over their lives, for, as the years passed, there was no child born of their marriage. As you must know, this is very important to a king, and his ministers began hinting that he put his love aside. The lady was aware of this and turned to the only one who could help. She became very devout and gave alms willingly, nourishing and clothing the needy, hoping that God would relent and bless them with a child. Year by year they grew further apart, the King becoming restless and roaming from tournament to tournament, yet was he always faithful to the love of his youth."

Subtly Phémie's voice changed as she went on. "Now we come to the fair Jehane. Her father was a knight who dwelt in the marshes of Flanders. He was honest and brave, and his good wife was virtuous. Their daughter was only twelve, but of such beauty that her mother sought to have her married. However, her father was so busy with tournaments that he gave little thought to his wife's complaints. So the mother went to her husband's squire, told him of her plight, and asked him to get the knight to discuss the matter. Robert, the squire, promised that he would do what he could. So it was, while they were traveling, the handsome young man finally had the opportunity to talk to the knight. The father suggested that since Robert himself was a goodly lad, and noble and brave, he would be a good husband for his daughter. Robert was dismayed, protesting that he had neither station nor monies, but the knight assured him that Jehane's dowry would bring him property and that it was time Robert was made a knight.

"When the knight told his wife of the plan, she fell into a swoon and shortly thereafter sought aid from their relatives to dissuade her husband. Anyone with eyes could see that Jehane's innocence and beauty would enamor a man with far more property than Robert could ever hope to possess. However, when approached by the relatives, the knight threatened to make war upon them if they continued interfering. Robert, himself, knowing how the mother felt, tried to dissuade his master, but to no avail. He did not love Jehane, seeing her only as a pretty child; but the girl secretly loved the squire and had begged her father not to reconsider.

"So it was that Jehane and Robert were married. Directly after the ceremony, Robert was going to leave on a pilgrimage, as all knights did when first knighted. There was another young man in the service of the father, Sir Raoul. Although he was extremely wealthy, he was jealous of Robert's good fortune. Upon hearing of Robert's intention of leaving his bride still a maid, he made him a wager of all his property, against all of Robert's newly acquired property, that he, Raoul, would have his way with Jehane, and she would not be a virgin when Robert returned from his pilgrimage."

Here a gasp went through the assembly, and the King merely nodded, leaning forward expectantly. Phémie continued, "So certain was he that the girl's virtue would render her incapable of such a wrong, and hoping to add Raoul's fortune to his own, Robert willingly made the wager. Shortly after the young man left, Raoul began making advances to the girl, and she refused him most virtuously. Now it must be explained that Raoul was an exceedingly handsome man, and very persuasive, but to no avail. He even bribed Jehane's personal serving girl to talk to her, and the woman did, telling her that this knight was very manly and handsome, and fair of speech. This, too, was to no avail. Again Raoul bribed her, and again she approached the girl. This time she told her that every lady, when her husband was away, had one or even two lovers, and that it was not only permissible, but fashionable. Again came the refusal.

"Raoul was at his wits' end when they received a message that Robert would return in a short while. At the cost of another large bribe, Raoul arranged that the serving girl would leave open a small door in the castle wall and he could come in and have his way with her whether she agreed or not. It happened that Jehane was preparing for her husband's return, and as she was stepping out of her bath, Raoul entered. Despite her protests and struggles, he picked her up and was carrying her to the bed when he tripped on the rug and they both fell. As she fought to escape him, Raoul noticed that she had a mole beneath her breast, before he was forced to flee.

"When Robert returned, he found that his wife, whom he'd thought a mere girl, had blossomed into a woman. The morning after their delayed wedding night, the father held a feast in celebration. As was the custom, there were only men present, and Raoul was forced to come to the board and confront Robert. Rather than tell the truth, he claimed that he had won their wager, and for proof, told of the mole he had chanced to see under the girl's breast. How else, he asked, could he have known it existed, if he had not had his way with her? For further proof, he offered the testimony of the serving girl, and the company present demanded that Robert go and see for himself. Jehane was sitting in the garden with her mother, apart from the feasting men, and Robert stormed upon them, tearing her bodice from her in his rage. Of a certainty, he found the mole and left the weeping girl in the arms of her bewildered mother.

"The father had been holding the wagers, and Robert conceded that he had lost, instructing the knight to give the winnings to Raoul. Without another word, the young man left, riding away with only what he'd possessed when he'd first come into the knight's service. When her father confronted her with the tale of her unfaithfulness, she denied it, but none would believe her. She was an outcast among her own people and had no recourse but to flee from her home. Cutting her hair, and wearing a squire's clothing, she set forth alone, intending to find her husband and convince him of the truth.

"It was several days before she met the knight on the road, and offered him her services as a squire. Robert, not recognizing the dust-covered boy as being, in fact, his wife, hated to refuse, for what was a knight without a squire; but he had no money. Jehane offered her own money until his fortunes bettered, and he had no choice but to accept, as he didn't have a *sou* for bread and was going to be forced to sell his only horse.

"Thus the two journeyed to Marseille, where they hoped to hear of a war in which Robert could find employment. However, there was no news of a war anywhere. Jehane, by now known as Jean to her lord, suggested that with their remaining money she buy flour with which to make bread, as she made the finest bread anywhere. Robert, despairing of his loss of property far more than the loss of his fair bride, was too disheartened to put forth any other plan, and agreed. In all the time they were together, Robert had never mentioned his tragedy, so Jehane was content to hold her silence, serving him as best she could and sharing his privation.

"Again we must turn to that villain, Sir Raoul, who unjustly held the lands and monies of Robert and who also had ruined the happiness of Jehane. Seven years after Robert and his bride had separately disappeared, Raoul became very sick, so sick that everyone feared for his life. One day, when the mysterious illness was at its worst, Raoul called for the priest and told the whole story of his villainy. The good father knew all the people involved and refused to absolve the man, insisting that he must travel to the Holy Land to confess his sins there, and if any asked him of his mission, he was to tell them. Raoul returned from death's door, but when a full year had passed, he had not yet taken the cross. The priest reminded him often, but the knight treated the reminder as a jest until the confessor threatened to go to Jehane's father with the tale. Raoul promised that in six months' time, he would undertake his journey."

At this point Phémie stopped, stretching, her eyes closed. When she looked at him again, Louis saw the pure devilry in her expression. "The story is overlong, Sire, and it's not my wish to bore either you or this goodly gathering."

There came an answering chorus of denial from the group surrounding them that they were far from bored.

"Perhaps you are tired, Your Majesty," she suggested, and Louis was suddenly undecided, looking down on her face. Should he give her aid in turning her hand against the fools who had tried to trap her, or should he indulge his own curiosity to hear the end of the story? After wrestling a moment with the problem, he decreed, "Continue your story, Madame."

At this, there leaped into Phémie's eyes an expression so unmistakable that his own eyes widened in amazement. It was a gleam of triumph; the victory was hers, and he could see that she had cast her net wide, not for the group about them, but for the biggest fish of all. No one but himself! She had bested him, and he leaned forward once again. "*Diablesse!*" he whispered, his eyes reflecting his appreciation of her cunning; and she began to laugh, rocking back and forth on her precious footstool, completely unafraid of his displeasure. He accepted this with good grace, calling for more wine; and when the servants had stepped out of the circle once again, Phémie returned to her story.

"Here we return to King Florus. The powerful nobles of the kingdom had finally persuaded their liege to set aside his wife and take another as queen who might bear him children. There was no other course for him, and with many tears, he set aside his childhood love. Rather than accept the lands and monies due her, she entered a convent, and there spent the remainder of her days. The new queen was found, and four years after their marriage, she gave birth to an heir, dying in her ordeal. The boy was sickly and died soon after. Poor King Florus hadn't the heart to marry again, and all the fair maidens brought for his inspection went away again with small gifts and firm refusals.

"We return once again to Marseille, where the squire Jean and the knight have done very well in their bread business, well enough to open their own inn. Here Raoul, on his way to the Holy Land, stopped while waiting for his ship. Jehane recognized him, after all the years since his treachery, and asked him the reason for his journey, while keeping up her own role as Jean. Raoul, pledged to answer any who asked, told it all, then presently boarded his ship and sailed. Once in the Holy Land, he confessed his sins and was told to return all the lands and monies he had stolen through his deception. Raoul promised to do so as soon as he returned to his homeland. But his villainy was so deep that upon his return, he foreswore his sacred oath, enjoying his property as he did before.

"Jehane, thinking that Raoul would, in his hope of heaven, continue to tell the truth, persuaded Robert to return to their own land. When they reached her father's home, she retained her disguise as a young man and told the whole story before her father's board in Robert's hearing. Raoul denied that he had ever stayed at their inn and that he had ever told such a story. Robert was convinced of the truth as told by his squire, for where else could he have learned it but from Raoul himself? Sir Robert hastily challenged Raoul, calling him a liar, and Raoul had no choice but to fight; otherwise he would prove by his cowardice that he was a traitor and villain. The battle was long and bloody; both men fought fiercely and both were wounded. But Robert, because of his just cause, was given the needed strength to overcome. When Raoul's sword was shattered, he ran from the field, begging for mercy and admitting to the truth for all to hear.

"After the battle, Robert was truly happy, having recovered not only his own property, but Sir Raoul's as well. His victory, however, was shadowed by the disappearance of his squire. He'd lost not only his bride but his best friend, and he fell into a depression. Jehane had fled to the house of her cousin, there to rest and prepare herself for the joyful reunion with her husband. When she returned to her father's house, she found Robert in the arms of death. His wound had worsened, his depression had deepened, and he'd given up his desire for life. He died without learning that his wife and best friend were the same. Jehane mourned her dead husband, entering her widowhood, doing many charitable works, and remaining, above all, virtuous. The story of her beauty and virtue was spread far and wide across the land, and there were many suitors for her hand, but she refused them all. The courtiers of King Florus heard of her noble qualities and, in their liege's name, commanded her presence. When the messenger arrived, Jehane told him that she was not to be summoned so easily. If the King should want her for wife, he should come to her himself, praying for her hand. Jehane did this not out of boldness but in hopes of putting him off, for we all know that kings do not like unruly women.

"It chanced that King Florus came across her reply accidentally and was curious about a woman who did not want to become a queen. So he traveled to the widow's home and at first sight of her, fell deeply in love. After many refusals, Jehane finally took pity upon the poor man and married him. God blessed them with two children: a girl who became a queen, and a lad who became Emperor. For many years King Florus and Jehane lived happily together, and when it was the will of God, he passed into Paradise, for his soul was stainless. But they were not long to be parted, for the fair Jehane endured but six months before she followed after him. And that is the end of the tale of King Florus and the Fair Jehane."

There was a long moment of silence, then suddenly the room burst into applause. Phémie was quite frankly surprised, for she had expected nothing but laughter and abuse for her tale of virtue and faithfulness. On the contrary, the courtiers loved it, voicing their approval in arguments concerning the foolishness of Robert for not believing his wife and whether anyone could maintain a disguise so long. Bewildered, Phémie looked about her and saw that several of the ladies were actually wiping tears from their eyes.

"Are you surprised that so unvirtuous a group can enjoy a story of virtue?" Louis took advantage of the turmoil to speak openly to her.

"I am indeed!"

"Don't you see? All of the ladies think of themselves as Jehane, and all of the men identify themselves as Robert."

"And you, Sire? Which of the men in the story are you?"

"I? Who else but the King, who finally wins the fair Jehane in the end."

"All of these Jehanes?" she teased, and he replied with great seriousness, "There is only one Jehane here—one true Jehane."

"Your next favorite?" she asked boldly, her eyes alight with curiosity. No one had dared ask him such a question before, and he was taken aback by it.

"Perhaps," he answered somewhat sternly, but she didn't notice his change of attitude.

"You know, I'm glad I don't number myself among all these Jehanes."

"No?" He was surprised, asking, "Then, as whom do you see yourself?"

"Jean, the squire." She laughed easily. "Let all these silly women be Jehane, with her fairness and virtue. Let me be Jean, serving a master faithfully and having all those adventures."

"But Jean is Jehane!"

"Not really. Jehane is lovely, with beautiful gowns and men wooing her. I don't see how she could return to being a woman after having her freedom."

"She did it for love of her husband, Robert, even if he was a fool."

"He wasn't a fool, Sire. He was merely a man. And don't forget, he didn't really love Jehane. He wanted her fortune."

"I won't forget it. I can only hope that you won't. Look to yourself, Euphémie. You're a very wealthy and beautiful woman."

"My wealth and my 'beauty' have not inspired any of your courtiers to approach me, Your Majesty. I just don't appeal to men. Even Charles, despite all the time we've spent together and the love he professes for me as a friend, wouldn't have me."

"What do you mean—have you? He already has a wife, or did he neglect to tell you that?"

"No, that was one of the first things we discussed upon meeting. Don't do him such an injustice, Sire. It happened not too long ago. I was lonely one night and asked him if he would want me as a mistress."

"My God!" he ejaculated, amazed that she would admit such a private feeling so easily.

"Oh, please don't concern yourself." She misinterpreted his expression. "He wouldn't have me."

"I have often, in the past, believed de Montais to be a fool, but never more so than now."

"You're misjudging him again. He isn't a fool. He is always thinking of what's best for me. I've never believed that anyone, other than my uncle and my husband, could really care for me. I was certainly glad the next day that he hadn't taken advantage of my momentary madness." She fell into a reflective silence, her gaze far away, then said, "I suppose someday I shall have to take a lover, if only to find out what it's like."

Louis stared at her, hardly believing his ears. Here before him was a young woman, presumably still a virgin, without a blush speaking not of innocent love but of the basest relationship between a man and a woman. He supposed that he would have to go about the weary business of finding her a suitable husband, perhaps one of the foreign princes who were forever hanging about Versailles seeking just such a bride.

She had brought a very puzzling thought to his mind. Usually his courtiers were so responsive to a beautiful woman, especially one with a fortune. But on the night of the ball not one had sought out a moment's conversation with her; and during the hunting party, no one had approached her. Even if they didn't consider her appearance attractive, perhaps because she didn't suit the type of beauty they preferred or were accustomed to, there was no denying the size of her fortune. She, herself, disclaimed any beauty, but Louis found her more than beautiful; he thought her fascinating. Perhaps the men of his court had such jaded tastes in women that even her fortune could not lure them. Here was no temptress; at least, not obviously so. She was certain not sensuous, with her long stride and healthy coloring. Her eyes were too direct for the womanly art of teasing. There was no sham of shyness. There was certainly no hint of proficiency in lovemaking. Yet there was something that appealed to Louis. Perhaps it was simply that she was so different from any other woman at his court. Where his courtiers fled from difference, he found it attractive. He tried to envision her in bed, but could not. Then a new thought came to him. Here was a true virgin—not just a girl who had not yet known a man. Euphémie, he realized, had not been awakened to sexuality.

"What do you want in a man, Euphémie?" he asked quietly, and she answered without hesitation, "A companion, mostly. Someone with whom I can share my interests and who will allow me to share his."

There was his answer, he thought to himself. "Then why did you want to become de Montais's mistress?"

"I didn't really want to, Sire. I just asked him if he believed that a man and a woman could be friends, and he said yes, but not for long; they would either become lovers or would drift apart. I didn't want to lose his companionship, so said I would become his mistress."

"And what did he say?" Louis restrained the laughter rising in him as he pictured de Montais being subjected to such directness.

"He said that we hadn't reached that point yet. I think he was uncomfortable."

"I can well imagine that he was." He laughed, unconstrained. "Poor de Montais!"

"I think I embarrassed him, as well." She smiled fondly, it

seemed to Louis. "May I tell you a secret, Sire?" She leaned forward, and he nodded. "I think he's still in love with his wife. Is she very terrible to him?"

"I've never seen a man so kind to a woman who treats him as badly as she does. I've often wondered how he bears up under the humiliation and pain she must cause him."

"Then I'm right; he must still love her, despite his denials. Poor Charles!"

Louis thought that the handsome allowance his courtier received from the erring woman's father might be the main force behind de Montais's behavior, but he didn't want to spoil Phémie's illusions. It would be otherwise if he saw a threat to her from de Montais. But since that gentleman had enough good sense to allow no deeper relationship with her than an innocuous friendship, Louis was content to remain silent for the moment. If ever circumstances did change, he would have a quiet word with his courtier. Of course, if she persisted in searching for a lover, he could wish for no one better or more harmless than de Montais. It was something, he decided, to watch closely.

"He becomes very angry with me, you know." The comment caught him surprised.

"De Montais?" The picture of de Montais angry left him incredulous.

"Oh, yes. One night he shouted at me about something silly I'd said. And he was very angry about the gown I wore to the ball. That's how I know he's just a friend."

"I don't understand."

"Well, if he cared about me, other than as a friend, he wouldn't get angry and tell me how silly I am. He gets very impatient with me, not at all as he reacts to his wife."

"Do you care very much about de Montais, Euphémie?"

"Is that another way of asking if I'm in love with him?" she asked, and when he nodded, she continued, "Not in the way you mean. He has become like my cousin used to be—very protective, very critical, and always telling me what I must do. I'm certain he thinks of me as a sister."

"I didn't ask you how he feels about you, but how you feel about him."

"It's difficult, because my feelings have changed. I used to think of him as another cousin. Then I considered him as a lover. But he's just a friend. He's growing further way from me in some way I can't explain. I don't like people thinking that they can tell me what to do and then expecting me to obey them. My cousin always said I'm very stubborn."

"You're a strange, wild creature, aren't you?"

"I suppose I am. I don't know what will become of me, but I do know that I'm not going to do what everyone else wants me to."

"And what's that?"

"Marry again and raise a pack of children. Other women, I realize, take their marriages lightly and leave their children to the raising of others while they sit in their furs and jewels awaiting their lovers. I must be free, away from the world as you know it. Does that sound foolish to you, Sire?"

"It would have to, I'm sorry to say. Women can't set themselves off from the world; not even men can do that any longer. We all have responsibilities, my dear."

"Yes, I know. But my responsibilities are to myself and to life. That's the greatest responsibility of all, wouldn't you say?"

"I would say that a woman needs the protection a good man can offer her. She needs children; that is what she was created for."

"And if she can't produce children, or her husband gets tired of her? What is she to do? Flee to a convent for his convenience?" Her reference was to the first queen in the story she'd just told, but he took the remark personally.

"Watch what you say!" he warned, thinking she was reminding him of an episode in his younger years involving a former mistress, but she was insensitive to his dark mood, and innocent of any knowledge of his past.

"And why not the convent?" she asked conversationally. "It's just fleeing from one prison to another. Listen, Sire, come with me riding tomorrow. Only then can you understand what I'm saying. Leave behind the world you've created for yourself and be free, if only for a few hours."

"You don't know what you're saying. No one can leave the world behind."

"I didn't say 'the world,'" she corrected him sharply. "I said 'your world.' Oh, there's no use in talking to you, either." She sounded defeated, as if she had been battling the inevitable.

"My God!" he roared, "dare you speak to me in such a way?"

The room fell into silence, but neither Louis nor Phémie noticed it. "Forgive me, Sire," she said bitingly, with no hint of apology in her tone. "I'd almost forgotten that you are a king."

"No one forgets that I'm a king."

"Especially Louis Bourbon. Let me ask you this." She hurried on, seeing him about to rise. "Have you ever tried to leave your world, if only for a short while?"

He sat back, his expression revealing that he was controlling himself with immense effort. "Yes, I have tried."

"How? In the arms of a woman? A creature of your own world? What kind of escape is that?"

"It is, at times, the only escape offered to a man concerned with the business of ruling. How much time do you think a king has in his day?"

"You're not at court now. Come with me, Sire," she pleaded sincerely. "You'll lose nothing more than a few hours you'd have wasted in hunting."

13

So it was that the next morning Louis awoke with thoughts of Phémie's challenge racing through his head. Throwing back the covers and getting out of bed, he went to the washstand, pouring the cold water into the basin. After splashing his face and neck and drying with a rough towel, he looked out of the window to see the first gray light of dawn creeping up. Soon she would be leaving for her escapade—her wild, mad flight from reality—but he was King, and kings had no hope of escaping reality, even for a few hours. From the hallway came the slightest of sounds, but he heard it, not wanting to admit even to himself that he had been waiting and listening for it. There it was again, passing his door and going on down the hall to the stairs. Well, he thought, let her go. It was all well and good that she could be mad; he could not.

Directly outside the door of the lodge he saw a groom, walking with the horses against the chill of the early morning air, but there was no sign of Phémie. Rolling up his shirtsleeves, Louis looked about, then mounted as the groom held his stirrup. The boy had made a mistake, bringing a particularly unruly black for the Duchesse, and further, by not saddling it as he had the King's white.

"Did the Duchesse d'Amberieu give you instructions, lad?"

"Yes, Your Majesty," the boy answered lowly, and Louis grew impatient.

"Then where is she? Getting her own saddle, I can barely imagine."

"She's not using a saddle, Sire." This time the groom's voice was louder, and Louis looked down in surprise. Laughing with delight, Phémie, in her boy's clothing and hiding under a wide-brimmed, disreputable hat, stood looking up at him. "Don't I make a fine groom?"

"What do you mean, you're not going to use a saddle?" He disregarded her question. "And why did you choose that black? He's not fit for most men to ride, let alone a woman."

"That's because they don't know how to talk to him. If they spoke to him kindly, he'd be as gentle as a child's horse."

"That I doubt very much."

"As you will. It's too fine a day to argue. But do let me say how much I approve of your outfit." Her reference to his leather breeches, boots, and shirt opened at the neck made him laugh, forgetting to scold her for her impudence.

"If my people saw me like this . . ."

"To the devil with them. Today you are merely Louis and I am Jean, your squire." She swept off her hat, making a leg to him. Then she went to the other side of the black, grabbing a handful of mane and vaulting gracefully up onto his bare back. At her sudden weight, the animal snorted impatiently, anxious to be off, but she held him in check, crooning softly to him and stroking his powerful neck. Rarely had Louis seen a man handle a horse so well, certainly never a woman. She didn't have the hands for such a strong horse, but it would seem that she wouldn't need them. "Shall we be off?"

"You lead the way."

And lead the way she did, not at a sedate walk, but touching her heels to the black's side, they were gone from the lodge at a full gallop. The pace was a hard one; it seemed that she wanted to get as far away from the place as fast as possible. Frequently, he glanced at her, watching her excitement grow. Before they'd left, she had stuffed the hat into the top of her trousers, and the wind ruffled her hair and flapped her shirt. Before long Louis was caught up in the magic and breathed freely, feeling the wind against his face and through his own loose shirt. Louis the King was back at the lodge, sleeping in his warm bed, while Louis the man was out, riding freely, and the feeling exhilarated him. At his side was not the Duchesse Euphémie d'Amberieu, but a wild, undisciplined boy who was living for the moment. She, too, had become her own man, so to speak, but she had done it before, many times before. Yet she didn't give the appearance of being accustomed to it. It seemed as if this, for her also, were the first time.

Not once had either horse slackened its speed, taking the logs and branches strewn over the road easily. It was madness, pure and simple. With each flying hoofbeat, Versailles, the court, the world became farther away. The enchantress at his side had taken his hand and led him into a world he had never known—a world peopled by two human beings and two god-like horses who could run like this forever and never stop. So completely had he lost his identity that he felt like a centaur, half-man and half-horse, descendant of Ixion, and that they were riding not through a forest in France, but were actually in the mountains of Thessaly.

Finally Phémie slackened their pace to an easy walk, and looking about him, Louis saw and felt the silence of the forest world. No longer were there chattering, laughing groups of people behind him; no longer were there armed soldiers clearing the path ahead. There were the trees, the real masters of the forest, whispering as the wind danced among their leaves. There were colors he had never really seen before—the greens and browns and golds that had been hidden from him before. As the sun came up, there was the sound of birds, and at their approach, rather than silence, the songs changed to scolding. No longer was the forest a hunting ground for his enjoyment, but a misty, mysterious entity that changed into a magic world filled with sunlight and peace. A deer startled across the road ahead of them, but not once did the thought of a kill come to his mind, nor did the thrill of the hunt send his blood rushing. The road stretched out before them, leading ever deeper into the forest, like a brown satin ribbon dotted with the gold sunlight filtering through overhead branches. There had been no need for speech between them, but now Phémie spoke, as if to herself.

"This is my heaven."

"What do you mean?"

"I believe that when a person dies, and the soul is spotless, he is allowed, by the Almighty, to choose his own heaven. Many choose the palaces and streets of gold with all their worldly wealth. Others choose the place of the angels, where all day long the world is filled with beautiful singing. When I go there, I will ask God to give me Lucifer, and all my dogs, and let us roam forever in the wilds of heaven."

"A strange request, asking for a horse by the name of Lucifer. Do you think God will see the humor of it?" He had to tease, feeling uncomfortable in the presence of such naked sincerity, but she only smiled at his witticism.

"You must remember that Lucifer means 'Angel of Light,' and that before he became Satan he was the highest among the angels in God's court. God will know that Lucifer, as a horse, is the finest of his subjects—his horse subjects."

What a disarming creature, Louis thought as silence once more enveloped them. Who would ever look at her as a man looks at a woman while she spoke with such childish simplicity of heaven?

"Why don't you like the courtiers, Phémie?" he asked suddenly, and she was silent for a moment, considering. When she spoke, it was with certainty.

"I don't dislike them, Sire; I pity them. They are so lukewarm in their attitudes toward life. They are bored and need constant entertainment. They don't even realize that all their entertainments distract them from real living. When I meet a person like that, I become very sad because there is so much living to do, and so many things are denied us, sometimes by others but most of all by ourselves."

"I'm one with you in that!" he commented with feeling, and she smiled at him once again, gently.

At a slackening of the reins, and a touch of her heels, the black was off at a gallop, and Louis found his own horse responding eagerly to the fast pace. In the years to come, Louis was to remember this ride, with Phémie at his side, her laughter mingling with the sound of the wind, her eyes shining with excitement, her honey-colored hair catching the sunlight and imprisoning it, her slender legs gripping Lucifer's sides like tender young saplings, her lady-like hands holding the reins loosely yet with the command acquired in many years' riding.

At noon they left the road, going deep into the forest. Once she stopped, listening, and, satisfied, led him to a small stream. After they had dismounted, she took a tightly wrapped bundle from the back of his saddle. There was bread, cold meat, and cheese. Instead of wine they drank water from the cool, clear stream. They lay side by side beneath the trees after lunch, talking of many things until Louis fell asleep in the warm sunlight. She woke him an hour later, and it took them all afternoon to retrace their way to the lodge. As the last light of day was failing, they reached the stables, leaving the horses to the grooms, and climbed the back stairs to their rooms. When Louis emerged, he was once again the King of France, yet Phémie knew by his expression that he would recall their day together with fondness. That night, before retiring, Louis announced that they would leave for the court on the next day. Phémie hoped that it was because he no longer had the heart to kill any of the beautiful creatures they had seen when they had entered the forest, not as masters of the world, but as enchanted visitors.

"Charles!" Phémie called, running into the house eagerly, but Madame Matilde was the only one there to answer her call.

"He is not here, Your Grace."

"Has he gone to Versailles, or to the city?" She pulled off her gloves and cape, trying to hide her disappointment.

"We don't know where he has gone."

"What is it, Madame?" Phémie became alarmed. "What has happened?"

"It was after you left—the very same day." She began hesitantly. "Monsieur was having his noonday meal, mentioning to me how empty the house seemed in your absence, a sentiment we all shared . . ."

"Go on!" Phémie insisted brusquely.

"A messenger arrived from the court. After he and Monsieur had spent a little time together, the messenger left. A short while later, Monsieur summoned me, telling me that his wife had died in her sleep."

"Holy Virgin!" Phémie paled, crossing herself. "I should have been here, Madame."

"It wouldn't have helped, Your Grace," she said firmly. "He left immediately to tell the lady's father and to arrange for the burial. He said that he needed some time alone."

"Poor Charles! How did he look? Did he leave any message for me?"

"He was grieving, of course, but controlled himself very well, as one would expect a gentleman to do. He said he hoped to return before you did, but if not, I was to explain to you what had happened and apologize for his absence."

"I only wish I could have comforted him during his time of need."

"No good can come from regretting something that couldn't be helped," she reminded her sternly, picking up the fallen cloak and gloves. "There'll be time enough to comfort Monsieur when he returns."

"You're right, of course. I must write Florimond and let him know what has happened. He expected Charles to be his groomsman at the wedding. It will be impossible for him to attend now."

14

Instead of returning to the d'Amberieu chateau, Charles made his way to Versailles. As he approached his room, his valet suddenly appeared from his hiding place behind a staircase newel, signaling him frantically. With cold fear clutching at his heart, Charles passed his own quarters and followed his man down a flight of the back stairs, which was usually reserved for servants. When he was certain no one was near, he warned his master, in a whisper, that there was a man waiting in his room; a man who had not left in almost three days, having meals brought to him there. For a moment Charles was indecisive. If he ran away, they would surely think him guilty, but of what? There was no way that they could have discovered anything. His wife's death appeared natural, and the Baron Lapalisse's demise was not yet common knowledge. To run would be insane, he decided; it could only be that the King had another errand for him.

He returned to his quarters, and when he entered, he saw

the familiar liaison who had so often come for him in the past and was pleased that his good sense had prevailed. Perhaps it was strange that the fellow wouldn't allow him the time to shave and change his travel-stained attire, but then the King wasn't known for his patience. Louis had already dismissed the bulk of his courtiers and was just ending the hour or so he spent in private conversation with his family at the end of the day. He would then proceed to his own bedchamber and be prepared for retiring by those few special courtiers who had purchased the privilege of undressing the King and emptying the royal chamber pot. But tonight, Louis interrupted his routine, going instead to the council chamber where Charles was waiting for him.

As the courtier straightened from his bow, he saw, even in the dim light, that Louis was not pleased to see him, as he usually was. His voice, when he finally spoke, was cold and distant.

"Our sympathy on the untimely death of the Comtesse."

"Thank you, Your Majesty," Charles said calmly enough, but he was quaking within. Had it been his imagination that the King had put heavy emphasis on the word "untimely"?

"What are your plans now?"

"I hadn't thought. . . ."

"Hadn't you?" Louis roared, his temper unleashed. "I won't permit it, de Montais. The Duchesse believes that you loved your wife and thinks of herself only as a friend. I'm not such an innocent."

"But, Sire, I had no intention of approaching Her Grace." Charles felt hopelessly trapped and knew that he could rely only on his wits to save himself. The King owed him nothing, really, and felt no special affection for him, as he did for his favorites. No, Charles was alone, and weaponless except for his quick brain.

"At least not until after the period of mourning, is that it?" Louis interrupted brutally. "It was all for nothing, de Montais. She won't marry you; she does not love you."

"I don't believe it!" Charles was stung to reply, but recovered brilliantly. "I won't believe that you think so badly of me, Sire. I give you my oath—"

"Don't blaspheme! You were seen entering and leaving Tremon's room. Your wife's maid had just left to get some fresh clothing for her mistress, who, she swears, was yet alive. Upon her return, the lady was dead. It was not she who saw your arrival and departure, however, but a maid-servant who kept the door across the hall open, waiting for her mistress's return. Your wife's maid didn't report the death, as she was too busy stealing the Comtesse's jewelry and attempting to run away. Do you have an answer to this accusation, de Montais?"

During the King's long narrative, Charles had had the opportunity to think; and when he replied, it was without hesitation.

"I admit I found my wife in Tremon's room, but I swear to you that she was dead when I went in."

"Why did you linger so long, and why didn't you report it?"

"There were some of my wife's letters in the possession of Tremon. He came to me, demanding money, but I refused him. When I heard that he'd disappeared, leaving his gambling debts unpaid, I decided I'd best try to find those letters. When I went to his room, I had no suspicion that my wife would be there. I saw that she was dead and searched for the letters, to no avail. As for not saying anything, I was afraid of the scandal."

"Excellent!" Louis commented appreciatively. "You have explained everything most reasonably. I'm amazed at your cleverness. There is only one occurrence that makes me continue in doubting you. Why did you, in the company of a friend, venture upstairs, suposedly looking for the Comtesse; go to her room, although you already knew that your search would be fruitless; and express your wish that she be told you were seeking conversation with her?"

Charles remained silent for a long moment before admitting, "I have no logical answer for you, Sire."

"That is what I thought."

"I told you the truth, Sire." Charles stubbornly maintained his innocence. "I was frightened and wished no suspicion to fall upon me."

"Why should suspicion fall upon you?"

"The trials are of recent memory. I was afraid," he stated simply, shrugging his shoulders. Louis, scrutinizing his courtier closely, conceded, "I have no proof, only suspicion. I want to believe you, de Montais, and it would help your cause if you would be amiable to helping me in a little plan of mine."

"Of course I would do anything in my power to aid you, Sire, without hoping to gain anything for myself."

"I'm pleased to hear that, for what I want of you will not be easy. I want you to prove to me that you have no desire to marry the Duchesse."

"What can I do, but give you my word?"

"There is one thing. You see, I want her to believe that you truly did love your wife. I want her to forget you."

"Perhaps if I went away for a while . . ."

"Exactly! But not with her awaiting the return of her old friend. She must believe that you are lost to her forever, that you'll never return."

"That sounds like death, Sire," Charles commented softly, and Louis suddenly laughed. "I said lost to her, not to life. I want you to enter a monastery. It will be very comfortable for you, and will only require a year, perhaps less, of your time."

Charles looked at Louis as if the monarch had taken sudden leave of his senses. Louis didn't take kindly to the expression on his courtier's face but held his temper in check.

"You have told me that you feel no affection for the Duchesse. I don't believe you, but she told me that she feels you loved your wife, and I do believe her. Even so, she is alone in the world now. She will have lost the protection of her cousin with his approaching wedding, and that is the way I want her. It would be too easy for her to turn to you, even in friendship, and refuse to agree to my plans for her future. Surely you can see that even your presence here at court could cause serious problems for me."

"May I ask what your plans are?" Charles was appalled by his own boldness, and fully expected a reprimand; however, Louis hesitated but a moment before confiding, "It is my intention to marry her to one of our allies. There are several eligible foreign princes who find Versailles pleasant and would appreciate such a wealthy wife."

"And if I were to remain near her?"

"Understand me, de Montais." Louis became threatening. "Your choice is not whether you remain here, or leave. It is a choice between a comfortable monastery, for a year, or a dungeon for life. If you help me now, I'll not be averse to calling you back to court, with honors, as soon as the Duchesse is married. You may even have her as a mistress; I'll have no objections."

Charles knew that there was nothing he could do at the present but capitulate.

"I will do as you say, Your Majesty."

"I didn't doubt it for a moment." As Louis turned to leave, Charles commented off-handedly, "When I collect my clothes tomorrow, I'll tell her of my grief, and my desire to take up the monastic life."

"That won't be necessary." Louis faced him again. "You'll write a letter, subject to my approval, and the men I send to pick up your clothes will deliver it. That way you'll not be tempted to warn her, or perhaps even attempt to escape with her. I don't want you placed in an untenable position."

"Your Majesty is too kind."

"It is nothing. Perhaps after your time of meditation and penance, we'll find a proper alliance for you, one more in keeping with your new title and position. Your reward will be a compensation for your disappointment." As an afterthought, he added almost mischievously, "With both of you safely married, there won't be the temptation to 'remove' an unwelcome spouse. At least, let us hope so."

The letter that Charles composed surpassed the King's expectations. It revealed a man unbearably torn by sorrow at his loss. The religiosity and nobility of sacrifice evidenced by the courtier, all for love of his dead wife, pleased Louis beyond measure. Above all, it was believable, and the King knew that Phémie would respect de Montais's request for solitude. Charles was told, when his belongings were returned to him, that the letter had been delivered; no more. There was a guard placed outside his door, which would normally indicate the strong displeasure of the King; yet, paradoxically, food from the King's own table was brought to him every evening.

The court was alive with speculation, but there was no answer forthcoming. De Montais never left his room, and no one on any pretext was allowed to enter. Only his valet was permitted free access, and, one night, a chambermaid bearing fresh bed linen. As soon as the door was closed behind them, the girl handed the valet the linen and rushed into Charles's outstretched arms. After kissing her soundly, he took her to the farthest corner of the room while the valet began stripping the bed.

"Thank God you've come. Did you have any difficulty?"

Phémie was breathless with excitement and, for a moment, could only shake her head. Finally she managed to say, "Madame provided this costume for me; no one ever looks closely at a chambermaid. What is wrong, Charles? Why are you under guard? You said in your letter that everything was well."

"We have little time, so listen carefully," he demanded, effectively stopping the flow of questions, and she looked at him trustingly. "You are in grave danger." As he went on, her expression changed from trust to dismay. "The King is planning to use you in a political marriage."

"If that is true, then he has conveniently forgotten a promise he made shortly after my birth."

"I know he promised that you would never have to live at court. And he has never broken a promise, but he would find a way to convince you that it is necessary for you to agree to his plan."

"Never!" she said sullenly, and he scolded her, "Don't be

a fool! Don't face him in an argument. And, above all, don't wait for him to tell you what he wants of you. If you don't know about it, he can't blame you for disobeying, can he? Go to see LeForge at his warehouse on the docks. My driver knows where it is, and he can be trusted to remain silent. Give LeForge this letter"—he pressed it into her hand. "It introduces you and instructs him to place himself and all his resources at your service. He will see you safely out of France."

"Oh, Charles, I'm afraid. You don't really want to enter a monastery, do you? It was the King's idea, wasn't it? Let's leave together. Now that your wife has gone, there's nothing left for you here, is there? We can fool the guard. He expects to see your valet pass in and out. You can wear his clothes, and they won't miss you for a long time."

For a moment Charles was tempted to tell her the truth but realized that it would only cause her unhappiness. He'd had many hours of agonizing thought, running the gamut from frustration to despair. Now he realized that in order to be truly secure, he had no choice but to accept the will of his master. It was tormenting to admit that there was no hope of making a life with her. Louis had used ruthless tactics in the past. To prevent a marriage he didn't approve of, he employed the simple expedient of throwing the poor fellow into prison for many long years. All that Charles could hope to salvage for himself was his own well-being. Once that was ensured, by obeying the King blindly, and without hesitation, he would be able to return to court with a new title and honors. Life had not seemed empty before he'd met Phémie; he was optimistic that life at court would, once again, seem worth living. Besides, he reasoned, her only chance of escape was in going alone. Charles doubted if Louis would pursue her as long as he believed that she was ignorant of his plans. He would, in all probability, merely wait for her return. Charles was confident that he was doing what was best for her, and said in his most convincing manner, "It is something I want to do, and I am content."

"Then why the guard?" she demanded suspiciously, and he replied lightly, "He's there at my request. While I am waiting for His Majesty's final approval to enter the religious life, I don't want my former friends besieging me with questions. Don't be concerned about me." He shook her gently. "The fate he has planned for you would be your death. Look to yourself and escape!"

"Where can I go?" she cried, feeling very much alone.

"When first we met, you told me you wanted to take a ship and sail to New France or the Indies, for 'real' adventures. Just think of this as your dream coming true."

"I never thought it would happen so suddenly. I'm not ready; there are letters to be written to Florimond and my people in Bretagne. I must meet with my bankers." She passed a hand over her forehead despairingly. "It's no good, Charles. The dream will just have to wait."

"You can't dictate terms to dreams. You must seize opportunities when they come. Most important of all, however, is that you can't be certain that Louis will wait. Once I am gone, I'll not be able to help you. Don't concern yourself with Florimond; he's out of your life now. And Madame Matilde can inform those in Bretagne. The danger is great, Phémie—so great that it would be unwise even to return to your house in Paris. Go to LeForge tonight; he'll be able to give you shelter in his warehouse, and you can write to Madame Matilde and your bankers from there."

"But my clothes . . ."

"Madame will pack your belongings and send them to you at the warehouse. Leave it to LeForge to make all the arrangements. The sooner you leave France the better."

"Very well, Charles." She took the discarded linen the valet held out to her, clutching it tightly, tears coming to her eyes. "Farewell, my friend. May your new life bring you joy."

"And may you find the adventure you've been seeking." Charles walked with her to the door, his arm about her shoulders. Kissing her once again, he stepped out of view as the valet and chambermaid left the room.

Phémie reached the coach without incident, telling Charles's driver to take her to the merchant's warehouse. As they started back toward Paris, she noticed that she was still holding the linen and began to laugh through her tears.

Monsieur LeForge proved to be an invaluable ally. Whatever his first thoughts were of a Duchesse in the cap and apron of a chambermaid, he kept them to himself. After their initial interview, he sent a number of empty crates in a cart with Phémie's sealed letter to Madame Matilde. The crates were returned the next night, fully packed and nailed shut. In her message, *madame* voiced her suspicion that the house was being watched and stated that she had cautioned the driver to return to the warehouse by a more discreet route. She regretted not being able to see her mistress before she left on her journey, but she was to be assured that the prayers of her faithful servant were with her. With the intelligence that her house was quite possibly being watched, Phémie felt reassured that she had done well in obeying Charles's instructions. Phémie was reasonably certain that *madame*, if she had found the boyish garb Phémie favored, had not packed it with the rest of her belongings. It was with little difficulty, however, that she found what she needed in the warehouse and stocked up on several sets of clothing. She even found Spanish boots that almost fitted and a long knitted cap of the sort favored by seamen. As for Monsieur LeForge, he put the "Elisa" at her disposal—the same ship that Charles used on his diplomatic missions. The "Elisa" was in port, waiting for a cargo, but the merchant declared that the only delay would be in provisioning her for a long journey. Phémie elected to hide on board the ship rather than stay in Paris. The transporting of her belongings was trusted to a fast wagon and expert driver. When the wagon left the warehouse, the driver was not alone on the box. Next to him sat a young man with a seaman's cap pulled down over his ears to protect them from the chill night air.

Phémie was quite prepared to live under conditions of

hardship once she'd reached the "Elisa," but the Captain, having been warned of her arrival, escorted her to Charles's cabin, insisting that it was not necessary to hide belowdecks as she suggested. The cabin was luxurious, with a large soft bed rather than the usual bunk, a small dining table and straight-back chair, a large, comfortable chair with a lamp overhead and table beside it, and a long, padded ledge underneath the windows where one could watch the sea. The cupboards contained the finest china, linens, silver, and crystal, and there was a finely stocked wine chest. There was even a glass-front cabinet containing a small but diverse library.

Phémie, once alone, unpacked only as much as she would need for her journey, her nightclothes, and one gown in which to leave the ship once they'd reached their destination. She was determined to wear only her boy's clothing while on board the ship. When she'd told the Captain this, it was obvious that he disapproved of a woman in men's clothing but admitted that it would be wisest since she was the only woman on board. After she had completed her preparations, she had the rest of her belongings taken below.

Finally the "Elisa" was provisioned, and they made ready to sail with the late tide. It was a foggy night, but Phémie refused to stay in her cabin, standing, instead, at the railing of the quarterdeck near the Captain as he gave the order for the anchor to be raised. On the heels of that order, a longboat thumped against the side of the "Elisa," and a man called up to them, "A passenger on the King's bounty. Have you a space for him?"

The Captain hurried to Phémie's side and quietly told her that they couldn't refuse a passage paid by the Crown. The newcomer, he explained, was probably a missionary priest, a soldier, or a minor civil servant being sent out to the colonies in the service of France. He did promise, however, that the fellow's quarters would be belowdecks, and his activities would be restricted. As the stranger boarded, Phémie instinctively stepped out of the circle of lantern light, melting into the shadows. Even though she was certain that she hadn't been seen, she had a frightening feeling that his eyes were searching for her. Ridiculous! she scolded, telling herself that she was merely imagining things. After the stranger had been taken below, the Captain returned to the quarterdeck with the fellow's travel permit.

"He's not dressed as a priest," he confided in a low voice, "and he's not in uniform. This is very strange, Madame. A man's occupation is always listed on the paper permitting him to use the King's bounty. But there is nothing listed here."

The feeling of dread swept over her again despite the Captain's dismissal of the irregularity. "I suppose it's just an oversight. I'll ask him to explain it in the morning."

"And if he can't explain it, Captain . . ."

"We'll put him off at our first landfall."

Being somewhat reassured, Phémie retired to her cabin, determined to remain sequestered until the matter was settled one way or another.

They were several hours out of port, and Phémie had been unable to sleep. Wrapping herself in a warm robe, she sat next to the windows, waiting for the dawn. The night was very quiet, most of the crew having gone off watch, and the only sounds were the normal creakings and groanings of a ship at sea. Suddenly she heard something else—footsteps outside, in the companionway. With her breath caught in her throat, she crept noiselessly to the door, putting her hand on the latch in the darkness, and leaning heavily against it. In a moment she felt the latch being lifted, and someone trying to push open the door.

"What are you doing there?" She heard a voice call out, and the man moved away from the door.

"I thought this was the galley; I've not eaten since early yesterday," she heard the other explain easily, no trace of guilt or fear in his voice as he went outside. So it was the stranger, Phémie thought, her heart pounding. She'd have wagered a bag of gold that he had known that it was her door he was trying to force, and that he hadn't been looking for the galley. As she climbed into bed, she found she was shaking, and not from the cold.

In the morning, after a sleepless night, Phémie waited anxiously for the Captain to make his report. In the interim, she'd decided not to tell him of the attempted intrusion until after he'd divulged the information he'd gleaned from the stranger. If his papers proved fraudulent, she'd tell the Captain of the incident to reinforce his resolve to put the stranger off the ship. If it proved otherwise, she realized that the stranger's explanation of searching for the galley might be a valid one, and she would look like a hysterical woman in the eyes of the Captain. When the Captain finally did arrive, she was in a high state of anxiety, but kept herself well in hand.

"I had a visit with the other passenger, Madame. His papers show him to be a civil servant in Paris, but his home is on Martinique. His father is ill, and he's been granted an extended leave."

"And you believe him?"

"There is no reason to doubt, Madame. I have heard the family name; they are prominent planters in the colonies. And his papers are signed by Monsieur LeReynie himself."

The name of the head of the Paris Police brought a chill to her heart, and all she could say was, "I have no more doubts, either, Captain. Thank you for your caution."

When she was alone once again, she began to think feverishly. What was she to do? She was certain the man was a spy; her instinct told her that, despite the lack of definite proof. The Captain was more than satisfied, and could no longer be relied upon to watch the fellow with suspicion. She herself must get the proof, and if she did, she asked herself, what could she possibly do with it? Her only chance was to prove to him that she was Madame Lapalisse, the name she'd given the Captain and crew. Once he believed that she was not his prey, he wouldn't feel the necessity of filing a report with his masters, and she would be safe on Martinique. There was a danger that Mignon, who knew her by her real name, would inadvertently betray her, but that danger wouldn't have to be faced for two months.

She certainly had the time to put the fellow at his ease, before they reached St. Pierre. With his arrival on board, all her plans had changed. No longer could she wear her boyish clothes nor could she eat her meals with the Captain and his officers. Sending for her belongings, she decided that she would, one day soon, meet the stranger "accidentally"— perhaps when she was strolling or speaking to the Captain. In the crates she even found the wigs that Théophile had purchased for her years before. They were hopelessly out of style, but that would add to her disguise as the widow of a provincial nobleman going to visit a convent school friend.

When the Captain arrived to escort her to dinner, she was wearing her new costume and explained to him that, with another passenger on board, she'd best follow convention. If the Captain had any suspicions regarding her sudden change of heart, he kept them to himself, agreeing with her plan, even to her taking her meals in her own cabin. As he left, the Captain assured her that his officers and he would be most discreet. Phémie could only hope that the poor man didn't suspect that she was some kind of criminal escaping justice, or a bad woman running away from her husband. As long as he didn't discuss her with his other passenger, she really didn't care what he thought of her privately. Nothing was going to stop her from preserving her freedom.

Phémie emerged from her cabin the next day, feeling extremely self-conscious, but she needed to have no fears as far as the crew was concerned. They were extremely well-trained to take little note of what their passengers were doing, and if there were any staring, it was not noticeable. At her request, an awning had been raised, creating a small oasis in the starkness of the ship's main deck. She had her chair and table brought outside, and would pass the afternoon with sewing, which she detested, and visiting with officers who paused in their rounds. As she was preparing to return to her cabin, the late afternoon having turned chilly, the stranger approached her boldly, his eyes, even from a distance, scrutinizing her. Phémie stood up, not wanting to be at a disadvantage, deliberately turning her back on him to pick up her sewing.

"Pardon!" he said brusquely, and she turned again, an expression of polite inquiry upon her face.

"What is it?" she asked softly, noting his faded clothing, darned stockings, and run-down shoes. He certainly was dressed for the role of someone on the King's charity, but his well-trimmed nails, his carefully queued hair and voice that suggested that he was accustomed to being attended, belied the poverty which his clothes were intended to convey.

"I want to apologize for disturbing you the other night," he said. When she made no comment, maintaining an expression of puzzlement, he restated his apology. "You know, the other night, when I thought your cabin was the galley." He finished lamely, "If I frightened you, I'm sorry."

"What is your name?"

"Raoul Soutiers, at your service, Madame . . . ?"

"Lapalisse," she stated simply, waiting politely for him to continue.

"You've not yet accepted my apology," he reminded her, uncomfortable in the presence of one who gazed at him with the expression of a contented sheep. A slight intelligence crept into her eyes as she, seemingly, finally understood what he had been trying to tell her.

"Oh, was that you making all that noise the other night?"

"Yes, and I am trying to apologize for it." His voice took on an edge and she noticed that his gray eyes became darker or lighter according to his mood. They were becoming very dark as she continued looking at him blankly.

"I heard you at the door. You threw yourself against it as if there were pirates on board. All you needed to do was tell me the cabin was occupied, or slide the bolt into place."

"I was too frightened to say anything," she admitted ruefully, "and I'd forgotten the bolt was already secured. This is my first journey away from home, you know, and one never knows what one will meet."

"Or whom?" He laughed in self-deprecation and she became flustered.

"Oh, no, Monsieur. I didn't mean to suggest that you . . . I mean, you don't seem to be the sort . . . Oh, I'm not saying what I want to say at all. I often do that, you know. And poor Hubert used to become so angry with me. The more I'd try to explain myself, the angrier he would become." She came to a full stop, drawing in a deep breath as if to continue, but the young man forestalled her, his eyes light with laughter.

"And what happened to Hubert that he's not with you on this journey?"

"He died, the poor man."

"Little wonder," Raoul said under his breath, and Phémie pretended not to have heard.

"I had to leave, you know. His sons disliked me and were extremely discourteous to me."

"You were his second wife, then?"

"Oh, no, his fourth. He'd outlived all the others, and I think he'd hoped to outlive me. I do think he was a remarkable man, for one past eighty, and I treated him far more kindly than he treated me. I was with him every waking hour; I never allowed him to suffer from loneliness. I do think it was unfair of them to say that I talked him to death."

"Did they really?" With great effort he controlled his rising laughter. Rather than answering, she sniffed indignantly, and he probed even further. "Do you have relatives in the colonies?"

"No, I'm very much alone. My only friend used to live in Fort Royal, Martinique. We attended convent school together, you know."

"What's her name? I know quite a few people in the capital."

"I'm not certain her name is still her name, you know; I mean, her own name. I do think she must be married by now. She was such a sweet, pretty girl. I'm certain that she was snatched right up, you know. And if she has children, perhaps I can be a governess to them."

"Didn't Hubert provide anything for you?"

"Only a meager amount. My fare took up more than I expected. And if Mignon doesn't need a governess, I just don't know what I'll do."

"Mignon?" he asked suddenly. "You don't mean the Governor's daughter?"

"Oh, but I do; I most certainly do. Are you acquainted with Mignon?"

"At one time, I shared that pleasure with most of the gentlemen in St. Pierre." There was something in his tone that was very distasteful to her.

"What do you mean?" she asked, her mincing tone forgotten, but only for a moment.

"Only that Mignon was extremely sought-after when I was last home." He covered his mistake gracefully and she nodded her head. "One would expect so. She would have no difficulty in finding a husband."

"I'm sorry I don't know whether she is living in Fort Royal or St. Pierre."

"I'm certain all I'll have to do is ask. Well," she sighed noisily, "it has been pleasant visiting with you, Monsieur."

"May I call on you after the evening meal, Madame?"

"Why, yes, I suppose you may, although I can't imagine why you would want to."

The young man watched the widow make her way across the deck and into the companionway leading to her cabin. She didn't look back; if she had, she'd have seen him grinning with pure amusement.

He was really quite handsome, Phémie admitted reluctantly. His features were almost too handsome, giving the impression of a mischievous choirboy. She doubted very much if he were even her own age; he was probably two or three years younger. Not that it mattered, of course. He was the enemy until proven innocent. There were too many inconsistencies about him for her to relax her guard, and she wondered if she'd made a mistake in allowing him to call upon her that evening. All in all, however, she was quite pleased with her performance and was looking forward to matching wits with him again.

"Have you no one to tend your door, Madame?" he asked harshly. "Is there no maid in your service?"

"My poor pension would not allow such an extravagance." She became wistful. "I had a maid all my very own once, but that was long ago."

"But you're gently born. Couldn't your husband provide you with that least of amenities?"

"I fear he thought that my lack of grace and beauty could get along very well without help. I was a failure, Monsieur."

"Soutiers!"

"Yes, I thought it was something like that. Please, do come in and sit down. Take the big chair, if you will."

As he settled himself comfortably, she fetched the straight-back chair for her own use, smiling to herself. If he'd any thought that she was other than she pretended, he'd never have taken the larger chair, let alone allowed her to see to her own seating. As she was pouring him some wine, he looked about him appreciatively.

"This is really beautiful. Did you furnish it yourself?"

"Oh, no, indeed! I believe it's the owner's cabin, and since I was the only passenger, they allowed me to have it at quite a reasonable cost for so much luxury."

"And a new gown, I would say," he suddenly observed, and she flushed, seemingly with pleasure.

"You noticed; I'm so pleased. Those little compliments do add so much to a lady's feeling of worth. I must say mine was shaken, being married to Hubert—oh! I really shouldn't say such a thing. It's almost disloyal, isn't it?"

"Not at all! I'm certain you'd never be disloyal to anyone. May I have another glass of wine?" he asked shamelessly, and she hesitated, obviously undecided.

"I'm not certain it would be proper. You know, it really isn't mine. It was here, in the cabin."

"Nonsense! You paid for it, didn't you?"

"For less than half, really. If you come by every evening, many glasses are contained in a bottle."

"There are only fifty-eight days left of our journey—that's two days and two glasses of wine. I've had one, so there is one to make up." He was mimicking her mercilessly, and Phémie felt a sudden personal dislike for the young man.

"I'm a woman alone, *monsieur*, and I don't think it kind of you to take advantage. Would you please leave?"

"Poor Hubert!" He got to his feet, looking down at her with derision. "Peace at last! He earned it."

"It's not necessary for you to be so rude. Must I call the Captain?" She was the height of outraged femininity, and he bowed. "I wish you long, happy evenings of counting glasses of wine."

She followed him to the door, reaching past him to open it. Suddenly he grabbed her wrist, spinning to face her. She was so astounded, she was speechless, and he laughed at the expression on her stricken face. "Poor *madame!* Married to an eighty-year-old man. Was there a wedding night? Did he succeed in piercing such fierce defenses as I find raised against me?"

"Release me this moment!" Phémie whispered her demand, not wanting anyone else to know of her humiliation unless it was absolutely unavoidable. Instead of obeying, he used his hold on her wrist to pull her against him, violently. As she crashed into him, her wig became askew and he laughed.

"Just as I thought." He pulled the wig off, tossing it away from him disdainfully. "You must really think I'm a fool! Madame Lapalisse, indeed! I met your cousin, the Baron, on the afternoon of his presentation. De Montais asked me to guide him through the gardens while he had an audience with the King. Actually he was an amusing, likable fellow; didn't seem ill at all."

"What are you talking about?"

"Your cousin. Do you know what he died of?"

"Died?" She couldn't believe her ears. "Surely not Florimond . . ." Without another sound, she fell against him in a faint. Picking her up, he carried her to the bed. In a short time he'd revived her by sprinkling rosewater on her temples and wrists.

"I've never done that before . . ." she murmured, and he became all contrition. "I am sorry; I thought you knew about your cousin."

"No, I must have missed any word of it. Poor Giselle! She's waited so long, and for nothing. It must have been an accident . . ."

"Are you all right now?"

"Yes, I think so. How long have you known about me?"

"Even before we met. When the Captain told me your name, I knew I'd succeeded in my quest. I only had to make certain . . ."

"Then the King is looking for me." The young man only nodded, and she asked, "Do you know why?"

"I thought perhaps it was because he hadn't completed his conquest. It's all over the court that you're the next favorite. I heard that the night he was told that you'd disappeared, he went into a rage."

"Are you to take me back?" Her question was fearful, and he laughed.

"I don't really know. We received our instructions from Monsieur LeReynie, and all he required was that we report where you are. He gave me the travel permit on the off chance you might have sailed back to Bretagne. If I'd come across word of you around the docks, I was to journey to Bretagne and make certain you had arrived there."

"Now that you've found me, what are you going to do?"

"I don't know yet. They don't know I'm here, you see. There was no word of you, but I did hear that Monsieur LeForge's ship was sailing without a cargo. Everyone knows that LeForge is de Montais's father-in-law, and that you are a friend of de Montais. It was not too difficult to arrive at the possibility you might be the reason the 'Elisa' was sailing without a cargo."

"What price your silence?" she asked bluntly, and the young man looked distressed.

"Gentlemen do not speak so frankly of certain arrangements."

"I am not a gentleman, and I'm offering you a bribe. Do you live at Versailles, or do you have lodgings in town?"

"I live in the town; a miserable, filthy place."

"And your patron? Hasn't he been able to secure a place for you at court?"

"He can barely afford his own. He got me this assignment so that I might further myself."

"There's little hope of that, Monsieur. LeReynie will report your findings to His Majesty, and it is doubtful that he'll even mention your name, not that it would do you much good even if he did."

"I know that, but little chance is better than none at all."

"There is only one thing that will allow you to take up residence at Versailles, and that is money to buy it. If I give you a letter to my bankers, instructing them to give you enough funds to establish you at court, within a certain reasonable amount, of course, would you continue your mission to Bretagne, and not inform anyone that you even know of the existence of the 'Elisa'?"

He took her hand, kissing it gratefully. "Your Grace, no one will learn of your destination from me, I promise you. When I return to Versailles, I'll report that I journeyed to Bretagne, as instructed, and that you, alas, were not there."

"My 'gift' would be very difficult for you to explain, if you are ever tempted to betray me later."

"I understand. As long as I remain silent, you'll remain silent. It's a bargain."

"In the morning you'll get your letter."

"I'll tell the Captain I wish to be put ashore. He's expecting such an order."

"What do you mean?"

"Only that I've allowed him to believe I'm in the employ of LeReynie, and he was only too anxious to assure me of his cooperation. I'll simply tell him that you are not the one I am looking for."

"It would seem that the Captain is not to be trusted," she

said more to herself than to him, but he commented on her remark.

"You must remember that Monsieur LeReynie's name is powerful in France, especially since the trials. There'll be no need for you to concern yourself with that, once you get to the Indies. Tomorrow or the next day you'll enter the Great Ocean, and the Trades will catch you up and carry you to Martinique. I wish I were going with you. It's been a long time since I've been home." He appeared very young and vulnerable, but only for a swiftly passing moment. In the next, he was once again the budding courtier, already in possession of some of the wiles and vices bred at that place. "Perhaps I'd best wait for the letter, Your Grace. I'll be put ashore long before you rise."

As she wrote the letter, she suggested lightly, "I was once told by an authority that if one wants to succeed at court, one must attend closely to the ladies. It is they who dictate the rules at Versailles." She signed the precise instructions to her bankers, sealing it with her signet ring. Raoul Soutiers kissed her hand once again, then left her life forever. Once she was alone, she had to force herself to remember her early life with Florimond in order to weep for him.

15

The passage of the "Elisa" had been considerably slowed, since they were expecting to sight Martinique at any time and the Captain ordered day sailing only. There had been some rough seas, but such times were easily forgotten with the ship riding gently at anchor and the sea like a giant sheet of glass. Rarely had she known such solitude, as the Captain persisted in his suspicions and influenced his officers against her. Many times she'd been tempted to reveal her true identity, not only to assuage her aloneness, but to see the Captain, in particular, toady to her title. Her ordeal was almost over, but she couldn't help wondering if she were only exchanging one misadventure for another. No matter how hard she tried to sleep, the suspense of wondering what she would find on Martinique kept her awake. Surrendering to it, she changed into her favorite clothes and settled herself comfortably on the window seat, waiting for the not too far distant dawn.

When she first noticed the light, she thought she was seeing the reflection of a star, but the stars had long since set. As time wore on, the light persisted, and grew larger, and she wondered if the watch had seen it. Hurrying out on deck, she found the fellow fast asleep, but a gentle kick to his foot soon remedied that. In the gray light of dawn she told him what she had seen, and her idea that perhaps they were nearing land. He reminded her curtly that they were riding at anchor and couldn't drift that far in so little time but went up to the quarterdeck with her at her insistence. To her embarrassment, there was no light to be seen. Her protests that there had really been a light were to no avail; the seaman simply didn't believe her and occupied himself with extinguishing the night running light. As she returned to her cabin she realized that the mysterious light she had seen had not been growing larger, as she first believed, but merely coming closer. She was certain that it was another ship and wondered if their courses would cross. She heard the crew shouting to each other as they came on deck for another day's work. The anchor was being lifted as she sat before the windows of her cabin, peering into the gray mist of early morning. It was impossible to see any appreciable distance, and she suddenly felt very tired. Within a few minutes of returning to her bed, she was asleep.

Suddenly she was awakened by the unfamiliar and frightening sound of cannon fire, and all traces of the dream she had had were driven from her thoughts. Once her eyes had cleared and her trembling was more under control, she went to the windows to see what was amiss. The view that greeted her took her breath away. Over to the side, but a short distance, was the biggest ship she'd ever seen. Tier upon tier rose high above them at the prow and stern, elaborately built and painted red and gold. Without thinking, Phémie pulled on her boots and rushed out onto the deck for a better view of the strange ship. So great was her excitement that she didn't notice how silent and ashen-faced was the crew. They had shortened sail and were waiting for the arrival of an emissary from the foreign ship. All Phémie had eyes for was the ship itself. Climbing onto the narrow railing, she wrapped an arm and a leg in the rope ladder and from her perch had a better view of the galleon. They, too, had shortened sail, but had left the topsail in place, with its figure of a woman holding forth a cross. Flags depicting the same scene were flying from all of the masts, and the ship was trimmed with white linen, adding to its festive appearance. The reflection of the sun against the breastplates and helmets of the soldiers lining the rails flashed brilliantly. All in all, it was quite a spectacle for Phémie and she was oblivious to the Frenchmen's fear. A longboat bumped alongside the "Elisa," and several soldiers, an officer, and an elegantly dressed gentleman climbed aboard. Jumping lightly to the deck, Phémie ran to meet them, reaching the newcomers before her own officers came down from the quarterdeck.

"Welcome, gentlemen, to the 'Elisa.' Forgive my curiosity, but is your ship always so gaily bedecked?" For a moment the Spaniards regarded her in blank amazement, unaccustomed to seeing a woman dressed in breeches, open neck shirt, and boots. The younger of the strangers, the one who dressed so elegantly, recovered from his astonishment first, saying, "Permit me to introduce myself. I am Rodrigo Bartolomé de Merades, and this is Captain Valasco of the 'Santa Barbara.'" Reminded so firmly of the formalities, Phémie had the good grace to blush slightly in embarrassment. She extended her hand to each, introducing herself as Madame Lapalisse.

"And Monsieur Lapalisse?" the nobleman asked with chilling politeness, looking at the door leading to the companionway as if momentarily expecting to see her husband appear. She explained shortly that she was a widow and was almost happy to see the French officers approach.

"Madame!" the Captain barked, his face suffused with anger. "Return at once to your cabin."

Phémie, smarting under the impact of his rude command, was nonetheless relieved that she could escape the mocking scrutiny of the Spanish gentleman. She had realized that she'd made a dreadful mistake in addressing them so boldly, forgetting that her costume was rather unconventional in the eyes of others. De Merades had been unfailing in his courtesy, but his dark eyes were filled with scorn. As she turned to leave, the gentleman called to her, "Please don't deprive us of your charming company, Madame."

Despite the graciousness of his invitation, Phémie knew full well that he was ridiculing her and pretended not to have heard. Once she was in the safety of her cabin, she felt the tears of shame burning in her eyes and gave way to her impotent rage. A short while later, when a knock sounded upon her door, she shouted that she didn't want to be disturbed and threw herself down on the bed.

"Why are you weeping?" De Merades had entered the cabin despite her stricture, and Phémie leaped to her feet, rubbing the tears from her eyes. With her characteristic forthrightness, she replied, "I don't like making a fool of myself."

"Ah, then you are angry!" The idea entertained him, and he laughed with amusement untainted by mockery. "And you are angry at yourself. I admire your honesty."

"If not my manners or my clothing," she finished for him, and he laughed again.

"Courtesy forbids me offering an opinion."

"But not in entering a lady's quarters uninvited?"

"Alas, no, as I am on a mission for my captain. He thinks that this might be a pirate vessel, since it is obviously without a cargo. We have inspected the papers for the ship, but they could have been taken by pirates, as well. Regretfully, I must ask to see your papers." With her back turned to him, she reached under the pillow, careful to remove the document made out in the name of Lapalisse. After he had read it, he returned it to her with a little bow. He seemed in no hurry to leave, sitting on the window seat, apparently admiring the view.

"Have you no wine to offer me?" he asked as a matter of course, and Phémie, despite her wariness of his attempt at companionship, complied with his request.

"Are you quite comfortable?" She couldn't resist asking,

with heavy sarcasm, and he took the question at surface value.

"But of course. Tell me, Madame Lapalisse, why do you wear such a costume?" He pretended to study his wineglass closely, as she was obviously disturbed by his question. "Comfort, I suppose. I never really thought about it."

"That is a mistake. You must think about everything you do, especially when you are living in a world of men, as on this ship. You are either careless or foolish; I can't decide which."

"You've no right to come to an opinion about anything concerning me," she challenged, and he looked at her directly.

"Your honesty is refreshing; I wonder how long it would take before it became embarrassing or simply boring? But that is not our concern at the moment. I shall answer you as best I can. You say I have no right, but you are absurd when you speak of such things. Politeness forbids me the right of voicing an opinion—"

"You said that once before," she reminded him with deliberate rudeness.

"So I did!" he admitted with undiminished good humor. "But to continue, nothing can prevent a person from forming an opinion. Even dismissing a subject as not being worthy of an opinion is, in reality, passing an opinion despite the individual's wishes."

"Please, spare me your rhetoric."

"Is it permitted that I compliment you on the excellence of your wine?"

"What nonsense!"

After a moment he decided to ignore her comment, asking instead, "Have you ever been to Spain, Madame?"

"No, I haven't."

"Would you like to attend a fiesta?"

"What might that be?"

"Today is the feast day of Santa Barbara, for whom our ship is named. And tonight we are having a celebration in her honor. Would you like to join us?" His kind invitation, tendered after so much rudeness from her, embarrassed her, and she had the sense to be ashamed.

"That's very kind of you, Monsieur de Merades," she remarked far more gently. "This voyage hasn't been very pleasant for me, and I would enjoy a diversion immensely. But I'm certain the Captain would forbid it."

"I shall insist!" he promised, draining the glass and handing it to her. When he reached the door, he turned, his eyes alight with mischief. "If possible, wear a gown tonight. Those breeches . . . your legs . . ." He shrugged eloquently, and she had the grace to blush. With a formal bow, he was gone.

As soon as the Spaniards had returned to their own ship, Phémie was subjected to an unwelcome visit from the French Captain. She had so wanted to be alone; to remember every word de Merades had exchanged with her, to envision his manly expressions and graceful stances, even his devastating mockery of her. So she sat very still, hardly attending, as the Captain angrily paced, berating her for interfering when the foreigners had first come aboard.

All the pent-up resentment he'd felt ever since Soutiers had left the ship without her came pouring forth unchecked. He criticized her manner, her clothing, every small detail he could think of; and all the while Phémie held her silence, thinking instead of the man who'd so fired her imagination. In his moment of heightened emotion, the Captain let slip his real reason for resentment—by sailing without a cargo he was ineligible for the reward over and above his regular pay, not counting what he could sell privately and mark off the lists as breakage. He was so filled with anxiety that he was completely unaware of the enormity of the inadvertent admission; and still she said nothing, neither in defense nor counter-accusation. He turned then to the Spanish Captain, Valasco, a man reputed to take great delight in sinking French ships on the slightest of pretexts.

"And now he suggests that we don't sail until morning. I don't understand it."

"He wants me to come to their festival tonight," she volunteered in a small voice, her gaze far away.

"Who wants you to attend their festival?" he demanded incredulously, and she replied calmly, "Monsieur de Merades."

He was silent for several minutes, weighing the import of the information she'd provided.

"It is easy for me to forget that you are a woman, Madame, considering your choice of clothing," he said at last, scrutinizing her closely. "Yes, I can imagine that you might seem attractive to a man who has been long at sea."

"He didn't seem so very desperate to me," she commented with heavy humor, but he didn't hear her, so caught-up was he with his own thoughts.

"But this is excellent. De Merades is obviously a person of consequence. That devil Valasco treated him with the greatest respect. If the gentleman is interested in you, perhaps you could arrange with him to influence Valasco to let us go in peace."

"This is nonsense!" She laughed derisively, not believing that she'd heard correctly, and protested, "The gentleman is not in the least interested in me; his invitation was offered purely out of courtesy."

"I can't believe that, but if it happens to be true, you must do all that you can to encourage his interest."

By his attitude it was obvious that he anticipated her acceptance of his plan as a matter of course, and he was totally unprepared for her reaction.

"What are you suggesting?" she demanded, standing to face him, all dreams fading.

"I am suggesting that you make yourself amiable to de Merades, and"—he added as an afterthought—"if that does not meet with success, you might give your attention to Valasco himself. I admit that he is getting old, but if a woman approaches him in the right way, any man can rise to the occasion." This last was said jestingly, and he laughed at his own cleverness while Phémie stared at him in astonishment.

"You're mad!" she stated with conviction, not knowing whether to laugh or to rage at him. "What ever made you think that I would be willing to . . . amuse any man in the way you suggest?"

"Why, it's for the 'Elisa' and the salvation of her officers and crew!" He was amazed that she hadn't grasped that fact by herself.

"And why should I be interested enough in your safety to sacrifice myself in such a manner?"

"We are Frenchmen, Madame; your own people," he reminded her, and she laughed harshly.

"After the way I've been treated on this ship, it would seem more that I've been among enemies than friends. I'll wager you told your men not to speak to me unless it was unavoidable." By the expression on his face, she knew she'd hit on the truth. "I have never been treated so shamefully in all my life," she said with carefully measured words so he'd be certain to understand. "And now I am expected to sacrifice my virtue to your enemy to save your ship and your life so that you can go on cheating Monsieur LeForge."

His face became suffused as he struggled to control his anger. "Is your virtue so much more important than the lives of these men?"

"So I've been taught by the good sisters. 'It is better to lose one's life than to lose one's virtue,'" she quoted dramatically, enjoying his discomfort as he blustered at her ineffectually. Still very much in control of the situation, and continuing in her dramatic stance, she held up her hand, cutting off his flow of words.

"You have made no effort to endear yourself to me, Captain, and now it is beyond my power to save you. I suggest you pray."

She spent the time left to her in choosing a gown and jewelry and otherwise preparing for the entertainment she anticipated a great deal less than meeting de Merades once again. There was nothing she could do with her hair; it was clean, short, and curly as ever. She attempted to paint her face, but each time thought the effect grotesque so had to be satisfied with darkening her lips slightly and putting a soft shade of color on her lids. She was tempted to wear her ballgown, but realized it was far too bold a costume to wear on board a ship of strange men and possibly stranger customs. Besides, she was without the protection of Florimond and Charles. At this reminder, the first since she'd heard of her cousin's death, the tears came to her eyes and she quickly turned her thoughts to the matter at hand.

In the end she chose the most modest gown she possessed; one that she had never worn and whose fit was uncertain. It was the color of old ivory and was trimmed lavishly in the most delicate lace. The skirt was full, the bodice tight, rising almost to her throat. The absence of jewelry was most dramatic, and she felt better without it. All in all, she felt very pure in her suitable choice of costume and was delighted by its simplicity. When the knock sounded at the door, she threw a black velvet cape over her shoulders and opened the door to the soldier escort. As she went out on deck, the Captain joined her momentarily, telling her how pleased he was that she'd finally come to her senses. The remark was so ridiculous that she ignored it.

When they reached the Spanish ship, she looked doubtfully at the impossibly high ladder she thought she'd be required to climb. But the Spanish were evidently accustomed to women in elaborate skirts; they lowered a rope sling. With only a moment's hesitation, she sat in it and found herself suddenly dangling between ship and sea as the sling was hauled up. It was an exhilarating experience, and as they set her gently down on one of the upper decks, she was met by de Merades and Captain Valasco.

"What a wonderful device!" She laughed breathlessly, taking de Merades's proffered arm. The Captain said something, and the other translated, "Captain Valasco welcomes you aboard the 'Santa Barbara' and hopes you'll enjoy our fiesta."

"With such a charming host, it would be impossible not to." She nodded smilingly to the Captain as her reply was translated.

"It would seem that a change of costume provides a change of manners," de Merades commented teasingly, and Phémie colored slightly, but bantered in return, "It's been so long since I've been in the company of a gentleman, like the Captain."

De Merades laughed appreciatively, and as he was translating to Valasco, Phémie took the opportunity to appraise her surroundings. Despite the gaiety of trimmings and colored paper lanterns hanging from the rigging, the "Santa Barbara" couldn't disguise what she really was—a ship of war. The decks were covered with great boxes of sand, vats of water, stacks of cannonballs in racks, and crates of grapeshot. There was no room for a promenade, or even a short stroll. Despite the apparent large size of the ship, it was crowded with men: soldiers, crewmen, gun crews, and brilliantly uniformed officers. De Merades was dressed most elegantly in black, with white lace at his throat and sleeves. The only jewelry he wore was a medal trimmed in diamonds over his heart and the gem-studded sheath of his sword. She was escorted to the dining cabin and was surprised at how cramped it was. Even she had to duck her head to avoid bumping it against the doorjamb. Her escorts had to keep their heads bowed because the ceiling was so low. As de Merades took the cape from her shoulders, several officers joined them. Everyone sat down very quickly, as standing was so uncomfortable for the men, and the introductions were quite informal. She was placed at the end of the table opposite Captain Valasco, and de Merades sat at her right. She was very impressed by the dinner service; the plates, goblets, and even utensils were made of gold.

"Are there no other ladies aboard, Monsieur?" she asked innocently, and he poured her some wine, answering in the negative. "How long has it been since you've seen a woman?" She smiled sweetly and de Merades laughed.

"Spare me your blushes and sighs, Madame. When I first saw you, you were hanging from a rope, looking very much like a monkey."

"It's unkind of you to remind me, and I don't think I look at all like a monkey."

"And even less like a boy tonight." He leaned back comfortably, openly scrutinizing her. "May I compliment you on your gown?"

"I was hoping you would," she said with a flash of frankness, and he added, "The customs of different countries vary in certain aspects. For example, only unmarried ladies of Spain are allowed to wear white. Once they are married, they are required to wear more somber, respectable colors, like black and brown."

"There are no such strictures in France, I am happy to say," she retorted with feeling, and he asked with a semblance of patience, "Doesn't it seem reasonable to you that the last day a woman wears white is upon the occasion of her marriage? No other color is so startling, nor attracts the eyes of men more readily than white; wouldn't you agree?"

"I must confess I've not thought about it very much. To be perfectly honest, I've never thought about it at all. But if I were pressed to give an opinion, I feel that white is the color of purity, and a woman can be pure after marriage as well as before."

"You are speaking of her soul, of course."

"I also believe"—she watched him closely as he was sipping his wine, looking about the table with a hint of boredom—"that simply because a woman lies with a man, she needn't dress herself as if she'd lost her soul as well as her virginity."

Her remark made him choke, and the next several minutes were occupied with his coughing fit. When it had finally cleared, and he sat back in his chair, his face suffused and his eyes running, she continued on an entirely different tack. "I do wish I could speak your language, Monsieur. It would be so enjoyable to converse with these gentlemen."

For a moment it seemed as if he were not going to allow her outrageous remark to pass without comment, but he wisely let it go, saying instead, his voice harsh from coughing, "I think they prefer looking at you rather than talking to you."

"And you, Rodrigo Bartolomé de Merades? Which do you prefer?" She was smiling, despite the challenge, and he replied slowly, "If I had the choice . . ." He went no further, his eyes dancing with laughter. "Tell me, how many masks do you possess, Madame . . . Euphémie Lapalisse?"

"I prefer the name of Phémie." She corrected him matter-of-factly, and he replied shortly, "I don't! Euphémie is a woman's name, and Phémie that of a child."

There was no chance for reply as their dinner was served, and she doubted very much if he would welcome an argument. The meal consisted of several dishes of fish and beef that, she suspected, had been dried but left to stand in water before serving. Everything was covered with a thick sauce, and de Merades scraped most of it from her plate. Even so, at the first mouthful, she felt as if a fire were raging in her throat and gasped for air, her eyes watering. The men were amused by her reaction, but de Merades spared her the necessity of suffering any longer by the simple expedient of drowning her food in wine. It was actually quite good that way, and she could finish the meal in relative comfort. Conversation was restricted drastically as the men applied themselves to the business at hand.

Afterwards, Valasco signaled that the meal was at an end, and when she'd stood, de Merades slipped the cape over her shoulders and led her from the room. He escorted her to where three chairs had been set up on a platform overlooking the main deck. Phémie sat between the Captain and the nobleman and became lost for a time in the songs and dances that members of the crew performed to perfection. She felt her heart quickening to the rhythms and sounds of what de Merades proudly attributed to the peasants of his country. He explained that the throbbing music reflected the passions of his people. She clapped her hands with the others and thrilled to the dancers' stomping feet and the singers' strangely unmelodic yet pleasant songs. De Merades translated, leaning close to her, pouring out the words of love that filled all the songs. His breath in her ear caused her to shiver while his words whirled through her wine-lightened head. After the singing and dancing, there was to be a religious play, he explained, but he wanted to show her something that would only take a few minutes. When she agreed to accompany him, although somewhat hesitantly, he took her hand to lead her away from the sleeping Captain.

"Perhaps he is ill," she suggested, not understanding how anyone could sleep through so much noise.

"He always naps after eating at night. We will return before he awakes, and he'll never know we were gone."

"Are you certain?"

"You must trust me, Euphémie," he stated simply, and she followed him, no longer hanging back. They went up several ladders until they were on the topmost deck, where he paused, looking to see if they were being followed. Certain that they had been unnoticed, he led her into the dark companionway, guiding her to the last door. Opening it, he pushed her gently inside, then bolted it securely behind him. As soon as she entered the darkened cabin, she sensed a trap and began to protest, "I really think we should return to the others. . . ." Without replying, he busied himself with lighting the overhead lamp. In its gentle glow her worst suspicions proved justified. He had brought her to his cabin and was now leaning against the door as if to dissuade her from escaping.

"It's quite simple compared to the luxury of your accommodations. But I have books to read," he motioned toward the case—"wine to drink, and a bed of sorts." His reference to the narrow bunk disturbed her profoundly, and she turned away in hope that he hadn't noticed.

"Have you no honor? I freely gave you my trust, and you betray it at the first opportunity."

"Will I ever cease being amazed by you?" He shook his head in wonderment. "You run about in breeches and a man's shirt, honestly believing that simply because you forget you're a woman, everyone else will. Then tonight, at table, you speak so lightly of lying with a man, like the loosest of tavern women. You can hardly blame me if I find you a mystery and am determined to discover which you are."

"I am neither. It's only that I have the unfortunate habit of saying whatever comes to mind. Now, will you please allow me to leave?"

"I have not finished with you."

"If you dare touch me, I'll scream so loud your Captain will awake."

"You are acting the fool again. I merely mean to say that I don't believe you are who you say you are. You speak too readily of honor. That word does not come easily to a simple widow. You lack maidenly modesty. You are completely undisciplined in your speech and manners. I think that you have been indulged as only the very rich and powerful are indulged."

"Rich? Powerful?" She forced a derisive laugh. "I don't even have any jewelry."

"A wise precaution while traveling in these troubled times. Forgive me for calling you a liar, but I believe you are someone very important."

"You're really very mistaken." She persisted stubbornly, and he scolded her.

"Don't think I am such a fool. Do you think me so blind that I failed to see the seal on your papers? Don't be ashamed of your birth, Euphémie. I, myself, am an *hidalgo* —the son of someone important. My father is a cousin to the King, but that is not what concerns us now."

"I am concerned only about returning to the entertainment. I beg of you, Monsieur, let us go now."

"Not until you tell me who you really are. I do not believe for one moment that you are who you claim. Will you tell me?"

"Please, we have only just met, and it is doubtful if we will ever meet again. What can it possibly matter to you who I am?"

"I am tired of this game, Euphémie. It is an easy matter for me to forget that I'm a gentleman if I do not believe a woman is a lady. I am capable of treating you like any tavern wench I have the good fortune to meet."

"Very well," she capitulated with no further protest, "my name is d'Amberieu." She admitted it with reluctance, but never suspected that he would recognize the name. At the mention of it, his eyes widened, and he whispered, "The old Duc's daughter?"

"No, his widow. I told you that I am a widow," she complained petulantly and he apologized.

"Forgive me, but I have rarely been so amazed. The Duc's widow in breeches and climbing about like a monkey. Now I can understand why you used the name Lapalisse. It would make quite a tale."

"You promised . . ." she began fearfully, and he deliberately misunderstood.

"Don't be concerned. I'll keep my silence."

"It's not that. You promised we could leave here." He looked at her for a long moment, then smiled wickedly. "You are really a beautiful woman. I imagine the old gentleman passed from this world with regret."

"You're a deceitful, cruel man, and I demand you open that door at once!"

Without a word he pulled her roughly into his arms, kissing her slowly. At first she was too startled to struggle, and by the time it occurred to her to do so, it was too late. With a sigh, the resistance left her and she surrendered to the very pleasant sensation. When he pulled away, she kept her eyes closed, afraid of seeing the laughter in his eyes.

"Euphémie, look at me!" he demanded breathlessly, and she obeyed. There was no laughter in his eyes, but a strange, new light she hadn't seen before.

"Oh, don't!" She buried her face in his shoulder as he stroked her hair with a semblance of gentleness.

"Please, Euphémie, don't deny me! I will be kind to you." Forcing her head up, he claimed her lips once again. His mouth moved to her ear as he pleaded with her, catching the lobe in his teeth and biting softly. His hands were careful on the ties of her dress, not wanting to frighten her, as he kissed her eyes, her mouth, her throat. She was fully caught up in his passion, straining against him eagerly, until he held her away from him to allow the gown to drop away from her. To his delighted surprise he found that he'd not have to struggle through layers of petticoats; she wore only a light chemise that offered slight resistance to his force.

"No, please . . ." she began to protest, but his kisses drove away all doubts and fears as he carried her to the bunk.

When he'd finished with her, he lay back, resting on her outstretched arm. At first there was only the sound of the sea, moving the ship rhythmically at anchor, and then de Merades began to laugh.

"So you were a virgin. Mother of God, you actually had me believing you. The Duc's widow!" His laughter began anew, and she held her silence. "I was mistaken, Euphémie. You would never become boring. But you must never wear breeches again. And that shirt! It hides all of this." He leaned over her, his finger tracing patterns on her breast, on her stomach, and along her ribs. She felt the fire spring to life again and caught at his hands.

"No more!" she pleaded, but he jerked his hands free, grasping her wrists in the same movement and pressing them into the pillow above her head. His eyes explored her body, and she tried to hide her nakedness but he held her firm.

"Exquisite," he murmured appreciatively, his head bowing lower and lower until he claimed her lips in a long, teasing kiss. He felt all resistance leave her and released her wrists. With a moan, she surrendered completely, her arms embracing him.

Rather than returning to the fiesta, de Merades firmly suggested that she return to the "Elisa," and he would make suitable excuses to their host. Infinitely relieved that she wouldn't be required to mouth inanities and be attentive to entertainments when all she really wanted was to be alone, she agreed to leave the galleon immediately. De Merades, kissing her fingers gallantly, assured her that they would meet again in the morning to make their plans. A few minutes later she boarded the "Elisa," the hood of her cape pulled over her hair. Only the watch saw her come aboard and felt no need to inform the Captain since he'd not been left any specific orders to do so.

Once in her cabin, she discarded the formal dress for her sleeping shift and took her favorite seat by the windows where she could see the "Santa Barbara." Now that she was alone, she didn't know what to think about; there were so many impressions crowding in upon her. Whenever she called de Merades's face to mind, her blood began to rush. There had been pain and discomfort, but pleasure such as she had never experienced.

She had no idea how much time had passed, lost in her reverie, but she was suddenly brought back to the present when she became aware that the "Santa Barbara" was moving. Throwing the cape over her shoulders, she rushed out on deck in her bare feet. The Spanish crew was busy in the rigging; she could see their occasional figures in the light of the paper lanterns. Running up to the quarterdeck, she demanded and received the Captain's glass. Anxiously she scanned deck after deck, wherever a light showed, but she couldn't find him. It couldn't be true; she rejected the obvious numbly. He had told her they would meet in the morning; she'd heard him. It couldn't have been her imagination. She had really heard him say it. They were going to make their plans. That was what he'd said. But there was the "Santa Barbara," slipping quietly away in the dark of night, bearing the thief whom she had hoped to love. Nowhere did he show himself as she searched for him once again. He was hiding in the shadows; she knew it. A coward! He was nothing more than a base coward, but she was worse. She was a fool. And she couldn't even cry, so complete was her shock.

The Captain joined her on the quarterdeck, and she handed him the glass without thinking. After making certain that the Spaniard was not simply maneuvering for a broadside but was actually leaving in peace, he crossed himself, saying, "Thank God!"

"Are you a religious man, Captain?" She asked with all semblance of calm.

"Yes, Madame. I have been praying, as you suggested." He was all of a sudden very respectful, but it no longer mattered to her.

"Who was Saint Barbara?"

"I believe she was one of the Virgin Martyrs, but I'm not certain."

"You are undoubtedly correct, Captain," she commented with an irony he didn't understand.

"If you wish, I can ask the second officer; he once studied for the priesthood." He was so anxious to please, but she shook her head.

"It doesn't really matter any more. Saint Barbara's feast day is over."

16

They stopped at Fort Royal only long enough for them to learn that the Governor-General's residence was in St. Pierre rather than in the official capital. As they sailed away, Phémie saw only wooden warehouses and flat-roofed shacks. She couldn't help wondering—if Fort Royal was so lacking in the amenities, what could the second city offer? But the port official, who boarded at Fort Royal, perhaps sensing her dismay, described St. Pierre in glowing terms, remarking that it was the financial, social, and cultural center for all the French colonies in the Caribees. Fort Royal's only distinction was in its bay, where ships could find safe harbor under the steep thick walls and gaping black cannons of Fort St. Louis, for loading the local products of the islands for transport back to the homeland.

As the "Elisa" came into sight of St. Pierre, Phémie was at the rail, looking at it through the glass. It was not protected by a natural bay, but was open to the sea. Here there were houses, real houses, with brightly colored roofs and clean white walls. At the edge of town, near the water's edge, was the marketplace, and all along the shore were fishing nets hanging out to dry. It was such a pretty sight because the sun made the still damp skeins sparkle brilliantly with a million drops of water. Here, as in Fort Royal, there was a predominance of blacks in evidence. Where, in the capital, there were mostly men working on the docks, here there were gaily dressed women at the market and naked children playing in the water and on the sand. It was not a Paris, but it didn't have the filth and mud and crowds of the city, either.

There was a great deal of noise as the women in the stalls and carrying their wares on trays hanging about their necks were all yelling, vying for the attention of those who would buy. As Phémie walked through the market, she avoided the fish stalls and purchased, instead, strange sweet fruits that she'd never seen before. Sharing her treasure with her escort from the ship, she bit into the fruit eagerly, the juice filling her mouth and running over her chin. Only by bending over was she able to keep her gown from being seriously stained. She was unable to understand the language the blacks were speaking, so when she saw the white woman waiting in the sedan chair, she approached her unhesitatingly.

"Pardon me," she began, and the woman looked at her, terrified. Phémie didn't understand why she seemed so shocked, but continued, "I've just arrived from France and I wonder if you could tell me where I might find accommodations?"

After staring at Phémie for a moment longer, she looked past her to the sailors who were carrying the heavy crates. The officer, carrying an iron-bound chest, whispered to her that they had better get directions elsewhere.

"But why?" Phémie asked, making no effort to lower her voice. "I'm certain this lady can give us the information we seek." Phémie turned to her again, "If you'll be so kind . . ."

"The only kindness I can give you, Madame, is to agree with your escort. You'd best seek your information elsewhere."

"Forgive me if I intruded." Phémie was puzzled and began searching the crowd with her eyes.

"One moment, Madame!" The woman got out of her sedan chair. "I didn't mean to be rude. St. Pierre is small, and you are new here. It would do you a great deal of harm to be seen overlong with me. There is only one hotel in St. Pierre, and it's not suitable for a lady like you. Have you no relatives or friends with whom you could stay?"

"There is a friend, but I wouldn't want to impose upon her. I thought if I had quarters of my own, I could tell her of my arrival without her feeling that she must make room for me. To be perfectly truthful, we attended school together many years ago, and people do change."

"We are talking too long." The woman looked about her nervously. "If you would like, you would be welcomed at my house for a cool drink, and we could, perhaps, find a solution." Before Phémie could reply, the other warned her, "You must know that my mother was a slave, like most of these women."

Phémie looked at her with surprise and interest. She was a beautiful woman, and if her coloring was a bit dusky, it could be attributed to the sun. There was no hint of dismay or hesitation as she said, "If you'll give me directions, I'll be most grateful for that drink."

With the help of her escort, Phémie found the gate in the high wall on a back street. A black woman, who was evidently expecting her, opened it immediately upon her arrival. The seamen were relieved at the respite offered by the tiny garden and welcomed other servants who bore trays laden with fruit and drink for them. Seeing that they were being well cared for, Phémie followed her guide into the house.

The interior was dark and cool, and she was greeted by her hostess. Phémie introduced herself as Euphémie d'Amberieu, deciding that she need no longer play that game, and the woman introduced herself simply as Celeste. There was little talk as Phémie refreshed herself, taking her ease in the charming drawing room. Finally she said, "I am simply not prepared for this heat. I see that my clothes are perfectly useless." Her complaint was so natural that Celeste timidly offered her the name of her dressmaker.

"What is the name of that stuff you're wearing?"

"It is called muslin, and is very cool."

"All my dresses shall be of muslin," Phémie announced, taking off her plumed hat.

"Oh, Madame, your hair!" Celeste cried out in pity, and was surprised as her guest laughed, running her fingers through the crushed curls.

"I always wear my hair like this."

"But why?" She was so amazed that she forgot her shyness.

"I suppose because it's comfortable, and I don't have to have a hairdresser dancing in attendance wherever I go."

"Don't you have a maid who could help you with it?"

"I don't have a maid to help me with anything."

"But your gowns! How are they laced?"

"By me. All my clothes are made with the laces at the side rather than the back."

Celeste could only shake her head, laughing with Phémie. Everything about her was quiet and gracious. Her voice had a husky-soft quality that was charming. She dressed with ruffles and bows. She was obviously adept in the art of cosmetics, although her beauty wasn't dependent upon such artifices. The bone structure in her face was exquisite, and her best feature was her eyes with their slightly oriental cast. Everything about her bespoke femininity, and Phémie realized how ungainly she must seem in comparison.

"This is a lovely house. If I could find one like it during my stay here, it would be ideal. Perhaps on this very street."

"You must not even consider it, Madame. This section of St. Pierre would be not at all suitable. There are residences around Government Square that are far larger and more grand."

"But I like this section. It's so quiet."

"That is because there are no men or children living here. Only women who are kept in these pretty little houses by gentlemen who need a place of retreat, a place of comfort, but most of all, a woman who lives for nothing more than to please him."

"I understood that down at the market. You made it quite clear then."

"I wasn't certain that you did. And I am still uncertain. If it was known that you'd been in this house, none of the white women would accept you. There would be a great scandal."

"I don't care about things like that."

"Forgive me, Madame," Celeste forestalled her next remark, "but I must care for things like that. If my gentleman found me involved in such a scandal, I would lose him."

"Do you love him, Madame?" Phémie asked softly, realizing that she was being rudely inquisitive, but Celeste didn't take offense.

"He is very kind to me. My children are well cared for, and I like my life here. If he were to withdraw his protection because of a scandal, I would lose my house and no other gentleman would want to become my protector. I would have to go to Fort Royal and live in one of those terrible shacks and have my body pawed by any animal that had the coin to pay."

"My God!" Phémie paled, touching her arm in unaffected sympathy. "I didn't understand."

"I have too many good years left, Madame. As long as I am beautiful, I will live in this house. If that is long enough, I'll be able to buy it and finish out my life here."

"Surely not all the women on the street are as beautiful as you. What will happen to them when . . ." She couldn't finish, and Celeste supplied, "When they are old? They become servants to the young girls who are just beginning. It is not a bad life, if they are taken in by a girl who doesn't think she's better than she really is. The best way with that is to have a beautiful daughter and teach her how to please a man." Suddenly she laughed. "It would seem that I am giving you a lesson, rather than helping you with your difficulty." Going to her desk, she took paper and quill and laboriously wrote something. Returning to Phémie, she handed it to her, and Phémie read the name of a Monsieur Alair written in a beautiful script.

"He owns several houses that would be suitable for you. I know of at least two that are empty."

"You've been very kind, Madame." Phémie tucked the paper into the neck of her dress, then retrieved her hat. "I don't want to be the cause of any trouble for you, but can't we meet again? You're my first friend here."

"Don't say that. There is your friend from school, whom you're forgetting, and you'll meet many ladies that would be more . . ." She paused, and Phémie teased, getting to her feet, "Suitable?"

"Exactly." Celeste smiled for a moment, then became serious. "Before you leave, let me make one more suggestion. Be careful when you buy your slaves. They love to tell tales, and before you realize it, your private life will be the property of St. Pierre."

"I haven't thought of buying any slaves." She was obviously distressed by the idea.

"Who will clean your house, cook your food, serve your table, and greet your callers? When you are settled, send for Monsieur Outelas. He is a very strange man, but can be trusted to supply anything for gold. He can get you the kind of servant you'll require, and it will be worth the price you pay him."

Much to her delight, Phémie found the perfect property for her sojourn in St. Pierre. It was located on the far side of Government Square, the last property on a quiet residential street. The main house was in excellent repair, and beautifully furnished by the former owner, a planter who'd made his fortune and had recently removed his family to France. There were the usual drawing rooms and small salon, as well as a large dining room and a kitchen more than adequate for entertaining on a large scale. There were quarters for the house slaves to one side of the main building, and a well-planted, large garden with cobbled walkways. At the back, out of view from the main house, was a charming little house of one room only, open on three sides to the garden. The place had obviously been well tended, and Phémie bargained with the estate agent, finally settling on a price that was satisfactory to them both.

Her escort left as soon as the estate agent arrived, and once that worthy had departed, the price agreed upon and the documents signed, Phémie found herself alone in her new house. The agent had promised to send Monsieur Outelas to her as soon as it was convenient for that gentleman, so there was nothing for her to do but wait.

When it was almost dark outside, she lit a lamp and realized too late that she had forgotten to make any arrangements for food. With night coming on, she hesitated going in search of someone who could help her. The estate agent had told her that hers was the only occupied house on the street, and, at the time, the idea of such isolation had seemed perfect. But alone in a deserted house on a deserted street in a strange place, she felt more than a bit frightened. When the knock sounded on the front door, she nearly jumped from her chair. Telling herself to be still, that it could only be Monsieur Outelas or the estate agent returning, she proceeded sedately to the door. She opened it to see a man with a large, covered basket over his arm. In the gathering darkness she was unable to discern his face, but knew he wasn't the agent by his general appearance.

"Monsieur Outelas?" she asked hopefully, and the man bowed slightly.

"At your service, Madame."

"Thank God!" She released her breath, laughing lightly at her own foolish fears. "These old houses can be frightening if one is alone at night." He seemed to understand, correctly interpreting the strange welcome, and she held the door wider so he could pass in.

"I'm so glad you've come," she admitted honestly, and he laughed, "I imagine that you're starved for food as well as companionship. That fool Alair shouldn't have left you alone like this."

"Do I smell bread?" she asked meekly, not daring to hope.

"Bring the lamp," he suggested; and after she'd fetched it, he led the way unerringly into the dining room. "Can you serve yourself?" he asked politely, putting the basket on the table, but not waiting for an answer as he disappeared into the kitchen.

"Are you joining me?" she called out to him, breaking off a chunk of still-warm bread, and finding a treasure hoard of fruit, cheese, and cold joint of beef, and wine.

"I've eaten," he returned her call, "but I'll share the wine with you."

"I didn't find any glasses," she managed to say despite a full mouth.

"We can drink from the bottle." He'd come back into the room bearing tapers for the wall sconces, which he put into place and carefully lit. With the formal light, Phémie could see her benefactor clearly. So far he had proven to be an excellent fellow, and seeing him in the light dispelled the last of the sinister image as suggested by Celeste. He was not very tall, but had the hard body of a man accustomed to work. His face was wreathed in an expression of good humor and polite interest. It was an unremarkable face except for the lively eyes. The forehead was not too broad, the cheeks full and ruddy, the mouth gentle and accustomed to smiling, the chin not too determined. A pleasant face and a pleasing expression! Phémie at once felt comfortable in his company, gladly sharing the wine he offered.

"Monsieur, you are sent from heaven." She sat back comfortably, replete and secure, drinking again from the bottle before passing it to him. He watched, amused, as she wiped her mouth with the top of a crooked finger.

"Yours is a famous name, Madame," he began, conversationally. "Are you related to the old Duc?"

"His widow," she volunteered shortly, but without rudeness. He was obviously impressed, his eyebrows shooting up in amazement.

"Ah, then I should call you 'Your Grace.'"

"I'd rather you wouldn't." Again she responded shortly, and he realized that she didn't want to discuss it any further. It did seem out of place, since they were drinking from the same bottle. From the moment she'd first spoken so naturally of her uneasiness he'd liked her. She was completely unaffected, and he could see the absurdity of addressing her by such a lofty title. "Very well, we have reached our first bargain. How else might I serve you?"

"I was told that you could arrange for some servants."

"You mean you want to buy some slaves."

"On the contrary, I do not want to buy slaves. I have no idea of how long I'll be here. I may decide to leave quickly and don't wish to be burdened with the necessity of disposing of possessions."

"But you have purchased this house."

"That's not quite the same thing. I need merely commission Monsieur Alair to sell it at some time or other, and that would be sufficient. But seeing to the placement of slaves with people who would treat them decently is an entirely different manner. Wouldn't you agree?"

It was her longest comment, delivered almost breathlessly, and he realized that she was eager for him to understand. He did understand, but not in the way she expected. Slavery was such an integral part of life in the colonies that it was easy to forget how repugnant it could be to a sensitive person.

"Yes, I would agree. But I'm afraid there aren't any servants available, only slaves. I might, however, be able to hire some of my own people out to you. That way you'd not have the responsibility of seeing them relocated before you leave."

"I shouldn't need many," she said, obviously relieved by his suggestion, "just a cook and a girl or two to keep the house clean."

"Madame, the people who occupied this house before you had over forty slaves. Even the children had two or three slaves apiece. You will need a cook, as you say, but several kitchen helpers, as well, depending on how much you entertain."

"Will I be required to entertain?" she asked, dismayed, and he patiently explained, "The women of St. Pierre are very social, and since they are restricted to the same companions, any new arrival of consequence is in demand. You'll be the guest of honor at innumerable dinner parties and even balls. You'll be besieged with ladies calling in the morning and in the afternoon, leaving their cards and praying for an invitation to enter into your presence."

"I'm glad I cautioned Monsieur Alair not to mention my arrival to anyone but you."

"And you may trust me to keep silent, as well," he assured her before continuing with the business at hand. "I would suggest five in the kitchen, and, if you need more, I will supply them as the occasion demands. You'll need three in the garden, and it will require at least six girls to keep this house clean, if they are good workers. How many will you need for your personal use?"

"None! I prefer caring for myself."

"Don't let any of the ladies know that! It would cause a scandal, and you'd be considered unnatural." He smiled to take the edge off his words, but she realized that he was very serious. "I'll let you have Jessamine. She speaks French as well as anyone from Paris, and the native tongue as well. She can be your housekeeper and personal servant. Other than that, you'll need a houseman and a seamstress."

"I have the name of a seamstress in town."

"I would suggest that you have one of your own unless you want to see your new gown on every lady in St. Pierre."

"Very well!" she capitulated. "I'll rely on your knowledge of these matters."

"That's very wise of you, Madame."

"Now, how much do you want?" she asked bluntly, and he was unsettled at the prospect of discussing money with a lady.

"I hadn't thought. . . . Let us discuss the cost when we

see how long you'll be using them. When you're ready to leave, you can pay me."

"Excellent! Did you bring an agreement for me to sign?"

"This is different from my usual dealings. I wasn't prepared."

"Whenever you find it convenient; you'll always be welcomed."

"There is something else, Madame. I was wondering . . . would you perhaps . . ." He hesitated, and Phémie asked, "What is it, Monsieur?"

"It's only that you mentioned you were without glasses, and when I was in the kitchen I noticed that it was bare of utensils. I can provide anything you might need. I have some excellent porcelain and crystal at the moment of a quality that would satisfy you."

"I'd be most grateful. Perhaps Jessamine could give you a list once we get settled."

"That would be best." He welcomed the suggestion that he deal with a servant about such matters. "And I'll present an accounting to the bank as soon as you've established funds there."

Since their business had been concluded to the satisfaction of both, Outelas thought he'd better excuse himself, but Phémie didn't seem disposed to let him go just yet.

"Could you tell me, Monsieur, why all these lovely houses are deserted?"

"The French are afraid. There have been some bloody rebellions on other islands, and so they are all clustered about Government Square with its garrison. Many of the slaves on the plantations were warriors or chiefs in their own country. It's not easy for a man like that to become a field hand, subject to a white overseer who likes to use the whip. So there has been some killing and some burning. Several of my neighbors have joined me in establishing a list of rights protecting slaves from certain abuses and have told them not to be afraid to complain if they are mistreated. They also know that if they are in the wrong, they'll be punished, as well. We have written to France to see if there can be some sort of law established that would be binding on all the owners. There are still many who would prefer locking their slaves up at night and standing guard over them during the day."

"Have there been any rebellions here?"

"In St. Pierre? No, only runaways. The poor fools are usually brought back and sold onto a plantation. To be a house slave is a definite advantage. The quarters are better and so is the food. Some have grown up with their masters and are treated like members of the family, as long as the black doesn't forget that he's a slave. You need have no fears about the people I'll send you, as long as you let Jessamine handle them. If you're too friendly, they'll get lazy, and if you're too harsh, you'll find your house plagued with accidents. They are very simple people but not stupid as so many whites like to believe. They are particularly quick to determine your strengths and weaknesses, and will use them to their own advantage. You must never interfere with Jessamine, once you give her authority, or there will only be confusion. If you wish to discuss anything with her, especially something you don't agree upon, do so privately and not in the hearing of others. If you remember these rules, you'll be very happy and well taken care of."

"I've never surrendered my responsibility to someone else."

"Madame, this is not France, but a new world to you. There will be enough for you to do in learning about the social customs of St. Pierre without thinking about domestic problems. If you have any doubts about anything, confer with Jessamine. She'll be able to advise you."

"Jessamine sounds like a paragon of capability. How can you part with her?"

"It will be difficult," he admitted honestly. "She is a woman of few words, sometimes frightening in aspect, but always loyal, even if she doesn't care for you personally. Do not take offense at anything she says, as she is usually right no matter how little you like it. And the more she scolds you, the more she likes you. If you can win her good opinion, you'll be very fortunate indeed."

"Have you won it yet?"

"No, and I've tried for years. I'm not respectable enough, I believe, and I never will be. She knows too much about me to think I'd ever change. She treats me like a very naughty ten-year-old."

"If it's respectability that's required to get into her good graces, I'm afraid I'm doomed to failure. I wear what clothes I please, my hair is unforgivable, and I don't like the companionship of women. Your Jessamine will not be the only one to disapprove of me."

"My dear Duchesse, if you were to shave your head and run about Government Square totally naked, the ladies of St. Pierre would think it's the latest fashion in Paris and follow your example."

He'd been so caught up in the ease of their conversation that he'd forgotten himself completely. His remark, he realized, was definitely out of place, and he braced himself for the upbraiding he felt he deserved.

"Can't I just tell them it's the fashion?" she ventured tentatively, and he was so taken aback that he could only stare in disbelief for several moments. There wasn't a trace of a smile on her face, but her eyes were alight with mischief.

"Madame," he began ponderously, getting to his feet, bowing, and sitting down again, "you are a gentleman."

"Is that a compliment or must I call you out?" she asked with mock severity, and he maintained his attitude of seriousness.

"The highest I can give."

"Then I thank you, Monsieur Outelas."

"There are few of us left, Madame. We are disappearing from the earth. If you are ever in danger, I will defend you with my life's blood."

"Is it likely I'll be facing any danger here in St. Pierre?"

"Not at all likely, else I'd not offer my life's blood."

"I suspect," she choked on her laughter, "that you are a rogue."

"And I suspect we were cut from the same cloth," he suggested boldly, and she considered before replying, "I only wish I had the courage to be a rogue. Alas, I am but a woman."

"And a woman alone." He sympathized with her. "Have you no friends here?"

"I don't know," she replied cryptically. "In convent school I became acquainted with a girl who said her father was governor here. She must be married now, but her family name was Chazelles."

Outelas masked his amazement, asking, "How long ago was this?"

"Six, almost seven years ago. I knew her for only a short time."

"I shall make inquiries and let you know when I discover anything. As for tonight, I shall send Jessamine to stay with you. It will take a day or so to bring the others to St. Pierre."

"From what you've told me of Jessamine, I'm certain we can manage."

17

Although she was nearing her twenty-fifth year, Madame Espalion was still an attractive woman, having escaped the harsh toll that the tropics usually extracted from her sex. She and her husband had sat through a private dinner with a minimum of polite conversation and now were sharing a scene of tranquil domesticity, tranquil only because they were not speaking at all.

When they were first married, Gaspard Espalion, completely in love with his bride, decreed that they would spend at least one evening alone each week. Even when they had moved to the plantation, taking up residence with his parents for their bridal journey, he'd insisted upon the ritual. Now, though there was a great deal more hate between them than love, the habit was so ingrained that neither questioned its validity. Even if their relationship was negligible, their evenings together offered respite from the constant round of social engagements.

Gaspard Espalion was a virtuous man—a rarity in his time.

By some horrible trick of fate, he'd married a harlot. He'd taken a virgin to his bed, but within a short time she'd outpaced him; he could no longer satisfy her. Being an intelligent man, he knew that they were having difficulty in the private aspects of their lives together and truly believed that it was merely a phase that would pass in time. What he did not realize was that his wife was seeking satisfaction elsewhere. He learned of it only after her activities had mounted to scandalous proportions and his only recourse was to remove her from temptation. They left the gaiety of St. Pierre, and his important position in the government, for the peace and boredom of his family's plantation. Instead of improving, however, she seemed to have worsened and was subject to long bouts of weeping and angry outbursts against her husband.

His priest abjured him to be patient with her moods, but not to relinquish his rightful place as her husband. Everyone, except Gaspard, was of the opinion that she needed a child to calm her. For a time she submitted to him, but he soon found her door bolted against him. She began taking long, lonely walks at night, and he grew suspicious when he noted the frequency with which their neighbor called upon them. In the house she was watched over by his mother, who knew of her son's unhappiness. When she chose to walk beyond the compound, a slave would accompany her.

As time passed, the security he assumed was assured at the plantation proved to be the opposite. Her personal maid, under the lash wielded by his mother, admitted in his hearing that his wife had taken up with a black, that at night, in her shift and barefooted, she would leave the house and meet with whoever took her fancy. Gaspard couldn't believe the testimony, protesting that the maid had been questioned under duress. But his mother was adamant, insisting that he keep watch to see the truth for himself. That very night he was waiting in the trees as she came from a slave's cabin and beat her until he thought he'd killed her. With a heavy heart, he took her back to the city and made no further attempt to curtail her activities as long as there was no open scandal.

Finding herself with a husband who not only understood her weakness but who had promised not to interfere in her activities inspired nothing but contempt within her. She despised his goodness, his long-suffering martyrdom. She had respected him for beating her, but when, as she was recovering, he'd fallen on his knees before her, begging her forgiveness, she'd spat on him. Once the restrictions were lifted, she would take a lover occasionally, but she was no worse than most of the younger ladies in St. Pierre. She was bored beyond endurance, but there was no relief. So once a week they would eat alone together and retire afterwards to a salon where he would read and she would sit with her sewing. Actually these evenings were quite comfortable, if they weren't required to converse. Sometimes she would go to his room late at night and allow him to couple with her passionlessly. He never asked her why, nor bolted his door against her. Looking at her as she bent over her sewing, he knew that she still had the power to arouse him, despite the sickness he felt when he lay with her. She wished he would get a mulatto woman like other men; then she wouldn't feel sorry for him at times. She had broached the idea to him once, but his virtue had been so outraged that she avoided the subject after that.

She was so engrossed in her sewing that she wasn't aware a slave had entered the room and was waiting patiently to be noticed.

"What is it?" Gaspard asked, and the girl, eyes downcast, replied in a soft voice.

"A note for the Maîtresse." Aurélie looked up, curious. All of their friends were familiar with the Espalion ritual and would never interrupt it.

"Well, give it to me and get out," she snapped, and the girl obeyed with alacrity. Gaspard watched his wife closely as she read the missive and was amazed to see her face become alive with excitement.

"By all the gods," she laughed, letting the sewing drop to the floor as she jumped up.

"There is only one, true God," Gaspard intoned piously, crossing himself, and she was distracted for a moment, looking at him incredulously.

"Sometimes I'm tempted to adopt the slaves' religion," she said.

"They are all baptized Christians and have no other religion."

"You are a fool, Gaspard," she remarked genially, her good humor returning.

"What has happened to lift your spirits so?"

"The arrival of a woman I'd forgotten. We were once friends, a lifetime ago."

"Am I acquainted with the 'lady'?" He sneered on the last word, and she was quick to retort, "She's more of a lady than you could ever hope to meet. We were at school together in France."

"Perhaps she has changed as much as you have from those days of innocence. I suggest you renew your acquaintance in her quarters rather than inviting her into our home, at least until you've discovered whether she is still worth knowing."

"No matter what she might have become, she is still worth knowing." She delighted in her husband's puzzled expression, and anticipated the metamorphosis that would come over him as she explained, "She is a Duchesse, my dear."

He didn't disappoint her, his eyes nearly bulged from his head. "Don't jest with me, Aurélie!"

"I know how important such things are to you. Perhaps she knows the King," she speculated mischievously, and watched him rise to the bait.

"That would be too much of a miracle. But she undoubtedly knows someone of influence who could be my patron."

"So you still dream of that."

"And why not? I am an able administrator; it's been through my hard work that your father retains his exalted office when he would otherwise have been replaced years ago."

"Oh, I agree. We'd all be lost without you. How does it feel to be so needed by so many?"

"And what of you, my wife? How often have I suffered through your complaints of boredom?" He was stung by her taunting. "You have made all your conquests, and your palate is jaded, except for blacks, of course."

"Of course!" Her expression was filled with fury. "You've allowed me to do anything except the one thing I truly desire."

"I don't care to discuss it."

"Then why did you mention it?"

"To see if your appetites have abated with time. I think Paris would be good for both of us. There may not be any blacks in the city, but there are a great many more men than here. I've never heard of anyone becoming bored in Paris."

"What are you suggesting?"

"Only that you renew your friendship with the Duchesse and do nothing to threaten this godsend. Does she have other friends here?"

"I don't believe so. It would seem that she's staying in the Cardenal house."

"I'm surprised that Alair didn't tell me that we have a member of the real aristocracy among us." The snide reference to her father's spurious use of the title Vicomte didn't bother her.

"If I remember correctly, Euphémie had no great love of her title. She probably neglected to tell him she's a Duchesse. Her note is signed with only her given name. She addresses me as Madame, and hopes that I am her little friend from the convent school."

"Why would she be so uncertain of who you are?"

"Because she knew me only by the name I bore as a child. I wonder who told her my married name?"

"Someone must have made inquiries for her. But surely we would have been informed." Aurélie, pursuing her own thoughts, hadn't heard him.

"I have never been invited to the Cardenal house. One of the daughters had the face of a horse, and she was the prettiest of the three. I remember that Madame Cardenal invited the handsomest boys and the ugliest girls to their parties."

"I thought they were rather nice people. The girls may not have been beautiful, but they were obedient and virtuous."

"Perhaps you should have married one of them. By now you'd have been surrounded by a pack of yowling, virtuous, and obedient brats."

"At least I would be certain they were mine, and white, as well."

"What good is that to a real woman?" she screeched at him, her expression twisted and ugly. He rose slowly and prepared to leave the room, but she blocked his passage, leaning against him, whispering, "There hasn't been a white man born who can satisfy a woman like a black."

"Enough!" he shouted, but she threatened a scene if he refused to hear her. He was even more afraid of gossiping slaves than he was of what she might tell him, so he returned to his chair. She sat on the footrest before him, anticipating the agonies she could inflict upon her prudish husband.

"On the plantation, when I was allowed to walk alone, I would go down to the slave cabins and watch them unseen. A man would roar like a bull, and the woman would moan and croon deep in her throat. He'd kneel above her, and she'd worship his weapon; that is what they call it, you know."

"No, I didn't." He tried to ridicule her, but she wouldn't release him that easily.

"The sweat made their bodies wet and they'd slip all over each other in their blind passion. It was marvelous to watch, but one night, weary with only thinking about it, I took a stout stick, one that your father walks with, and went down to the cabin of a buck I'd particularly admired." She leaned forward, her eyes glowing darkly. "He had a woman with him, as he usually did, and they both were terrified when a *maîtresse* came in. Their eyes rolled, showing white, and the woman began to scream, but I beat her into silence. As she huddled in the corner, I let the man know what I wanted, but he couldn't do it. So I began to moan and croon, and had him kneel above me. I handled him as I had seen the other women do, and soon he forgot I was white. I have been used by every young buck on the plantation, and some of the older ones as well."

"You must be possessed!" he croaked harshly, wiping the palms of his hands on his trousers. She noticed the gesture and smiled slowly, her tongue moistening her lips.

"Gaspard, let me show you how they do it!"

"No! Aurélie," he pleaded, aroused despite his repulsion. When he whispered her name, she knew she had won; she knew that she could at last humiliate him beyond her fondest wish.

"You can't refuse me. Perhaps if I worship you, you'll become a real man. Let us go up now, Gaspard."

18

Phémie regretted the note as soon as it was gone, but gave no sign to Auguste Outelas as he sat opposite. During the ten days she'd been in St. Pierre, he had been her only visitor, calling upon her at least once a day. Something told her that he was not the simple, well-meaning planter-merchant he pretended to be. Madame Jessamine, who was a treasure, despite her intimidating manner, refused to talk about Outelas. Phémie sensed that he was a power within the colony, but suspected that he was not quite respectable. He was intelligent, witty, and admired her unabashedly. Not once did he try to tell her what to do, as Florimond and Charles had. He would offer suggestions, but never in opposition to what she had already stated as a course of action. When she expressed doubts about becoming involved in society, he would evidence amazement, reminding her that she was a Duchesse and thus was required to take her place.

Despite her own feelings about such "nonsense," she tried to appear as befitted his notion of a Duchesse. She dressed formally, with all the accoutrements. Every day Madame Jessamine would dress her hair, and Phémie would spend a great deal of time before her mirror, practicing with her cosmetics. This was a bore, but well worth the time and frustration when she saw the frank approval and admiration in his expression. This was a new experience for her, dressing not only to impress a man, but to please him day after day.

"Well, it is done as you wished, Auguste." She broke a long silence, and he nodded. "This is the way it should be, Your Grace." He teased gently. "It is not for your sake alone. All these people here are truly impressed with such things, and I include myself among the first. Someday, many years from now, they'll be able to tell their grandchildren that they had known a real Duchesse."

"Do you want grandchildren, Auguste?" she asked, realizing too late that she was intruding on personal grounds.

"To want children, or grandchildren, just for oneself is the height of vanity. But to love a woman, and to see her face in hers . . ."

"Have you ever loved a woman like that?"

"Once," he answered shortly, and, not to be put off, she asked, "Won't you tell me about it?"

"Why do you want to know?"

"Because you have become a very dear friend," she confessed, slightly embarrassed, and his expression reflected disbelief.

"You know nothing about me, and if you did, you'd not welcome me to your house."

"You do me an injustice!"

"But you're a Duchesse."

"I wasn't born a Duchesse; and even if I were, it wouldn't impress me as much as it has you." She scolded him with a flash of temper, and he laughed. "I have been terrible, haven't I?"

"Yes, terrible!" She laughed with him. "All this talk of society and personages and Duchesses . . ."

"I think I'd like to tell you about my past, Euphémie. I've never told anyone before, but I think I can trust you.

"My father was a merchant in Marseille and fairly wealthy. I was a late child, and both my parents doted upon me, if not upon each other. After my father died, my mother married again. The fellow was an obnoxious fool who tried to discipline me, as he told my mother, for my own good."

"Was he very mean, Auguste?"

"Not really. Actually, he was quite well-meaning, and very good for my mother. He loved her as my father never had.

"I was thirteen then and too big for my mother to coddle any longer. Her husband wanted all her attention for himself, so my mother gave me money to go to a school in Paris. I had ideas of my own about that and got off the coach at its first halt and returned secretly to Marseille.

"Fired by the stories I heard there about the opportunities for adventure that were available in the colonies, I bought passage on the first ship going to the new world."

So, thought Phémie, that's why I found Auguste so attractive from the first. He's an adventurer like me. "I imagine," she said, "that you and your bag of gold were soon separated after you left France."

"No," Auguste replied. "Surprisingly, we both arrived intact. I gave part of my money to a hunter in return for his teaching me his trade. Several boys I'd met on the ship had sold themselves to hunters for just such a reason.

"I soon learned how to kill wild cattle and prepare their hides for sale, but, more than that, I learned how to survive in this strange, cruel, new world."

A haunted look filled his eyes as he continued. "The year I turned sixteen, His Majesty decided that his loyal subjects in the colonies could improve their lot by taking wives, and he could improve his position against the Spanish with a larger, more stable population in the islands.

"I went down to the coast, mainly to deliver my hides but also to watch the women arrive. It was an exciting occasion. The hunters bathed and shaved and put on clean clothes for the event.

"I never expected to be chosen as I didn't look my sixteen

years, but, out of the crowd of women, as if guided by a heavenly hand, she came and stood before me, her eyes modestly downcast. The only women any of us had seen since coming from France had been Indians, so to be chosen by the youngest and prettiest woman there was like a dream. She was no older than I, and her hair was like gold and her eyes the color of the sea. I couldn't believe my good fortune. Over the objections of older and richer men who desired her, my wife and I were married by a priest, and I took her back to the camp.

"A year or so later, I earned enough to build a house on some land I'd been buying. It was hard work, and I remembered how I'd left my home so I wouldn't become like my father. But it was different with us. We talked, laughed, and cried together. We found joy in life even when everything was against us. She gave me two sons, both with hair the color of gold and eyes as blue as hers.

"I had cleared the land and planted a crop of tobacco. At harvest time, I took the crop to the coast and sailed to Martinique to sell it. When I returned, a wealthy man now, I was told of a raid by the Spanish. When I reached the farm I saw the burnt-out shell of our house and the three graves where my friends had buried my wife and my sons. I joined the Brotherhood after that, and it took a lot of Spanish blood to quench the fires of hatred that burned within me. I went back to the land, after making my fortune. Now I grow cane rather than tobacco. Although I'm not quite respectable, I am welcomed into the finest houses because of my money. It has been fifteen years since my family was killed, so the scars have healed and the pain has lessened with time."

"Fifteen years?" she repeated, amazed. "And you haven't married again?"

"Spare me that!" He struck a prayerful attitude, laughing. "I have been assailed and besieged with the daughters of every planter, every official, and every officer in the colonies." He sounded weary and disgusted. "A few years ago,

I was even honored with an offer from the Governor for his daughter's hand," he said slyly, and her eyes widened.

"Not Mignon!"

"And why not? She was of marriageable age and looking for a fortune."

"You misunderstand me. Why did you claim not to know her when I first asked you, and why didn't you tell me about her, as you have about so many people in St. Pierre?"

"The people I told you about are not friends of yours. And I think it best that you form your own opinion about Madame Espalion."

"Has she changed that much, then?"

"How can I say, since I didn't know her when you did?"

"You know full well what I mean," she accused, becoming angrier as she saw how amused he was.

"Of course I do, Your Grace, but you must leave such things to my judgment. Aurélie Espalion is your friend, and I'll not slander her to you. Anything you want to know, you must find out for yourself."

"What an irritating man you are!"

"Absolutely true!" He replied to her exasperation with good humor.

"What if I don't like her any more?"

"The same holds true for her; what if she doesn't like you? All that she has to do is walk out of your house, but that's not likely, is it? One doesn't walk out of a Duchesse's house, especially if one has an ambitious husband who wants to try his talents at court."

"What else should I know?" she asked, no longer angry, and he matched the seriousness of her mood.

"If you find the friendship an embarrassment, all you need to do is arrange for a patron in Paris to sponsor them at court. It has long been Espalion's dream."

"I have no friends, either in Paris or at the court."

"How can that be?"

"I told you I wasn't born a Duchesse. The Duc was an old man when he married me, mostly out of pity and the desire to keep the Crown from inheriting when he died."

"Didn't he want an heir?"

"I was his heir, his daughter in spirit. The only way he could give me his name and fortune was by marrying me. So we were married and I was sent to a convent."

"Did you want the title and the fortune so badly—at least, enough to marry in that way?"

"There was someone else involved, and it's very complicated. Let us just say that it made a dear friend happy; and, other than the inconvenience of the convent, it hasn't caused me any unhappiness."

"I should think not!" He laughed shortly, and she found it an effort to hold her temper.

"After all your revelations I have a feeling that I know as little about you as you know about me."

"I'm glad." He was perfectly sincere, but before she could decide whether to be relieved or insulted, he leaned forward, catching her hands in his. "I don't want to know you too well, Euphémie. I don't want to feel compassion, or impatience, or admiration, or . . . interest. You're a charming companion, and that is where your safety lies."

"Why, Auguste, are you afraid of me?" The smile was hovering about her mouth, and her eyes were bold with speculation.

"Not 'of you,' but 'for you.'" He corrected her in all seriousness, then had to laugh, "And don't you try any of your Parisian flirting with me. I may not be as harmless as you would like to think."

"If you weren't, I wouldn't welcome you to my house." She tried to pull her hands free, not liking the turn the game had taken, but he wouldn't release her. "Auguste, let me go this moment, or I'll . . ." she threatened vainly, and he answered her challenge, "What could you do if I decided I wanted you? Who would hear your cries for help? Jessamine? The slaves? Perhaps the Governor in his mansion so far away." Suddenly he let her loose, leaning back again in his chair. "You trust too easily, Your Grace."

The change in his tactics left her head spinning, and she answered without thinking, "What can one do when one is without friends?" It was such a naked plea that he was touched, but not enough to change his course.

"Learn to live without friends. Therein lies safety, as well."

"You frighten me sometimes," she complained, and he shrugged, the gesture indicating how little it mattered to him.

"Fear is an excellent teacher. You won't forget tonight's lesson so easily, will you?"

"This is not my first encounter with fear," she reminded herself softly, then turned on him with a flash of anger. "Did you deliberately frighten me just to teach me a lesson of your own devising?"

"I've been thinking of it for several days, and now that you'll be facing the wild cattle alone, I want you to realize that you can't be so easy in your friendships. Your best protection is in your title, but you forget it too easily and allow others to forget it, as well. No, it's more than allowing—you actually encourage them to forget it. So whatever happens, if you're not careful, will be on your own head."

It was as if she hadn't heard anything he'd said except the one word that she now repeated almost dumbly, her eyes filled with dismay.

"Alone?"

"Well, not really alone, I suppose. There will be your friend, Madame Espalion, of course."

"From what you've said, I should probably number her among the cattle."

"I've said nothing to disparage your friend."

"You've hinted broadly enough." She was regaining her balance. "But that is not what I asked. Why is it I'll be alone? All the time you were telling me about them, you kept saying that we would see them together. What has happened so suddenly to prevent your being here?"

"Don't you think I've played court long enough?" he asked harshly, brutally, and she recoiled as if he had struck her.

"I don't understand."

"My dear Duchesse, I have many commitments. There are many matters that need my attention, and I have been neglectful."

"I do beg your pardon." She rose to her feet, trembling with rage, although her voice was calm enough. "I had no idea that I was keeping you from matters of such great importance. However, I don't remember requesting your presence at any time. You'll correct me if my memory is faulty."

"No, it's just that I felt so sorry for you, and now that you'll be surrounded with other people, I'll be free to pursue my own interests."

"Don't let me detain you for a moment longer."

He got up, walking toward the door leading to the garden.

"You should have told me your time was so precious," she shouted angrily.

"Expensive is the word," he returned over his shoulder. "But you needn't concern yourself. I'll submit an accounting to your banker."

As he passed out of sight, she hurried after him. Rushing into the dark garden, she felt his arms go about her waist, pulling her against him. Turning within the circle of his arms, she leaned back laughing breathlessly. "Oh, you fool!"

As he looked into her animated face he was almost tempted to apologize, but drew her against him instead. He closed his eyes, his face in her hair, the scent that had taunted him from a distance driving all thoughts from his mind. Finally he said, "I have to go away for a short while, Euphémie."

"Why couldn't you have just told me like that? Why did you have to hurt me so?" The laughter had turned to tears, and he held her even tighter.

"This has always been the way with me. From the first, when I left my father's house, it was with angry, ugly words. That way, if I don't come back, there'll be no weeping for me."

"But you'll come back here, won't you? Surely you aren't going into danger?"

He didn't answer, kissing her lightly on the lips. They

walked together to the gate, where he took her into his arms once again, but this time gently. "You don't love me, do you?" he asked in a whisper, and she shook her head.

"Forgive me, Auguste. I don't mean to hurt you, but . . ."

"You don't hurt me; I'm relieved. You see, I've been unable to love a woman since my wife. I just don't want you to be hurt."

"I don't want you to love me, either," she said sincerely, and he smiled kindly.

"It's so much better this way. When I return . . ."

"I'll still be your charming companion. Hurry back, please."

Without another word, she broke free, running into the house. Outelas made his way down the deserted road, whistling softly. Charming companion—it wasn't exactly what he had in mind, but they could discuss that when he returned. All in all, he was pleased with his success. She had responded to his deliberately varying moods much as a beetle does when touched with a stick, scurrying off in another direction. She was infinitely more interesting.

Phémie stood before the mirror, looking at the reflected outlines of her body through the transparent nightgown. Turning this way and that, critical of her image, she pursed her lips thoughtfully. So he'd never love again. That, she decided, would remain to be seen.

19

When she arose the next morning, Phémie took extra pains over her toilette and choice of costume. From what Outelas had hinted, she had reason to be very nervous about renewing her acquaintance with Mignon. In school she had been such a pale, frightened little creature, but people somehow changed over the years. Phémie could only speculate as to how much Mignon had changed.

Near the official hour for morning calls, Phémie started down the stairs. She approved of the effect the minimum of cosmetics and cool, green morning gown provided. She felt almost confident as she waited in the formal drawing room, more anxious than she would like to admit. When the hour passed with no sign of Mignon, Jessamine told her that if she were to call at all that day, it would be in late afternoon. Phémie debated with herself as to whether she should change her gown, but decided against it. She didn't have any doubts that the woman to whom she had sent the note was, in truth, her friend from school, although she had only

Outelas's word for it. She strolled aimlessly in the garden for a while, then had a light lunch in the little house. After eating, she settled on the chaise and was just dropping off to sleep when she heard the sound of voices as the women approached.

"I won't have a slave telling me when I can call on my friend. If you were mine, I'd find a good, thick leather strap."

"The Maîtresse is sleeping . . ." Jessamine protested to no avail.

"Don't you lie to me, you black baggage," Mignon insisted. Phémie closed her eyes, carefully pacing her breathing to feign sleep. Mignon was deliberately attempting to take her off balance, and Phémie was determined that she wouldn't be the one in an awkward position.

"How tiresome!" Mignon complained, bending over and shaking Phémie's shoulder.

"What is it?" Phémie sat up, rubbing her eyes.

"I'm here, Phémie. Your friend, Aurélie."

"Aurélie?" She peered up at her. "Oh, Mignon." She yawned, sinking back on the cushions. "This is too bad of you. I've not changed my gown or fixed my hair. You were never late at school."

"I'm not late, Phémie. I'm early." At this pronouncement, Phémie could not help but laugh, getting to her feet. "You are impossible!"

"Then I'm forgiven?" Aurélie pleaded charmingly and the two embraced. Aurélie stepped back, appraising Phémie. "You haven't aged at all, you wretch."

"I haven't thought of age," she admitted, and the other winced playfully.

"I've thought of little else."

The changes in Aurélie were in degree rather than anything startling. Her hair was still the beautiful glossy brown it had been, and her eyes were still large, almost overwhelming the rest of her face. But now she wore a thick layer of cosmetics and a heavy perfume. She conveyed a sensuousness that had not even been hinted at in the past. She was totally female, graceful, and charming. Phémie felt very big and awkward next to her.

"Before you say another word," she instructed with a firm sweetness, "you must tell me who has helped you so much. You should have come to me as soon as you arrived."

"I didn't know whether you were still here."

"Of course you didn't. How silly of me! Now, tell me who has taken such good care of you."

"Monsieur Outelas."

"I should have known." She laughed delightedly, but Phémie sensed an undercurrent of disapproval. She continued with the same lightness. "You must be careful of him, Phémie. He's very, very wicked."

"Do you know him well?"

"Very well!" she suggested broadly, still smiling. "He is the only man I've met who ever puzzled me. I don't know whether he conquered me, or I him. But enough of that!" She saw by her expression that such conversations met with little approval in Phémie's eyes, and had tact enough to leave it at that point. In many ways Phémie seemed totally familiar, but she took little comfort in it.

"I can't believe that you're really here."

"I said I would come to visit one day. It's good seeing you again, Mignon."

"You mustn't call me that any more. I'm known as Aurélie, and I hope you'll never mention the other again."

Phémie was startled by her vehemence over so small a matter, but only said, "I can't promise, but I'll try."

"Tell me, Phémie, what have you been doing in all these years? Is the old fellow still alive?"

"No, I've been a widow for several years now."

"What a dreary state that must be! It's the same as being unmarried. People frown on your taking lovers."

"Do you mean to say that it's respectable to have a lover only if one has a husband?"

"It's almost required, my dear. What else would we have to talk about in this wearisome place?"

"How boring for you. Come into the house where we can be comfortable."

"Did you bring many clothes with you?"

"Enough for my needs." She led the way as Aurélie chattered.

"My one passion in life, at the moment, is clothes. Is that one you're wearing something you brought with you?"

"No, I had it copied when I arrived. It is so warm here, and everything I have is so heavy."

"I think the only way one can stay comfortable is by going without clothes altogether. If you don't mind, I'm going to steal your most fashionable gowns and have them copied for myself."

"Just so you leave me enough to cover myself. I don't ascribe to your belief in going without."

"Then you wouldn't mind?"

"Of course not."

Aurélie squeezed her hand impulsively, "You're as generous as ever. What are your plans?"

"I believe the proper procedure is for me to present myself and my papers at the Governor's residence."

"Oh, we're not like that here. Anyway, he wanted me to sound you out on whether you'd be receptive to a ball in your honor. There is so little for him to do, the poor dear, and I didn't think you'd be averse to such a scheme."

"I think that's an excellent idea, if it wouldn't be too much trouble for everyone."

"Trouble? Oh, dear Phémie, we are all so bored with one another's company that it would brighten up our dull lives. A formal ball! St. Pierre is suffering from such ennui that we celebrate His Majesty's birthday with a toast after dinner. Can you imagine such a thing? We're becoming so provincial that we didn't even have a ball on the great day."

"I went to Versailles for the occasion." She tried to be casual and hoped that she didn't sound boastful.

"You didn't! But of course you did, if you say so. After all, you're a Duchesse." They passed through the house and started upstairs. "Did you faint with excitement?"

"Good God, no!" Phémie laughed, and Aurélie was amazed. "I would have, or been sick all over myself. Did you see him?"

"His Majesty? Of course. He's still the handsomest man in the world, or so the ladies all claim."

"Who was your escort?"

"I was escorted by a very special friend, who has now retired to a monastery." Phémie laughed at the expression on the other's face. "I seem to have that effect on men."

"How wonderful for you! Has any man killed himself for you yet? Or fought over you in a duel?"

"The first is forbidden by the Church, and the second by the State. I should hope I'd never be responsible for anyone's death. And I didn't want Charles to enter the religious life, but he loved his wife so much."

"A man who loved his wife? What a rare creature!" she commented sarcastically, and Phémie turned to her.

"For shame! He did love his wife, more than anyone really knew. She treated him horribly, but he suffered her insults and infidelities without complaint. And when she died, he was so grief-stricken that he gave up his life and position at court to live in solitude."

"It sounds like a romance." She was unconvinced, and Phémie had to admit, good-naturedly, that it had all the elements of an improbable love story.

"It doesn't matter whether you believe it or not. How do you like my house?"

"I have been here often. The former owners used to give wonderful parties." She lied easily, and Phémie was taken in.

"I hope to entertain on a modest scale once I've been introduced to St. Pierre. It's really very kind of your father to want to welcome me so lavishly."

"He's as bored as the rest of us," Aurélie said unthinkingly, and Phémie could only laugh at her frankness. "Whatever the reason, it will serve my purpose quite well."

"Then everyone's happy about it."

Phémie took her into the room that served as her wardrobe. One part of it was filled with gowns and underthings brought from France, as well as the lighter-weight clothing made since she had arrived. In addition to the seamstress provided by Outelas, she had engaged the freedwoman who had been suggested by Celeste when she first arrived. Both women had several girls serving as apprentices, so the rest of the room was filled with cutting tables and other paraphernalia necessary to the successful completion of their tasks. As soon as the two women entered the room, the sewers fell silent, their heads bent over the work, and Aurélie eyed them suspiciously.

"You must count your gowns every day before they leave. They're not above stealing, you know."

"Madame Jessamine takes care of such matters for me," Phémie replied, and the other wisely let the subject drop. As Aurélie examined the clothes brought from France, Phémie held a consultation with the two seamstresses. When Aurélie left, clutching the gowns she had chosen to have copied, Phémie wearily returned to her own room, discarding her morning gown in favor of a light robe. Madame Jessamine came in, closing the jalousies to darken the room, and picked up the clothes thrown carelessly about.

"*Madame!*" Phémie called sleepily from the bed, and the housekeeper approached her.

"I am here, Maîtresse."

"You have been in St. Pierre for a long time. Is there anything you can tell me about Madame Espalion?"

"It is not right for me to speak of your friend."

"I don't know that she is my friend. She was once, many years ago, but she has changed so much that I scarcely know her."

Jessamine understood her plight and took pity on her. "*Maîtresse* must be careful of that woman. She is not to be trusted too far." She would say no more, and left Phémie with her own thoughts.

When Gaspard returned from a long day in the Government offices, he found his wife in her room, admiring the gowns she'd borrowed. She was more animated than he'd seen her in years, and after he'd given enthusiastic approval of the gowns, as was expected of him, he asked, "How is the Duchesse?"

Aurélie turned away from her treasures and reclined on her chaise, indicating that he was to sit with her. For a moment he couldn't believe that he'd actually been invited to remain, then hurriedly pulled a chair closer.

"I've been thinking of what you said about Paris last night, but now the royal residence is at Versailles."

"The court has moved, then."

"Evidently. Phémie attended the Grand Ball there, rather than at the Louvre. You know, Gaspard, I think you've helped Father for quite long enough. It is time that we give some thought to your own career in government. Your idea of going to France is an excellent one. I could be of great help to you in your work."

He understood from her little speech that they were to be allies, and he welcomed the change in their relationship. "What do you think of the Duchesse helping us? Did you mention anything today?"

"About wanting to go to Paris? That would have been foolish, wouldn't it?" She continued without waiting for his answer. "When we see Father tonight we must persuade him to give a ball to welcome Phémie to St. Pierre. I told her that such was his wish, to see how she would like it, and she liked it exceedingly well. Now all we have to do is tell Father that it is imperative that he do so in his role of Governor."

"That won't be difficult. He takes my counsel now without questioning it."

"We'll leave early so you can talk to him before the others arrive."

"What do you think of our chances, Aurélie?" he asked anxiously, and she smiled with a degree of kindness, putting her hand on his arm.

"I think we will be at Versailles very soon."

"Will the Duchesse be that easy?"

"Of course; we're good friends." She reassured him, but inwardly realized that her footing was not as firm as she'd like it to be. Phémie would take some careful handling, but Aurélie had no doubt as to the outcome.

Whenever she occasionally thought of de Merades, Phémie's thoughts would become very dark indeed. She spent hours imagining how she would wreak revenge upon him. She could see them meeting again, but then she would no longer be in the awkward position. She would have become very beautiful, of course, and desirable. When he saw her for the first time after such a long separation, she envisioned him begging her for her favors. How she would take delight in spurning him! She imagined herself looking at him with withering contempt, proud, haughty, unreachable. As his pleas became more desperate, she would laugh at him, then turn on her heel and walk away without a backward glance. Never, never would he recover from such rejection; he would go through life a broken, despairing man, unloved and unwanted. It was a lovely dream, one that she encouraged when she was alone. If only it would come true, she prayed, although she realized that she had little experience in such matters. How could she, unschooled in the art of flirtation, humble a man who was so certain of his powers over women? She would just have to learn, and she sensed that Aurélie Espalion would be an excellent teacher.

Every day Aurélie visited and talked with growing excitement of the magnificent ball that she was so instrumental in planning. Each visit passed without Phémie finding the courage to broach the subject she wished to discuss. On the eve of the great day, Aurélie made a second call, late in the evening. As they sat in the small salon, Aurélie chattered on at interminable length about the preparations and her own gown, which, she claimed, was the best-kept secret on the island.

"Everyone knows that you're here," she was saying, "but they haven't dared to call, knowing that your official recognition isn't until tomorrow night. I handled that quite well, don't you think?"

"Indeed I do," Phémie answered automatically as the other went on without a pause.

"Father is dreadfully poor. He receives only a token recompense from His Majesty, but the King sees to it that his representatives live well. No, more than well. Lavishly! We are supplied everything: the finest wine, food, clothing, and even slaves. In Paris Father would live like a middle-class merchant if he had to depend on his own funds to keep him alive. Euphémie d'Amberieu!" She shouted, clapping her hands because Phémie had drifted away.

"Forgive me; I was thinking of something else."

"How well I know it! I've known it for quite a few days now. I thought if I just kept talking, you'd finally make up your mind to trust me and tell me what is concerning you."

"I didn't want to bother you with a problem of mine. It's so silly."

"Nothing is silly if it's a problem. We are friends, you know."

The word "trust" decided Phémie against confiding in her. To even begin the story would stimulate her curiosity; and knowing Aurélie as she did, she knew that she'd keep at her until she'd dug it out. Following hard upon this realization was the knowledge that there was a source she could go to and rely upon silence. To be perfectly honest with herself, she had no confidence in Aurélie to remain silent about anything, if speaking of it was to her advantage.

"It's my gown," Phémie said. "I wanted to wear the same one I wore to the Grand Ball, but I'm afraid it's not appropriate. Would you come upstairs with me and help me decide?"

Aurélie could appreciate such a problem and rose to do battle for a solution. Between the two of them, a gown was chosen, and Aurélie returned to her home feeling that she'd finally broken through Phémie's reserve.

Calling for Madame Jessamine, Phémie ran upstairs to her own room. By the time the housekeeper had joined her,

Phémie had stripped off her gown and was thrashing through the wardrobe. Far at the back she'd found what she was looking for, and she came out with her hands full.

"Do you know where the street of women is?" she asked, knowing no other name by which to call it.

"What does the Maîtresse know of such a place?" Jessamine asked, staring horrified as Phémie dressed herself in trousers, open neck shirt, and boots.

"Don't look so stricken!" Phémie laughed, exhilarated, then explained briefly how she'd met Celeste.

"You cannot go there!" Jessamine protested. "If someone should see you, and in those clothes . . ."

"All they'd be seeing is just another boy roaming the streets. Anyway, you'll be with me, and you can answer any questions if we're stopped."

"I'll not go there."

"But you must. I can't go to the door and ask for her. What if her protector is with her tonight? It would cause her trouble."

"How do you know of these things?" Jessamine scolded fiercely. "You're not like that other woman, who should be living there herself and not with such a fine gentleman as Monsieur Espalion."

"Have you met Monsieur Espalion?"

"He often comes to the Maître's house, as does anyone of worth."

"Do you know Celeste?"

"I know her."

"Then you know that she is a very kind person, and it is not shameful to know her."

"It would be very bad if the Maître knew that you went to that street. I will go and bring her here, if you must see her."

That plan took away a great deal of the excitement, but Phémie could only approve the wisdom of it. When she nodded her agreement, crestfallen, Jessamine smiled slightly, her opinion of the Maîtresse reaffirmed. "I'll leave now, and while I am away you must change your clothes. Celeste will run away if she sees you in such a costume."

"May I serve her wine and cheese, or wouldn't that be proper, either?"

"In the small house it will be proper. It is well to receive her there. I'll bring her in the gate, and when I return, I'll take care of the other things."

When the two women came in the gate, they found Phémie rushing down the path toward them.

"Madame Celeste!" she greeted her guest, taking her by the arm and leading her into the small house.

"This is madness!" Celeste couldn't help but laugh, shaking her head in disbelief that they were both there.

"The only madness is that we have to meet in secret," Phémie explained, "but I won't say anything more. I know you don't approve of talk like that."

"After we met, I told myself that I must never again be so foolish, but my protector is away and it is the dark of night."

"Are you really that frightened? But of course you are." She rushed on, "You told me before. I'm sorry."

"It must be very serious, whatever it is you wish of me."

"I want another lesson." Phémie stated bluntly, and the other raised her eyebrows slightly, in surprise. "Here's Jessamine," Phémie warned as the wine and cheese were brought in. The housekeeper left as quickly as she came, and Phémie acted the part of hostess. When the ritual was completed, she continued, "I want you to teach me how to humble a man; how to bring him to his knees." She said this with such vehemence that Celeste looked at her more with pity than amazement.

"I have never learned such a thing myself, so I'd be unable to teach you or anyone how to hurt another." This was said so gently, and with such compassion, that Phémie felt her eyes sting with tears.

"I've done it again!" she said helplessly. "I'm such a fool, and I'll never learn to be otherwise."

"Were you badly hurt, Madame?"

"It was my own fault. I know so little of men and the ways of men with women. I don't even know how to flirt," she admitted abjectly, and Celeste smiled, saying, "Flirting is a young girl's game. Men like it because it makes them feel young again themselves, and witty. Your best weapons are your honesty and your humor. Do not pick up a tool that is not suited to your strength or weakness. I am sorry that I cannot help you."

"You have helped me. What do you do to attract a man?" She blushed, embarrassed, rushing on before the other could answer. "That's an unnecessary question. You're a beautiful woman."

"But so are you, Madame."

"With spots on my face, and my hair like this?" She pulled at it angrily, but still laughing.

"You do not use your cosmetics properly. If you wish, I could show you what to do in that way. I could help you choose the proper gown for the ball tomorrow night, and I can even suggest the man you try to conquer."

"Conquer?" she asked, a frown creasing her forehead.

"Just for the evening. You'll be pursued by every man there, so you must choose just one to whom to direct your attention. That is the best protection for a woman alone."

"Who will he be?"

"Oh, someone very romantic and exciting. I'll tell you about him while we practice with your paints."

"How do you know he'll be there?"

"It is common gossip that although Madame Espalion always invites him to various occasions, he has never accepted until now. You can spend the evening with him and be assured that he'll not pursue you to your home or even approach you again unless you want him to, of course."

"Is he handsome?"

"So handsome that every lady in St. Pierre wishes him for a conquest."

"Oh, dear, I hardly think he'd be interested in me."

"Perhaps not interested now, but certainly curious, as everyone is. I'm certain that when he sees you, his attitude will change."

"Just so he won't think . . ." She stopped, blushing again, and Celeste laughed, "He'll think only what you'll allow him to think. In that you must be careful. Most men are certain that every woman alive thinks them terribly attractive; it can be difficult at times. But Jacques Bordeaux knows that he is terribly attractive and is not impressed with it."

"Jacques Bordeaux." Phémie laughed at the improbable name, and Celeste laughed with her, shrugging, "It is what he calls himself. He is the captain of a pirate vessel."

By the time Phémie rose from her late afternoon nap, Jessamine had prepared a special bath for her. Slipping off her robe, she stepped into the tub gingerly, sniffing at the heavy, strange odor that permeated the rising steam. After the bath, she allowed the black to rub her with a thick, odorless preparation that Jessamine refused to describe. It soaked into her skin like water into the parched earth, and Phémie decided that she approved of what it did to her skin. Even if the evening had not promised to be cool enough for it, she would have worn the gown Celeste had chosen anyway. Aurélie had chosen a gown that was entirely unsuited to her, while Celeste had picked one that was daring yet simple. Her gown was red taffeta, with taffeta and velvet in alternating panels, in the full skirt. The bodice was close-fitting, revealing the outline of her full, young breasts. Her shoulders and bosom were bare, and there were no sleeves except for small bands of cloth halfway between her shoulders and elbows. Under the flaring red skirt she wore heelless red satin slippers.

If Celeste had been surprised that she hadn't brought her jewelry, she gave no sign of it. Phémie was very pleased with the results of Celeste's art. Her freckles had been completely covered, taking away her girlish look. Her lips were as bold and as red as the gown. Her brows had been darkened, the lids colored with green paint and the eyes outlined in black, giving them an exotic, oriental appearance. A short, white satin cloak, much like the ones cavaliers wore, covered one shoulder while the other side, dropped low in back, was brought up under the arm and tied with a golden strand. It was ermine-lined and charmingly complemented the rest of her ensemble. As she stood before the mirror, making one last inspection, she asked over her shoulder, "Do you know Captain Bordeaux, Madame?"

Jessamine's eyes widened, but she showed no other sign of surprise.

"I know him," she replied shortly, and Phémie laughed. "What? No warning of disaster? Come now, Madame, surely you must have one caution tucked away somewhere."

"You need no warning from me. If you see him, you will stay away from him like a fer-de-lance."

"Is he that deadly?" she asked, exaggerating fear, and Jessamine shook her head. "Don't play any games with him, little one. Leave him to Madame Espalion. She considers him her own, and will not welcome any encroachment, especially from you."

"I consider myself warned, thank you, Madame," she commented with a hint of mischief. "The only safe man is probably Monsieur Espalion."

"Yes, he is a kind man, both safe and respectable."

Phémie arrived early, as requested by her friend. Aurélie was acting as hostess, as she had at all state functions since her mother had died. Phémie had met the Governor when he had called officially, and he greeted her like an old and dear friend, taking her hand in his and fondling it. Her moment of discomfort passed as Aurélie introduced her husband, Gaspard. The Governor, at a stern look from his daughter's husband, excused himself until the other guests began arriving.

"That's a lovely gown," Aurélie said flatly. "It wasn't among those we looked at, was it?"

Before Phémie could reply, Gaspard interjected, "The gown is not as beautiful as its wearer. Come, Aurélie, don't be so meager with your praise."

"You won't mind if I leave you with Gaspard, will you,

Phémie? There are several things that need my attention."

"Of course not, if Monsieur Espalion won't be inconvenienced."

"My dear Duchesse"—he took her arm possessively, leading her into one of the drawing rooms—"I assure you it will be a pleasure to entertain you."

Aurélie nodded approvingly as they disappeared from her view, then hurried off to the kitchens.

Phémie had been worried about conversing with so many people until Celeste had told her that she need not be concerned; people make their own conversation, she said. Nod at the right time, put in a word or two of agreement, and a person would come away feeling that it had been a very satisfactory, two-sided discussion. So it was with Espalion. Later he would tell his wife that he had certainly impressed the Duchesse; not once did she disagree with him.

At the appointed hour, Phémie took her place in the receiving line, directly after the Governor and before the Espalions. It seemed to last forever, but she held up under the strain well because it was such a novel experience for her. The rooms filled rapidly, and still there was no sign of anyone even vaguely resembling a pirate captain. The moving mass of brightly dressed planters, officials, officers, and merchants and their wives looked and sounded more like a jungle full of parrots than a house full of human beings. Finally the main stream had come to an end, and Aurélie whispered that any late comers would have to come in unannounced and without introduction.

The Governor claimed the honored guest, and the two of them led the others into the ballroom. After the first dance she was claimed by Espalion, who, with great consideration, led her to a special chair placed for her near the windows and hurried off to get her a cool drink. She was not required to dance, and no one approached her. Espalion, who was gaining in favor, reminded her that he was at her service if she should wish to dance, thereby establishing himself as her unofficial escort. Occasionally he would bring a few favored people up to her chair for some light conversation.

After a time, when Espalion had excused himself to dance with his wife, Phémie quickly ducked out the open doors into the darkness of the terrace outside. The air was refreshingly cool, and she strolled along the terrace, thankful for being out of the crowd's sight, if only for a moment. A man stood at the end of the terrace looking away from her toward the garden. On the low stone wall beside him was a bottle of wine and two goblets. He was obviously waiting for someone, but after strolling past him several times, she saw that he was still alone. He'd not turned while she was walking, and didn't do so as she approached him boldly.

"Are you waiting for a lady, Monsieur?" She spoke to his back, and he answered, without turning, "It would seem that she has come at last." Phémie looked about, but could see no one approaching them from any direction.

"Perhaps she has forgotten that you are waiting. It might be wise to go inside to find her."

"But she has found me." He turned, laughing quietly. "All the beauty in the world is before me. Why would I want to go elsewhere?"

She stepped back, peering up at him in the darkness, a light smile playing about her mouth.

"Captain Bordeaux!"

"Your Grace!" He bowed gracefully. He was a tall man, well over six feet, with broad shoulders and powerful chest and arms. In the light streaming from the window she could see that his eyes were as dark as his black hair. From long hours out of doors he was tanned to a rich bronze. There were tiny white lines at the corner of his eyes where he had squinted into the sun. His face was undoubtedly the handsomest she had ever seen. The jaw was strong, the mouth not too full, the nose rather prominent, the forehead broad below slightly tousled hair. His eyes were his most remarkable feature—black, shining, and expressive. He had chosen, for the occasion, to wear a pair of fawn-colored trousers, a white shirt tucked into the broad, jeweled belt, and a short, embroidered jacket.

"Have you been waiting long for me?" she asked laughingly, and he stepped closer, his low, melodious voice almost a whisper.

"All my life, I think."

He spoke with complete sincerity as his eyes were filled by the proud, willful, and hauntingly beautiful woman before him. Her eyes, the greenest he'd ever seen, betrayed a sensuousness, a deep warmth that drew him yet closer. Her mouth, softly full, smiled slightly in apparent confusion.

"You're late," she said for the lack of something better.

"My manners are notoriously bad," he bantered, and she laughed, relieved that he had turned away from her to pour the wine. Handing her a glass, he watched her closely as she sipped the wine, her eyes unable to look up into his. The moment of respite was all she needed, and when she looked up again, her eyes were filled with merriment.

"Alas, mine cannot be. Thank you for the wine . . ." She held the glass out to him, and his hand closed about hers.

"You cannot escape so soon, and without payment."

"But I must return, and my thanks were payment enough for our host's wine." She rebuked him stingingly, and he released her hand, taking the glass from her.

"Only beautiful women can inflict such cruelty."

Phémie had turned to depart, but upon his words, she stopped, saying good-naturedly, "You must be mad, or perhaps at sea too long. May I have your arm, Captain?"

"You ask for so little, when I would gladly give you the world."

"A poetic pirate! Such gallantry is wasted on me. Spare me your compliments and your promises, Captain. I have the world already, and there's nothing else you could offer."

"Those are unkind words, Your Grace."

"And your words are unnecessary."

"Euphémie!" She heard her name called, and recognizing Auguste's voice instantly, was relieved.

"Over here, Monsieur," she answered his call, and in a moment he was by her side.

"I've apologized to the Governor and Madame Espalion for my lateness. There remains only you . . ."

"You're not an instant late, Monsieur. May I present Captain Bordeaux?"

"We are acquainted." Auguste nodded in the friendliest manner to the scowling man. "I'm certain you'll excuse us, Captain, but Her Grace is the reason for all of this, and the other guests must not be deprived of her presence for too long."

"Perhaps you would join me in a glass of wine out here, Outelas, once you have delivered the Duchesse to her admirers."

Phémie scrutinized the pirate; he was so much taller than Auguste and broader of girth. No, she would not allow her friend to return alone to the terrace. As they left Bordeaux, she whispered, "You're not going to fight that man."

"It would not come to that. His welcome here is dangling by a slender thread. He'd not dare attack such a respectable citizen."

She hugged his arm affectionately, completely reassured that he'd not have trouble on her account.

"Will you always appear just when I need you?"

"What was he saying to you?" He was not to be distracted from what he considered a very serious matter.

"Oh, just some nonsense about giving me the world. And I'd been told he wasn't taken with himself. That was certainly false information."

"Who told you about Bordeaux?"

"Aurélie!" she lied quickly, feeling Auguste's arm tense. "She said that he was terribly handsome, and not a bit impressed with himself. Can you imagine any man talking like that to a woman he'd never seen before?"

"You are very beautiful tonight. It's enough to make any man lose his head."

"Any man except you," she complained, and she felt warm as he laughed lightly. "There must be one man left standing, if only to dance with you."

"Will you dance with me, Auguste?"

"They have announced dinner, Your Grace," he mocked her gently, "and the musicians have already left the ballroom." He lowered his voice to a conspiratorial whisper, leaning close to her ear, "They're all waiting for you so they may eat at last."

As they moved inside, Phémie smiled graciously, noting the stares of the revelers with a slight embarrassment. Auguste delivered her to the Governor and then dropped back to follow them into the dining room at a discreet distance. Bordeaux must have come in through the front, for he was among the guests as people searched for their places.

After dinner there was a complete, and very noticeable, change in the Duchesse. She danced often and had become less forbidding and more accessible. She mixed with the people, rather than sitting isolated at the front of the room. Outelas had replaced Espalion as her escort, and the obvious warmth and gaiety he brought out in her raised more than just a few eyebrows. They were an incongruous couple; she tall, long-limbed, and fair, while he was a bit shorter than she, darker of visage, and more somber. He brought her down from her throne and among the people, where she would talk to anyone Outelas chose. Always he was by her side, but unobtrusive and saying little. Finally he led her out into the garden, and as soon as they left the room, those remaining gathered in little knots, their conversation filled with speculation as to the demonstration of obvious affection evidenced by the Duchesse toward Outelas.

As they walked, Phémie began to hum a little song, and Outelas smiled to himself. But she was aware of his mood and asked suddenly, "Why do you smile?"

"Why do you sing?" he countered, and she was content to reply, "Because I'm happy."

"Perhaps that is why I smile."

"Oh, no!" She laughed, executing a little dance step as they progressed. "Nothing about you is that simple."

"Ah, then you know me that well?" He was hugely amused but kept his expression bland, almost innocent.

"I don't know you at all well. I just know you occasionally."

"Come, let us sit for a while. There is a bench behind the

hedge. Wait here while I see if it's been claimed before us."

Phémie did as she was told, watching as he left the path and crossed the grass to the place he'd indicated. Before he rounded it, to make his inspection, he stopped, leaning close to it as if listening. In a moment he turned to her, motioning that she should join him, his finger to his lips. Lifting her skirt, she crossed the grass as quietly as possible, the taffeta making only a slight noise. When she reached the hedge, he slipped his arm about her waist, pulling her close against him, whispering that she should remain silent. As she nodded her agreement, he released her, and she followed his example, leaning against the hedge and listening. At first the voices were too low to be distinct, but in a few minutes they began to rise in heated argument.

". . . and she thinks me a fool. Who wouldn't, after what I said to her?"

"You were a fool coming to me for advice in the first place. What ever made you think I would give you any honest suggestions in seducing my friend?"

"Hardly seducing! And even if that had been my intention, you had no right to lead me so far astray. No man likes to be made a fool of."

"Neither does a woman, and you've been making a fool of me ever since the beginning."

"I've not neglected you."

"No, but you were beginning to bore me. Now I can laugh when Phémie tells me of . . . what was it she called you . . . the 'Poetic Pirate'? It will make a good story, one I'm certain St. Pierre will enjoy."

"Don't do it, Auréliel" His voice became sinister, but she only laughed, "What's to stop me?"

"There are some interesting stories I could tell about you as well. I can live without people's good opinion."

"As can I!" she challenged, and his voice became more excited.

"But can your husband? What of his chances if there's a scandal about you? A scandal whose stink would reach all the way to Paris. You may be Espalion's wife, but you are still your father's daughter. If he were removed from his position because news of his corruption reached the ears of the King, how much of the muck would be thrown on your husband?"

"Gaspard has no knowledge of that." She sounded afraid.

"Who would believe it? You'd best do what I say if you want to see your husband advance."

"What do you want me to do?" Her voice became lower, and Phémie moved right to the edge where she could hear better.

"I want you to install me in Her Grace's good opinion. I want to be able to call on her without being laughed at. And I want you to find out if she has become Outelas's mistress."

"And if she has?"

"Then the other won't be necessary, as long as she doesn't talk about tonight to anyone."

"You mean that if she's his woman, you won't challenge him for her favors?"

"It wouldn't be honorable," he stated stiffly, and she laughed.

"I didn't know you were acquainted with the word."

Something in his face must have warned her that she was on dangerous ground, for she immediately began to soothe him. "All right, I'll do as you say. I'll somehow convince her that you're a fine fellow."

"And if she's not Outelas's woman . . . ?"

"I'll sing your praises until her ears ring with it, and she'll fall into your arms when you present yourself."

Phémie felt Auguste's hand close about her wrist, and he led her away quietly. She followed unprotesting as he led her to the back wall. Jumping up, he got a handhold on the top, and pulled himself up. Straddling the wall, he instructed her to raise her arms, then pulled her up beside him. Phémie would never have suspected him to be so strong, and she looked at him with amazement. As she balanced herself, swinging her legs over to the other side, he leaped down.

"Jump!" he commanded, and she protested.

"You'll never catch me. I'm too heavy."

"Do as I say."

"You're mad!" She laughed nervously, still holding tightly to her perch.

"You're afraid," he challenged, and she hesitated only a moment longer before pushing herself off the wall. He caught her with as little effort as he had pulled her up.

"Won't they miss us?"

"By the time they do, the men will be too drunk to care and the women will be too delighted with a possible scandal."

"Where are you taking me?" She hitched up her skirt with a show of willingness to follow him anywhere he might lead.

"I thought for a sail. There's a little cove I know of not too far distant, and a beautiful strip of beach."

"It sounds wonderful."

"You don't lack courage, Your Grace. I'll try not to betray your trust."

It was almost dawn by the time they reached the waterfront. Outelas's boat was a sleek, well-made sloop that was built for speed rather than comfort. There was one cabin below deck with only a narrow bunk, a table with charts secured on it, and a sea chest. As Outelas sailed away from St. Pierre, under the curious eyes of the fishermen readying to go out for another day of harvesting the sea, Phémie found a disreputable pair of trousers, a shirt with tattered ends, and a long sash in the sea chest. She used the sash to hold up the trousers, and tied the tattered ends of the shirt at her midriff, considering the costume modest enough despite the amount of skin that was showing. She went up on deck in her bare feet, and Outelas didn't seem dismayed by the spectacle she presented. The place was less than an hour away from St. Pierre, and the entrance to it indistinguishable in the long shadows caused by the rising sun. When Outelas had thrown the anchor overboard, Phémie followed it almost immediately into the water. When she surfaced, her hair streaming in her face, she saw

Outelas was still on the sloop, looking down at her. He wasn't laughing, but was obviously amused.

"Why are you waiting?"

"To see if you're attacked by a shark."

"If I am attacked?"

"I'll have the priest say a mass for the repose of your soul. I'll even light a candle for you."

"That's very generous of you." She laughed, treading water as she brushed hair out of her face.

"Once you're safely on shore, I'll change my clothes and join you."

She did as he bade, and it wasn't too long before she saw him dive off the boat and swim to join her. As he flopped down beside her, stretching out, she saw that his upper torso was criss-crossed with scars.

"Mother of mercy!" she ejaculated, tracing the marks on his back with her finger. "What happened to you?"

"Do my scars offend you?" he asked without a trace of rancor. "I'll go back to the boat and get a shirt."

"Of course they don't offend me. You must have suffered great pain."

"The lash is a cruel weapon."

"Turn over." She knelt above him as he obeyed and saw that the scars ran around his ribs and ended in blobs across his chest.

"What are these?" She outlined one of the blob-scars, and he answered calmly enough, "That's where the weighted end of the lash bit into the flesh."

She shivered, not appreciating his calmness.

"How can you be so casual?"

"I wasn't at the time, but the years have dimmed the memory of it."

"I'd never forget! Was it done to you because you were a pirate?"

Her shirt clung revealingly to her wet body, and he looked upon her with pleasure.

"The day is too beautiful to be talking of such dark things."

"Forgive me, I shouldn't have asked." She sounded sincere in her regret as she lay beside him, close but not touching.

"You're a heady draught, Your Grace," he commented softly after a long, companionable silence, and when she didn't answer, he pushed himself up on an elbow, and saw that she was asleep. He remained there, propped up, drinking in the sight of her in the safety of sleep. With trembling hands, he untied the ends of the shirt, laying them open and exposing her to the warmth of the sun and the heat of his own gaze. She didn't stir, nor did the slow, even pace of her breathing change. Several times he reached out to touch the perfection of her breasts, but stopped short, fearing to wake her. He could only look, and ache with hunger. After a while he heard her voice and looked up at her face to see her eyes still closed but her lips moving slowly.

"Have you looked your fill, Auguste?"

He felt embarrassed, guilty at being caught out, like a small boy, but strangely exhilarated at the boldness of her reaction.

"Never, Your Grace, could I get enough of it." She moistened her lips with the tip of her tongue, smiling slightly, but not opening her eyes.

"I feel like a wanton, letting you look at me like this."

"And if I touched you?" His hand closed over her breast, and he felt her tremble, but she made no move to dislodge it. Slowly, gently, so as not to frighten her, he began to caress her, watching her face closely all the time. Her eyes fluttered open and a sigh escaped her as she put her arm about his neck, pulling him down to her with sweet insistence. He kissed her lightly, teasingly, exercising the greatest control over himself.

"And if I were to touch you?" He breathed the question into her ear, and she whispered,

"I would act the wanton."

"I'll be good to you, Euphémie," he promised, feeling his control slipping away from him as she began moving beneath him, returning his kisses with a passion keeping pace with his own. She helped him with equally awkward hands at the sash about her waist and allowed him to strip the trousers from her. It took him only a moment to divest himself of his own, and then he was with her again. Her nails raked his back with exquisite pain as he led her to the height of passion. And when it happened, a cry was wrenched from her, and she lay still, broken beneath the burden of pure, physical pleasure. After a few minutes, he picked her up, with some difficulty as his strength had not yet fully returned, and sat down, waist deep in the water, cradling her in his arms as the gentle motion of the waves rocked them and the coolness of the sea revived them.

"How do you feel?" he asked, concerned, and she arched over his arm, trailing her head in the water, replying slowly, "For the first time in my life I am glad to be the maiden."

"Hardly a maiden!" He laughed, and she laughed with him, but for a different reason.

When he returned her to the house, he promised that he would come back later for dinner. Phémie called for Jessamine, discarding her clothes one by one as she went upstairs, until there were only her underthings to be taken off. The black woman helped her, and as she climbed into bed, she warned her that Outelas was coming for dinner, and to make it something very special. Almost at once she fell into a deep sleep, and Jessamine, noticing the marks upon her body, nodded approvingly.

"It is good," she whispered, and left the room quietly.

20

Aurélie stayed away from her friend's house for several days, hoping to show her disapproval. It was just as well that she did, for Phémie was deluged with callers, asking about France, about relatives, fashions, court gossip, all to no avail. Phémie simply didn't know the answers, and admitted it freely. Some did not return, finding her a very strange duchesse to say the least, but there were a few who persisted, not for information or gossip, but hopeful for a letter of introduction to some powerful personage at court. They, too, were disappointed in time, and after a while, ceased coming as well.

The one who did persevere was Gaspard Espalion, who never taxed her on anything. He simply called every day, chatting amiably, and Phémie did nothing to discourage him as she did the others. She felt sorry for Gaspard, for although he wasn't witty or otherwise entertaining, he was certainly not objectionable in any way.

When Aurélie heard that the Duchesse was not playing

"You have caused me great suffering, and I think it's bad of you to be so heartless. My friends come to visit, and you pretend to know nothing of Paris and the court. I told them you'd been to the Grand Ball at Versailles and they won't believe me, saying that you're nothing but an *hobereuse* who's more suited to a pigsty than society."

"Poor Aurélie!" Phémie laughed, a trifle unkindly. "I didn't come here to regale your friends with tales from our homeland, but to visit with you. It would seem, however, that my presence has failed to enhance your standing in society, and you're suffering from disappointment on that score. Forgive me if I can't sympathize with you!"

"You're shameless, speaking to me like that. You're the one who has embarrassed me, and yet you act as if I should apologize."

"There's no need for apologies on either side. I am content with my behavior, and see no reason to consult with anyone about what I do."

"Not even with Outelas? Why did you choose him for a lover? He's rich enough, perhaps, for a husband, but hardly respectable as a lover."

"Whom would you suggest?" she asked sarcastically, but Aurélie had an answer for her. "There's Captain Bordeaux! He's very attractive, and everyone would approve of such a match."

"There is much in what you say. He's tall, well-made, and very handsome. He's also something Outelas is not."

"What is that?"

"A fool! Any man who would talk as he did upon first meeting a woman is absurd."

"That was my fault, not his," she admitted with proper contriteness. "I told him what to say, but it was for your sake."

"I don't understand."

"I thought it would be so lovely for you to have a romance, a real romance with a real man. It would have been a diversion for you while you were here, and when you returned to France, there would have been no regrets."

"Oh, a sensible affair of the heart."

"Yes, that's it. Being what he is, he'd have no pretensions in regard to permanence or marriage. It just couldn't happen, so he wouldn't have false hopes. I wanted only to see that you were entertained."

"I have been, and I truly appreciate your efforts. I realize that you look upon such a conspiracy as part of being a good hostess, but I don't need to be encouraged by someone else to accept a lover. Perhaps I was a bit hard on the Captain."

"Then you'll forgive him."

"He did nothing to be forgiven for. It was highly amusing."

"Will you allow him to call?"

"I've allowed all your friends to call, Aurélie. I don't see why the Captain should be any exception."

"Just don't be rude to him, please."

"I've never been rude to anyone, despite what they might have told you. I've simply been unable to answer their questions, much to my regret. It's been very uncomfortable for all of us, but I made no promises."

"Well, if you'll accept Jacques, just as a caller, of course, that will make up for everything."

"You plead very well for the Captain. I can't help but wonder why you've placed such importance upon it."

"I promised that I'd do everything that I could on his behalf. He's quite taken with you, you know. He truly thinks you're the most beautiful woman he's ever seen."

"If I hear anything like that again from him, I'll never change my bad opinion of him."

"Doesn't Outelas tell you that you're beautiful?"

"He has more sense than that." Phémie laughed, feeling very warm as she always did when thinking of him.

"If you meet disaster with that man, remember that I warned you."

"Why Outelas and not Bordeaux?" But before she could reply, Phémie held up her hand, stopping her with, "Never mind! I'll not forget your warning. Now I have another matter I wish to discuss with you. I want to have a small, intimate dinner for just a few friends. Your father, of course, and you and Gaspard. Outelas, if he returns soon enough."

"What about Captain Bordeaux?"

"Do you think that would be proper? He hasn't even called on me yet."

"He'll call on you later today or tomorrow, if it would be more convenient. You could ask him then, in reparation for your rudeness."

"I most certainly won't. You can bring him as your guest, if you wish. It would be better for you to invite him, anyway. That way he won't have any false hopes." She parodied the expression, and Aurélie smarted.

"You were never like this in convent school."

"Only to the others, my friend. You've forgotten."

"Have I become the enemy, then?"

"You've been acting as though I have deliberately set out to do you harm. I've neither questioned nor commented upon your private life, and I expect the same courtesy."

"We're having an argument!" Aurélie laughed with surprise. "And about what? Your choice of lovers. How ridiculous."

"I don't want you to ever mention that again." Phémie didn't see the humor of the situation; her eyes narrowed dangerously.

"Considering whom you've chosen, it's not worth discussing, anyway," Aurélie conceded ungraciously, then changed the subject hurriedly. "I'll bring the Captain, but you'll need two women to balance your table. There's a very respectable older woman who'd meet your high standards. She'd be perfect for Father. As for the other free man, I suggest a woman he already knows, and would not feel awkward with. Her name is Celeste, and Outelas has been her protector for over a year now."

"You're lying! You're just trying to hurt me," Phémie cried, paling. She knew, by the expression of gleeful malice in Aurélie's eyes, that her accusations were true.

"Hasn't he told you? I wonder why not. It's common

knowledge in St. Pierre, but no one ever talks about it, as most of the men keep such women. It's really quite acceptable. In fact, I would say that Gaspard is the only man who hasn't, at one time or another, indulged in the practice."

"I'll never forgive you for this, Aurélie."

"My dear, I'm just trying to save you from a heartbreak and public ridicule. You should thank me for being such a good friend." She stood up to leave, patting Phémie on the shoulder companionably. "I'll be delighted to attend your little dinner party. I'll bring the lady I mentioned, and you can make whatever arrangements you wish with the concubine. It should be quite amusing."

As Phémie sat there, unable to move, the tears streaming down her face as she wept silently, Gaspard Espalion came in unannounced.

"Oh, Your Grace, she has hurt you!" He knelt on one knee before her. "She is capable of great cruelty. What has she said?"

"Monsieur, I'm so sorry. I know how much you want to leave here, and go to Paris."

"I was ashamed to tell you. I was afraid you'd think that I was as self-seeking as the rest. I don't want the introduction, anyway."

"But why not?" His distress was so great that she forgot her own.

"At first I did. Aurélie and I made great plans; she said that she would be a great help to me in advancing. I believed her for a time, but after talking with you, I realized that she would be a detriment."

"But I never said anything against your wife."

"No, but you told me how His Majesty feels about scandal. Remember, when we were discussing the poison trials?"

"It was not my intention to suggest that—"

"Please, Your Grace," he interrupted firmly, "I realize that you're blameless in this. A man would have to be blind not to realize that a woman like Aurélie would be his destruction at court. There were other things that decided me, as well. I don't bear a title and would have no chance against nobles seeking positions in government."

"Nobles don't seek such positions, Monsieur. I learned at least that much. His Majesty's advisors are all men such as yourself. You shouldn't give up so easily."

"It's useless to speak of it, although I'll always remember your kindness. You see, I'm going to be involved in the biggest scandal of all. I'm no longer going to be living under the same roof with my wife."

"A separation?"

"I've already filed the papers with the Governor. I've only to tell Aurélie."

"Where will you be going?"

"To my father's plantation, although it is a place of unhappy memory for me."

"Why don't you go to Paris? I have a house there, where you can stay until you've been accepted by His Majesty."

"Do you mean it?" The tears sprang to his eyes, and she reassured him.

"Of course I do. I have but one request, however."

"Anything."

"Tell Aurélie that I gave you the letter of introduction the morning after the ball. And never, never tell her that I knew of the separation."

"Is that all you wish of me?"

"It's a great deal, Monsieur. Tell me, when do you plan to leave?"

"I hadn't planned. I mean, when do you think it would be best?"

"In the spring, when the world comes alive again. It's a time of renewal and good feelings. Your chance will be best then."

"I'll do as you say, of course. May I ask who my patron will be?"

"I only know one man who lives at Versailles that could be of any help. Your introduction will be to the King."

"My God!" He sat down abruptly on the floor, his face filled with wonderment.

"I can make you no promises," she warned fairly. "It will be on your own merit that you'll succeed. The letter will only get you in the door."

"It is enough! It is more than enough! It's a miracle!"

"I've invited you and Aurélie to a small dinner I'm giving soon. Will it cause you any embarrassment?"

"Aurélie might make a scene, so I'll not tell her of my plans until afterward. You've asked so little of me. Isn't there anything worthy that I can do?"

"Perhaps when you've become well-known and powerful, I might need a favor."

As she was writing the letter to Louis, she felt some of the hurt leave her and wondered if she were wrong to take comfort in Aurélie's misfortune. It was no one's fault but her own that she lost her husband, and what he did with his life after he left her was his own concern.

When she was finally alone, Phémie fled to the solitude of the small house in the garden. Falling on the chaise, she gave vent to her grief, her anger, her hurt. When she'd wept all her tears, she gave over to thought and began to understand Celeste on the eve of the ball. She had a reason for praising Captain Bordeaux and encouraging her to make his acquaintance. She must have known that Outelas was spending time in her company, yet she didn't evidence any resentment or jealousy. That first day she'd claimed not to love her protector, saying that he was kind to her. The picture of Outelas being kind to her almost drove Phémie mad. Celeste was so much more beautiful than anyone she'd ever seen. How could she compete with such a woman? She paced about nervously, reaching no satisfactory conclusion, and so went in search of Madame Jessamine.

"Why didn't you tell me that Maître and Celeste . . . ?" She couldn't finish the question, and Jessamine closed the door so they wouldn't be overheard.

"Did that woman tell you?"

"It doesn't matter who told me," she interjected. "It only matters that it's the truth."

"It is not the truth. Maître has not been with her since you became his woman."

Phémie understood that she was not deliberately insulting her, but was using the only language she knew.

"Are you certain?" She felt such an overwhelming relief that she almost wept. "You mustn't spare me."

"Maître went to Celeste and told her. He bought the house for her so she would never have to worry again."

"Oh, I'm so glad. You'll never know how I felt, and how happy I am."

"I know." She nodded, smiling small as was her custom. "White women cannot share a man. They must have him for themselves. But it was not right for that woman to tell you about the Maître and Celeste. She did it only to make you sad."

"She will soon know more sadness, although I can't help feeling sorry for her."

"Maîtresse is tired; she doesn't know what she is saying." Jessamine acted as if Phémie wasn't there to hear her. "Maybe if she sleeps for a while, and then dresses pretty, the Maître will come for dinner."

"Is he back, Madame?" Phémie grasped her by the shoulders, shaking her excitedly.

"He will be back soon. What will you say to him, Maîtresse? Will you tell him what that woman said to you?"

"No, I think it best that I pretend I never heard it. Am I right, Madame?"

"You are learning to be a woman, and will find that the fewer bad things you say to a man, the happier you will be."

"Even if the bad things are true?" She asked seriously, and the housekeeper replied in the same vein. "Especially if they are true."

"I wish I were as wise as you." She yawned, stretching wearily.

"Now you need sleep, not wisdom." Jessamine scolded affectionately, and prevailed upon her to nap until it was time for dinner.

The dinner party was only a partial success as far as the

hostess was concerned. Outelas was called away the night before, and Phémie found the pirate Bordeaux in close attendance. He had been to the house several times and had proven to be an amusing companion. Once he'd learned that she had a taste for adventure, he would tell her stories of the Spanish plate ships, fabulous wealth from the silver mines of Peru, gold mines of Mexico, and emeralds the size of chicken eggs. When she repeated these tales to Outelas, he told her that only nations had a use for wealth like that; the pirates who risked their lives on such prizes usually lost it to the merchants, tavern keepers, and the women in pirate ports.

"If you really were a pirate, what prizes did you pursue?" she asked him once, and his reply, as always, was eminently practical.

"Rather than the treasure ship, I attacked the fat-bellied merchant ships bringing goods to the colonies. A bolt of cloth and a bag of salt will bring more gold than an emerald the size of an egg." But she didn't care if it were true or not. A tale of fabulous treasure, beautiful women held for ransom, and a pitched battle with the Spaniard was far more exciting than a bolt of cloth and a bag of salt. Despite his tales, his romantic appearance, and his air of command, Bordeaux, however, remained merely an amusement to the Duchesse. She made no pretense of where her interest, if not affection, lay. Her relationship with Outelas was completely satisfactory in all facets, and there was no way for another man to capture her attention. The pirate recognized this without being told, but he was stubborn and determined that one day she would be his, no matter what the cost.

Outelas had been mistaken about Phémie's reception in St. Pierre. The balls, galas, fashion setting, and popularity had all failed to materialize, as did everything else he had predicted. The people of St. Pierre simply did not like her. They were uncomfortable in her refusal to be one of them. Her frankness, her unforgivable lack of subtlety, offended and repulsed them. So when the scandal of the Espalions' separation became public knowledge after Gaspard had left for his family's plantation, the women of St. Pierre were eager to believe whatever Aurélie told them of the stranger in their midst. She met with her friends, telling them of her husband's attendance on the Duchesse, exaggerating their meetings all out of proportion. Her friends found it easy to see how Outelas had actually been used as a dupe by the wicked woman, concealing her true relationship with Gaspard Espalion. None of the women listening to her stories were free from blame, especially Aurélie. Affairs with even their dearest friends' husbands were common occurrences, and in no way unsettling to the community. Husband-stealing, however, was an entirely different matter—something that could not be tolerated. Aurélie attacked her former friend with relish, weeping copiously, putting herself on public display rather than retreating to voluntary confinement. She was rewarded with universal sympathy and support for her outraged virtue.

Never had St. Pierre been favored with such a notorious scandal. Everywhere people met, it became the only topic of conversation. Pressures were being exerted against the erring Duchesse in subtle ways. In the marketplace her servants were the last to be served and were given the poorest-quality goods. The seamstresses from town no longer came to her house. The bank returned her marque without explanation. She was without callers since Bordeaux, who'd returned to sea, Espalion, and Outelas were no longer in St. Pierre. All she could hope for was Outelas's swift return. Never had she been so alone and friendless.

Her only information as to this sudden reversal in her fortunes came from her servants, who overheard snatches of gossip in the marketplace. At first she couldn't believe what they were telling her, so she wrote a letter to Aurélie, asking for the truth. She never received a reply. When members of her household could no longer go into St. Pierre without receiving physical abuse, Jessamine begged her to send for Outelas. Phémie was loath to accept her suggestion, but couldn't do otherwise. The reason for the success of her relationship with Outelas was that both of them were without bonds or responsibilities to the other. She anticipated his return every day, however, and although she missed meat and bread from her table, there were vegetables from the kitchen garden and fruit in abundance. But there were quite a few mouths to feed, and Jessamine was instructed to dole out the food fairly; she wasn't to give the Maîtresse any more than she gave to the others.

The blacks were frightened, and began whispering among themselves. The housekeeper knew their mood, but did nothing to discourage them. They began slipping away, a few at a time, to hide in the hills, until finally there remained only the loyal Jessamine. Phémie noticed the defections each day, but said nothing. Jessamine looked upon them with relief. The servants had become useless, hiding in their quarters and whimpering with fear whenever approached. They were taking food out of her Maîtresse's mouth while serving no purpose, so she was glad to see them gone.

Three weeks after the scandal broke over St. Pierre, Phémie was paid a late-night visit from one person she'd never expected to see again. Since the supply of tapers was exhausted, Phémie met her guest in the small house in the garden with the moon providing the only available light.

"Celeste!" Phémie embraced her warmly, grateful for the visit. "You shouldn't have come."

"I have little time, Madame, and there is great danger."

"I know. If you had been seen, they'd not have spared you."

"You are in far greater danger than I."

They sat down as Phémie apologized, "I've no wine to offer you. Perhaps some fruit . . ."

"There is no time. I left my protector asleep and must return before he awakes."

Phémie understood the import of what she said, and only nodded, waiting for her to continue. "Tonight he told me that they are conspiring against you; they are going to harm you."

"I have done nothing!" Phémie protested futilely, and

Celeste tried to impress her with, "That does not matter. They are mad, without reason. Madame Espalion and the others have taken their complaints against you to the Church. The priest has joined their number and has added his voice to your condemnation."

"Mother of God, what have I done to him?"

"You've not been to Mass or to confess since you've arrived. You've not sent for him to minister to you. And most of all, you've not made a gift to the Church."

"What of the Governor? Hasn't he tried to stop Aurélie?"

"My protector didn't say anything about that. He only said that they, the men of St. Pierre, were at first amused by their unvirtuous wives casting stones at another woman, but now, with the Church entering into it, they are afraid to interfere."

"I had best send for Outelas. He'll know what to do."

"It is too late. If you had gone to the priest as soon as the whispers began, you could have avoided it."

"But I didn't know about it. I heard nothing until my servants came home from the marketplace with pieces of gossip they'd heard. What can I do?"

"I could hide you in my house. There is a concealed room where certain runaway slaves have taken refuge."

"Is the danger that great?"

"My protector overheard their plans. They know that you are alone, without protection, and want to strike before Outelas returns."

"What is their plan?"

"At dawn tomorrow they are meeting at Government Square. They are going to march to your house and capture you."

"My God!" Phémie paled with fear. "Do they want to kill me?"

"The priest will not allow that." She offered cold comfort.

"Is he marching with them?"

"At their head, with a cross. They will come here and drag you out into the road. They will strip the clothing from you, smear your body with ashes, dress you in a hair robe, and march you to the wharf at the end of a rope. There you will be put aboard a fishing boat and taken to Fort Royal, where you'll be given over to a ship's captain to be returned to France."

"Do they know what will happen to me on such a ship?"

"They know, and welcome it. Your clothes will be divided among the women, although the priest thinks they should be burned, along with your papers. He is hoping for your gold, for the Church coffers, but Madame Espalion expects it to be given to her in return for the loss of her husband."

Blindly Phémie stretched out her hand, calling, "Jessamine!"

"I am here, Maîtresse." The black stepped out of the shadows from where she'd been listening unseen. She took the young woman's hand, pressing it reassuringly.

"You heard?"

Jessamine nodded, and when she spoke it was with hard determination.

"They will not harm you, Maîtresse."

"What must I do?" She was depending completely upon the wisdom of the slave.

"You must go to the Maître. Celeste is a good friend, but it would not be safe for either of you if you were to hide in her house."

"When they find you gone, the first place they'll look is the road to Outelas's plantation," Celeste protested, then fell silent under the gaze of the housekeeper.

"There is much to do, Maîtresse," Jessamine gently reminded Phémie, who was still distressed. "You go and change into those clothes you have kept hidden from me."

Phémie had to smile when Jessamine revealed her knowledge and she thanked Celeste with tear-filled eyes, then rushed away, glad to be doing something rather than just thinking of what could happen if she were caught.

Once they were alone, the housekeeper sat down while Celeste remained standing respectfully.

"We will go to Outelas, where she will be safe. And the eyes of the French will not see our passing."

"Yes, Mother." She addressed Jessamine by the title all the blacks called her when in their own company. "She's not like the others, is she?"

"You would not be here if she were." Jessamine smiled at her, and Celeste knelt before her, overwhelmed by such a blessing. Jessamine continued, "You have done much, girl, but you must do more."

"I'll do anything you say, Mother."

"At the marketplace tomorrow morning you will find the Governor's cook. Her name is Janne. Any of our people will tell you who she is. You must be very careful that there are no French watching when you give her this."

Reaching into her pocket, she pulled out a crudely carved female figurine, with great, pendulous breasts, one of which was painted black and the other white. Celeste, at the sight of it, fell back, terror-stricken, and Jessamine nodded approvingly. "It is good that you are still one of us. You've not forgotten the power your people possess."

"Is that for the enemy of your Maîtresse?"

"Yes, for her who called herself friend and then wounded the Maîtresse cruelly. I have been working every night since, after the house was asleep, to put strong magic into this." She caressed the figurine with strong fingers, almost as if she were kneading her will into it. "This figure represents woman bearing child." Celeste lost enough of her fear to become curious, and began to ask, "But why . . ."

"One is white," she touched the breast mentioned, forestalling the question, "the color of her own people. The other is black, the color of our people."

"I don't understand, Mother."

"It means that she carries the seed of a black man, though she doesn't know it yet. He is a great warrior, newly brought here from our homeland. He does not speak French and he does not carry a French name, nor will he ever. Soon he will try to run away, and will die like a warrior, to be reborn in our land. It is right for him to do this."

"And the child the enemy carries beneath her heart?"

"She will try to kill him, as she has killed others before they came from her womb, but she'll not succeed. She will give birth to the son of a warrior who will never know the word slave, nor will ever feel a band of steel about his leg."

Unconsciously, Celeste crossed herself, fearful of this woman who had the power to know what was to come. Many strange tales had been told of Jessamine, but never had Celeste seen it for herself.

"He will lead many of our people to the freedom of death and the promise of rebirth. He will destroy the woman who bears him, but will never lift a hand against her. Everyone will know of his birth, and of his mother; the evil that she has committed will be seen by all, and she will be alone."

"Is that the magic you have put into the figure?"

At her eager question, Jessamine merely nodded, holding the figurine out to her balanced on the palm of her hand. With hardly a moment's hesitation, Celeste snatched the carving, secreting it in the bosom of her dress. She remained kneeling long enough for the woman to place her hands on her head, mumbling a blessing for one who had returned to her own people, then Celeste was gone, running out the gate and swiftly down the road. Jessamine turned her thoughts to the poor hunted creature upstairs.

Phémie had not been idle nor helplessly fearful while the two women talked in the garden. Throwing open the jalousies to take advantage of the bright moonlight, she searched out her forbidden clothing. As she dressed, she felt more sure of herself and her chances for survival. By the time Jessamine joined her, she had wrapped her papers in protective covering and tucked them safely into her shirt. The feeling of panic and fear she'd first felt was gradually being replaced by the nervous excitement of adventure. She knew, without a doubt, that they would never take her. She would escape to Outelas's plantation and find warmth and security within his embrace. She refused to think about what could take place between the time she left St. Pierre and the time she arrived at the plantation.

At Phémie's insistence, they took all but one of her gowns and burned them in the huge kitchen fireplaces. The heat became so intense that Jessamine thought the house might catch fire but didn't communicate her fears to her Maîtresse. She was glad to see that Phémie was determined to fight, that she wouldn't allow her pursuers even the pleasure of possessing her clothes. It was dangerous to take so much time, but Phémie was adamant. When all of the gowns were either destroyed, or ruined beyond any possibility of repair, Phémie took the last gown, the one she had worn to the Grand Ball so long ago, and packed it into a heavy chest. They buried it outside the thick back wall, then artfully covered the spot with undergrowth. When they were finished, there was no way to determine that the area had ever been disturbed.

While Jessamine hurriedly gathered as many water containers as she could carry in a pack, Phémie, in the light from the fire in the kitchen, wrote a short note to Aurélie, promising her former friend that she would return shortly and settle the score between them. She secured it to the front door with a knife. While Jessamine was carefully extinguishing the fire, Phémie went upstairs for the last time. She had known such kindness, such warmth in that room, and prayed that someday they would return to it, and she would once again experience the excitement of hearing Auguste's tread on the stairs, the joy of their reunion and the exquisite exhaustion at the completion of their lovemaking.

When Phémie returned to the waiting housekeeper, she had a rapier buckled about her waist and a dagger caught under her belt. It was shortly after midnight, and, as if conspiring with the fugitives, the moon hid its light behind the clouds to obscure their passage from the house where she'd known so much happiness. Jessamine had not told her their route, and Phémie had not asked. They walked down the middle of the road, where their footsteps would be obliterated by the crowd coming on their dreadful mission at dawn.

At the crossroads, Jessamine led her into the undergrowth, which closed after them like a curtain. If what lay behind them had been less terrifying, what lay before them would have been unbearable. Whenever they paused to rest, Jessamine would listen carefully. Phémie could hear the sounds of the creatures who lived in the jungle. There were croakings, slitherings, flappings and cryings. There were sudden, startling sounds, and eerie, far-away sounds. She was always glad to start out again so all she would hear were the noises of their own making. There were things that touched her in the dark of night, and she was thankful she couldn't see them. She and Jessamine moved slowly and with utmost care. Jessamine cautioned her not to fall nor to grab at anything, whether it be a vine or the limb of a tree. Every step had to be placed carefully and firmly, before the next could be taken. In the six hours before dawn that they had been traveling, they'd not gone any appreciable distance, but they were safe, and that was all that mattered to Jessamine.

As the day's light filled the sky, Phémie saw a massive green wall behind them, and realized that no one would suspect them of taking this route. With the light, they could move more quickly, but the heat was increasing by the minute. Jessamine signaled for a rest, much to Phémie's relief. The black woman was scarcely affected by her exertions, but Phémie was panting for breath and running with perspiration. They found some shade where it was slightly cooler, and Phémie leaned against the tree, not daring to sit down in the slime under her feet. As she drank from the container Jessamine handed her, slowly and in small amounts as she had been shown, Jessamine again seemed to be listening to the sounds about them, cocking her head first one way and then another. All that Phémie could hear were the buzzing insects and the distant sound of rushing water.

"Are we near a river?" She asked in a whisper, and Jessamine turned a beaming face to her.

"We have come through the night safely."

"Is the plantation close?"

"No, it is two days away, if we move quickly. But we

have found the river, and across the river is the road that leads to the Maître."

"Are we going to the road?" she asked hopefully, but the black shook her head.

"No, that would be unsafe. But the road and the river travel together. As long as we can hear the river we will find the plantation. If we go too far away from it, and become lost in the jungle, we'll never find our way out."

"But what if they come along the road looking for us, as Celeste said? Won't they hear us?"

"We will hear them before they hear us. All we need do is wait until they pass, and then continue our journey."

"What do you think they'll do?"

"I think they will go to the plantation and watch for us. I think that when they don't see us, they will think we escaped to the sea. We will move closer to the river so we may hear them as they pass us. No matter what happens, stay close to the river. If I cannot be with you, the river will be your guide and see you safely to the Maître."

"What do you mean?"

"Only that we have far more enemies in the jungle than pursue us by the road. If the devil snake bites me, I'll die very quickly and you must go on alone." It was the only time Phémie had ever seen the black frightened, and she wished that their ordeal were safely over.

Now that they had found the river, they traveled in easier stages, resting for longer periods and not moving at all during the heat of the day. They took turns sleeping, although sleep was elusive and she was tortured by the thought that she might not awaken. Finally she had grown so exhausted that the thought of death was no longer a torment and she fell into the arms of sleep gratefully. There was an endless supply of food provided by the jungle; Jessamine always chose the familiar fruits and avoided those she had not previously tasted. They were only a short distance from a source of fresh water. Yet death was their constant companion in the form of the huge, flat-headed devil snake. Its brown and gray markings helped it blend into its background so effectively that often she didn't see it until it moved. But no matter how fearful she became, no matter how heavy her legs, no matter how weary, the thought of her enemy gave her the strength and the will to go on.

"Aurélie," she would whisper again and again, like an incantation, and the black added her own prayer to it.

Jessamine was worried about her Maîtresse. The rigors of their escape were taking their toll, and the girl did not look well. Many times she was tempted to risk traveling by the road, but there was unusual activity upon it and they couldn't take the chance of coming upon another party unwarned.

Finally their ordeal was over. They had come to the edge of Outelas's plantation. Hurriedly crossing a small clearing, they plunged into the protection of a sugarcane field. The cane was planted in orderly rows, so that all they had to do was follow a narrow corridor between the tall plants. Phémie began running, stumbling, often falling, to reach, at last, a place of safety—a refuge from the nightmare that had overtaken her and had pitched her into darkness. Now there was hope; just a few more steps, her fever-ridden brain promised; just a few more steps, and Outelas would gather her up into his arms and carry her into the light. When they came to the edge of the field, Phémie could see the wall of the house a short distance away. Jessamine told her to wait in the protective covering of the field while she went for Outelas. When she returned, she found the girl mercifully unconscious.

"I never took you for a coward" were the first words he addressed to her as she joined him after her long sleep. Upon awakening, she'd found herself in Jessamine's cabin, a short distance from the main house. Though puzzled, she'd resisted the temptation to ask the slave what had occurred, and Jessamine told her only that she was to join the Maître for dinner. He didn't rise when she entered the dining room, and he had already started his meal. Phémie ignored the chair being held for her by a slave, instead standing proudly at the end of the table.

"We were both mistaken, it would seem. I always thought you were a gentleman."

"You were a fool to run away." He ignored the barb. "Why didn't you stay and face them?"

She stared at him incredulous, as if she couldn't believe her ears. "Do you know what they had planned for me?"

"It would never have happened. The Governor was waiting at the wharf to rescue you, thereby earning your eternal gratitude."

"In the meantime my papers would have been burnt, my clothes dispersed, and my gold secreted in the coffers of the Church or Aurélie's chest. How, if I may ask, was I to know the Governor would be waiting to save me?"

He disregarded her query, saying only, "You shouldn't have come here."

"Where else was I to go? Who else was my friend, and would be happy to offer me safety?" The sarcasm was biting, but had no apparent effect on him.

"I instructed Jessamine to find you a gown suitable for dining at my table."

His criticism stung, and she fought to retain her dignity.

"I'll not wear another woman's clothing, and I've no intention of sharing your board."

"You have found your courage, I'm happy to see." He didn't sound or look at all happy.

"If I were a man, I'd challenge you."

"It's a pity you aren't, because you certainly don't challenge me as a woman."

It was a cruel blow and struck her with the same impact as if it had been physical. She saw a stranger sitting at the other end of the table, and it was impossible to believe that there had been any warmth between them. She understood that she was as much a stranger to him, and worse, she was an intruder. There was nothing else to say to him.

"If you'll excuse me . . ." She began to leave, but he signaled to a burly slave, who closed the doors, leaning against them. "I haven't excused you, and I won't until the meal is finished. If you don't wish to partake, you may do without, but you'll not leave."

She stayed as she was, standing near the table, her gaze on the floor. Finally she asked, miserably, "Why are you punishing me? What have I done to deserve such cruelty?"

"You have presumed upon my hospitality, dear Duchesse. You have made me break a promise to the only woman I could ever love."

"If you'll give me supplies, I'll leave here in the morning." She overlooked his remark about love, wishing only to be gone.

"I'll think upon it, but for tonight, since you're under my roof, I'll tell you the story you've been after me to tell."

"It's no longer necessary, Monsieur, since our relationship—"

"Don't speak of such things here!" He leaped to his feet, overturning the chair. Grabbing her by the wrist, he spun her around viciously. "Look about you, Your Grace. Do you see the tile floor, the paneled walls, the beamed ceiling, the leaded, colored glass windows, the crystal sconces? Now come, let me show you all the rooms of my house, and then I'll regale you with a story."

Holding her arm in a vise-like grip, he yanked her from one luxurious room to the next, pointing out tapestries, paintings, massive stone fireplaces, exquisite statuary, and the finest of furniture. Upstairs he showed her his own room, strangely resembling a monk's cell, and absurd in its contrast to the luxury surrounding it. There were two children's rooms, a nurse's room between, and a play room. The last room, at the end of a long gallery, was fit for a queen. Everything in it was pink and white. There were huge wardrobes, filled with clothes, and a floor chest overflowing with a treasure in jewelry. The canopied bed was turned down, and the scent of perfume wafted from the fresh bedding. There was even a nightshift of fine lace spread at the bottom, ready for the Maîtresse of the house to retire.

"Remember what you have seen!" he commanded as he

led her downstairs once again. He left her standing in the middle of the drawing room while he made himself comfortable in a chair before the hearth. Despite the heat of the evening, there was a small blaze burning, and she suspected that it was more for effect than actual use.

"I shall now tell you the truth as only one other person ever knew it."

"I don't want to hear it." She pleaded, "Please, let me go."

"I want you to know it, Your Grace. I want you to know that I was born a Huguenot, and was sent to the gallows because of my religion. I spent two years in slavery and finally escaped because the Captain had a kind heart. I sold myself into bondage to come to the colonies and became a hunter of wild cattle. Everything I said about my wife was true. We used to sit together and dream about this house. Everything you see here was planned by her. I never forgot how she wanted her house; and when I built here I made a promise that no other woman would live in her place, whether in this house or in my heart. All these years I've kept my promise to her, until I met you. I used to close my eyes and see her face. I used to be able to hear her laughter in the wind. But you have come between us, Euphémie. It is your face I see and your laughter I hear. Did you know, when I came here I was never going to see you again? I promised her that. But you had to come here, and now I've broken another promise. I must purify myself; I must pray for her forgiveness. I must do everything in my power to rid my life of your influence. You must come to mean nothing to me, and then she'll forgive me."

"I'll go away from here, from St. Pierre, even from Martinique." She felt the cold clutch of fear in the presence of madness.

"She was so warm, so alive. . . ."

"You must stay here and be close to her. If you don't go away from her, she'll know you still care for her. You never loved me, nor I you. I meant no more to you than Celeste.

Surely she'll understand that and not punish you for being only a man."

"She always understood." He looked at her, his voice eager, asking, "Do you believe that her spirit came here, to this house, to be close to me?"

"I have heard of such things. One of the sisters at school was from England, and she told us of spirits that inhabited houses where they had been happy."

"You are kind to comfort me like this, Euphémie. You may go in the morning."

Phémie looked at his face as he stared into the fire, his thoughts far away from her, and she was amazed to see how much older he'd become since she'd last seen him in St. Pierre. It was as though he'd laid aside the last vestiges of his youth and had surrendered to age. He was still lost in the fire as she quietly slipped from the house.

When Phémie returned to the slave's cabin, she told Jessamine everything that had passed between her and Outelas. All during the telling, Jessamine sat unmoving, with the peculiar stillness that only she could affect. At the end, she commented sadly, "I had hoped that you could bring him back to life, but her hold on him is too strong."

"You've known all the time about his wife?"

"I have seen her in the house."

At this Phémie crossed herself, her eyes wide with fear.

"Why didn't you tell me?"

"Did you have the eyes to see him tonight? Did you see how he has aged since being away from you? He has seen more than fifty years, and you brought him youth and life. Now he will live with the dead."

"I'm afraid of her, Jessamine. Perhaps if I really loved him, I would fight her for him."

"No, she has already won. She is my Maîtresse now."

"Jessamine"—she lowered her voice to a whisper—"you needn't stay here. Why don't you come away with me? I'll buy your freedom for any price he asks." The black regarded her with affection, reaching out and touching her.

"You are a good woman, and mean well, but it is not possible."

"Why isn't it? Won't he let you go?"

"He gave me my freedom many years ago. I stay with him because his need is great."

"I need you, too," she argued, but Jessamine shook her head.

"No, you are strong. You feel weakness now, but that is only because you are alone. You will find your strength again."

"But I need help now!"

"Have Monsieur Espalion help you. He is your friend."

"Gaspard? Do you think it's wise? Won't it prove that Aurélie was right, after all?"

"No one need know. His plantation is but a short distance from here. Call on him before you continue to St. Pierre. It will do no harm."

21

If Phémie had had any fears about her reception at the Espalion plantation, they were put to rout by Gaspard and the senior Espalions. Gaspard blamed himself for Phémie's misfortune, despite her absolving him of any fault; thus he was grateful for any chance to be of assistance. They had heard of the disaster that had befallen her, and warned her against returning to St. Pierre. So it was agreed that while she proceeded to Fort Royal without delay, the Espalions would arrange with the agent to sell her house and would have the funds transferred to her bank in Paris. In the meantime, she had enough gold to see her comfortably home. And so they parted—Phémie to Fort Royal and Gaspard to St. Pierre, to meet once again on the "Good Sea," the ship that would take them to France.

Phémie didn't want to return to France; the King and his plans for her were a very real danger. Yet she had nowhere else to go. With a healthy bribe, she would be put off before the ship reached port, thereby avoiding the officials who examined the papers of travelers. Louis would never suspect that she was back in France, especially since Gaspard's letter would suggest she was still in the colony. There was no other alternative open to her, and she was too weary to start running again. She would be unable to use her own name and had cautioned Gaspard to pretend that they were strangers. There was no reason to jeopardize his own position. How different was her journey to Fort Royal! The road over the mountains was wide and deeply rutted by the carts bearing the products of the many plantations in the area. The party moved swiftly, and Phémie found herself feeling lighter with each step away from the scene of tumultuous happenings. She had arrived on Martinique with few hopes, and now, as she left, with St. Pierre retreating into the past, she had none.

The party moved through Fort Royal shortly before dawn. The blacks found a fisherman who would be willing to take her to the ship she was seeking, and, without farewell, started back to the plantation. The "Good Sea" was riding at anchor in the bay. Hailing the Captain, who had to be roused from his bed by the watch, she asked if he had room for another passenger. Since Gaspard Espalion was his only passenger, and not a well-paying one at that, he welcomed her aboard. Once in his cabin, she explained that she'd lost all her clothes and papers in a fire, and he accepted her tale, whether in sympathy for her or for the gold she was willing to pay for the main cabin didn't matter to her. The Captain knew by her speech that she was of the nobility, and sensed that there would be more gold coming his way when they neared France.

The cabin on the "Good Sea" was far different from the luxury of the "Elisa." There was a narrow bunk instead of a wide bed. There were no books or casks of wine, or comfortable chairs and a table. It was, however, clean, and there were cushions on the ledge under the windows, so she was content. As she closed the door behind her, safe in the dim cabin, she knew that once again the sea had offered her a refuge when all else had failed. It was like being home again.

By the time Espalion came aboard, Phémie was well rested and impatient to be going. The Captain introduced his passengers to each other, and was relieved to see that they responded with courtesy and friendliness, despite the gentleman's obvious surprise at seeing a lady in trousers. When the Captain left them exchanging pleasantries to get the "Good Sea" underway, Phémie waited until she was certain he was out of hearing before asking, "Did all go well?"

"Yes. Alair has agreed to buy the house. He will give you less than you paid for it, and charge twice his usual fee, of course, but at least you are rid of it. When we reach Paris . . ."

"My plans don't include Paris. I'm going to get off before we reach port. I'm certain the Captain will be very amenable to a bribe. If you're questioned concerning me, say only that we met in St. Pierre, where I gave you the letter. It is important to me that certain people think I am still there."

"I will do as you ask, have no fear on that count."

"You're a good fellow, Gaspard. Now tell me, what has happened in St. Pierre? Are they still searching for me?"

"Only the Governor. Despite Outelas's denial, everyone believes that he has you hidden at his plantation. He's never allowed anyone into his house, but his refusal this time has become very sinister, and they're certain it's because you are within."

"And Aurélie? I was unable to keep my promise to her."

"I heard about the dagger and the note. It has a great many of the ladies ill at ease. As for my wife, she betrayed herself. When they found your clothing ruined, Aurélie went mad, running through the house, calling your name. She searched every cabinet, every drawer, between the mattresses on your bed."

"Looking for me, undoubtedly," she commented grimly, and he laughed shortly.

"Many of those present became suspicious that her cry

for revenge was not very noble or pure. The whole town is in a state of confusion. I was questioned by the priest when I went to confess before embarking upon this journey, and I assured him that you had shown kindness to me out of friendship for my wife. I believe he realizes that his role was not very priest-like, so it was not difficult to convince him that there was nothing personal between us. As I was leaving, he hinted that the Church would be willing to give you sanctuary until the matter was explained to everyone's satisfaction. I suppose he expected me to send you his message."

"There were times in my struggle to reach Outelas that death was as close to me as you are now. Yet I would rather take sanctuary in a nest of devil snakes than expose myself to the mercy of those people."

"I've lived with them for most of my life. They aren't really bad people—just bored and easily led."

"God save me from becoming so bored that I'd raise a hue and cry against someone simply for entertainment."

"If it were in your power, what would you have befall Aurélie?"

She was thoughtful for a moment, and the expression on her face was not pleasant.

"I'm not an unjust person, Gaspard. All I would ask is that she take a journey similar to mine; that she be routed out of her home in the dead of night and forced to march through the jungle for days, not being able to sleep except for brief snatches while standing, putting her hand out to balance herself on the limb of a tree and seeing the black, glittering eyes of the devil snake about to strike. Then, having survived the nightmare, reaching the place where she had hoped for safety, the refuge from all the dangers that had pursued her, to have the door closed in her face, to be more alone than ever before."

"Is that what happened with Outelas? Was he truly so heartless?"

"It wasn't that he was heartless; it was simply that he had no heart left for me."

"I can't believe that. I saw the way he watched you. Never have I seen a man more in love."

"I think you exaggerate, but that's not important. All I can say is that he's fallen in love with his wife again, and there wasn't room enough for both of us."

"I didn't know he's married. Does Madame Outelas live at the plantation?"

"Inhabit would be a better word, I think, and indeed she does that."

She certainly had a strange way with words, he thought, but didn't question her about it. Instead, he asked, "What are you going to do now?"

"My most immediate plan is to have the sailmaker fashion me a few shirts and trousers. He's very clever with a needle and thread, they tell me, and I could certainly do with a fresh change of clothes."

"I have more than enough clothes with me. Perhaps he could cut down some to fit you. Or better yet, there's a cloak or two he could make into a gown . . ."

"Spare me that!" she laughed, then softened her tone. "You're very kind to offer, but I prefer the simple sailor's garb. Far more practical for shipboard than satins and velvets."

"I suspect you're quite happy to be leaving Martinique, though you certainly can't be blamed for that, and looking forward to returning to your home."

"You're mistaken, Gaspard. I am relieved to be leaving your island, it is true, but I dread returning to France. My only happiness is to be at sea once more. I would be content to sail all the seas of the world and never touch land again. It would be difficult to surrender that kind of freedom simply for the company of one's own kind. You know, my friend"—she leaned on the railing, watching the water below—"ever since I can remember, I've wondered who my own kind are. Do you suppose I'll ever find out?"

It was not a question that could be answered, certainly not by him, and he looked at her closely while her attention was elsewhere. She resembled any other woman, though her beauty was different from any he had ever seen, and he simply did not understand her. It was not his place, however, to understand the nobility, he admitted to himself. For some reason, the Duchesse had taken the effort to be kind to him, and one no more questioned the favors of an aristocrat than one would the favors of God. One could only thank the benefactor, whether Divine or human, and use the gift to full advantage. It was his prayer that he would be permitted to do just that. She was so absorbed in her own thoughts that she didn't even notice him leave her side.

"Monsieur Espalion . . ."

He heard his name being called as if from a great distance. In the next moment a hand was laid upon his shoulder and rudely shook him.

"What is it?" He sat up, eyeing unkindly the sailor who had dared awaken him in such a manner.

"The Captain requests your presence on deck, Monsieur." He repeated the polite form awkwardly, his expression filled with fear. Gaspard's resentment faded, and he pulled a robe over his nightshirt.

"Is there trouble, boy?"

"We've been boarded by pirates. They came on us just after dawn, and there was no way to escape them."

"My God, we're only two days out of Fort Royal! He's a bold one, whoever he is. Did you wake Her Grace?"

"Pardon, Monsieur?" The fellow looked at him blankly.

"I mean the lady, Madame Lapalisse."

He counted himself fortunate that the slip was made in front of an unlearned seaman and not the Captain. It showed him that he had best keep better watch over his tongue.

"No, Monsieur. The Captain asked only for you."

"Excellent! There's no need to concern the lady. I'm certain we can do everything that's required. Tell me," he said as he put his arm companionably about the young man's shoulder, "don't pirates usually board a ship with the discharging of pistols and a great deal of shouting?"

"That's what I've heard, Monsieur."

"Perhaps they used stealth so as not to awaken the company. They must have known that only the watch would be about at this ungodly time."

"Aren't you afraid, Monsieur?" he asked, standing aside so the gentleman could pass through the door ahead of him.

"I don't think there's anything to fear. If they wanted to harm us, we'd all be dead in our bunks by now. I am acquainted with several numbers of the Brotherhood. If our pirates are French, we have little to worry about."

"I pray that you're right, Monsieur," the seaman mumbled, not at all reassured, as he followed the other out onto deck.

In the growing morning light, Espalion spied the Captain in earnest conversation with a familiar figure. Without hesitation he approached the two, saying irritably, "Jacques, this is really too bad of you." The pirate looked up, his expression changing noticeably.

"Gaspard!" The pirate was taken aback by his presence. "I had no idea you were on board. Accept my apology, I beg of you."

"There's no need of an apology. How could you have known?"

"So you're finally on your way to France after all these years. I'm pleased for you, but sorry for myself; now I'll have to bargain with that fool of a Governor. Tell me, how did you leave Her Grace?" He asked the question that had occurred to him from the beginning.

Espalion realized that he was on dangerous ground with the Captain overhearing everything spoken between them, and chose his words carefully.

"It's because of her kindness that I'm here. She gave me a letter of introduction and has lent me the use of her house in Paris until I can find quarters at Versailles."

The pirate laughed, clapping him on the back.

"Ah, that's what comes from having a wife with powerful friends. I imagine Aurélie is excited beyond containment.

Where is she? Still abed, I would imagine, even with the ship in pirates' hands."

"No, I left her in St. Pierre . . . until I am settled . . . then she will join me." He lied awkwardly, but Jacques paid him only half a mind.

"Are you the only passenger, then?"

"No, there is one other. A Madame Lapalisse."

"Lapalisse?" He repeated the name, his forehead furrowing with thought as he tried to remember. "I thought I knew everyone in St. Pierre."

"She was visiting her aunt, old Felleson's wife." He lied desperately, and Jacques noticed his distress and frantic side glances at the Captain.

"Of course, old Felleson," he agreed, realizing that no one of that name existed in their circle of friends.

"Don't misunderstand, my dear Jacques, it's a delight to see you anytime, but a bit uncomfortable under these conditions. Why have you stopped the 'Good Sea'? Her only cargo is sugar and tobacco."

"I thought perhaps the Captain would be willing to make a donation. But since you're his guest, he may keep his gold."

The Captain saluted the pirate in gratitude and left the two friends alone.

"Now, what of this Madame Lapalisse of yours?"

"She's not mine, Jacques."

"Whatever you say, old friend." He humored him, winking rakishly. "Who is she?"

"Euphémie d'Amberieu!" he whispered to the pirate, whose expression betrayed his emotion at the news. Gaspard continued, "I'm sorry, Jacques. Aurélie told me how you felt about her. It must be terrible for you, seeing her slipping away from you."

"Why is she leaving so soon? What of Outelas?"

"That's over and done with, the fool. Let me tell you the whole story."

He did so, quickly and concisely, and Bordeaux's face become dark with anger. At the end of it, he commented, "If

Aurélie weren't your wife, Gaspard, I'd gladly wring her neck. And the others! How could they be so blind? But more than any of them, what possessed Outelas to act so falsely?"

"It's all over, Jacques. She refuses to talk about it. I wish I could understand her. She's anxious to leave Martinique."

"With good reason!" Bordeaux interjected humorlessly.

"But I feel she doesn't wish to return to France. Her use of another name, her bribing the Captain to keep even that name out of his log, and her desire to be put on the French coast before we reached port in order to avoid the official inspection of her papers . . . If I didn't know better, I would say she's afraid."

"From what you say, it's fairly obvious that she's frightened of something or someone."

"That may be true, but she's no coward." He defended her heatedly, and Jacques soothed him. "Fear is not the proof of cowardice; only a fool knows no fear. I think I'll offer my greetings."

"Don't frighten her, Jacques," Gaspard pleaded, and the pirate laughed. "I'm far more afraid of her than she is of me."

When he knocked gently on the door, he heard her clear voice telling him to come in. Entering, he saw her sitting on the window seat, looking at him over her shoulder.

"Oh, it's my poetic pirate! Good morning, Captain Bordeaux."

"Your Grace!" He swept her a bow before approaching her. "You don't seem surprised to see me."

"But I am. I knew we had visitors on board because I've been sitting here watching the ship without a flag ever since we were hailed. She looks very fast."

"She needs to be fast."

"So I should imagine."

It was unreal to him, the two of them exchanging pleasantries as if he had just dropped in for a visit. She hadn't evidenced any relief when she'd learned that it was an acquaintance who'd interrupted her journey, and he doubted if she would have shown any dismay if he had been a pirate on earnest business.

"Gaspard told me of your misadventures in St. Pierre."

She laughed at his description of the disaster that had befallen her.

"I have learned not to cast myself upon the tender mercy of others," she said lightly enough, but even in the dim light of the cabin, he could see the pained expression in her eyes.

"You've not been treated kindly. I suppose it will be a relief to return to your home in France." He threw this out casually enough and saw the expression change to something akin to fear. No, it wasn't fear; it was more the expression of a hunted creature when it hears the pursuers.

"There is nowhere else I can go," she said softly, as if accepting her fate, and he was quick to disagree.

"That is not so. There are other islands that belong to France. They don't contain the amenities that St. Pierre offers, but you could find a place of respite, a place where you could gather your strength again before continuing on."

"I can do well enough without the 'amenities' of St. Pierre. What makes you think"—she watched him closely, almost with suspicion—"Captain Bordeaux, that I couldn't find such a place in France?"

"I have eyes to see, Your Grace. You're not overly anxious to return to our homeland."

Her eyes gleamed with mischief as she commented drily, "And you know just the place where I could rest, and gather my strength, as you say?"

"Yes, I do know of such a place."

"I suppose Gaspard told you of what happened to me in St. Pierre."

"He told me all he knew of it. I can't understand why Outelas refused you shelter."

"He discovered that he was in love with his wife."

"His wife is dead," Bordeaux said shortly, and Phémie shook her head. "You would have difficulty in convincing him of that."

"He's gone mad, then."

"Mad or no, I trusted him. What makes you think I would be willing to trust you?"

"You trusted him because he was your—" He pulled up short, realizing that he'd overstepped his bounds.

"Don't be afraid to speak the truth, Captain. It is as you say; I trusted him because he was my lover. If one cannot trust one's lover, whom can one trust?"

"One who has nothing to gain from being of assistance. I pride myself on being an honorable man, Your Grace. I'll not deny that I find you a beautiful woman, but then you know that. You know exactly how I feel about you, but I've never forced a woman to my will."

She scrutinized him closely for a long time, and he returned her gaze unflinchingly. Finally she said, dropping her bantering tone, "It's true, what you say. I dread returning to France. The danger that awaits me is great, and I'm without friends to aid me. But how can you expect me to trust you? I know what is ahead of me in France, and will do everything I can to avoid it. But with you I would face the unknown. I don't know you, Jacques Bordeaux, and without knowing you, I cannot bring myself to place any trust in you."

"You knew Outelas, and look what happened. It doesn't matter how long you know a person, Euphémie, but how you look at him. If you look at him through the eyes of love, your judgment is impaired beyond hope. Look at me through the eyes of reason."

"You shouldn't have said that!" She laughed lightly, gaily, for the first time since the nightmare began. "What kind of reason would I possess if I placed myself in the hands of a pirate? A man I scarcely know?"

"Ask Gaspard Espalion if I'm worthy of a personal trust. We have been friends for many years now, and he knows I've never betrayed anyone. Or do you feel Gaspard is unworthy of your trust?"

"Hardly that," she commented cryptically, then asked, "What is this place you would have me go?"

"It is a small island called Désirade. There is a house on a lagoon, hidden from the sea. You would find peace, and time to think; to make a plan instead of just running back into danger."

"It's madness," she whispered, deep in thought, and he saw that she was actually considering it. Wisely he kept quiet, knowing that if he said anything more it would damage his cause. He could almost see the arguments chasing across her mind, and she seemed to be wavering for a moment. But then she found a new thought, and she became firm in her resolve.

"I think not, Captain, although it was kind of you to offer. I will have an ally in France. Gaspard will be my eyes and my ears in the camp of the enemy."

"I can't let you go, Euphémie. Don't you see, it was meant that I caught this ship before you escaped me forever."

"Nonsense!" she scoffed unkindly. "It is pure chance that you're here. I recall you saying that you've never forced a woman against her will."

"And I won't, in that way. You know full well what I meant."

"Then why do you want me to go with you? Now that Outelas no longer occupies a place in my life, do you hope to fill that place?"

"No, it's for your own good. Have you seen your face? You have the look of some pitiful wild creature almost run to earth. Give me the seventy-five days it would take this ship to reach France. If you're not content, I'll put you aboard another ship without protest."

"I don't mean to sound so cruel, Captain, but you would be the last man I'd trust."

"Why am I so different from Outelas? We share the same profession . . ."

"Please, spare me your comparisons. It is simply the way I feel. I can't explain it any other way." He watched her closely as he took another tack.

"You want to come with me, but you daren't," he said, as if inspired. "What do you want me to do? Abduct you so your honor won't be tarnished?"

She almost laughed, it was so ridiculous.

"What is it about this place? There must be something here that causes madness wherever I turn. Aurélie, Outelas, and now you."

There was nothing more he could do. She had stripped away his masks one by one, and there remained only himself. He resorted to the only argument he was familiar with.

"You're going to come with me, Euphémie, or the lives of this crew will be on your soul."

"Oh, stop! You're acting the fool again."

"I'm not jesting, believe me. If you don't willingly accompany me, I'll sink this ship."

Something in his manner told her that he was perfectly serious, and she became frightened.

"You can't do that; I couldn't have been that mistaken about you."

"I've tried it your way; I came bowing and humble, my hat in hand, for the privilege of a few moments in your company. I've never done that before, and no one will ever know how difficult it was for me. But for all that, I've earned your scorn and disgust for my pains. Now that we're in my waters, we'll play by my rules."

There was something very wrong, she realized. His eyes were no longer filled with admiration and kindness. They had become bold and determined; he was changing from one man to another before her eyes, and she felt stunned at the transformation.

"By what right . . ." She almost choked on the words, so great was her dismay.

"By right of conquest, my lady." He addressed her possessively, so certain was he of his success. "No longer the fool's role for me. It's little wonder you hold me in such contempt. But no more!" He approached her confidently, grasping her by the wrists and pulling her to her feet. "Do you know what the Spanish call me?"

She shook her head numbly, powerless to escape his grasp.

"The Savage! If you don't do as I tell you, I'll show you how I earned the name."

"You were so kind before. I thought you meant all those things you said." When he didn't reply, she asked, "What do you want of me?"

"Obedience," he answered simply, and she retorted, "In exchange for what?"

"Your freedom."

"When you're finished with me?" she asked defiantly, and he answered her in all seriousness, "Exactly! Now that you understand me, what is your answer?"

"What answer could I have? If I go with you willingly, the 'Good Sea' continues unharmed. If I refuse, you carry me away protesting and sink this ship. Either way, you get what you want. My pride is not worth all these lives. I'll do as you wish."

"You're being very sensible. Where are your clothes?"

"I have only what I wear, except for my sword and dagger. May I bring them along?"

"Only if you'll promise not to use them on me," he said half in jest, but she didn't see the humor of it.

"What of Gaspard?"

"I suggest you explain to him that you wish to return to St. Pierre and face your accusers. Say that you don't wish to have such ugly accusations following you for the remainder of your life."

"That's very clever of you," she interrupted. "It is just the sort of thing he would believe, and approve of. Of course, I'll tell him that you've kindly offered to take me back, and that I'll follow him to France as soon as my name is pure again."

"And in that way we'll avoid any foolish heroics on Gaspard's part. Do you agree with the plan?"

"It will be done as you 'suggest.' I'll have to write a letter to my housekeeper, with your permission, of course."

"Write your letter, but you'll forgive me if I read it before you pass it on the Gaspard."

"I have no paper or ink . . ."

"I'm certain the Captain does. I'll return with it in a moment."

While he was gone, she quickly retrieved her papers and bag of gold from under the mattress, secreting them securely on her person. Upon his return she'd just managed to complete her task. When the letter was finished, and he'd read the harmless list of instructions regarding her estates, he escorted her out onto the deck. With the whole crew as an audience, she found it easier to dissemble before Espalion. He thought her action in keeping with his image of her and applauded her courage. He was certain she would find the attitude toward her changed drastically, and assured her that the matter would be expedited so quickly that she'd be on the next available ship to France. She requested that he carry out their former plan, to place himself in the capable hands of Madame Matilde, and to deliver her letter. With a brief farewell, she climbed over the side and down the rope ladder into the waiting longboat, the pirate following close behind.

Despite her feeling of desolation, she did take some notice of her surroundings as they boarded the pirate vessel. There was only one cabin left standing, and the railings were raised breast-high. It was quite a bit smaller than the ships she'd traveled on, but was much less ponderous. The men she managed to catch sight of before he deposited her in the cabin, while he issued orders for their sailing, looked no different from the crewmen on a merchant ship. The cabin was not unlike the one she'd just left, with the exception of a few more pieces of furniture. There was a wide table covered with charts and a wooden, unupholstered chair. There was a chest at the end of the bunk containing nothing more interesting than his clothing, most of which, it would seem, was left where he had discarded it. There was a row of crudely built cabinets lining two walls, and she inspected these, as well. Here she met with more luck, finding some bottles of wine and a goblet. There were no cushions on the ledge beneath the windows, but she found that the more wine she drank, the less uncomfortable she was as she watched the "Good Sea" retreating into the vast blueness of the sea. By the time he returned, knocking and waiting a moment before entering the cabin, she felt prepared to face him.

"Well, Captain, has it been decided?" she demanded brusquely, her voice laden with wine.

"Pardon, Your Grace." He was puzzled until he saw the bottle and goblet on the ledge beside her. "I'm a poor host, it would seem."

"It would, indeed."

"I'm glad you felt comfortable enough to help yourself."

"There are places where, if one does not help oneself, one is not helped at all."

She didn't seem disposed to say anything further, so he asked, "Has what been decided?"

She had been waiting for the query, and replied calmly enough, "Am I yours or do you have to share me with your crew?"

"My God!" He was taken completely off balance. "Do you really believe—"

"Spare yourself and don't ask what I believe. It wouldn't be very pleasant for you."

"You don't belong to anyone, Your Grace." He was fighting to keep his patience. "If I let the men think that you are my woman, it's for your own protection."

"I feel only a little better on that point, but have no other choice than to take you at your word. I think I would like to sleep now." She rose unsteadily to her feet, taking his arm for support, and he led her to the bunk. "I've had too much wine." She stated the obvious as she lay down. "It was either that or jumping out of the window." Her voice became more sluggish as she turned over, cradling her head in the crook of her arm. "I do hope I've done the right thing."

As he covered her with a light blanket, she was already asleep.

When she awoke, night had fallen. The lamp hanging from the ceiling over the desk swayed slightly, and in its dim light she found the convenience and relieved herself before stumbling back to the bunk and sinking into oblivion. She slept soundly until the heat in the cabin awoke her at mid-morning. As she sat up, the cabin spun, and she lay back again, the wave of dizziness passing. When her stomach was reasonably settled, she tried again, getting to her feet successfully. The cabin was entirely different from when she had first seen it. The table was cleared, and decorated with a crudely painted pottery bowl filled with vegetables. The scattered clothing had been removed, and there was a narrow mattress on the ledge beneath the windows. Above all, the convenience was rigged in the corner, screened from the rest of the cabin by blankets so she would have privacy while answering her calls of nature. Unwillingly, her resentment faded, and she found herself actually thinking of her captor with kindness. On the sideboard, hastily constructed, was the goblet and a bottle of what proved to be a very satisfying fruit punch. She had a deep thirst after her indulgence of the day before and finished the entire bottle. Her next concern was relief from the heat and a light meal, so, taking a deep breath, and her courage in hand, she opened the door and stepped outside. The bright sunlight blinded her, and she had to cover her eyes with a hand for a few moments. When she removed it, Bordeaux was beside her, and she felt infinitely reassured, smiling up at him weakly.

"How do you feel?"

"Absolutely terrible! I've never had a white wine like that."

"It wasn't wine, but rum. Ladies usually drink it in a fruit punch."

"I'll wager they don't remain ladies, no matter how they take it."

"Are you hungry?"

"What do you have to offer?"

"Nothing you're accustomed to," he warned laughingly, leading her over to the mast where several men were sitting. It was here, he explained, that they did their cooking. He showed her the low-sided box of sand where the cookfire had been kindled. The meat that had been cured and salted on land was stewed until it was soft and ready to drop apart, at which time it was poured into wooden pannikins and eaten with the fingers. She confessed that she wasn't ready for such a heavy meal, so he promised her something that wouldn't do violence to her stomach. When they returned to the cabin, he found a large wooden bowl and rubbed it with garlic. Then he chopped up raw herbs, palm hearts, a little of the dried meat, and cooked eggs. To this he added oil, salt, and the juice of a sour fruit. Despite having to eat with her fingers, she found the dish excellent. She could wish only for some bread to soak up the liquid mixture, but otherwise it was perfect. When she was finished, she washed her hands in a bucket of salt water, then felt ready to talk about her situation.

"What are your plans for me, Captain?" She was comfortable on the window seat, and he sat on the chair opposite, ready for her questions.

"I'll take you to my house on Désirade, as I promised. It's very quiet there, and you'll regain your strength."

"Where will you be?" Her question had an edge, and he hoped to reassure her as he replied, "After I see to your comfort, I'll be away for a time. I must go to Habana . . ."

"That sounds Spanish."

"It is. The plate fleet will be leaving from there in the spring. I'm going to try to discover when."

"Isn't it dangerous for a Frenchman to go into a Spanish port?"

"Only if they find out he's a Frenchman. I speak their language as well as they do and look far more Spanish than French."

"Have you tried such a masquerade before? Has anyone you know gone into a Spanish city on such an errand?"

"Yes, it's been tried by others," he answered carefully, and she was quick to say, "But not successfully, I'll wager."

"I have a plan that removes all danger from my visit. It will be as safe as walking through St. Pierre."

"Isn't there a chance you'll be recognized? Didn't you say

that they've called you The Savage? What will be your fate if you're captured? Have you thought of that?"

"I refuse to discuss it any longer with you. I won't have you so concerned about my welfare that I begin to worry as well."

"Forgive me for sounding so heartless, but my main concern is for myself. If you don't return safely from this place, what will become of me? Will I become the property of the man who replaces you as Captain? Am I to spend the rest of my life being passed from one pirate to the next until I'm so old no one wants me?"

"I'll return for you, Euphémie," he said simply, and she shook her head, not hearing him. "Am I to die by my own hand? You can't just leave me somewhere without a friend or a means of escape. It was wrong of you to take me off the 'Good Sea.' I must sound like a terrible coward."

"No, you're a very brave girl." He was filled with tenderness. "It's my fault; I just hadn't thought how you'd feel. I'll see that you're protected while I'm gone and put on a ship to France if I don't return."

"Not all men share your honor, Jacques, even if they enjoy your friendship."

It was the first time she'd called him by his given name, and he was warmed by it. "You must trust me."

"So we've come back to that." She sounded disheartened; then, as she continued, she became angry. "I've not had a choice until now. When you took me off the 'Good Sea,' you became responsible for my safety. I'm going to hold you to that, not some stranger you appoint in your place. You, Jacques Bordeaux! No one else." Her expression was fierce as she gazed steadily at him. "If you're not willing to accept those terms, you'd best turn this ship about and overtake the 'Good Sea.' What's it to be?"

"You're without mercy, Euphémie," he said softly, his eyes glowing with admiration. "I wonder which of us is truly the captive."

"You needn't say those things to me any more. You no longer have to win me."

"I mean what I say." He reached out to her, and, without thinking, she put her hand in his. "You tempt me to put aside my dreams of the plate fleet."

"Is it so very important? Do you desire the wealth so desperately?"

"It's important, yes; but not in the way you think."

"In which way, then?"

When he didn't answer, she suddenly understood, and answered for him, "It's the adventure, isn't it?"

"Partly, yes."

"I can understand that. If I were a man . . ." She shrugged, disheartened.

"I would not have you a man, Euphémie." His smile was gentle, but she commented with her usual honesty, "No more than I would have you a woman, I suppose."

"Yet I don't wear a gown and carry a mirror and rouge pot wherever I go."

Although she made no comment, he felt the gulf between them widen. "I meant no criticism."

"Didn't you?" she challenged, and he was thoughtful for a moment before replying, "I must have, or I wouldn't have said it, would I?" At this they both laughed, and Phémie relaxed once again.

"You're not offended by plain speaking, are you?" he asked carefully, afraid of driving her away again.

"As long as it's not against me, I'm not," she teased, and he laughed appreciatively.

"Do you know, some of the most enjoyable moments of my life have been spent in your company."

"That's very kind of you to think so, and I'm sorry to disappoint you."

"You've not disappointed me—" he began his denial, but she interjected firmly, "but I have. I know what it is to believe someone is just as you'd like him to be, and then discover he's something else altogether. We seem to see people through our own eyes, and not according to their lights. When they are themselves, it's little wonder we're disappointed."

"Outelas has hurt you, hasn't he?"

"You've not been listening to me. I'll admit I was hurt, but it was my own fault. I was warned that he was dangerous. Even if I hadn't been alone and friendless, I think I still would have trusted him. I believed him possessed of certain qualities because I wanted to believe, not because he actually possessed them. When we first met on the 'Good Sea,' I told you I would never trust a man again. That's not true. I'll never trust my opinion of a man again."

"That will avail you nothing. If a man wants to impress you, or win you over, he'll be anything you want him to be. I went about it the wrong way. Rather than waiting to meet you, to see what kind of woman you were, I listened to Aurélie. If I had been right in taking her advice, you'd have accepted me as a 'poetic pirate' with good grace. And I wouldn't be starting off at such a disadvantage now. Don't you agree?"

"If you are correct, when can a person trust another?"

"Never! You can trust a man only to be a man. No one ever remains the same, even if he is as honest with you as you are with him. Anyone is capable of treachery if the reason is important enough."

"Then why do people bother to impress others?"

"Because they all want to be thought of as fine fellows. Tell me, if Outelas should regain his senses and regret what he has done to you, would you return to him?"

"Never!"

"You're not quick to forgive a weakness, are you?"

"It's not very Christian of me, is it?"

"You are doomed to disappointment. Were you very much in love with him?"

"I didn't love him at all."

"There must have been something between you," he protested, and she commented calmly, "There was. He understood that he couldn't possess me. We didn't expect anything from each other."

"Until the end, when you went to his plantation?"

"With all the hounds of hell pursuing me, where else

could I have gone? I went there, not as a woman, but as someone sorely pressed by her enemies. If it weren't for Jessamine taking me into her cabin, I would have lain in the field without any aid. And when I awoke, I was told I could have a meal with him. Tell me, Jacques, would you have treated a friend like that, let alone a lover?"

"I am not mad, as Outelas must be."

"So you defend him yet. Why is that?"

"I have no answer for you."

"I don't believe it. Is this an example of the honor you were speaking of to Aurélie? It's no longer necessary to waste such a virtue on Outelas. He is not my lover."

"Honor is never a waste. But it's true. I promised myself that I would not touch you as long as you belonged to him. I had to know how you felt about him. I had to know whether you were merely angry, or whether you really didn't care for him. I still don't know, Euphémie."

"And what am I to answer to that?" She laughed harshly. "Should I use your honor to my advantage and tell you I still care for him? Or should I tell the truth at the risk of being ravished by you? You want the truth? I'll tell you the truth, the real truth. There's not a man alive strong enough to possess me. It will be by my desire whether a man makes love to me or no, not his."

"Perhaps it is not strength that you are looking for, Euphémie. Perhaps it is gentleness, and that is, indeed, a rare virtue among men."

"I have saddened you with this nonsense. Here we sit like a couple of graybeards in search of the secret of Truth."

"A goddess who is as elusive as you and who also refuses to be possessed."

"I think you are correct, Jacques. The truth is not to be possessed. Let us leave it at that. I am weary of all this talk about such serious things. Tell me some more of your adventures. If you tell it well, I might decide to become a pirate and join your crew."

"What reason do you have for hating the Spanish? For that is the first quality needed to become a member of the Brotherhood."

"I would not have to look very far for a reason, although hate is such a strong word."

"As is love?"

"Perhaps you have found the answer to your question! Both love and hate are strangers to me. I think that you would find love as stifling as I would. Tell me truly, do you want me to love you?"

"I would never ask that of you or of any woman. A man like me has to be free of that sort of thing when he goes into battle."

"Why is that?"

"Only because a man like me needs a woman, but cannot be needed as a woman needs a man."

"So you want a woman's body, but not her love."

"I think I said it more graciously," he baited her, and she laughed.

"My apologies for being so ungracious."

"I presume you don't approve of such an arrangement."

"Why ever not? Life would be so much simpler and more pleasant that way. You would enjoy life at court with your attitude."

"You don't approve, then?"

"Of course not. The relationship between a man and a woman should be based on something more than physical pleasure. I think two people should be able to enter into an affair of the heart because of common interests and respect—perhaps even the love of romance. But neither of them should have any hopes of being together forever. And when it's over, let it end as it began, in joy rather than in ugliness. They should make love, and part without sadness or bitterness." It was as though she was reading him a lesson, and sounding very superior about it. He couldn't resist saying, "That sounds very reasonable. I accept!"

"Oh, you fool!" She laughed, regarding him with impatient amusement. "It is reasonable, and it would save people a great deal of pain."

"There would be one difficulty in your eminently sensible plan. What if one is ready to end it before the other?"

"Their relationship would have been such that the one could approach the other and tell of the disenchantment. The other would understand, and allow the separation."

"But what if the other didn't want to end it? What if it was still good for the other, and the other had hopes of making it good for the other?" He was deliberately speaking nonsense, but she was so caught up in her ideal plan that she was unaware of his ridicule.

"Then she—it's usually the woman who holds on so desperately, isn't it?—is hoping for forever and has broken one of the rules. On that occasion, she has brought the pain upon herself and doesn't deserve consideration." Her interjection was heavy with sarcasm, and his tone matched hers.

"Did you learn all that at court?"

"No," she answered proudly, "I never thought about such things until I came to St. Pierre. Actually, my relationship with Auguste was my inspiration. I thought it was perfect. Neither of us made any demands on the other. If Aurélie had not gone mad, we would have parted good friends with no sadness."

"Or bitterness," he supplied impatiently. "You talk about your private affair very publicly, as if you were discussing the mating of a prize stud to a brood mare."

"Oh, no!" she objected heatedly. "That is your preference; a woman, any woman, who will give you pleasure but not love."

"You misunderstand me, deliberately I suspect. Be that as it may, your ideal sounds as romantic as two merchants arranging the trade of a bolt of cloth for a bag of flour. Each looking for the best bargain but remaining very polite about the whole thing."

She couldn't decide whether to be insulted by the disparagement of her philosophy or entertained by the image he painted. Before she could make up her mind, he added,

"By your own words, you've admitted that we would be very well-matched in an affair."

"How can you say that?" She was interested in his reasoning.

"I would make no demands on you. I hold you in the highest esteem. And I would certainly never hope for forever, as a man in my profession has no forever. What else is required?"

She gave his suggestion her earnest consideration, finally saying, "Nothing! According to the things I've been saying, you would be perfect, if I were seeking such a relationship at this time. But Outelas was my first affair, and it's only just over. I can't allow myself to become wanton. If I were to bed with you so quickly, the next man would have an even easier time, until I would become like those women at court. Can you understand?"

"But of course! You're not averse to taking me as a lover on my own merits, but your sense of timing won't permit it."

"I'm so glad you understand."

"You would be amazed at how much I understand about you, Your Grace." His whole demeanor changed; no longer did he regard her with kindly amusement. Leaning forward, resting his elbows on his knees, he asked, "Tell me, how much time must pass before you permit us to become lovers? How much time to soothe your sense of outraged virtue and prevent you from being overwhelmed with a feeling of wantonness?"

"Oh, you're cruel!" Her expression betrayed how much he had hurt her.

"And what of you? Sitting here, teasing me with your 'mayhap I will . . . mayhap I won't.'" His disgust was obvious. "That's far more wanton than an honest bedding. You know little about life and less about men. After listening to your 'philosophy,' I've decided that you're not a woman at all."

"You've no right to speak to me in this manner." She tried to sound indignant and succeeded only in sounding very young.

"Whatever possessed a man like Outelas to attach himself to you? Did you spend your time together in weighty discussion?"

"We talked a great deal, of course."

"I'll wager you never told him your philosophy. You wouldn't dare! He'd have laughed you out of hearing. How could he have left a woman like Celeste for an infant? It's immoral!"

She was holding up badly under his scathing attack, but he felt no mercy for her. "It must have been the title that attracted him."

This final insult was too much to bear, and she demanded, "Return me at once. I won't go another league with you."

"Have no fear, Your Grace. Your virtue is safe with me."

"I'll never forgive you for this, Captain Jacques Bordeaux," she said at her dramatic best and he shrugged, as he made his way to the door.

"I know; you've brought your dagger and your sword so I'd best not turn my back on you. I hope you enjoy your solitude."

"Get out!" she screamed, and he bowed gracefully.

"I was just leaving, my lady."

The door was closed on the sound of his mocking laughter.

When she had cried all her tears, and exhausted her prayers, she was calm enough to assess her situation. How lightly she had spoken of adventure with Charles. And now that she had realized her wish—for what could be more of an adventure than being the captive of a handsome, daring pirate?—she was completely miserable. If only she had remained at the chateau in Bretagne. If only she had refused the King's invitation. She would not have been forced to flee a desperate situation. Her bad fortune had relentlessly pursued her to the colonies. There was something about her, it would seem, that aroused anger in people, that made them antagonistic, and even dangerous. So she had fled another impossible situation, and found herself in yet a third. There was only a slight chance that she would ever see her home again if her predicament remained unchanged. Despite the humiliation she'd suffered at her captor's hands, she began to realize that his contempt for her could be worked to her advantage. Only Bordeaux could save her; only he could be persuaded to put her on a French ship, or at least take her to Fort Royal. Thus, she had to make her presence so uncomfortable to the pirate that he'd welcome any opportunity to be rid of her.

Her first thoughts were all destructive. His charts were in the cabin, but to ruin them would be endangering lives, her own included, so she began to look elsewhere. She didn't want to ruin anything really important; she just wanted to annoy him. She finally decided on his clothing, and poured a bottle of the fruit punch into the chest at the end of the bunk, closing its lid on the staining, sweetly sticky mess. Next, she dropped overboard, one by one, every bottle of the white liquor he seemed to prize so highly. As that was the end of her resourcefulness for the time being, she settled back to wait for his reappearance.

All day long he'd stayed outside, working with the few men who were sailing with him for the first time. It had been his policy from the beginning to recruit younger men, barely into their twenties, who weren't suffering under the misconception that they knew more than their captain. A man signed on with him for three years—no longer, but sometimes shorter if he didn't prove himself. At the end of his tenure he found himself in great demand by other pirate captains, as Bordeaux picked his men for loyalty and the ability to take orders without question. Consequently, he'd never been confronted by a mutinous crew. His plan stood him in good stead for the future as well as for the present. The men didn't forget their former captain, nor the time spent learning their trade.

Bordeaux had never used the lash on a man. The malcontent, thief, or murderer was merely put in chains until the end of the voyage, when he would be released in some pirate port with the story of his crime public knowledge. To kill a Spaniard was an execution, but to kill another member of the Brotherhood was murder most foul.

Jacques was well pleased with his present crew. They would be sailing into enemy waters soon and would be without a Captain while he was in Habana, so they would have to be good in order to survive. The only thought he spared for Euphémie was when the mid-afternoon meal was ready. Beyond the courtesy of having a seaman take her a portion of the fish stew they were all eating, he put her from his mind. Finally, after dark had fallen, he turned the ship over to the watch and retired to the cabin. She'd left the lamp burning, but was soundly asleep in the bunk. As he stood looking down on her as the shadows cast by the swaying lamp played across her innocent face, he felt the stirring of pity in his heart. She'd not had an easy time of it in St. Pierre. Not many of her breed would have had the courage to even attempt such a journey through the jungle, let alone complete it. Yet for all that, she was not his sort of woman. He realized that now. It was his vanity that had prompted him to act so rashly when he'd met her on the "Good Sea." It wasn't only that she was so ill-suited to his way of life, but that he preferred lusty wenches whose only pleasures came from entertaining men like him. Her talk of ideal love on the pure basis of respect and dignity was far beyond his experience, and he couldn't imagine a relationship of that sort. His anger when they had been talking earlier had been aroused because of the casual way she had spoken of her affair with Outelas. She was an unnatural woman as far as he was concerned, and the sooner he returned her to her own kind, the better it would be for him.

But how to do it? The "Good Sea" was beyond his easy reach. Fort Royal would entail his reversing his course and losing precious time. There was simply too much to do, so she would just have to wait until they set sail for Habana. Never had he been so uncomfortably trapped by his own vanity. It was a difficult lesson, but one well learned. He would not soon forget the Duchesse d'Amberieu.

When Phémie awoke in the morning, she saw the hammock in which he'd slept still hanging a short distance from the bunk. Surely, she thought, he couldn't have found his ruined clothing; she would have been awakened by the disturbance. Brimming with curiosity, she lifted the lid of the sea chest. To her amazement, the soiled clothes were gone. There hadn't been an uproar when he had discovered her maliciousness; no outcry of disgust. So, with no slight feeling of apprehension, she waited all day for his return. Her meals were brought to her by silent crewmen, and she couldn't bring herself to ask about the Captain. When he came in, late that night, she awoke from a fitful sleep, sitting up in the bunk and complaining, "You made me feel like a child."

"Believe me, Your Grace, it was not my intention to arouse any feelings within you."

"I've acted badly, I know, and I'm ashamed of myself," she admitted despite his chilling demeanor.

"Before I found my clothes last night, I had decided I'd made a terrible error in bringing you here. It was my vanity, and nothing else. I'll take you to Fort Royal as soon as I have prepared for my voyage to Habana. I'm telling you this now so we can arrange a truce between us. If you can control your unruly temper, and refrain from any more vengeful acts, I'll cease burdening you with my unwelcome presence."

"I'll honor my part of the bargain, but please, don't deprive me of companionship. Why can't it be like it was in St. Pierre? I so enjoyed your tales of the sea."

"I have my duties to perform, Your Grace," he commented shortly. All the while he'd been talking, he had been hanging the hammock and otherwise preparing to retire. Finally he extinguished the lamp and in the darkness she heard him climb into his makeshift bed.

"Very well." She sounded really disappointed. "I can understand how I've not endeared myself to you. But at least allow me to go outside. I can't bear another day in here."

"You'll have to 'bear' it. There is no privacy out there, and I assure you you'd be far more ill at ease than my men. I think you'd be much more comfortable if you remained inside. Now, if you'll pardon me, I'll get whatever sleep I can until dawn."

"Jacques, I am truly sorry about your clothes," she apologized in a small voice, but he didn't reply.

For the remaining few days of the voyage, she had a great deal of time to think. She didn't see Bordeaux, unless she happened to be awake when he came in at night, but then she'd pretend to be asleep so he'd not feel required to speak to her. She'd played the fool once by apologizing, and vowed she'd not seek any further conversation with him. She'd been ridiculed, humiliated, and shunned. It was punishment enough for her misdeeds.

If she had thought to be bored in her solitude, she was mistaken. Their passage through the Caribbees was strewn with islands of all sizes—from a rock a man could stride across in several steps, to a lush, jungle-covered mountain. The sea itself was never-ending in its fascination. Yet being physically inactive was very hard on her. She turned to mental activity, writing a history of her adventures from the moment she first met Charles. She hoped that she might gain a better understanding of herself and the people she met by reliving it. Thus, she spent a great deal of time at Bordeaux's desk, using a blank logbook she'd found in one of the cabinets. Unbeknownst to her, Bordeaux came across it and began reading it. Each night, after making certain she was asleep, he would read with real interest what she had written during the day. To his amazement, the characters of her tale were etched in life-like, realistic poses, and she was far kinder to them in the telling than she was to herself. By the time Désirade was sighted, he understood why she was so hesitant in returning to France. Despite the compassion he felt for her in her dilemma, there was nothing he could do for her. Besides, by her own statement, she had an ally and could avoid the fate planned for her. So he absolved himself. His vanity had played him false once; he was not going to allow it to happen again.

22

Upon reaching Désirade, they sailed to the far side of the island, where a boat was put over the side and Bordeaux and his captive were rowed ashore. Phémie looked in vain for the house he'd mentioned but didn't break her silence to ask. Rounding a hook-like curve in the coast, Phémie saw that there was a spur of tree-covered beach, behind which was a wide lagoon. The inlet to the hidden body of water was very small and not easily seen from a distance. Once inside the lagoon, Phémie saw the two-storied house. It was a white, wood structure with green trim with a balcony around the whole of the second floor, much like the Lapalisse house. There was little else to distinguish it. There were no outbuildings, and there was no other residence in sight.

When the boat touched ground, Bordeaux helped Phémie out, and the two of them proceeded to the house alone. When she looked back, she saw that the men in the boat were rowing away, obviously not waiting for their Captain to return. It was late afternoon, the worst heat of the day over, yet the interior of the house was stifling. While she waited in the entrance hall, Bordeaux went through the silent rooms, opening windows and throwing back shutters. It was the simplest of residences from what she could see. The one large drawing room was almost bare of furniture. The more intimate small salon directly next to it was, in comparison, lavishly furnished with several easy chairs and a highbacked couch. There was a darkened room he'd not gone into, and she wandered, seemingly aimlessly, into it. It proved to be a library of the old order. There was a huge desk, on which she placed her logbook, a comfortable chair behind it, and, lining the walls, floor to ceiling cases that were actually filled with books.

At the sight of such an extensive library, she was startled out of her long silence, saying to him enthusiastically, "I had no idea you so enjoyed reading. At last I have found something we hold in common."

"Do you know," he began, with deceptive mildness, "in all the years I've been here, I've not read one of these volumes. They belonged to the planter who built this house. His widow didn't wait long enough to pack them."

"You must take delight in disappointing me," she complained, and he laughed. "I have to confess, it does give me pleasure."

"But why?" She swung to face him, her expression bewildered.

"Simply because I made a fool of myself when we first met. A man can never forget when he appears foolish in the eyes of a woman."

"Yet that wasn't my fault. I had nothing to do with it. You should take your revenge out on Aurélie."

"It's not so bad when a man does something foolish in the presence of another man," he continued conversationally, disregarding her protests of innocence. "Another man will either laugh, thinking it's a jest, or will sympathize and try to make it easier for him. A woman doesn't have the grace to do either. And she won't forget! She's forever reminding the poor fellow until he sickens of both the occurrence and her."

"Are all women like that, or just me?"

"No, not all; only the stupid ones," he said with a twinkle of mischief.

"You needn't become so insulting. Unless, of course, it soothes your vanity. Then nothing I say will cause you to be at least polite." Her retort hit on the truth, and his sense of humor left him in a rush.

"If that is all you have to talk about, the less said between us the better."

Too late he saw the gleam of triumph in her eyes as she shook her head in mock sorrow.

"You're in the wrong profession, Bordeaux. You've made a fine art out of being a fool and should be paid for it. 'The Poetic Pirate,'" she announced to the empty room, "has become 'The Piratical Fool.'"

"Take care," he warned ominously, starting toward her slowly. But she only laughed, backing away from him and shouting, "Have no fear of fools!" It would seem that all good sense deserted her as she taunted him even further. "A fool today is a fool tomorrow! What counts the vanity of a fool?"

He was almost upon her, and she put her hand out, as if to stop him. "Who but his mother could love a fool?" She saw how dark his expression had become, and whooped with glee. "An angry fool is twice foolish."

At this he smiled unpleasantly, saying softly, "I will make you pay dearly for this."

"A threat from a fool is a . . ." She got no further as he grabbed her violently by the shoulders in a sudden lunge, halting her retreat.

"I've warned you."

"What price does one pay for speaking the truth?" She threw the challenge in his face contemptuously.

"There is only one way to humiliate a demon like you." He drew her closer until she was trapped within the circle of his arms. As his head bent lower, he felt a sudden pricking sensation at his chest. Evidently she had concealed the dagger in the belt of her trousers, underneath her loose shirt.

"I think not!" She pressed the point until blood was staining his shirt, "My charitable feelings have completely deserted me."

He dropped his arms, stepping back from her, his eyes filled with a mixture of appreciation and anger. "This is not the end of it, Your Grace," he drawled lazily, and she responded softly, "If you touch me again, I'll kill you."

Despite the calmness of her voice, he knew full well that she meant what she was saying.

"You'd best sleep with a dagger in one hand and a sword in the other."

"Where, now, is the honor you spoke of so freely? I didn't ask to be brought here."

"Your mouth is so lovely, Euphémie; far more suited to sweet kisses than such dark threats."

"You must be jesting, or are you really a fool?"

"You allowed Outelas to dip his fingers into the honey pot."

She disregarded his crudity, saying instead, "I'll light a candle for your soul. Now, which is my room?" She circled him widely, keeping the dagger pointed.

"There is only one room with a bed."

"Then that one is mine." As she started up the stairs, keeping her eye on him all the while, he asked, "We eat at sunset. May I look forward to your company?"

"Of course! My appetite remains healthy despite your presence."

"And mine has been increased because of yours."

She hurried the rest of the way upstairs, trying to escape the sound of his laughter. She found the room he'd spoken of at the end of the long hall, and slammed the door shut, leaning against it while trying to catch her breath. The encounter had left her more shaken that she wanted to admit even to herself. Her first concern, however, was to make certain that the door was secured before throwing herself across the bed. She was still trembling inside from his touch.

The violence that was only hinted at caused a great weakness within her. He was an animal; a healthy, brutal animal, and her body responded to the pressure of his against it as it never had to Outelas. Auguste had been a gentleman, a polite, considerate lover. Bordeaux gave a promise of animal passion, and she was suddenly afraid. What if she hadn't had her dagger? She knew that she wouldn't have been alone on the massive bed at that moment. But he wasn't her enemy. Her only enemy was her weak, trembling woman's body that was crying out for him to take her. It demanded her surrender, yet she knew if she did, he would accomplish her humiliation. No matter what happened between them, if she fought him with all her strength, he would never be the victor. There would be nothing between them other than a declared war. All she could do was make him pay for his conquest. There was no escape.

To her surprise, and secretly, her disappointment, he made no further overtures in her direction. Other than at meals, she never saw him. Being left to her own devices, she turned once again to her logbook, and to take long walks on the lagoon beach. She never saw anyone else, and wondered where his ship and crew had gone and where he spent the daylight hours. After a constrained dinner, she would retire to her room, listening for his footsteps, which never followed. Despite his lack of attention, she wouldn't relax her vigilance; the dagger became her constant companion, although she doubted if he would give her the chance to use it. Still, she would have to try, if for no other reason than to save her pride. Waiting for him to make his move was wearing, but she didn't have a moment's doubt that he would carry out what he had threatened that first day. It wasn't at all like waiting for the return of a tender lover. Rather, it was like waiting for a storm to break. There was that same mixture of anxiety and excitement when one sees the first flash of lightning and knows that the thunder is following on its heels.

* * *

One night in the second week since their arrival on Désirade, Bordeaux was absent at dinner. Night had fallen and she had retired to the salon to await his return. When the front door opened, she started out of the dark room into the hallway, then suddenly stopped. The man who walked in the house was not Bordeaux. He was a young man, barely into his twenties, with a bold swagger that belied his nervous expression.

"Hallo!" he called loudly. "Is anyone aboard?" Phémie laughed at his unconventional hailing and stepped into the light.

"If you're looking for Captain Bordeaux, I'm afraid you'll be disappointed. He's not here at the moment."

"Your pardon, Madame. I hope I didn't startle you."

She was amazed by the easiness of his address. Obviously he was a young man of breeding, despite the flared canvas breeches and knitted shirt that were common to the seaman. His hand rested on the hilt of his cutlass in much the same manner she'd seen young men pose at Versailles.

"I'm only startled to find a gentleman so far from Paris."

"I knew you were a lady when you first came on board our ship; a real lady, you know. Not a planter's wife or some foreign creature that has pretensions to that title." He was so proud of his observation that she had to smile, deciding to play out the game to break the monotony.

"May I offer you some wine, Monsieur?"

"You are too kind, Madame." He bowed gracefully before following her into the library. Taking the chair before the desk, as she indicated, he kept up a steady stream of conversation while she fetched the wine. "It must be terrible for you, being separated from your servants. I know how lost Mama was when she wasn't surrounded by them. A lady, like yourself, wasn't meant to live like this. I think it was barbaric of him to bring you here. The poor creature has probably never been in the presence of a real lady, and you undoubtedly blinded him to the foolishness of his action. Which reminds me, he sent me here with a message." He accepted the glass she handed him graciously. "This is really too kind of you. After being so long in the company of vagabonds and thieves, if not worse, I was afraid that I'd lost my polish."

"Some people never lose it," she commented mischievously, controlling her laughter.

"Ah, you are so right. Birth will always tell, won't it?"

"It will, indeed!" She sat down behind the desk as he crossed his legs with all the elegance of a dandy. "What is the message the barbarian wanted you to deliver?"

"Only that he is detained in the village and won't return for several hours. To tell you the truth, he is in his cups pretty deeply and is looking for a woman."

"Need he drink heavily in order to find a woman?"

"If you saw the women in the village, you would understand it. Personally I would prefer remaining celibate."

"And have you remained celibate?" she asked, enjoying herself hugely; in fact, she couldn't recall a time in her recent past that she'd enjoyed more. It was undoubtedly only because the lightness the young man brought with him was contrasted with the darkness in which she had found herself from the moment she had to flee St. Pierre.

"It was either that, or getting the sickness."

"I'm certain your mother would be proud of you."

"It would be the first time, I can assure you. I've not been a good son, Madame. That is why I am here, posing as a pirate."

"You're not here by choice, then?"

"No more than you, Madame. There were certain charges of cheating at cards in my regiment. They were completely false, but the fool who lost was the son of a magistrate. As it happened, I was dismissed from the service, my father disowned me, and I was forced to flee. It was either the colonies or prison; perhaps even the gallows."

"All that for cheating at cards?"

"I neglected to mention that I killed the fellow in a duel. After all, he called me a cheat!"

"But why did you become a pirate? Surely you could have found a position as a tutor, or keeping the accounts of merchants and planters. You've been well educated. I'm certain your services would have been in demand."

"They were. I tried tutoring; the children were all right, but the parents were impossible. Do you have any idea how many mothers have daughters of a marriageable age?"

"I think I do." She laughed understandingly.

"I tried the other as well. My 'employers,' however, were always trying to prove how much more intelligent they were than a young, disgraced nobleman with an education."

"It must have been terrible."

"It was!" He agreed fervently, then added, "Even if it weren't terrible, even if I had found a decent fellow to work for, I'd not have stayed long. I'm too anxious to return home, and the only way I'll be able to do that is by having a mountain of gold. If you're rich enough, Madame, they'll forgive you anything."

"So you've become a pirate?"

"And a good one, too. That's one thing about our Captain. He knows how to teach his trade."

"Then you haven't had any qualms about the killing?"

"We kill only Spaniards, and that's not like killing real men."

"Tell me about some of your adventures with Bordeaux." She poured him another glass of wine, setting the bottle near his hand, then settled back for a long evening of conversation. When he left, it was after midnight. At their parting, he took her hand, kissing it as only a true gallant could, and suggested that they remain nameless to each other, as he was certain neither of them would want anyone else to know where they had met. Phémie appreciated his point, bidding him farewell and good fortune. Even if they saw each other again, they'd not be able to acknowledge their acquaintance. Despite his outrageous snobbery, Phémie appreciated his charm and wit; both were the products of a society she had never much admired. Perhaps, she thought, watching him disappear into the night, she was just as much a snob as he was. It would not surprise her if that were the reason she alienated people so quickly. But as her head was aching from so much laughter and so much wine, she decided not to think about it.

That was how Bordeaux found her; sitting on the steps outside, leaning her head against the post of the railing, and in a delicious state of not thinking. He had come in through the back and gone directly to the library because the lamp was still burning. Instead of finding her there, he saw an eloquent scene laid before him. The two wineglasses, the empty bottle, the disorder of the desk where they must have reached across to touch each other. He ran upstairs quietly, moving down the hall listening for their voices. Hearing nothing, he threw open the door, thinking to catch them out. The room was empty, of course, but the bed was in disarray. It never occurred to him that she might have neglected to straighten her room that morning. She was obviously not in the house, and he wondered if she might have run away with him, hoping to escape. After all, he was of her own class. He could see what had happened almost as if he had been there. The fellow delivered his message. She recognized him as one of her own and invited him to join her in some wine. Then she must have begged him to help her escape; the only bribe she had to offer was herself. The two of them went upstairs, where he made free use of her charms. Then they ran off. It wouldn't be too difficult to find a small boat. The village was populated by fishermen and women. One group supplied the food; the other satisfied appetites of a different order. As he hurried out the front door, he almost fell over her.

"Merciful God in heaven!" she cried as he accidentally kicked her.

"I'm sorry," he said shortly, sitting down beside her.

"Is that all you can say?"

"It's enough, and you're not likely to hear it from me again."

"I'll wager you don't say it often." She wrinkled her nose distastefully. "You smell as though you poured your wine over yourself, instead of drinking it."

"I notice you were drinking my finest this evening."

"I had only a glass or two. That nice boy you sent with your gracious message drank most of it. The way you came out of the house just now suggests that you're in a hurry to rejoin your 'friends' in the village."

"What do you mean?"

"The women who are honest in their bedding," she reminded him spitefully, and he was just drunk enough to answer back.

"And what of you with my messenger? Did you have to prick him with a dagger or did his sweet manners pry open your legs?"

"Save that kind of talk for your 'honest' women. It's not appreciated here. Now, if you'll excuse me . . ."

She started to rise, but he gripped her wrist, pulling her down again. "You think you're better than everyone else, don't you?"

"I don't think it, Bordeaux. If you remember correctly, you're the one who's always evaluating people and judging their worth."

"Do you want to go for a walk along the beach?" he asked, changing course suddenly, and she could only shake her head.

"Why not? Have I offended you that much with my unfortunate language?"

"Sharing the same world with you is offensive, Captain. As to walking on the beach with you, I don't think it would be wise. It would remind me of the first time Outelas 'pried open' my legs. If I had to make a comparison, I'm afraid you'd come out far worse than you do already." She got to her feet unencumbered, starting into the house. At the door she paused, looking down at his back. "You'd best go back to the village and console yourself with your 'honest' women. But don't come scratching on my door with the sickness."

As she closed the door behind her, he seemed to have made up his mind about something. He had tried to sport with the women in the village. It was the first time he'd ever considered such folly, and he wasn't dismayed when the mood left him as suddenly as it'd come. The woman was disappointed that she'd gotten him no farther than the door of her room, but he soothed her wounded feelings with gold. No, he usually did his whoring with women like Celeste; women who knew how to keep themselves free of the sickness. There were also the respectable whores, like Aurélie Espalion, whose black maids knew how to keep them clean.

He'd always had remarkable success with women. They either pursued him, or put up only token resistance to make the game more interesting. Never before had a woman laughed at him. It had been easy to keep his boast about not having to force a woman; no woman had ever seriously resisted him. Phémie wasn't playing the game when she repelled him with the point of a dagger. She had ridiculed him past endurance, and, in doing so, was forcing him to humiliate her in return. Whatever happened between them, he decided, would be her fault. She had to learn that a man's self-respect wasn't a mere plaything. Any blame would be on her shoulders alone.

He admitted to himself that he had drunk too much. He couldn't go to her in his present state; he would need all his wits. As he walked away from the house, he discarded his clothing, piece by piece, so that by the time he'd reached the lagoon, he was naked. Without pausing, he dove into the cold, dark water. The first shock of it drove the rum-laden fumes from his brain. As he swam vigorously, he began thinking clearly. He climbed out of the water feeling refreshed and renewed. His body came alive as the warm blood rushed through it. He left his clothes where they had fallen as he strode determinedly to the house. His bare feet made no sound as he went up the stairs and down the hall to her room. For a moment he paused, his hand on the latch, to take a deep breath. He threw open the door and he took in the scene in one quick glance. The lamp was burning; she was lying unclothed upon the bed, reading; the dagger was on the table beside the bed; the blanket was at her feet. So startled was she by the sudden intrusion of a naked man into her room that for a moment she was incapable of movement. When that moment passed, they were both in motion; Bordeaux, understandably, attempting to reach the dagger; Phémie, inexplicably, diving for the blanket. With a laugh, Bordeaux reached the weapon, opened a window and threw it out. Phémie had succeeded only in covering her nakedness. The pirate stood over the bed, laughing, as she tried to voice her outrage.

"How dare you? You're either drunk or mad. Get out of here at once!"

"When I am finished with you, Madame." He spaced his words effectively. His hand hooked in the blanket and he tore it from her grasp. "In our last meeting, you had a dagger and I had none. As you can see, our positions are reversed. I am the one with the weapon and I don't mean to just tease you with it. The first lesson is: Never take up a weapon unless you intend to use it."

"You are mad, and an animal as well!" she hurled at him vainly. "You spoke of honor."

"You stole that honor from me. Now you will pay for it, as I promised."

"I'll not fight you," she said, resigned. "You'll have no conquest. You'll have no joy in my surrender." She lay flat, her limbs rigid and her eyes closed.

"You're the maddest woman I've ever met."

"To you I am just a statue. You'll find more warmth by sticking your 'weapon' into a hole in the sand."

"I have no doubt of that, even if you were at the height of your passion." He stretched out beside her, luxuriating in the sight of her beautiful body. For a moment he hesitated, tempted to try to arouse her so there would be pleasure rather than hatred in their mating. But such weakness, he realized, would fail to punish her, and he wanted that even more than he wanted a woman. Without a word he separated her legs, then mounted her. There was no cry of protest, nor any response as he took her with even less feeling than an animal. When he climaxed, shuddering as he ejected his life's seed into her, he felt sick at what he had done. He rolled off her, and she left the bed, not looking back, and walked proudly from the room. A few moments later he heard the front door close. Looking out of the window, he saw her take the path to the lagoon.

As he waited by the window, watching for her return, he knew that he'd not humiliated her, as he'd wished. All he had accomplished by his act was to destroy his own honor. By doing absolutely nothing, she was the victor; her pride and honor were restored.

Phémie, too, was examining her feelings. As she cleansed herself in the cold water of the lagoon, she experienced an odd sensation of exhilaration. That she'd bested Bordeaux meant less than nothing to her. She'd proven to herself that she wasn't a wanton woman. She had exercised selectivity and control when it would have been so easy to capitulate. For that one moment, when she saw him standing in the doorway in all his manhood, a wave of passion and excitement had swept over her. Then she'd felt shame in her nakedness—something she'd never experienced with Outelas—and could think only of covering herself.

All the waiting and anxiety were over now, finished by that worthless scene in the bedroom. Somehow she sensed that he would never touch her again. If he were any sort of man, he would be burdened with his guilt for a long time to come. He'd created his own purgatory, she thought, and if he expected any easing of his conscience from her, he'd be sadly disappointed.

When she returned to the house, she found him sitting on the top stair, waiting for her. She started to pass without a glance at his dejected figure, when he spoke. "We'll sail with the evening tide. Can you be ready?"

"I'll be ready," she replied briefly before continuing to her room.

He'd been busy while she'd been gone. The bed was freshly made, the dagger prominently displayed on one of the pillows, and on the table she found a heavy purse of gold. At first she was inclined to throw it in his face, but realized that it might cost her more than she possessed to return to France. Let him try to soothe his vanity. Let him allow himself to consider her a prostitute by accepting his money. She had more important things to think about, the foremost being home. Home! She sighed, allowing herself to wonder which home would be safest. Since Florimond hadn't married, the Lapalisse estate would remain in her ownership. Her beautiful sanctuary would be waiting for her there, but so might be the agents of the King. The same could be expected at the house on the cliffs above the sea, although any strangers in the area would be far more subject to suspicion than in the country. The safest place would be the one closest to the enemy camp, the one least likely to be watched. Besides, she wanted to hear anything Gaspard might have to report. From Paris she could decide what her next move should be.

As the day on which she expected to see Martinique wore on, and finally passed without her sighting any landfall at all, she became concerned. By mid-afternoon of the next day, she boldly left her cabin and approached Bordeaux.

"Where is Fort Royal?" she demanded unpleasantly, and before answering, he took her aside to the railing, where they would not be overheard.

"We are not going to Fort Royal. The next landfall you see will be Cuba."

"You promised that I would be put ashore at Fort Royal, and I insist that you turn about immediately."

"I can't do that. You know too much about our plans, and I don't think you'll keep the secret."

"I know nothing about your plans, except that you're going to Habana to find out something about the plate fleet. Even if I did know something, why do you think I would reveal it?" The question was hardly spoken before she laughed, answering it herself. "Ah, you think I'd betray you for the sake of revenge. You seem to be overly concerned with that, and punishment. Do not credit me with your own qualities, Bordeaux. I am not like you; I'm not the one seeking revenge."

"I wish I could trust you, but this mission is far too important to rely on an injured woman's silence."

"But you don't hesitate placing me in a highly dangerous situation. Perhaps you won't be satisfied until you see me dead."

"Don't be absurd! There is a risk, but I'd hardly call it dangerous. You'll be safely hidden in a quiet cove." There was such contempt in his voice that she became really angry.

"It may please you to think me a coward, but in my opinion your promises have proven worthless. Sweet Jesus, am I to be undone by such a vain fool? I cannot share your conviction that the Spanish are so witless as to allow you to sail into their port nor so gullible as to tell you their secrets. You may be willing to gamble your life on such an improbability, but you have no right to gamble mine."

"There is no threat to you, Madame. Even if the ship were taken, you could claim you were on board against your will." He was becoming exasperated, but she continued doggedly, "What if they don't bother to take the ship? What if they decide to fire on us before asking for our papers?" She shook her head, her tone heavy with frustration. "What good is it to argue? You're an unreasonable man bent on your own destruction and the destruction of any who are unfortunate enough to be with you. Since you'll not listen to reason, I must look to my own survival."

"Hasn't it always been so?" he retorted, and she held her temper remarkably well, considering the provocation.

"No, not always, but this time I shall. And don't pretend I should be grateful for finding myself in this situation. If it weren't for you, I'd still be on the 'Good Sea.'"

"I wish to God you were! Of all the shrewish, harping, disagreeable women I've ever seen, you are far and away the worst. Accept the fact that you are here. There is nothing you or I can do about it now. At least have the goodness to hold your tongue so I can get this business over as quickly as possible. Leave me in peace, woman!" He felt infinitely better after his outburst, and was even amused as he watched her flee from his anger. He doubted very much if anyone had ever talked to her in such a manner. If her behavior toward others was as intolerable as it was toward him, she had deserved such a lecture for a long time.

The scathing accusation was more effective than he'd imagined. Phémie was completely subdued and neither pouted nor wept. When they chanced to meet on deck, they exchanged polite greetings but never engaged in conversation. If she thought badly of him, her expression did not reveal her opinion. In a moment of weakness, he instructed the nobleman who'd acted as messenger that evil night to keep her company whenever she came out on deck. The arrangement proved so satisfactory that he could turn his mind to other more important things.

After several nights of sailing without running lights, a very risky business, they came in sight of the Cuban coastline. The navigator, an older man on board only for this voyage because of his knowledge of the island and its waters, quickly found the cove he was looking for and anchored the shallow-draft pirate vessel in the secluded hiding place. An uneasy quiet fell over the company as Jacques disappeared into the cabin. Phémie sat on the ledge under the windows, the silent question in her eyes. Without hesitation, the pirate began stripping off his clothes, his voice brimming over with excitement.

"This is the safe haven I promised you. There's not a Spaniard in this part of the world who'll come even close to this place. They believe it to be haunted."

"Is it truly?" she asked, really interested, as she looked out of the window, to avoid watching him undress. "How did you hear of it?"

"Our navigator. He was the captain of his own ship until the Dons took it away from him and gave it to one of their own."

"And you believe him?"

"It doesn't matter whether I believe him or not."

"Would you betray your country for such a reason?"

"No, but then I'm not a Spaniard. The man's a good seaman and has earned a captain's share of the prize if my plan succeeds."

She shrugged, feeling that he knew more about such matters than she, then mentioned her fear.

"I have a strange dread about this place. It isn't safe here for any of us."

"I told you it was haunted." There was a teasing tone to his voice, and she turned to look at him. Her protest died on her lips as she saw before her a Spanish priest.

"Holy saints!" she ejaculated, and he laughed, pleased with himself.

"How do you like my costume? Look! I even had my head shaved." He bent over, showing her the clean-shaven spot. "You wear trousers, and now I'm wearing skirts." He walked back and forth in front of her, the brown friar's robe swaying just above his sandaled feet. The white rope, as a belt, and a long rosary completed his disguise. "I have learned the rituals of the mass and the confession. No one will suspect that I'm not a priest, and I shall have answers to anything I ask."

"But that's sacrilege! You can't say the mass and hear confessions." Her voice dropped to a whisper, "Have you no fear for your soul?"

"Such nonsense means nothing to me. I'm not one of you; I'm a Huguenot, as are most of the Brothers."

"Those men will truly believe that they're receiving absolution. You can't play them so false, even if they are the enemy."

"I'll hear no more arguments from you, Madame." He'd not expected such piety from her, and was disappointed that she hadn't praised him for his cleverness. Seeing that she was crossing him and that he was in a dangerous mood, she quickly changed their conversation.

"Did your navigator tell you why this place was haunted?"

"Only that it was the site of one of the first settlements, and all the people disappeared mysteriously."

"He must tell the story better than you do. I'll ask him while you're gone."

"You'd best not do that; my men don't know about it, and I want to find the ship here when I return. Don't speak to him at all. I've told him that you're a young nobleman I captured for ransom. If he hears your voice, he'll learn the truth."

"But surely one of the crew has told him by now."

"I'm the only one on board who speaks his language, and he has no French. Will you, just this once, do as I ask without arguing? You'll be safe here, as I promised." He left the cabin rapidly, without looking back, and Phémie was a woman alone on the ship of strange men. The feeling of dread renewed itself, and she moved to the door to bolt it.

It was evident that when Bordeaux left the ship he appointed the young nobleman her guardian. It was he who brought her mid-afternoon meal, but rather than merely leaving it on the table and excusing himself after a few pleasantries, he closed the cabin door behind him.

"I think there's going to be trouble, Madame." He kept his voice low, and she answered in the same way,

"I haven't heard anything amiss. What is it?"

"Our navigator has gone over the side. He left shortly after the Captain and has not yet returned. I told the man left in command, but he refuses to heed my warning. It seems that the fellow told him of his intention to spy out the land, to make certain there was no one about who would notice our presence."

"Wait! You say he told the man?" When he nodded, she asked, "Was it in Spanish or French?"

"Why, French, of course. None of us speak his language."

"Bordeaux said that he had no French!" she announced in a dreadful whisper, and the nobleman instantly saw the implication.

"I fear we have been betrayed, Madame."

"What can we do?"

"This ship is no longer safe for you. Bordeaux's men know full well what will happen to them if they're taken by the Spanish. They'll try to run, but if they're trapped, as we are now, they'll fight to the death. Bordeaux must have lost his senses to trust a Spaniard."

"I can't believe he'd risk so much if he'd not been certain. Maybe it's just this place that gives us such misgivings."

"I think not; even if we are needlessly fearful, there is no harm in your going ashore and concealing yourself until I signal that it's safe to return."

"Will the others let me go?"

"No, so we won't tell them. I'll let a rope over the side. Do you think you can climb down?"

"I don't know. If I fell, they'd surely hear me."

He nodded, going to the windows. Leaning far out, he reached the dangling rope and pulled it inside. Motioning her to his side, he started to tie it about her waist.

"Wait!"

From under the mattress on the bunk, she brought out the thickly wrapped packet of papers, and, turning her back, stuffed it into her canvas trousers, flat against her stomach. Next she secured the dagger in her gold-laden belt and pulled the shirt over it. Finally she buckled on her sword and was ready to go.

"This is the plan," he whispered, tying the rope about her. "Conceal yourself well someplace where you'll be able to see the ship. I'm going to try to get permission to search for our navigator. If I succeed, I'll leave the ship in the longboat. If not, I'll slip over the side after dark. I'll come ashore near those two rocks." He pointed out the landmark, and she nodded her understanding. "I'll be nearby."

"I wish I could give you the time to eat, but I must get back or they'll come looking for me."

"I couldn't keep any food down anyway," she said breathlessly with a mixture of fear and excitement. "I don't know your name yet."

"It is Pierre."

"And I am Phémie."

He kissed her hand quickly, then assisted her out of the window.

"Do not take the time to untie the rope. Use your dagger. And remember, you're not strolling along the streets of Paris, so be watchful."

"Until later, my friend." She swung out from the ledge, and he lowered her slowly into the water below. Luckily the water was shallow, and, after a few floundering moments of panic, her feet touched bottom. If it had been any deeper, the heaviness of the gold would have ended her adventures forever. With relief he saw her leave the water and disappear from sight.

Phémie easily found a place of concealment from where she could see the ship and yet not be seen. She remained hidden for the rest of the daylight hours, damp and irritable, but watchful. The longboat was not lowered over the side. At twilight, just as the last of the day's light was fading, she made her way carefully to a location close to the two rocks her ally had indicated. The cover was sparse, but she was within hallo-ing distance and the night would soon blanket her. She waited what must have been several hours, and there was still no sign of him.

As the first thin gray band of light appeared on the horizon, heralding a new day, she knew that something must have gone wrong, and he'd not be joining her. Reluctantly she returned to the undergrowth as dawn's light filled the sky and the birds began their daily fight for existence. She wondered if the pirates had missed her yet; and if they had, whether they would pursue her. She doubted it very much, as Bordeaux had probably left very definite instructions about not leaving the ship. For the moment, she was safe, and if luck held, she could return to the ship when Bordeaux returned from his fool's errand.

Her first concern, however, was finding fresh water. From her trek through the jungle on Martinique, she'd learned which fruits to eat, but not how to find water. There was no immediate danger, but the sweetly thick juices she'd been relying on were beginning to make her thirstier than she'd been before. Soon she'd be forced to return to the ship if she didn't find her own supply of water. With a feeling of foreboding, she began her search, moving inland and trying to fix landmarks in her mind.

Bordeaux squirmed uncomfortably, trying to ease his bonds. It was the second day of his captivity, and he'd had a great deal of time to ponder his mistake. He had been taken as soon as he was a safe distance from the ship. Three men had been waiting by the path to which the navigator had directed him. So total was his surprise that he was captured without a struggle. A short time later, the small party was joined by the man he'd been so eager to trust, and one of his captors left with a message to Habana. They had tied him securely against a tree, but had otherwise treated him gently, seeing to his feeding and watering at reasonable intervals. Their talk was the same as that of men everywhere, mostly about women. Occasionally, however, they spoke of the man whose arrival they awaited. At such times, their voices betrayed the fear in which they held him. It was he who had commanded them to treat their prisoner with care, and they responded as if their lives depended upon their obedience.

On the morning after the ignominious capture, the navigator left the small camp, taunting Bordeaux with his plan of returning to the ship and telling the crew that all was well. He claimed that Bordeaux, in his folly, had traded the quarterdeck for slave's chains in the mines of Peru. Despite his being left with only two guards, it was impossible to slip his bonds and escape. He could only wait until his condition somehow changed, praying that they would make a mistake before the arrival of their master.

What galled him more than anything else was that even a chit of a girl like Phémie had sense enough to suspect the Spaniard. He had not wanted to suspect the fellow. He wanted to go where the rest of the Brotherhood feared to go. He wanted to make his way to the heart of the enemy's camp, and return safely and successfully. The ambition to do what others had failed to do had impaired his judgment, blinded him to the very real possibility of betrayal. He'd made the deadliest mistake of all; he'd underrated the strength and wit of the enemy. The navigator had reversed the tables on him, doing successfully what Jacques had hoped to do himself. He'd walked boldly into the pirates' stronghold, and had found one vain enough to follow him into a trap.

Phémie had seen it all, even without knowing the whole plan. She had warned him that the Dons weren't witless. She'd mistrusted the navigator without ever seeing him. And, above all else, she'd recognized the pirate captain for what he truly was—a vain fool. His vanity had cost him his ship, his crew, and his freedom, in exchange for a living death in the silver mines from which no man escaped. It was a hard price, but he'd pay it in full measure. He knew what fate awaited him; he could only wonder what would befall the woman who had tormented him from the beginning. With a flash of humor, he wished her upon the Spanish; that would be more than enough revenge for what they were about to do to him.

The smell of cooking meat attracted Phémie to the fringes of the small encampment. She saw the two Spanish soldiers, bent over their cooking pot, and Bordeaux tied to a tree at the edge of the clearing.

As quietly as possible, she circled the camp and came up on her hands and knees behind the captive. She whispered his name and was relieved that, in his surprise, he didn't betray her presence. Her dagger made quick work of the rope that held him, and he extended his hand for a weapon. Without looking around, he heard the slight sounds as she slid the sword from its scabbard and placed the hilt firmly in his hand. The first soldier was dead before he fell into the fire; the second had just made it to his feet before he was cut down. Phémie avoided looking at the slaughter, feeling more than a little sick. Death came so easily. Jacques wasted no time, stripping off the friar's robe and availing himself of one of the dead men's trousers and shirt.

"I must overtake the spy before he reaches the ship. Do you think you can find your way alone?"

"Do what you feel you must," she said wearily, and he added, "I'll keep your sword for a time."

"Keep it forever or fling it into the sea. I'll never wear it again." She unstrapped the scabbard, handing it to him.

"Follow me as quickly as you can, and bring the priest garb. I'll make use of it yet. Do not tarry! If I'm not mistaken, the men were expecting their commander at any moment, and this place won't be safe."

Without another word or backward glance, he plunged into the jungle, taking the same direction as the man who'd had the courage and the wit to entrap him. Phémie watched him go, then collected the robe, rope belt, and rosary before leaving the encampment.

She hurried, hearing Jacques ahead of her, but could not maintain the grueling pace with which she started out. Soon the silence of the jungle closed about her, yet she had no real difficulty in following the trail of bruised and broken undergrowth. It was humid and hot, and the small flying creatures were thick and persistent in their biting. The sweat running down her face would have blinded her if she hadn't continually wiped it from her forehead. How she yearned for the clean, cool air of the sea. As each gasping breath drawn caused a stabbing pain in her chest, she imagined, in a panic, that she was losing the trail, that the impenetrable green wall would block her and she would never reach the sea. She lost all conception of time, her whole existence centered on the placing of one foot in front of the other. When she finally stumbled upon the fly-covered, staring-eyed body of the navigator, she knew that Bordeaux had succeeded in his effort.

A long moment elapsed before she realized that the pirate had not waited for her to join him. After killing the navigator, he'd just gone on. A fearful suspicion came over her. Despite her exhaustion, she pushed on, frantic with fear.

The sun was lowering in the clear, blue sky when she caught the sound of the sea not too far distant. She trudged on, her eyes streaming with tears, until she broke out of the jungle and onto the beach. There she saw the pirate vessel, its sails catching desperately at the slight breeze, moving slowly out of the cove. She tried to shout, but her parched throat was incapable of any sound but a sob of despair. She sank wearily down onto the cooling sand, still not able to credit Bordeaux with such treachery. She had saved his life, and in return, he was leaving her to the tender mercies of Spanish soldiers. As she watched the departing vessel across the widening distance, she heard the first cannonade of a ship she couldn't see. The pirates had just reached the open sea, preparing to escape, when the shots hit the pirate ship broadside. There followed one cannonade after another, almost deafening in its roar, and the pirate was defenseless. Bordeaux's ship shuddered violently, the sails in tatters, the mainmast and rudder splintered, and fire engulfing the decks. Still the pounding shot continued mercilessly until there was nothing left of Bordeaux and his swift, proud ship. Only then did Phémie see the two clumsy warships as they maneuvered close to the spot where the pirate had gone down. There had been one on each side of the cove's mouth, and they had caught Bordeaux in their crossfire.

She had little feeling for what had happened to Bordeaux. He had died a clean death with his ship, and among his comrades—the best kind of death for a man of his trade. She felt a stirring of regret for Pierre, the young nobleman; but he'd chosen to be there and must have known the dangers involved. Her own fate now lay in the balance. She might die in the jungle, the victim of the devil snake or the sun; or, if she were found by the Spanish soldiers, death would come by her own hand. At the moment, however, she was beyond caring. The evening was turning cool, and she was unutterably weary. Covering herself with the friar's robe, she lay back on the sand. After crossing herself, she began saying the beads and was asleep before she reached the third Ave.

So deep was her sleep that she didn't hear the jingling of bridles as horses approached. In the twilight, the leader of the soldiers could barely make out the form on the beach. It could have been a shadow, or perhaps a fallen tree. The tide was coming in, but had not reached high enough to pull a body under. He remained where he was, ordering one of his men to investigate. The soldier ran over to the spot, then quickly returned.

"It looks like a youth, sir, but he's wearing a priest's robe."

"Dead?"

"No, but sleeping like the dead."

The leader dismounted, covering the short distance to see for himself. If the boy belonged to the French pirate crew, he'd have escaped into the jungle. If he were Spanish, surely he'd have heard the battle and avoided the cove, finding someplace else to sleep. Perhaps he was the captive nobleman the navigator had mentioned to the messenger.

Night had fallen abruptly, and the men were lighting their torches to begin searching for any of the pirates who might have escaped. Calling for a torch bearer the leader stooped beside the sleeping form. Peering down at the tear-streaked dirt on the face the leader put his hand on the tangled hair and stroked it gently.

"Euphémie!" he whispered softly, not wanting to awaken her.

23

How often de Merades had thought of Phémie since their brief meeting at sea. Closing his eyes, he would call to mind the picture of her hanging on a rope ladder, balanced precariously on the narrow railing, the breeze blowing her ridiculous hair back from her face, and molding the shirt against her young body. When she had approached them on the deck, she had not intended to be bold. She was being natural and open. Many a quiet moment he had spent remembering. It filled his empty, meaningless personal life with warmth and joy. How imaginative, refreshingly honest, and alive she was. He'd come to believe that she couldn't possibly be the paragon he recalled. The real Euphémie Lapalisse must be a pale shadow beside the creature he had endowed with so many virtues. For all the time separating them, he'd hoped that one day they would meet again. All too often he'd paused at the door of his wife's bedroom, only to turn away when Euphémie's face came unbidden to fill his thoughts and his eyes. Even his confessor became impatient with the frequency with which he admitted to lustful dreams involving a woman he'd met but once.

Relations had not been good between him and his wife before he'd left for Spain; since his return, they had become impossible. She bore his neglect in martyred silence, spending as much of the day in the chapel as her duties allowed.

A pious woman, this Señora Mercedes de Merades. No one wore her black dress more proudly, attended mass more devoutly, or made charity visits among the poor with more regularity. Everything about her life was well ordered, including her husband's weekly visit to her room. He knew that she was distressed by his lack of attention, but he comforted himself with the belief that her distress stemmed from the disruption of her schedule more than from a personal hurt. As the Governor's daughter, she was the shining example to the other women of their class. To the misplaced aristocrats, she represented stability, as she carried on the customs of their homeland. Since the Governor lived alone, it proved convenient for his daughter's family to take up residence with him. Thus, she presided over and held court in this extension of the royal palace with as much dignity and sociability as an ungraceful, humorless woman could.

Unknown to de Merades, his wife had been intimidated by his self-confidence, the surety with which he handled other people, from the beginning of their marriage. Those in his service feared him. His equals admired and emulated him. Her own assurance lay only on the surface. Her stiff stature and unyielding manner were her shield and buckler. To others, it seemed proper that she should be so aloof. In actuality, she was a quaking, frightened woman far more suited to the convent than to be the wife of a politically ambitious man who was more interested in himself and his own pursuits than anything or anyone else.

With his usual lack of thought or consideration, de Merades brought the fever-ridden, delirious Frenchwoman he had found on the beach to his wife for the care she needed. Without question, or complaint, Mercedes de Merades did as she was told. For almost a week she nursed the stranger with her own hands, sleeping a few fitful hours each night in a chair beside the bed. Her husband was a frequent visitor, far more frequent than was seemly, often standing at the foot of the bed and staring at the woman without comment. At these times he was either unaware of or inconsiderate of his wife's presence. His obvious concern for the strange woman was unnatural and puzzling to Mercedes, but she held her silence.

After a particularly long period of sleep, Phémie awoke clear-eyed, the fever broken. Her last memory was of falling asleep on the sand after Bordeaux's ship went down. How she came to be in a comfortable bed with a strange, black-gowned woman hovering over her was a complete mystery. She attempted to speak with her, but the woman shook her head, indicating that she didn't understand French. Since Phémie had no Spanish, it would seem that conversation was futile. She realized that she had been ill, yet her first concern was for her papers. There was no sign of her clothing, and the nightshift had no places of storage or concealment. Using gestures, she patted her stomach, and the woman pointed to a tray of fruit. Shaking her head, Phémie picked up her pillow and pretended to be writing on it, then patted her stomach again. The woman smiled frostily, bringing the packet of papers from a dresser drawer. Phémie took the proffered packet, hugging it close to her and lying back against the pillows again. Smiling up at the woman, she pointed to herself, enunciating carefully, "Euphémie d'Amberieu."

The woman nodded, repeating the name, then gave her own as Mercedes de Merades. Phémie couldn't believe her ears; it was a name she'd never expected to hear again.

"Rodrigo Bartolomé de Merades," she said softly, as if to herself, and Mercedes exclaimed, her eyes burning, pointing to herself, "Señora de Merades!"

Phémie suddenly sighed, closing her eyes and feigning sleep. She was not tired; she simply didn't want the woman to see the expression of dismay in her own eyes. In that one moment, so much had been explained. A short while later she heard the door open and close, and considered it safe to come awake again. The first sight that greeted her was Rodrigo Bartolomé de Merades standing at the foot of the bed.

"Euphémie. Thank God!"

"Monsieur de Merades?" She pretended to be amazed by his presence. "How came I here?"

"I brought you, my dear. This is the Governor's residence in Habana."

"And the lady who has been caring for me?"

"You must mean Mercedes."

"I want to thank her for all her kindnesses to me."

"It is quite unnecessary, Euphémie. She is the housekeeper here and expects no thanks for doing only her duty."

"I still owe her my thanks."

"I will extend them to her if you insist."

"I do insist, and I would prefer thanking her myself." Her tone of voice, though sounding weaker than he remembered, gave no room for disagreement. "What is the word for 'thank you' in your language?"

"Oh, very well. All you need say is *Gracias, Señora*."

"Gracias, Señora." Phémie repeated the simple phrase several times, using different inflections, until Rodrigo, at the end of his patience, complained, "I've prayed for hours on my knees that the Good Lord would allow us to meet again, and all you can say is '*Gracias,* Señora'!"

"It is difficult for me to imagine you upon your knees, even before God." The retort was said without insult, merely as a statement of fact, and Rodrigo recognized the spirit behind it.

"It must have seemed so on the 'Santa Barbara,' but I have changed, Euphémie. I have learned humility."

"Humility is a difficult lesson, but perhaps you should have better spent your time learning honesty."

"Why are you so cruel? Why must you—"

"Please, Monsieur," she interrupted him, "I wish to thank your housekeeper before I forget the words. Will you call her for me?"

"There is no need; she has been here all the time."

He called for the woman who had been standing just out of Phémie's range of vision to join them.

"Madame . . . I mean, *Gracias*, Señora de Merades." Phémie kept her gaze on the woman's face, and saw Rodrigo, out of the corner of her eye, swing about on his heel and leave the room noisily. Mercedes sat in the chair next to the bed, looking at Phémie with the first sign of kindness she betrayed—a nervous little smile that was far different from the coolness she'd displayed before.

"You're a good woman, Madame d'Amberieu."

Other than a slight start, Phémie showed no particular surprise.

"I am sorry, for your sake, that you speak my language, Señora. It is strange, isn't it, that your husband doesn't know of your ability?"

"My father was ambassador to France when I was a child. It was long before our marriage was arranged, so there was no way Rodrigo could know. Pardon, Madame, but does he know you're a duchesse?"

"I told him when we first met, but he didn't believe me."

"You are not angry that I read your papers?"

"No, it's small enough price for keeping them hidden for me. You must be wondering how I came to know your husband."

"Spare me that, I beg of you! You're an honest woman, and I would prefer not knowing. But you are also a woman of honor. When I told you that I am his wife, I saw that you had not known he was married. Now that you do know, I believe that you'll not repay my hospitality by allowing my husband undue liberties."

"Be assured of that, Señora."

"I am only partially relieved. My husband is a very determined man and will not be denied anything he truly wishes."

"If only there were some way I could escape, but he will be watchful."

"Not after what you've done to him, Madame. You caught

him out in a lie; he'll not be able to face you for some time."

"It is in both our interests then that I return to my own country. Perhaps you know of some way, or some friend who would aid us in this cause."

"There is a man I have known for many years. We played together as children." She paused, lowering her eyes, and Phémie detected the blush that colored her face and neck slightly. When she looked up again, her eyes were glowing, and the change that had come over her transformed her into a lovely woman. With a shock Phémie realized that Mercedes didn't love her husband, as she had first supposed.

"I am certain that he will think of a plan."

"Do not wait too long to speak with him, Señora."

"It will be done tonight," she promised without hesitation. "No one knows better than I how little patience my husband possesses."

During the next few days, Phémie concentrated on regaining her strength. The fever had taken its toll, but she was not nearly so weak as she had first supposed. The delicious thick soup that Mercedes had recommended was working wonders. As each hour passed, she feared a visit from de Merades, but it seemed that he lacked the courage to face her. Phémie remained in her room even when she was well enough to leave it. Since the fever had broken, she didn't need constant care, and Mercedes would disappear for hours at a time on some mysterious errands she'd not even disclose to her fellow conspirator.

On the fourth night, without warning, Mercedes crept stealthily into Phémie's room. As the two women changed into their costumes—nun's habits—Mercedes quickly outlined the plan in a whisper. With great care, they would descend into the kitchens, using the back staircase, and leave the house shortly before dawn. They would make their way to the church adjoining the convent, where they would fade into the crowd of nuns hearing the first mass of the day. After mass, they would use the crowd of nuns as a shield and slip through the door leading to the rectory garden. Once outside, they would conceal themselves in the ruin of the ancient church that had first been built on the site. Inside they would find Mercedes's black gown and a seaman's uniform for Phémie. After changing their clothing, they would be joined by her friend, who would take Phémie to the ship on which she would leave the island. Mercedes would return to the church to attend mass at her usual hour. By the time the ship was out of the harbor, she would be back in her home, about to take up her daily chores. If Rodrigo, in his search, which would certainly ensue after he learned of Phémie's disappearance, hoped to follow the trail of a lone young woman who was without the language or decent clothing, he would naturally be disappointed.

Phémie silently feared that the plan was too involved to succeed as easily as Mercedes hoped, but had no other alternative. Only with the arrangements for her passage already made and with a guide to accompany her to the ship would she ever see France again. It had suddenly become very important to her to see France again, and not only because it offered her a place of refuge among her own people. It was also because she was tired of being a stranger wherever she traveled. She'd realized at last that France was not merely Louis's kingdom; it was her home. So she would follow the twists and curves of Mercedes's plan; and she would trust the man Mercedes called friend. In her present desperation, she would have bargained with the devil if it would get her home. As if Mercedes sensed the Frenchwoman's doubt, she chose that moment to attempt to reassure her. They were not alone in this. The habits were loaned to them by the Mother Superior, who knew of the plan and approved of it. It was the priest who had suggested the church ruin as the place to change their costumes and rendezvous with the guide, promising to see that no one strayed into the garden. And, finally, her personal maid would see that the kitchen door was barred after their departure and would meet her mistress for mass so as to return home with her as usual. That made three people who were unnecessarily, in Phémie's opinion, privy to the conspiracy. But she could only congratulate Mercedes on her plan, securing the packet beneath the overblouse of the habit. Into the deep pocket she dropped the heavy purse of gold returned to her by the strange, unsmiling woman. Someday, Phémie vowed, she would repay the full debt, even if she had to return to Habana to do it.

Reaching the church without mishap, the two women faded into the group of nuns filing into the pews specially held for them. After mass, the nuns were the last to leave the church, and there was no one present to see the women slip out the side door. After they had changed into more comfortable clothing, they were joined by the guide, as Mercedes had promised. With only a smiling nod in his direction, Phémie went outside to give the friends a few minutes alone. The garden was quite pleasant even in the early morning dew, and she took a short walk. Upon returning, she called out in a soft voice, and receiving no reply, became alarmed. Surely they hadn't deserted her, after bringing her all this way. Again she called out, in a louder voice, and, to her relief, she heard Mercedes asking her to come in. Although time was flying, she did as she was asked. The two had moved deeper into the dark interior, and she could scarcely discern them standing near the raised dais where the altar had been.

"We must hurry!" She approached them rapidly, unmindful of their stiff attitudes. "The next mass will be starting soon—"

Too late she saw the third figure step out of his place of concealment, the sword nakedly threatening in his hand.

"There'll be no more masses today, Euphémie. The priest is ailing with a broken head."

Phémie stayed as she was, knowing that escape was impossible.

"Forgive me," Mercedes begged, her tears flowing. "I should have warned you, but he would have killed Miguel."

Moving even closer, Phémie saw that the young man had

indeed been wounded, his arm hanging uselessly at his side, his sword still in its scabbard.

"Imagine my surprise," de Merades began pleasantly, "discovering that my dull, chaste wife not only speaks French, but has a lover."

Mercedes denied the latter accusation in Spanish, and de Merades reminded her of "their guest."

"If you are wondering how I happened upon this elopement, you've only to ask your trusted maid. She has been in my service from the beginning."

"Then you'll know I am innocent of your charge. I've never had a lover."

"Oh, I know that, my dear wife, but who will believe you when I present the testimony of your maid, along with the dead body of your childhood friend?"

"And what do you intend doing with me?" Phémie asked lightly, belying the panic that gripped her. She knew that he had no intention of harming her, but the danger to Mercedes's friend was very real. She desperately needed time, praying that the priest would recover enough to summon aid.

"After attacking a helpless priest and killing a man who's unable to defend himself, you wouldn't hesitate to dispose of a witness who could give the lie to your tale," she taunted. "A priest, a wounded man, and a woman! Rather dangerous adversaries for a man of your courage. Hadn't you better call for assistance in your butchery?"

"You needn't fear me, Euphémie. Once my wife has been confined to a convent to do penance for her misdeeds, you and I—"

"You and I?" she interrupted, disbelieving that she had heard correctly. "You must be mad if you think I'd have aught to do with you after your acts of cowardice and betrayal."

"At first my attentions may be distasteful to you, but that will change with time. Stand aside, Mercedes, unless you wish to die with him."

"In the holy name of God, Rodrigo, have mercy on him."

She fell on her knees before him, her arms encircling his legs to impede his progress. "I'll go to the convent; I'll do anything you say, only spare him."

Phémie, taking advantage of this moment of distraction, threw herself against Miguel, as if to shield his body, her hand closing about the dagger in his belt and pulling it free. A moment later de Merades had shaken his clinging wife loose, kicking her aside brutally, and gripped Phémie by the shoulder, spinning her around to face him. As her arm arched over her head, he dropped his sword, grasping her wrist and squeezing until she cried out in pain and the dagger fell to the stone floor with a clatter. With her free hand, she dealt him a stunning blow across the face, and he needed all his wits to subdue her. Phémie fought with the fury of desperation as she felt her strength leaving her. Quite suddenly, just as he was winning over her, he stopped the struggle, his eyes bulging from his head. Without a word, he released his hold on her and stepped back. His eyes, filled with pure terror, glazed, and he fell dead to the floor, the dagger plunged to its hilt in his back. Mercedes couldn't take her eyes from the man she'd just killed until Phémie grasped her shoulders and turned her away.

"Look to the priest; he may need your aid," Phémie said, leading Mercedes firmly from the ruined church. "I will take care of your friend. You must meet your maid in there and pretend that nothing has happened. Miguel will call on you later and tell you what has been done."

"But what of Rodrigo?"

"All that you can do for him is pray for his soul. The living need your concern now."

Even in her distress, Mercedes could see the wisdom of Phémie's words, and she returned to the main church, her face a bit pale, but otherwise outwardly composed. After binding Miguel's wound, Phémie dragged de Merades's body behind the dais. The young Spaniard indicated that he would dispose of it after Phémie was safely out of Habana. Fortunately, his jacket was a dark color, and the stains were not too noticeable from a distance. Their journey to the docks was uneventful, and they were welcomed aboard the ship that would take Phémie to a Spanish port. Upon arrival she would have more than enough gold to buy some respectable clothing and to hire a fast coach to take her across the frontier into France. After bidding Miguel farewell, confident that he would see to the protection of Mercedes, she gave in to the exhaustion that overwhelmed her. Mercifully, she slept without dreaming.

It was a long voyage to Spain, and Phémie had more than enough time for reflection. At first her thoughts were very morbid. She was quite convinced that she brought disaster to every man who crossed her path. Florimond, dying shortly before the wedding for which he had wished so ardently. Charles, she imagined, still in a monastery. Auguste, absolutely mad and living with the ghost of his dead wife. Bordeaux, speaking so fervently of honor, having betrayed himself far more than he had betrayed her. And, lastly, de Merades, willing to do murder to gain what he wanted. In regard to that episode, although she was ashamed of the feeling, she was thankful that it had been his own wife who had done the deed; Mercedes would find comfort in the fact that if she had not killed her husband, an innocent man would have died at his hand. Phémie's conscience was burdened enough with the knowledge that de Merades would not have died, the young man would not have been wounded, and Mercedes would not have to suffer with her dark thoughts, if it had not been for the intrusion into their lives of the Frenchwoman. All she could do now was pray for them all.

Toward the end of her voyage, however, the horrible memories faded and she began planning how to escape Louis's keen surveillance and avoid the hateful alliance Charles had warned her about, an eternity before. She would retreat to her Paris home, as she'd originally planned, living in absolute seclusion until she felt reasonably safe in venturing out once again. Her papers were secure; she would use the name of Lapalisse when she crossed the frontier. The Duchesse d'Amberieu's arrival in France would be reported to Versailles as a matter of course. Mademoiselle Lapalisse could pass without notice or comment. How she looked forward to the peace and quiet of her own house, and the exquisite pleasure of sleeping in her own bed. In her opinion, it was a blessing to be prayed for, but one which she hardly deserved.

Madame Matilde just happened to be passing through the front hallway when the knocker sounded against the door, heralding the arrival of some late guests, no doubt. Since she was the closest to it, she opened it herself. Other than the slightest raising of the eyebrows, she gave no hint of surprise when she saw the young woman dressed entirely in black standing before her.

"We are relieved that you have arrived at last, but the front door is not for servants. You must go around to the back."

If Phémie hadn't known that something was amiss when she saw all the carriages lining the drive, Madame Matilde's frosty greeting would have aroused her suspicions. After the door was closed in her face, she dismissed her coach by the gate and carried her one small case up to the brightly lit house, sensing that her adventures were not quite at an end. Thanks to her housekeeper's quick thinking, she'd been forestalled from uttering any greeting that would have betrayed her. At the presence of possible danger, her weariness dropped from her like a burdensome cloak, and she picked up her case, walking to the back of the house briskly. Every room in the house, with the exception of the master's quarters on the uppermost floor, seemed to be occupied. Madame Matilde had reached the kitchen before her mistress, and had warned those who would recognize her to ignore her. When Phémie walked into the multitude of people preparing for a large dinner party, she saw that her own servants were in the minority. No one paid her the slightest attention as Madame Matilde directed her into the servant's quarters. Once in the housekeeper's room, the woman embraced her mistress, tears in her eyes.

"Thank the good Lord you've come back to us!"

Phémie returned the embrace, saying, "There were times when I thought I'd never see you again. But tell me, did Gaspard ever arrive?"

"Yes, but he could not remain, as you can see. I arranged for his quartering in a respectable house in the city." She paused, looking at her closely in the dim light. "You have suffered much, my child. It has made a woman of you."

"No, Madame, you hope for too much. It has only robbed me of my childhood."

"Past time, I would say," she stated gruffly, wiping the tears from her eyes.

"Have I changed that much?" Phémie laughed, infinitely comforted by finding Madame so unchanged.

"You've let your hair grow, praise God, but that is nothing. The difference is in your eyes, I think."

"It would seem that other things have changed, as well. What, in the name of heaven, has happened to my house?"

"We have been invaded by foreigners, Madame. Shortly after you left, we received an order from Versailles to make welcome the Vatican Ambassador. When His Highness arrived in Paris, the King gave him your house until such time as you should return. I suspect that His Highness refused to live at the palace; there's no love between His Holiness and His Majesty, as you must know. Now that you are back, we can send them all on their way."

The last was said with a sniff of disdain, and Phémie was amused.

"Don't you like the gentleman, Madame?"

"I do indeed, Your Grace." She realized that she was being teased, and fell back on her dignity. "And I can't complain about the work, because he brought his own servants, none of whom speaks our language. Other than his man, that is, who thinks his master is the lord of the earth, and himself lord over us. An impossible man, too full of his own supposed worth, and hardly granting a nod or a word to any of us lesser beings. But His Highness is very kind. If he asks for anything, it's always with a 'please' at the first, and a 'thank you' afterward. And he being a nephew of the Pope!"

"Are all those carriages his?"

"Oh, no, those belong to his guests. At first no one would come near him, considering the bitterness between his uncle and the King. But His Majesty made it known soon enough that His Highness was held in the highest esteem, and the house has been flooded with notes and invitations ever since. Despite his openness, and friendly appearance, he has been very particular in allowing only invited guests admittance. I've turned away more people in this short time than ever visited the Duc in the many years I've been here."

"How is Gaspard doing? Has he found a position with the King yet?"

"Your letter did it for him, and most grateful he was, as he should be. He has taken quarters in the city, near his work. There is one visitor who has been very persistent; I think you knew him once." She was being sly, but Phémie didn't jump to the bait and waited patiently for her to continue, which she did shortly. "Do you remember Monsieur de Montais?"

"Charles?" She was truly surprised. "I thought he was grieving in a monastery."

The housekeeper made a rude noise, before commenting, "Only women were created for grieving. I never saw a man hide himself away because he lost his woman to death. All that sorrow; it wasn't natural to a man."

"I thought you liked Charles."

"I did, but he was different when he was with us. Now you would hardly know him. He stayed a scant three months in the monastery; hardly a decent time of mourning for his wife, still warm in her grave."

"How curious."

"You haven't heard it all. He rejoined the world of the living by marrying again, and wearing the title of Marquis, a wedding gift from His Majesty."

"You don't mean it!" The expression on Phémie's face

satisfied the housekeeper that her story was not without interest.

"He's here tonight, with his bride. Do you wish to see him?"

"Yes, but I don't wish him to see me."

"It's wise not to place too much trust in a man who owes the King a whole new life."

"What service could Charles have performed to have merited rewards?"

"His Majesty has been even more generous to your friend. Not only did he endow Monsieur Charles with the hand of a distant cousin, and a new title, but he has given him several rich estates owned by the Crown, and the Blue Coat of King's Gentleman."

"Those are honors indeed." She was thoughtful for a moment, then agreed with her. "You're correct; I can no longer trust him."

"He often comes here, on the King's business, but has been unable to ingratiate himself with His Highness. He once presumed on his friendship with you, and asked me to keep a list of callers, and any messages that arrived through secret means. I told him right then that I was not in His Highness's confidence, and I didn't hang about the hallways spying on the Ambassador from the Vatican. Whenever we have met since, Monsieur Charles has had nothing but a long face for me."

"It's difficult to believe. I've come home, hoping to find rest and seclusion, and find high politics and intrigue. What are they doing now?"

"They sat down to dinner just before you arrived. It's a small party, the kind His Highness prefers. There will be conversation with the meal, so it usually takes well over two hours for him to eat."

"And then?"

"There'll be a concert in the main salon and dancing afterwards. His Highness considers gambling a waste of time and money."

It was obvious that the Vatican Ambassador had met with

Madame's approval, if not stolen her heart, so Phémie said with a semblance of seriousness, "A sensible man! When would be the best time to see Charles and his bride?"

"The safest moment would be when they come from dinner. If you stay in the shadows at the first level stairs, you can see him without being seen."

"Perhaps you'd best get me a white apron. If I am seen by people, they'll think I'm a servant." The housekeeper turned to leave, then paused in the doorway for a moment, saying, "Monsieur Espalion told me what happened in St. Pierre. I took the liberty of having some new gowns made for you. And your rooms have been untouched. You may retire there without fear that someone will intrude. You need only be careful that a light doesn't show."

"You're so thoughtful, Madame," she said appreciatively, and the dour woman smiled briefly. "It is good that you are home again. I will return soon with your apron."

"And something to eat, please. I haven't had a decent meal since I left. Oh, and some cool milk, if you will. You can't imagine how thirsty one becomes when there's no milk."

"I will bring it all. You rest now, Madame; there is more than enough time until they leave the table."

After eating the rather informal meal, Phémie allowed her travel-stained gown to be brushed thoroughly before putting on the stiff white apron that helped her fade into anonymity. The housekeeper brushed her hair back from her face in a severe fashion, tying it securely and hiding it under a maid's cap. The disguise was so effective that if de Montais met her face to face, it was doubtful he would recognize her. As the time neared for the end of dinner, the two women went up the back stairs to the first landing, hurrying to the front staircase. Phémie took up her position, and Madame went downstairs, stationing herself just outside the dining room doors. Looking up, all she could see was a maid standing in the shadows. The face was indistinguishable.

Nodding, Madame disappeared into the back of the house, and Phémie waited alone.

It was not a long wait. Before too many minutes had passed, the doors were opened, and the guests began filing out. Phémie felt that familiar spurt of excitement as her eyes scanned the faces below her. She was not surprised that Charles was beside his host, among the last to leave. She paid her former friend slight attention; he'd not changed in the least. The woman hanging on his arm was a pasty-faced creature, who wore her cosmetics to a disastrous disadvantage and was pitifully obvious in her emotion for her new husband. But the bulk of Phémie's attention was captured by the man de Montais was trying to impress. He wasn't particularly tall, but he was extremely masculine, making his guests look foppish and gaudy in comparison. What caught her interest to such a degree was the way he laughed, or rather the freedom with which he laughed. It was not the polite, restrained laughter of court but an expression of true amusement. His face was wreathed with pleasure; his eyes, large and luminous and brown, were alive with it. It filled the whole house, and Phémie found herself laughing as well, not only with the Italian, but at the poor, pale excuses of humanity surrounding him. Somehow she had expected great dignity from an Ambassador, and great solemnity from the representative from the Vatican. His Highness, however, was an Italian, filled to overflowing with the juices of life, and ready to laugh and enjoy himself at the slightest provocation. In an instant she saw why Charles would fail with this man. The courtier was too earnest, too serious; his laughter was empty, and rang hollow next to the laughter of his host, just as he, himself, was empty and hollow next to the Italian. Too soon had Charles forgotten all he had learned from his association with the girl he'd once loved.

As the last of the revelers were lost to sight, Phémie left the shadows and ran with light feet up the main staircase to her room, unaware of the man who came out into the hallway on the third floor at the sound of her footsteps. Giovanni waited until she disappeared into the suite reserved for the owner of the house, before turning back to his chores in his master's room. He listened in vain for the sound of the maid returning from her errand, then decided that she must have gone back down again with far more decorum and quietness than she'd gone up.

He tried to put it from his mind, but he was an observant fellow, and he knew that there had been something wrong about the woman he'd seen but briefly. The more he thought about it, the more it seemed to evade him, until he happened to catch sight of one of the other maids. The woman he had seen had been wearing a morning cap on her head! His curiosity about such an incongruity prompted him to climb the narrow staircase leading to the top floor.

When he had first arrived, he'd gone and explored the owner's suite, thinking it proper that his master should occupy it. The housekeeper had appealed to the Ambassador directly, and his overindulgent master had granted her wish: no one would disturb her mistress's quarters. Now, as he approached the door leading to the disputed territory, for he'd never forgiven the housekeeper for her interference, he listened for any sounds that would indicate the presence of an intruder. There was nothing. However, when he tried to open the door to investigate further, he found it bolted against him. For a moment, he was tempted to knock on the door, demanding entrance, but thought better of it. The situation would require diligence, and he knew which of his people he could entrust with such a delicate mission. When he'd gathered as much information as he needed, he would then approach his master with his suspicions. Until that time, the door leading to the owner's suite would be under unobtrusive, but constant, surveillance.

Late one night, more than a week after his successful dinner, Alessandro Scarcini was bidding farewell to an entirely different set of guests. Despite their peasant clothing, these men still took every precaution that they should not be discovered. They were priests who'd come surreptitiously to the chateau in order to make personal reports on Louis's encroachment upon church property and prerogatives of the Pope's representative. They were frightened men, seeing in Louis a monarch who might become another Henry of England if pushed too far or denied too much. The men had left as stealthily as they had come, through the side windows of a small study, avoiding the gravel drive and keeping to the cover of the trees. Once he was alone, Alessandro unbolted the door, signaling to Giovanni that the way was clear. He returned to his desk to secrete the reports in the hidden chamber as Giovanni came in, closing the door behind him.

"What is it?" Scarcini asked.

"Your pardon, Highness, but I'm certain there is a spy in the house."

"What have you learned?" he whispered to the man who posed as his servant, and Giovanni replied in the same tone. "He must have entered the house during the confusion of the official dinner. I was in your room when I heard someone running up the stairs. When I reached the hallway, the person was on the stairs leading to the owner's quarters. The person was dressed in a black gown, white apron, and a cap that the maids wear only in the morning, when dusting. When the person entered the owner's quarters, I went back to my duties, thinking that it was only a maid sent on some errand. I waited, listening for her return, but she never came back. Suspicious of the cap and the haste with which the 'maid' ran, I mounted the stairs to the door. When I lifted the latch, thinking to investigate, I discovered that the door was bolted."

At this Alessandro's eyes narrowed, but he kept his silence. Giovanni continued, "I had guards posted, to keep watch day and night. No one came out of the rooms. Only the housekeeper went in; after she sounded a peculiar knock, the door was opened to her." He duplicated the knock on the desk softly, and his master nodded.

"A signal."

"The housekeeper always carries a bundle. My men suspect that it contains food and drink. She visits but once a day, shortly before the rest of the household is up, long before you stir from your bed. She goes up the back stairs to the third floor. Since yours is the only room occupied up there, she runs little risk of meeting anyone unexpectedly. Despite these strange occurrences, we were not certain that the housekeeper wasn't sheltering some woman up there, perhaps a runaway wife or a young relative who has shamed the family. We didn't wish to concern Your Highness until something happened that made it imperative that we take action." He paused, swallowing hard and clearing his throat, before continuing, "The housekeeper left the suite above this morning carrying a pair of trousers, a shirt and jacket, and a pair of boots."

The significance of this information was not lost upon the nephew of the Pope.

"Do you think Louis has sent a spy into the household?"

"No, Highness. The clothes and boots were those of an officer in the Spanish Navy."

Alessandro whistled softly, his expression growing in concern with each revelation. "Are you certain of this?"

"Yes, Highness. The housekeeper had them buried in the kitchen garden. Our men just dug them up again."

"What could Spain want in this house?"

"It has been many years since an Ambassador from the Vatican took a place in the French court with such friendliness and favor shown him. They may suspect an alliance."

"Between my uncle and the French king? Ridiculous!"

"There have been stranger alliances than that, Highness," Giovanni reminded Alessandro gently, and the younger man nodded.

"Very well, let us say that their suspicions were aroused. Why would Madame Matilde give aid and shelter to a Spaniard?"

"Perhaps he bears a letter from her mistress, as did Espalion. Perhaps the Duchesse found refuge at the Spanish court."

"How could she? Espalion brought his letter from the Caribbees."

"We have only his word that the Duchesse didn't leave the colonies."

"We seem to be in a dangerous situation, Giovanni. What do you suggest?"

"I thought we had best do something before the real reason for our visit to France becomes known. So I have placed the housekeeper's room under guard. If she attempts to leave it before we are finished, our man will see that she doesn't go very far, or try to reach our unwanted guest. While the house sleeps, I think we should see who the intruder is. I thought you might like to accompany us."

"I most certainly should," he said with feeling, pushing his chair back abruptly as he rose to his feet. "It's my head that's on the block."

Phémie heard the light tapping on the door when she was about to fall asleep. It was far too early for the housekeeper's usual visit, but perhaps something was amiss. So she got out of bed, slipping a robe about her shoulders, and went to the door. There it was again—the correct signal. Sliding back the bolt, she pulled open the door. Before she realized what was happening, she was sent sprawling by a heavy blow to the shoulder, and was surrounded by men with drawn swords. As she struggled to a sitting position, fighting to regain the breath that had been knocked from her, she again heard the laughter that had so enchanted her the night she had arrived home. Now she found nothing amusing in it. All she could see were two hands stretched out to her, as if to help her stand, and she slapped them aside, enraged. Someone gave an order in Italian, and the men who had rushed in withdrew as quietly as possible. There remained only one man, stooping before her, his hands held out once again. This time she took them and he stood, pulling her to her feet. He wrapped her fallen robe about her shoulders with great solicitude. There was only the one candle lit, beside her bed, and he retrieved it, taking it into the library.

"Won't you join me?" the man asked lightly, and

Phémie, her dignity restored, went in. Without thought, she sat behind the desk, wincing as she came into contact with the chair. The man sat opposite.

"I am Alessandro Scarcini," he offered hopefully, but she merely nodded.

"I know."

"I must apologize for my men. They thought you were a spy."

"A spy secluded behind a bolted door? What could I possibly spy upon?"

"Nothing from here, I admit. But the housekeeper could have brought you messages and reports. To be quite honest with you, we thought you were a man. But who could blame us when Madame Matilde left here with the uniform of a Spanish officer and buried it in the garden?"

"I didn't know it was gone. Poor Madame . . . she means so well."

"As does my Giovanni! But neither of them suffers from their well-meaning efforts, as we do."

"I know where my pain lies, but what of yours?"

"Embarrassment, Madame, and until I can make amends for the brutality of my men, I shall continue to be in great pain."

"I can see why you were chosen as a diplomat, Monsieur Ambassador. I shall let you suffer awhile longer, at least until I can sit comfortably once again. But for now, allow me to offer you some wine."

Reaching under the desk, she pulled a concealed lever, and he heard a door swing open. She lifted out a tray containing a bottle of wine and several glasses and placed them upon the desk. The bottle was very old, and he studied the label while she cleaned two glasses.

"This is indeed a treasure, Madame."

"The Duc had a fine cellar, but he kept his best up here. Madame Matilde has a map of all the hiding places." She suddenly stopped, laughing ruefully. "I don't think I should have told you that."

"But why not? Do you think I would rob you of your wine?"

"No, but for a man to be so afraid of spies might mean that he has something to hide. You are probably a spy yourself."

Alessandro smiled, his pretense of amusement almost believable. "Of course I am a spy. Why else would I refuse to live at Versailles and choose instead a house so far from all the secrets of state?"

She smiled with him, commenting, "I didn't care too much for the new palace myself."

If he had any doubt about her identity, her remark dispelled it completely.

"They are still talking about you, Madame, and your strange disappearance."

"They have little to do but gossip."

"I know very little about your travels, but I think I know how you returned. You must have first come into a Spanish port from the colonies, disguised in the officer's uniform. When my men first saw you, you wore the costume of a maid." He applied his attention to opening the bottle, and she supplied the information he was lacking.

"Madame Matilde gave me the apron and cap. I had crossed the frontier in the plain black gown that the women of Spain are so fond of. You don't seen to be disturbed about a woman dressing in men's clothing."

"There!" He was successful in opening the bottle and hesitated to pour it. "This should be decanted gently, and with great love."

"You may pour it gently, and drink it with great love. I'm afraid I don't share your reverence for wine."

"Of course not. I wouldn't expect it of a woman."

She wasn't offended; on the contrary, she laughed in self-deprecation. "Personally I prefer milk, or clean, sweet water from a spring."

He poured slowly, exclaiming with delight when the liquid proved clear rather than cloudy.

"It is a miracle! Madame, I drink to the wine, with felicitations to the great God who created it." She lifted her glass, bowing toward him, saying simply, "To your pleasure."

When he'd finished his first glass, sipping slowly with appreciation, he referred to her earlier comment. "I am not disturbed by your choice of costume, Madame. I find your courage and determination to survive at any cost truly remarkable. Personally, I am grateful that you have returned safely." He raised his eyebrows comically, indicating the wine as he poured a second glass. She saw no reason to disenchant him by disclosing the fact that she was more comfortable in men's clothing than women's. Almost too late, he noticed that her own glass was empty and moved to fill it. Swiftly she put her hand over the glass, shaking her head. "Don't waste it on me. I honestly don't appreciate it as you do. Please, accept it as a gift."

"What can I give you in return for such a treasure?" he asked in all seriousness, and she replied in like manner, "Your silence."

"About your presence in France?"

"Yes. If you but give me your word, I shall find the rest I need so desperately."

"I think you have had a very difficult journey, Madame. Your lovely lips smile and even laugh, but there is sorrow and weariness in your eyes."

"All I ask is for a little time."

"Before you return to battle?" he asked with great kindness, and she felt the tears stinging her eyes.

"You understand so well."

"I know what it is to fight until one is too weary to lift a sword. You may have your time of rest, Madame; you have my promise on that."

She released her breath, sighing with infinite relief. "I'm so grateful."

"I ask for one favor in return," he interrupted, smiling to remove the chance of any misinterpreted threat from his words. "It is only that I be allowed to visit you in your tower whenever my duties permit."

"Towers are very lonely places. I should welcome your company."

"It is agreed then; we have a bargain."

"We have a bargain," she said, clasping his outstretched hand warmly. He drank the rest of his glass of wine, then resealed the bottle as best he could.

"I shall have Giovanni decant what remains immediately. Tomorrow I must go to Versailles, but I hope to be back by the early evening. Would you share my board, Madame?"

"I would be delighted, Monsieur."

He bade her good night formally when she saw him to the door, and she returned to her bed feeling more safe and secure than she had in a very long time.

In the beginning, Giovanni heartily approved of what he considered the harmless dalliance that his master was enjoying with the young woman who had been found hiding in the house. An occasional intimate dinner, a late evening walk after the gates had been barred, if the weather allowed, an earnest, quiet chat, or a conversation punctuated by laughter. As long as Alessandro remembered his responsibility to his uncle, and the real reason they had come to France, there was nothing to complain about. But soon Giovanni became suspicious that perhaps the Prince's involvement with the woman was neither harmless nor a dalliance. He cherished a very high opinion of his theories, and when the person hiding on the top floor failed to be a Spanish spy, Giovanni fell back on his other theory; the young woman was some relative of the housekeeper's, eminently suitable for a dalliance, but certainly not for anything more serious. So satisfied was he with his theory of her identity that it never occurred to him to pursue it any further. But when his master began neglecting his duties, when he put off going to Versailles, or holding audiences, or attending social functions, Giovanni became concerned. What finally seriously alarmed the good servant of the Pope was that the Prince now on occasion relegated the business of gathering reports of the priests to Giovanni.

Although he was loath to do it, Giovanni wrote a secret report to His Holiness complaining of Alessandro's dereliction of duty. Before he could send it, however, the entire situation had changed. Alessandro suddenly left off his romance, throwing himself with a fury into his work. Every day he was either at Versailles, or Versailles seemed to come to the house. His dinners became more frequent than they were before he'd met the woman. He drank dangerously, and flirted outrageously, but kept a clear head for his clandestine meetings with the clergy. Sometimes, when the Prince was away, the woman would take a long, lonely walk on the grounds. Or she would just sit in the main salon until she heard his carriage approaching, at which time she would quickly run upstairs. It was obvious to even such an unromantic fellow as Giovanni that the two had had a falling out, and nothing could have pleased him more. At night, upon accompanying his master to his bedchamber, Giovanni would, at times, see Alessandro pause at the stairs leading to the fourth floor, then turn away in disgust. Sometimes he would see the woman standing in the shadows at the top of the stairs, straining for a glimpse of his master. As long as neither of them made an attempt to heal the breach, whatever it was, Giovanni could rest easy.

Then one night, disaster struck. The Prince was in a particularly black mood. He ate sparingly, drank even less, and was completely unresponsive to Giovanni's feeble attempts at humor. Without warning, he suddenly stormed from the dining room, taking the stairs two at a time as he rushed up to the top floor. Giovanni followed on his heels, begging him to reconsider. It was as if the man was deaf, so intent was he upon reaching his destination. When he reached the door, he tried to open it, but found it bolted.

"Phémie!" he yelled, pounding on it, and her voice could be heard on the other side of it. "Leave me in peace!"

"You dare ask for peace? Stand back," he warned, throwing himself against the door. When it didn't budge under his assault, he screamed at Giovanni, "Get me some men. I want this door chopped into firewood."

At this the woman opened the door, saying with great dignity, "There is no need for such violence."

The Prince advanced upon her threateningly, and she retreated before him. "I don't recall inviting you in." Her bravado sounded false and her dignity was crumbling. His hands shot out, grasping her by the shoulders. She winced with pain, but did not cry out. In fact, her face glowed as she looked up into his.

"Say that you made up the tale of your wanderings!" he demanded, shaking her mercilessly. "You did it only to tease me."

"I've told the truth," she confessed, but not quite truthfully. "If I had known it would drive you mad, I'd never have told you."

"Why did you tell me? I didn't want to know."

"I had to tell you."

"Why?" His anger left him suddenly, and he was desperate for her answer.

"Because I love you," she whispered, her head bowed.

"What did you say?" He couldn't believe that he'd heard aright.

"Because I love you," she repeated, raising her voice, but not her head.

"Look at me!" He shook her by the shoulders, but more gently this time. When she obeyed his command, he saw the laughter, the love, the joy, the tenderness in her eyes.

"You're a willful woman." He passed the judgment on her helplessly, and she sympathized with him, "I know. How can you abide it?"

"I don't know if I can, but I can't let you roam about by yourself, can I? Someone has to look after you."

It had been an unusually quiet morning. The meeting with his ministers had been uneventful, and, for amusement, he was contemplating an afternoon of hunting if the weather remained suitable. When one of his secretaries brought him a sealed letter, his quick eye spotted the mark of a signet he'd not seen in a long time. Breaking the seal anxiously, he unfolded the parchment and read the simple statement:

> Her Grace, the Duchesse Euphémie d'Amberieu, and His Highness, the Prince Alessandro Scarcini, have been married under special dispensation by the Bishop of Paris. Upon their return from their wedding journey, they will present themselves at Versailles for his Majesty's blessing.

Louis leaned back in his chair, unable to believe that the secret plot formulated by himself and his old enemy had actually succeeded. That Phémie had not seen her monarch's fine hand at work, nor Alessandro his uncle's, seemed incredible. The plan had been so ridiculously simple, and its improbable success dependent upon the improbable attraction of two very obstinate young people to each other. Chuckling to himself, he called for a secretary and began dictating a letter to His Holiness, the Pope in Rome.